A Simple Change

Books by

Judith Miller

FROM BETHANY HOUSE PUBLISHERS

The Carousel Painter

DAUGHTERS OF AMANA

Somewhere to Belong • *More Than Words*

A Bond Never Broken

BELLS OF LOWELL*

Daughter of the Loom • *A Fragile Design*

These Tangled Threads

LIGHTS OF LOWELL*

A Tapestry of Hope • *A Love Woven True*

The Pattern of Her Heart

THE BROADMOOR LEGACY*

A Daughter's Inheritance

An Unexpected Love • *A Surrendered Heart*

POSTCARDS FROM PULLMAN

In the Company of Secrets

Whispers Along the Rails • *An Uncertain Dream*

BRIDAL VEIL ISLAND*

To Have and To Hold • *To Love and Cherish*

To Honor and Trust

HOME TO AMANA

A Hidden Truth

A Simple Change

www.judithmccoymiller.com

*with Tracie Peterson

HOME TO AMANA

A Simple Change

Judith Miller

BETHANYHOUSE
a division of Baker Publishing Group
Minneapolis, Minnesota

Published by Bethany House Publishers
11400 Hampshire Avenue South
Bloomington, Minnesota 55438
www.bethanyhouse.com

Bethany House Publishers is a division of
Baker Publishing Group, Grand Rapids, Michigan

Printed in the United States of America

Library of Congress Cataloging-in-Publication Data

Miller, Judith.
A simple change / Judith Miller.
pages cm
Summary: "When unforeseen circumstances drive Jancey Rhoder to move to the Amana Colonies, she'll be forced to reconsider everything she wanted out of life—and love"—Provided by publisher.
ISBN 978-0-7642-1001-3(pbk.)
I. Title.
PS3613.C3858S56 2013
813′.6—dc23 2013010856

Scripture quotations are taken from the King James Version of the Bible.

Cover design by Lookout Design, Inc.
Cover photography by Aimee Christensen

Author is represented by Books & Such Literary Agency.

13 14 15 16 17 18 19 7 6 5 4 3 2

To Wendy Lawton

Thank you for your godly wisdom,
creative spirit, boundless encouragement,
and unfailing friendship.

A man's heart deviseth his way:
but the Lord directeth his steps.
—Proverbs 16:9

CHAPTER 1

February 1881
Kansas City, Missouri

I lifted the lid of the gaily decorated story-day box sitting beside me and glanced about the semicircle of children surrounding my chair. Their eyes sparkled with anticipation as they looked at the box and then peered at me. When I didn't immediately remove anything from the box, the youngsters—six boys and four girls, ranging in age from five to ten years—craned their necks forward, hoping to catch a glimpse of what might be inside. Before they could meet with any success, I placed the lid back on the box. Ten little chests deflated, and a unified moan escaped their lips.

None of them had developed any patience, at least not when it pertained to the story-day box. For the orphans who lived and attended my classes in the Kansas City Charity Home, the weekly story-day event had become an enchanting time that rivaled even recess.

Nettie stretched her arm and pointed her index finger toward the box. "What did you bring, Miss Jancey?"

Matthew folded his body forward and turned his head to face Nettie. "Mr. Ludwig said we're supposed to call her Miss Rhoder, not Miss Jancey. He said 'Miss Jancey' wasn't proper for a schoolteacher, didn't he, Miss Rhoder?" The nine-year-old sat up and brushed the dark strands of hair off his forehead.

"He did, Matthew. I believe Nettie merely forgot the new rule."

The six-year-old towheaded girl tucked her chin against her chest. "I'm sorry, Miss Rhoder."

"It's quite all right, Nettie. Now that we have a different director, we all must learn the new rules."

Although I thought this particular regulation a bit silly, I'd been silent about the change when Mr. Ludwig, the new director, made the announcement. My decision had been strategic. Except for insisting the children address teachers and other staff by surnames, Mr. Ludwig's regulations were less strident than those of the previous director. This particular rule didn't warrant making waves in the rather calm sea of change we'd experienced since his arrival. Besides, in the three years I'd been working at the orphanage, I'd learned that challenges were best saved for important issues—ones that most affected the children's care and education.

Matthew scooted to the edge of his chair and squared his shoulders. "I already know all of the rules."

Caroline lifted her arm and waved in my direction. Once I nodded for her to speak, Caroline turned toward Matthew. "You don't know all the rules, Matthew Turner, or you would have raised your hand before speaking." After directing a smirk at Matthew, Caroline patted Nettie's arm and whispered in the girl's ear.

John raised his hand. "Are you going to tell us a story, Miss Rhoder?"

"I am, but first we're going to do something different. Instead of bringing a lot of my belongings from home, I thought it would be fun to make some of the things we need to help us act out our story today."

My idea met with mixed emotions. The girls appeared pleased by the idea of participating in the activity, while the boys wanted to begin the storytelling.

Matthew folded his arms across his chest. "What's the story and what do we have to make?"

"Today we're going to combine history with storytelling. We're going to reenact George Washington crossing the Delaware with his troops." I looked at Matthew and the other boys. Their frowns turned to smiles at the mention of George Washington and his troops.

While reaching into the story-box, I looked around the group. "Who can think of something we might want to make for our journey across the river?"

"I know. I know!" Charlie shouted. "We need boats."

Matthew jabbed the younger boy with his elbow. "We can't build boats, Charlie."

I stood and motioned to Charlie. "I think we can form some pretend boats with chairs. Would you like to take charge of the boats for us, Charlie?"

He bobbed his head and smiled. "Want to help, Matthew?"

Though I hadn't expected him to agree, Matthew jumped to his feet and pulled a chair to the far side of the room. "Let's do it over here."

Once the boys were busy arranging chairs, I pulled a sheaf of newspapers from the story-box. "We can make tricorne hats out of the newspaper, and I brought some butcher paper we can paint blue for the water." I tapped my chin. "I don't know what we can use to create make-believe ice in the water. Any ideas?" I glanced around the room.

Bertie waved toward the dining room. "We can lump up some of the towels and napkins."

The other girls applauded her suggestion, and soon the children were hard at work creating the mock scene. Once the scene was completed, I related the story of how General Washington had rallied his men, and how, in the freezing weather, they'd successfully crossed the frigid waters.

When I finished explaining the history, I looked at the group of boys, all of them eager to participate in acting out the story. "Who would like to play George Washington?"

To my surprise, Matthew motioned to Charlie. "I think it should be Charlie. He's the one who figured out how to make the chairs into boats."

My heart swelled at Matthew's suggestion. He'd suggested Charlie instead of himself for the major role. Such a thing wouldn't have happened a year ago, but throughout the past year, with a bit of coaching and encouragement, Matthew had made strides in the right direction.

Moments later, I pulled him aside. "I'm proud of you, Matthew."

His cheeks flamed red from the praise, and he ducked his head. "He deserved it."

I squeezed his shoulder. "Why don't you take charge of the second boat?"

Nodding, Matthew hurried forward and motioned for several

of the children to join him. These slight modifications in the children's behavior had become a measuring stick for me. When I saw changes for the good, it confirmed that this orphanage was where I was meant to teach.

At the time I'd accepted the job, my parents had expressed concern. They'd anticipated that upon completion of my education, I would accept a position at a finishing school for a year or two and then marry. Instead, I'd returned home, accepted a post at the orphanage school, and remained single—at least for the present.

If Nathan Woodward had his way, we'd already be married. Nathan had proved to be the persistent sort. My father said that was a good thing, but I wasn't so sure. At times, I thought him too impatient, too eager, a bit too sure of himself, and a bit too sure of me, as well. He never seemed to doubt that we would one day marry, but I remained uncertain. I had yet to sense the stomach flips and heart flutters my girlfriends spoke of experiencing when they'd fallen in love.

"How does this look, Miss Rhoder?" Bertie had scrunched frayed white napkins into clumps and placed them on the blue butcher paper. "Henry says they don't look like ice, but I told him he's supposed to use his imagination." She inched closer to my side and peered at me with eyes nearly the same shade of blue as my own. "The chairs don't look like boats, either. How come Henry didn't say that to Charlie or Matthew?"

"Let's overlook what he said for today. I don't think he meant to hurt your feelings." Although Bertie didn't appear convinced, she agreed. "Everyone put on your hats and gather at the shoreline."

Henry perched his small hands on his hips and shook his head. "There weren't any girls on the boats, Miss Rhoder."

Bertie jutted her chin. "There weren't any boys, either, so if we can't get in the boats, neither can you, Henry."

After a few minutes of explanation and arbitration, the children gathered to listen while Charlie gave a speech and rallied the troops. The children rowed with brooms and mops, pushing aside the clumped-up napkins while pretending to shiver from the freezing temperatures.

I pretended to wave from shore. "What month and year is it?"

Matthew raised his hand and I nodded at him. "December 1776."

"Excellent! And what war are we fighting?"

Bertie didn't wait for me to signal. Instead she cupped her hands to her lips. "The Revolting War against the Bristish."

Henry shook his head. "It's the Revolutionary War and it's British not 'Bristish.'"

Bertie's lip quivered, and I turned to Henry. "She may have mispronounced the words, Henry, but Bertie's answers were correct." I stepped through the make-believe water and stooped down beside Henry. "What is our rule about correcting other students?"

"We let the teacher do it," he mumbled.

I nodded and returned to the imaginary shoreline. "I'm glad I didn't sink and drown while I was out by the boats."

The children giggled, and I soon continued questioning them about their history lesson. I knew when these questions appeared on their next test, they would all remember the answers. Story time and play acting had become my most effective teaching method, a technique I enjoyed as much as the children. And while Miss Manchester, who taught the older children, thought my system a silly waste of time, she did admit my children retained much of what they'd been taught during these sessions.

I hadn't learned this method in college, but rather during my childhood, as my mother entertained me with stories on rainy days or on evenings when my father worked late. Those times remained some of my favorite memories. I hoped our story times in school would give these children many fond memories to carry throughout their lifetimes, for I was certain that my memories of these children would always be important to me.

"We need to pick up all of our materials and put the chairs back in place. We have only a few more minutes until end of class."

The chorus of *aws* that filled the room caused me to smile. "You all did a wonderful job of learning today. I'm very proud of you."

"Can you bring the story-box again tomorrow, Miss Rhoder?" Charlie stood beside the row of chairs he'd helped carry across the room.

"Tomorrow is reading and arithmetic, but perhaps if you do well with those subjects tomorrow, we can do a story the following day." The children clapped their approval while I placed materials back inside the box. "Maybe you should help each other with your reading and math homework this evening just to be sure you do well tomorrow."

A ringing bell in the main hallway signaled the end of the school day. The children lined up in a snaky row and bid me good-bye before heading off to the dining room, where they would each be served a slice of buttered bread to curb their hunger until suppertime. Like most orphanages, this one operated on a meager budget. And though the children received three meals a day, the food was simple fare and the servings scant. Soon after I accepted the position at the orphanage, I found going home to a table laden with well-prepared food a mixed blessing.

As I waited for the horse-drawn trolley, a chill whipped at my skirt and tugged strands of my ash-blond hair loose from the spiral bun I'd carefully pinned in place early this morning. Tucking the hair behind my ear, I watched in earnest as the horses plodded down the street at a slow yet steady pace. After waiting in the chill February wind, I looked forward to the warmth of a blazing fire and a hot meal.

I boarded the trolley and rubbed my hands together. Even my gloves couldn't ward off the surprising chill in the air. Tonight I wouldn't feel a twinge of guilt that my father had employed a cook and a housekeeper to tend the preparation of meals and the household duties. I'd struggled with the idea when my mother had first taken ill, and I still wondered if my parents thought it would be better for me to quit my teaching position and help at home. Though they both professed otherwise, I knew Mother sometimes felt uncomfortable having Mrs. Oelwine prepare meals and clean the house, but with her failing health, there had been no choice. Either I quit my job or we hire a housekeeper. Understanding how important the children had become to me, Mother decided Mrs. Oelwine would be a fine choice. And she had proved to be a perfect fit. Not only could she cook and clean to perfection, but Mrs. Oelwine also enjoyed conversing in German and sharing stories of her family with my mother.

Reaching my destination, I stepped off the trolley and walked the short distance to our home, a large house with a sweeping front porch and giant columns—a stark contrast to the small spaces allocated to the children in the orphanage. This house was far more magnificent than any home my parents had ever expected to own. God had been gracious to them—at least that was my father's opinion. Even though I believed my father deserved some of the credit, he vehemently disagreed.

When I attempted to argue, my father would always say the

same thing: "Many men are industrious, but most have not been rewarded with so many blessings. God has blessed us: There is no other explanation."

Sometimes I wondered what he truly thought about Mother's illness. If he considered his financial success a reward from God, did he believe her poor health a punishment? Only once did I broach the subject with him. He'd opened his Bible to John chapter sixteen, pointed to verses twenty through twenty-three, and told me to read the passage.

When I finished, he looked at me over his wire-rimmed spectacles. His words remain etched in my mind. *"We are not promised a life without suffering. That verse reveals that we* will *suffer. But we can remain filled with joy because we have a Savior who has overcome the world. It is suffering that makes us grow and cling to the Lord. It reveals our need for Him. When life is easy, we tend to forget how much we need the Lord. Do you understand?"*

Although I'd nodded my head in agreement, I hadn't totally understood. And I still don't. My mother was a good and faithful woman who deserved good health and happiness. Surely God knew that. How could she be filled with joy when she experienced such pain? My father said I should simply accept the ways of the Lord, but late at night I continue to question Him.

"Is that you, Jancey?" My father's voice drifted toward me as I stepped into the hallway.

"Yes, it's me, Father." My stomach tightened. Why was he home so early? His days never ended until six o'clock—sometimes later. "Is something wrong?" Quickly removing my brocaded velvet cloak, I rushed up the stairs and down the hallway toward the upstairs sitting room. Still feeling the winter chill, I rubbed my arms as I entered the room.

My parents sat side by side, my mother's dainty fingers secured between my father's callused hands. She appeared to be doing well. I inhaled a deep breath and released the tenseness that pinched my muscles.

"I was afraid your health had taken a downward turn." I smiled at my mother and stepped closer to the fire burning in the heating stove. "What brings you home so early, Father?"

Deep creases that I hadn't initially noticed lined his forehead. "For a while now, your mother and I have been considering a change." The two of them exchanged a quick glance, and I saw the worried look in my father's blue eyes that were a clear match of my own. "Come and sit down, Jancey."

My earlier apprehension returned in an unexpected rush. I stepped forward and settled beside him. "What sort of change?"

We'd already made a number of changes to the house in order to accommodate Mother's declining health. The current sitting room had once been a guest bedroom, and we'd even moved the dining table to one end of the room in order to take our meals together when Mother couldn't navigate the stairs. There didn't seem to be any other changes we could make.

My father massaged his forehead, but the deep creases remained. "We are planning to move away from Kansas City. To Iowa. Back to the Amana Colonies."

My mouth turned dry and I stared at him. Surely I'd misunderstood.

CHAPTER 2

I attempted to make sense of what I'd just heard, but I simply couldn't. My father's announcement made no sense. My clenched fingers ached and turned chalky as I waited for further explanation.

My father patted my hands. "I know this comes as a bit of a surprise, but we didn't want to say anything until we'd made a final decision. Of course, we haven't received permission yet, so there is a possibility we won't be able to return. But your mother thought we should tell you so that you would have time to make your own plans."

My mind spun like a whirling top. "I don't understand." At the moment, I couldn't even think of an intelligent question.

"Of course you don't." My mother touched my father's sleeve. "You must start at the beginning, Jurgen."

My father frowned. "I'm not so sure where the beginning is,

but I will do my best." He leaned back and inhaled a deep breath. "I suppose this all began with the onset of your mother's illness."

I nodded and urged him to continue.

"The doctor was here again today. Over the past few weeks, he has told us that your mother's condition has worsened, and there is nothing that can be done for her."

Fear and anger collided like a raging storm within me. "Then we should find another doctor. I don't believe him."

My mother shook her head. "You don't want to believe him, but what he says is true. I have no desire to be probed and checked by any more doctors. Each one has told us the same thing." Her gaze rested on my clenched hands. "Becoming angry at the doctor or my illness won't change my condition."

How could she remain so calm? And why were they thinking of returning to Iowa? Neither of them had mentioned the Amana Colonies in years—unless they'd been privately talking about the past. That must be it. Making such a drastic decision couldn't have been something they'd decided in the past few hours. Though they hadn't included me, there was little doubt they'd been making plans for some time now. I'd usually been included when my parents considered matters of importance, especially those that would affect all of us. I wanted to ignore the feeling of betrayal, but a pang of resentment had already taken hold.

"If you are as ill as the doctor says, you should be here where you can receive proper medical care. Why would you even consider traveling? To move at this time would create a tremendous hardship on both of you."

My father tapped his index finger against his lips. "If you will let me talk, I will tell you."

I curled my lips inward, determined to remain silent, and nodded for him to speak.

"Your mother longs to spend her final days in the familiar surroundings of the colonies. We still have friends living there, and it would give her joy to reunite with them. There is a simple life in Amana that she longs to experience once again." My father stood and crossed the room. He stared out the window for a moment and then turned to face me. "The move will not be difficult. We won't take much. I'll have some of the furniture shipped, but our needs will be supplied once we are there. Unless you want to remain in the house, we'll sell it. My lawyer can handle the details."

My throat caught at his casual mention of selling the house, and I shuddered at the idea. All our family memories were in this house. "You plan to sell it?"

My father arched his brows. "Not if you wish to remain here."

I didn't know a great deal about the Amana Colonies. My parents had told me bits and pieces, but I'd never questioned them about their life in Iowa. It had never seemed particularly important to me. Until now. Question after question raced through my mind, yet my lips wouldn't move.

My father's eyebrows settled low on his forehead as he waited for me to respond. "Do you think you would like to remain in the house, Jancey?"

"Yes. No. I mean, I don't know what I want. This is so unexpected. The two of you have had time to weigh your decisions, but this is all so . . . so . . . unbelievable." I turned to my mother and looked deep into her gray eyes. "This is what you desire? To live the remainder of your life in Amana? To leave everything behind?"

In a period of only a few minutes, my life had been turned upside down. In spite of the warmth from the blazing fireplace, a chill settled over my bones. In that moment I was certain nothing would ever again be the same for us. I wanted to run from the room and return to yesterday and the day before. I didn't want to continue down this path to an unknown world filled with strangers and a different life.

My mother bowed her head. "I know this is hard for you, Jancey, and I will understand if you decide to remain in Kansas City. This is the only home you've ever known. Adjusting to a different way of living is very difficult, and unless you truly want to come, it is better that you remain here."

"But why, Mother? Why do you want to go there after all these years? I don't understand." My voice cracked with emotion.

She looked up, tears glistening in her eyes. "I wish I could explain this need that has come over me." She patted her hand on her chest. "It is a feeling deep inside that tells me I should return home to Middle Amana. I have tried to ignore the urgency that's come over me, but it's been impossible. Your father and I agree that such strong conviction should not be ignored. By us." My mother added the final two words as she glanced at my father. "And though I would prefer to have you come along, your father and I agree that you should pray and decide what is best for you."

I couldn't imagine God sending me an answer to the many questions that now deluged my mind. "I'd have to leave the children at the orphanage. And there's Nathan." I twisted around and looked at my father. "What about the construction company? Are you going to sell the business as well as the house? What will happen to those men who depend upon you for their jobs?" My attempt to speak in a calm manner failed. Instead, my voice tremored in an eerie pitch that exposed my chaotic emotions.

Father returned to the couch and sat beside me. "I can see your distress. I think we should have waited to tell you until after we received word from the elders. If we don't receive permission to return, we will have caused you great worry for nothing." He peered over my shoulder toward my mother. "Your mother and I debated about when was the best time to tell you, but I fear we came to the wrong conclusion."

I shook my head with enough vigor to send one of my hairpins flying onto the Axminster carpet. "I disagree. You should have told me much earlier. Had I known from the beginning, I could have digested the news in small doses. Instead, I must swallow it all in one giant gulp." I touched my throat. "And it isn't going down very well."

My father reached down, retrieved the hairpin, and handed it to me. "It wasn't our intention to hurt you. We were trying to protect you."

The sadness in his voice tugged at my heart. My parents would never intentionally hurt me. Yet how did my father think he had protected me? To argue against what they had done would change nothing for the better. Already I could see my mother flagging under the strain.

I clasped her hand. "You need to rest. Let me take you to your room."

She didn't disagree and willingly permitted me to help her to bed. When I returned to the sitting room, I expected my father to postpone further discussion until later, but he motioned me forward.

"Your mother is very tired today. Between the doctor's visit and her worry over telling you our plans, she's exhausted." He glanced toward the hallway. "Would you prefer to stay up here, or shall we go downstairs and finish our talk?"

"We can go downstairs and I'll make a pot of coffee." His smile was enough to tell me I'd given the answer he desired. "But I have many questions."

He nodded. "And I will answer them as best I can."

The expectation of a warm meal waiting at home had disappeared while I was upstairs with my parents, but once I neared the kitchen and smelled the aroma of a hearty stew, my mouth watered in anticipation.

I glanced over my shoulder at my father. "Mrs. Oelwine has already gone home?"

"Yes. Your mother explained that we would be eating late and asked her to prepare something that would remain warm." He raised his nose and sniffed the air. "Smells like soup or beef stew."

Although Mrs. Oelwine could prepare fancy dishes, extravagant meals weren't served unless we entertained. Neither of my parents enjoyed the social gatherings that had been thrust upon them when my father had become the owner of Forsythe Construction Company, and he'd done his best to expand the business without the trappings of elaborate parties and other social functions attended by business owners in the community.

After grinding coffee beans and filling the pot with water, I sat down at the kitchen table opposite my father. "I'm not certain what I want to ask first."

My father's eyes radiated understanding. "Upstairs you appeared surprised I would sell the house, so let me explain. Your mother and I agreed that if you decided to come with us, it would be preferable to place the house for sale, as we would no longer have the necessary income to pay taxes or insure the property. In addition, if no one lived here, the house would fall into a state of disrepair. We also considered the possibility of renting it, but that poses an additional set of problems. The rental moneys would not be ours to keep. I would be obligated to donate those funds to the community. In addition, we would still be responsible for taxes, insurance, and maintenance of the property. However, if you decide to remain here, we will deed the house to you."

My stomach churned at the thought of such monumental decisions. I stood and walked to the cabinet and removed two cups and saucers. "But then I must worry about all of those expenses you've mentioned, and with no salary from the orphanage, I couldn't possibly manage the upkeep on the house."

He nodded. "So now you more clearly understand why I said we would sell the house?"

While placing the cups and saucers on the table, I halfheartedly admitted my understanding, though I wanted to argue that if they would remain in Kansas City, our lives could continue as usual. Rather than ask God for guidance, perhaps I should pray that the elders deny my parents' request. A sudden pang of guilt caused me to push the thought aside.

"You also asked me about the business, and that is an even greater dilemma to solve. With Simon Hartzfeld's help, I am working on a plan."

My father's lawyer had provided Father with capable guidance for many years, so I was sure Mr. Hartzfeld had developed an excellent plan.

"What sort of plan, Father? Do the workers already know about this?"

A slight gleam shone in my father's blue eyes. "Are you asking because you are concerned about the workers, or because you wonder if Nathan has been keeping secrets from you?"

"Both." My one-word response sounded more austere than I'd

intended, and I hurried to expand my answer. "Most of the men are married and have families. For them to suddenly hear the news I have just learned would be devastating. How could all of them expect to find work?" Without giving him an opportunity to answer, I continued. "Forsythe Construction is known throughout Kansas City as a flourishing company. I'm certain your employees believe their jobs are secure. You will be dealing a terrible blow to men who have been loyal to you and your business. As for Nathan keeping secrets, I can say it would cause me unease."

"Nathan knows nothing of this, so you can lay aside those worries." My father folded his hands atop the table. "I appreciate your concern for those who work at the construction company. Other than the impact this move would cause for you, those men and their families have been at the forefront of my mind. That is why I've been working with Simon. He believes that by the time our current construction contracts have been completed, a qualified buyer will step forward to purchase the business. As part of that contract, we will insist that the workers be retained for a period of one year."

Soon the aroma of coffee filled the room, and I pushed away from the table. Wrapping a towel around the handle of the pot, I carried it to the table.

"And what happens to them after the year has passed?" I inhaled the fragrant aroma as I poured the hot coffee into my father's cup. "Do you think the new owner will retain them?"

"Of course. Once the owner observes their abilities, he'd be a fool to let even one of my men go." He chuckled. "Well, there may be one or two who need to work a little harder, but I think a change in ownership will be just the thing to light a fire under them."

After pouring coffee into my own cup, I returned the pot to the stove. "It does sound as though you've been giving this a great deal of thought. When do you think you will hear from the elders in Amana?"

My father shrugged his shoulders. "I can't say. It could be weeks or months, or it could be tomorrow."

"Tomorrow?" I inhaled a sharp breath and dropped into the chair.

"I don't think we will hear as soon as tomorrow, but you should give the matter much thought and prayer so that you can be at ease when the time arrives." My father took a sip of his coffee. "I plan to make an announcement at work tomorrow. Simon doesn't think it's wise to wait any longer. We need to be fair to the workers. If any of them are fearful about the prospect of a new owner, they will be free to seek other employment. Though I hope that doesn't happen, there may be some who are unwilling to risk the possibility of change." His shoulders slumped as he leaned back in his chair. "Of course, I've been curious about what course of action Nathan might want to take once he hears the news."

Leaving the children would be more difficult for me than leaving Nathan, but I didn't say that to my father. I doubted he would understand. From his earlier comment, I concluded that he and my mother expected Nathan would propose marriage once he heard the news. Did they believe I would marry Nathan in order to remain in Kansas City? Surely they realized I would want to be with them.

While the children loved me with an unconditional zeal that couldn't be questioned, my relationship with Nathan ran warm and cold, depending upon his mood. If I said or did something that displeased him, he could remain aloof for days. But when he was satisfied with me, he behaved quite the opposite. While he'd avowed his love for me on two occasions, the declarations had both been made after we'd disagreed and I'd suggested we put an end to seeing each other. To marry Nathan while still unsure of his love for me—or mine for him—would be foolhardy.

"There's my work with the children. To leave them . . ." My voice trailed off as I recalled the fun we'd had earlier that afternoon.

My father nodded. "You should let the director of the orphanage know that you are considering a move so they won't be surprised if you decide to come with us. Unless, of course, you arrive at another decision after you have prayed." His lips curved in a lopsided grin. "And after you have spoken to Nathan."

In my heart, I was certain of my decision. To be away from my mother during the remainder of her life was unthinkable. If I didn't go with my parents, I'd forever regret the decision. Yet they had asked me to pray before making a decision, and I intended to honor their request. Maybe God would change my mind. But Nathan? I didn't think so.

I wondered what my future would be like in Amana. Women couldn't be teachers in the colonies, a fact my parents had pointed out to me when they'd told me to seek God's direction. They didn't want me stepping into a new life without knowing the truth. And that particular truth caused me more concern than I cared to admit. No matter if it was a fact in history, geography, reading, or arithmetic, nothing gave me greater joy than to see the light of understanding shine in a child's eyes. I would miss teaching, and I prayed God would somehow fill that void in my life.

CHAPTER 3

I startled when the doorbell rang. After supper I'd gone to my room to read the Bible and pray. I'd promised my parents I would seek God's direction. If they should inquire, I wanted to truthfully tell them I'd kept my word. I didn't believe God would direct me to remain in Kansas City, but I was trying to remain receptive to the idea.

Not that I wanted to leave. I was quite content here. Unlike many young women, I'd never been in a hurry to marry, and being single afforded me the opportunity to spend more time with my mother as her health declined. I enjoyed occasional outings with Nathan, and I adored my work with the children.

Living at home also permitted me the luxury of teaching at the orphanage, where I volunteered my services. I loved the children and would miss them greatly. Each one held a special place in my heart, but I needed to be with my mother during her final days—both for her sake and for mine.

When the new director of the orphanage arrived in Kansas City, he'd wanted to change my volunteer status, saying it was improper for a teacher to work without pay. But after a cursory review of the orphanage's budget, he had changed his stance. Unless a replacement could be located, my resignation would leave the orphanage with a limited teaching staff.

I glanced in the mirror, patted my hair into place, and hurried downstairs as the doorbell chimed for the second time. Over and over, I'd asked Nathan to be patient when he arrived. Since Mother's condition had worsened, the doorbell could disturb her rest. Yet he continued to ignore my requests.

Nathan removed his brown felt hat. "You appear troubled."

His slicked-down brown hair was a perfect match for his brown eyes, brown hat, brown coat, brown trousers, and brown shoes. I pictured him standing beside a leafless tree and suppressed a smile. In that attire, he'd be a perfect match for the dormant elm in our front yard.

"Mother is sleeping. The ringing bell might waken her."

"Sorry." He ducked his head. "I thought maybe you hadn't heard it." He stepped inside and I closed the door.

"The bell is loud enough I can hear it anywhere in the house." I gestured for him to hang his coat on the hall tree.

"Did you have a bad day?" Using his thumb and forefinger, he reached forward and pretended to push my lips back into a smile. "Any coffee in the kitchen?" He winked. "And a piece of cake or pie?"

So much had happened since my return home that afternoon that I didn't wish to act the hostess, but I waved him forward.

"There may be a cup left. I don't think there is any dessert. Mrs. Oelwine left early today."

He chuckled. "You'll have to put a stop to that. I enjoy her desserts."

"Of late, desserts haven't been a matter of high priority to Father and me, and Mother can seldom tolerate rich food."

My answer had been curt, and I was surprised when he stopped short and stared at me.

"What is wrong with you? You're not yourself this evening."

I walked to the cupboard and removed a coffee cup. "I apologize, but there are times when I have more to worry about than coffee and dessert."

"If you'd like me to leave, just say so. You did invite me, didn't you?"

I sighed. Nathan was right. None of this was his fault. "I'm sorry, Nathan." I poured coffee into his cup and carried it to the table. "This has been a day filled with unexpected news that will change our lives."

His thick eyebrows lifted on his forehead like two brown wiggly caterpillars. "Our lives? Yours and mine?" He pointed first at himself and then at me. "What news? I haven't heard anything."

"The doctor told Mother there is nothing he can do to restore her health and her condition will only worsen." I couldn't bring myself to say she was dying. "Father and Mother have decided to move back to the Amana Colonies in Iowa. It's what Mother wants, and my father has agreed."

At first he grinned, but when he realized I was serious, he turned somber. "How can they even think of such a thing? When is this supposed to happen?"

I explained what my father had told me only a short time ago.

With each remark, he interrupted me with a host of questions. Many of which I couldn't answer. Finally I said, "You'll need to ask my father to further explain his arrangements concerning the business. I've told you everything I know."

"Did he mention any particular plans for my future at the company? He must have some idea in mind, since we'll need a reliable income if I'm going to support you."

"Support me?" My mind reeled. Did he think that I would remain behind and marry him? We hadn't discussed marriage. What was he thinking? "Why would you think you would need to support me?"

He studied me for a moment. "You know I have feelings for you. I've hesitated to mention marriage because you told me that you believed couples should know each other for a long period of time before taking their vows." He wrapped his hands around the coffee cup. "Have you considered the possibility that this is a sign we should move forward with wedding plans?"

I shook my head. "No, I don't think it's a sign we should marry. I promised my parents I would pray about my future, though I believe I know what I should do."

His brow creased, and I didn't miss the concern shadowing his eyes. "You're not thinking of going with them, are you?" He pushed aside the empty cup.

I nodded. "Of course I am. To be honest, I believe there's little choice to be made. I can't imagine being separated from my mother when she's ill and needs me."

He leaned forward and extended his hand. "You don't need to move there. You could go and visit from time to time. I'd go with you. If you don't want to marry right away, you could make some sort of arrangement with one of the other teachers at the orphanage. Maybe remain here in the house and rent rooms to some of them."

"Rent rooms? I don't want to operate a boardinghouse when my mother needs me. Besides, my parents plan to sell the house. They'll contribute the proceeds to the society when they go to Amana. It's the way things are done."

"I understand you want to help your mother, but I'm sure she wants you to have a life of your own." He stood and paced the kitchen. "What about the children at the orphanage?" Wheeling around on his heel, he pinned me with a hard stare. "You've always said you wouldn't give up your work with them."

Like a spade in soft dirt, his words dug in and cut to the quick. "Sometimes people say things without realizing what the future holds. How could I have ever imagined such a possibility as this?"

"But if they mean so much to you, how can you so easily decide to leave them—and me?"

"As much as I care for the children, the love for my mother goes much deeper. Surely you can understand there is a vast difference."

One look and I knew he didn't understand. How could he? Nathan's parents hadn't showered him with love and protection. His father had been a stern and cold man who'd left the family when Nathan was only ten. His mother had expected much from her only child and had given little in return. At the age of fourteen, he'd left home and never looked back.

A part of me could understand his desire to strike out on his own, especially when there had been no encouragement at home, but his lack of compassion and his indifference haunted me. How could he push aside any concern for the mother who bore him? He didn't know if she was alive or dead and harbored no desire to discover what had happened to the woman. At least that's what he'd told me, and I had no reason to doubt him. Those thoughts had given me pause. Did Nathan possess the ability to love in a true and meaningful manner? He'd seemingly erased his mother from his life. Would he do the same if his wife ever displeased him?

He twisted around as though the statement caused him discomfort. "There comes a day when we must cling to our mates and leave our parents. This could help prepare you for our future marriage."

"Right now I don't have a husband or children of my own, and I believe this to be a time when I can put my parents first. Unless something drastic should happen to change my mind, I plan to go with them."

His sigh signaled his displeasure. "As much as I don't understand what you're thinking, I'm even more baffled by your parents, especially your father. As far as I can see, this plan is impulsive and unwise. A complete destruction of everything they've worked for all their lives."

"Facing death can change a person's attitude about what's important. Besides, my parents have never considered wealth their ultimate goal."

Nathan returned to his chair. "Maybe not, but they've achieved more than most. It seems strange that they're willing to hand it over without a thought of providing for your future."

His tone surprised me. "Whatever they've earned is theirs. I have no claim to any of their property. If it gives my parents peace and happiness to contribute their assets and return to the colonies, who am I to say otherwise?"

"You are their daughter. Are you willing to live in poverty?" He raked his fingers through his hair. "I had hoped one day to purchase the business from your father, but it seems that dream will fade along with all the other aspirations I've ever had. There's no bank that would loan me enough money to purchase the construction company."

Nathan hunched his shoulders and looked every bit as despondent as he'd sounded. This conversation had become about him rather than about me, my parents, or my mother's illness, and the thought grieved me.

I forced a smile. "Would you like more coffee?"

He shook his head. "Tell me about Amana. I want to understand what it is that appeals to your parents and why they would want to return."

"You should ask my father. My knowledge is limited since I've never lived there and never questioned my parents much about their life before they came to Kansas City. It didn't seem particularly important." My thoughts raced back in time. I recalled a few times when my mother had mentioned things that had happened in the colonies, but I'd been more interested in my playmates and school than in hearing about my mother's past. "Beyond telling you that it is a communal society where they still speak a German dialect and live a simple life based upon their religious beliefs, there's not much I can tell you."

Nathan rubbed his jaw. "And you believe you will be happy living in this sort of place?"

I hesitated and considered his question. I prided myself on my ability to adjust to new circumstances, but living in a communal society would require drastic changes. Adjustments that would likely prove much more difficult than anything I'd ever encountered.

"I don't know if I'll be happy, but I'll be with my parents and I want to care for my mother during this time when she needs me."

His lips tightened into a thin line. "I can't believe you can so easily make this choice."

I understood his surprise and dismay, but I had hoped he would honor my decision—that he would understand and support me no matter my choice. Yet I didn't believe Nathan had the ability to push aside his own wants and needs. For most of his life, he'd had only himself to depend upon—and only himself to please.

And though we'd made no commitment to each other, he expected me to say that I'd remain in Kansas City and convince my father to retain Forsythe Construction. That way Nathan could someday become the owner.

CHAPTER 4

April 1881

The much anticipated letter from Amana arrived on a beautiful day in the middle of April. The contents of the missive were much like the spring weather: warm and welcoming. The elders' words of encouragement appeared to fortify my parents' decision. Like the sprouting trees outside my bedroom window, they were prepared to begin a new season of their lives.

In the garden below, fearless daffodils and crocus bloomed in full array, while the less hearty flowers peeked through the soft dirt as if uncertain whether to push up or remain hidden belowground a little longer. My behavior remained more aligned with the bulbs hiding beneath the dirt—tentative and unsure about the future.

Since my father's initial announcement that they would return to the colonies if granted permission, Mother had created a list of belongings she wished to take when we departed, and I'd been doing my best to sort and separate the items to remain from the items to be packed. Mr. Hartzfeld had located a buyer for our house. A family moving from the East wanted to purchase not only the house but as many of the furnishings as we wished to leave for them.

Mother declared it a sure sign that the proper decision had been made. Though less effusive, my father had been pleased by the transaction. "One less thing to worry over," he'd said after gaining my final assurance that I wouldn't later regret the sale. On the other hand, Nathan had been unhappy when I told him, expressing dismay at Father's plans to sell.

As the days passed after the sale of our home, I'd seen less of Nathan. His constant efforts to discourage me had created a breach of sorts, and when he'd last come to call, he told me he wouldn't return unless I sent word that I wanted to see him. Last night I wrote a note and asked Nathan to come to the house this evening if he was free.

I hurried downstairs before my father left for work and handed him the envelope. "Please don't tell Nathan we've received the letter of permission. I prefer to tell him myself."

Father tucked the envelope into his pocket. "I won't say a word. I plan to speak with Mr. Hartzfeld, but I'll be going to his office. We need to make final arrangements regarding the business and the house as soon as possible."

"Do we need to be in a great rush? There hasn't been any noticeable change in Mother's health. Of late I've even wondered if the doctor's assessment of her condition is incorrect."

"Unfortunately, I'm sure the doctor is correct. He assures me he's spoken to his colleagues. They affirm they've seen other patients who experience this same muscular weakness, but they simply don't have a cure. Like your mother, their patients have periods when they flourish and appear to be on the road to recovery, but it isn't permanent. He admonished me not to fall into the trap of believing she would get well." A shadow of sadness veiled my father's eyes. "The doctor was clear: The best thing we can do is provide her with good nutrition and tranquil surroundings. Our new home in Amana will provide both."

He sighed. "I have been praying we will be able to get settled in the colonies before I detect any further changes in her condition." He squeezed my shoulder. "Thus far, God has heard and answered my prayers. I'd like to be prepared to depart by the end of the month."

"And I am thankful for that, Father." I waited until he'd left and then hurried to gather my cloak and the cloth tote bag I used to carry books and papers between school and home.

The elders' letter had placed a note of finality on my decision to leave Kansas City. Today I would tell Mr. Ludwig the awaited permission had arrived. When I'd originally told him of my plans to move, he'd expressed concern for the students. But since then, he'd made little effort to find a replacement. I had hoped he might secure a new teacher before I departed so the transition would be less difficult for the children. He later advised he hadn't put much effort into the task, since locating a qualified teacher willing to volunteer her services would likely prove impossible.

I had personally inquired among some of the unmarried young women who devoted their time to charity work, but none had been interested in assuming a full-time volunteer position. I'd momentarily taken heart when Mary Wolff had pulled me aside after church services last Sunday and made inquiry, but once she learned of Mr. Ludwig's engagement, her interest ceased and our conversation abruptly ended.

In the end, I'd been disheartened. If nobody stepped forward to help, it would make leaving all the more difficult. For a day or two I'd even considered remaining in Kansas City until a replacement could be found, but I soon realized that could take months—or even a year. I couldn't take a chance someone would soon be located—not with Mother's health on the decline.

Telling the children would be my most difficult challenge. I didn't want them to feel that I was deserting them, but I needed to be honest. To build false hope and tell them I would return to the orphanage wasn't fair—only time would tell what was in my future, and theirs.

As usual, Mr. Ludwig had taken his post outside his office door. He greeted each of the children by name as they passed him on the way to their classrooms. I wasn't certain if the morning ritual was a test of his memory or if he thought it bolstered the children's self-esteem. After the first few weeks, I'd expected him to cease the practice, but there had been no sign he intended to quit.

"Good morning, Miss Rhoder. How are you this fine day?"

"Fine, Mr. Ludwig." I slowed my step as I approached and stopped beside him. "If you have a moment, I'd like to speak with you in private."

His jaw twitched at the prospect of changing his daily habit, but he ushered me inside. "Is there a problem?"

Knowing he wanted to return to his regular post, I quickly explained this would be my final week at the school. "I do hope you can locate someone to replace me. Perhaps an ad in the newspaper might prove beneficial."

He shook his head. "I don't think a newspaper advertisement would succeed in bringing a volunteer teacher to our doors. We will have to wait for God's provision."

I wanted to tell him that sometimes God expects us to take action while we wait but decided such a comment might do more harm than good. "Then I will pray for Him to provide the perfect teacher."

Seemingly pleased with my answer, Mr. Ludwig nodded and hurried back to his post outside the doorway. Sorrow weighed heavy on my shoulders as I trudged toward my classroom. Nettie Wilson skipped toward me, her wispy blond hair flying in all directions.

"Are we having story time today, Miss Jancey—I mean, Miss Rhoder?" She flashed a worried look toward Mr. Ludwig.

"Yes, but not until later this afternoon." Telling the children during story time might help soften the blow. At least that was my hope.

We walked hand-in-hand to the classroom, where the other children had already gathered and were shuffling to their seats. For the remainder of the morning and early afternoon, I did my best to conduct classes in my usual manner. If the children noticed my inability to concentrate or to display my customary enthusiasm, they didn't comment. After they returned indoors from their afternoon playtime, I pulled my chair to the middle of the room and motioned for them to form a semicircle around the chair.

"We're going to end the day with story time today because I have a very special tale that I want to tell you."

Caroline's hand shot into the air. "Is it a story we've heard before, Miss Rhoder?"

I smiled and shook my head. "No, it isn't."

"Is it from a book, or is it one you're making up in your head?" Matthew Turner didn't bother to raise his hand before asking, but I didn't reprimand him.

"This isn't from a book." As I looked into their expectant

faces, I burned this moment into my memory. I didn't want to forget any one of these children. Each one had become precious to me. Hot tears burned my eyes, and I pulled a handkerchief from my pocket.

"Why are you crying, Miss Rhoder?" Bertie wiggled forward, her lips quivering with concern.

"I think there's something in my eye." I didn't tell Bertie it was tears. That wouldn't help matters in the least.

After inhaling slowly, I folded my hands in my lap and glanced around the room. "Many years ago, a young man and woman fell in love with each other and decided they wanted to get married."

"*Eww*. Is this going to be a love story?" Matthew curled his lips and wrinkled his freckled nose.

I chuckled. "I won't talk about kissing. Does that help, Matthew?" He bobbed his head and grinned.

"As I was saying, this young couple decided to get married. They first lived in Iowa, but then they decided to move to Kansas City. Who can point to Iowa on the map?"

The map and globe, along with numerous other school materials, had been purchased by my father when he'd learned how few supplies we had at the orphanage school. Several of the children waved their hands and then watched as Caroline walked to the map and pointed.

"Excellent." I gestured for her to remain where she was. "This young couple lived in southeast Iowa." Turning in my chair, I looked at Caroline. "Now, point your finger to the southeast section of the state." She hesitated only a moment before moving her hand. I nodded. "Good. Now, slowly move your finger until you reach Kansas City." Caroline studied the map and then did as I'd instructed. I looked back at the circle of children. "That doesn't look very far when you trace it on the map, but it's quite a distance when you're traveling by wagon over bumpy trails." I motioned Caroline back to her place with the other children.

"Why'd they leave?" As usual, one of the younger children had forgotten to raise his hand.

"They'd been told they had to wait for a year before they could marry, but they didn't want to wait."

"So they runned away?" Nettie's eyes were as big as saucers. "Were they scared?"

"I'm sure they were frightened, but they didn't want to give up their dream to get married right away, so they left their homes and everyone they knew and came to Kansas City." I continued with the story, telling the children how my parents had struggled to make a life in a new place and how an older couple had extended both kindness and generosity to the young couple and later to their baby daughter.

"Many years later, the older couple made it possible for the young couple to purchase their business and live in a beautiful home, where they raised their daughter."

"Then what happened to them?" With a bored expression, Matthew folded his arms across his chest. "Did they live happily ever after?"

"Almost. They sent their daughter to very fine schools, and she became a teacher."

"Just like you," Nettie chimed.

"Yes, just like me. But one day, the mother became very ill and she wanted to return to her home in Iowa so she could be close to former friends that she hadn't seen for many years. So her husband said that was what they would do. They would sell their business and their house, and they would return to their old home."

Caroline waved at me. "What happened to their daughter? If they sold their house, where did she live?"

"She went with them," Matthew replied. "That's what girls do—they live with their parents until they move in with their husband."

Caroline leaned forward and glared at Matthew. "Not all girls! Some live in boardinghouses, don't they, Miss Rhoder?"

"That's true. Some young women do live on their own."

Caroline shot a triumphant look at Matthew. "See? I told you."

"However, that isn't what happened. In this story, the young woman leaves her teaching position and goes to live with her parents in Iowa."

"Ha!" Matthew assumed a victorious pose. "Told you so."

I held my finger to my lips. "No more interruptions, please." I glanced around the room. "The daughter prayed and asked for God's help with her decision because she didn't want to leave the children at the school, but she wanted to be with her sick mother and help care for her, too." I leaned back in my chair. "Let's create an ending for this story together, shall we? Who'd like to go first?"

Matthew shoved his hand into the air, and I nodded at him. "I think she should do whatever she wants."

"That sounds like something a boy would say," Caroline declared. "If she believes God wants her to go with her family, she should go. If not, she should stay behind and live at a boardinghouse, where she'll meet a single man, fall in love, and get married."

I chuckled at Caroline's far-reaching solution.

Nettie poked Caroline in the arm. "I don't want her to get married. I want her to keep teaching the children forever, so they won't miss her."

"Forever?" Matthew chortled. "The children will grow up and

leave the school, so why should she stay forever, Nettie? That's not a good ending to the story." He turned toward me. "How are you going to end the story, Miss Rhoder?"

My stomach clenched in a tight knot and I forced a smile. "This story isn't really make-believe. You see, it's about me and my parents."

"Oh no!" Nettie squealed. "You're not going to leave us, are you?" Tears glistened in her brown eyes. "Is Mr. Ludwig going to be our teacher?"

"I'm not certain who will be your new teacher, but I'm sure it will be someone you'll like even more than me—at least that is my hope. Until a new teacher begins, you'll probably go into Miss Manchester's class."

A rumble of moans and gasps circulated around me. I knew the children would be unhappy joining the older children in Miss Manchester's class, but I believed it to be the only solution. Although he'd done nothing to find a substitute, Mr. Ludwig wouldn't step in to fill my position. He'd consider it beneath his position as the school director. Even though Miss Manchester was strict, she did exhibit occasional affection toward her students. Neither of them would be a good fit for this class, but the children would adapt to Miss Manchester with greater ease.

Bertie's lower lip quivered and she stood. "Will you ever come back to see us, Miss Rhoder?"

Making false promises wouldn't be fair, yet I couldn't leave these children without hope. Their eyes were filled with anticipation as they awaited my answer. I sent a silent prayer heavenward that my words would be filled with truth and hope.

"We never know what each day will bring, but if there is any way possible, I will return to visit you." I held up a finger when the children started to cheer. "You must remember that I don't know when that might be. It could be only a month or so after I depart, or it could be a very long time. While I'm away, it would make me very happy to know that you are all doing your very best in your studies."

Caroline pulled Bertie onto her lap. "Maybe you could write us a letter once in a while and tell us about Iowa and your new students."

"You won't like them more than us, will you?" A tear rolled down Bertie's plump cheek.

"I don't know how often, but I promise I'll write to you as time permits." I held my arms open to Bertie and she raced forward. She crawled onto my lap and I rested my chin on her head. "You need not worry about other students just yet, Bertie. I won't be a schoolteacher in Iowa."

After dealing with the children's questions and tears earlier in the day, I hoped my talk with Nathan would go well.

Standing in the doorway, he removed my note from his pocket. "I hope this invitation to come to the house this evening is good news."

I sighed and ushered him inside.

"From that sigh, I'm surmising you have nothing pleasant to report."

"Did I sigh?" I did my best to sound cheerful. "Would you care for something to drink? A cup of tea or coffee?"

His frown returned. "You've obviously forgotten I don't drink tea."

"Of course you don't. I know better." I nodded toward the parlor. "Would you prefer to sit in the parlor or on the porch? It's a lovely evening."

"The parlor is fine. We're already indoors and I'm curious about why you sent for me." He tapped his finger on the note I'd sent earlier in the day. "Your father has heard from the elders, hasn't he?"

I sat down on one of the chairs and Nathan sat opposite me. "Yes. He received a letter yesterday. They've agreed to our return."

His eyebrows dropped low. "This may be a return for your parents, but it isn't a return for you, Jancey. You've never even seen that place." He leaned forward and rested his arms across his thighs. "I hope you're going to tell me that you've decided to remain in Kansas City."

There was a pleading tone in his voice—one I'd never before heard. This wasn't going to be easy. "I can't, Nathan. For now, I must go with my parents."

"Does that mean you're going only for a short time and then you'll return?"

A dull ache spread across the base of my skull, and I massaged my neck. "I'm going to repeat what I told the schoolchildren earlier today. I don't know what the future holds in store for me. There may come a day when I return, but I don't know if or when that will be."

"And you expect me to wait indefinitely?" He pressed his lips together and waited.

"No. I could never ask that of anyone. We have no formal commitment to each other."

"We would if you'd agree to marry me. You know how much I care for you. We could have a good life here in Kansas City, and I think your parents would approve. I'm sure they believe you deserve a life of your own." His anger vanished and he pinned me with a soulful gaze. "I'm asking you to stay here and marry me."

I didn't know which was more difficult to bear: his anger or his beseeching proposal. "Marriage is for a lifetime, Nathan. This period of separation could prove beneficial for both of us. If we are truly meant to be together, our feelings for each other will withstand the time we are apart. There's a saying that absence makes the heart grow fonder." I hoped my response would ease the pain I'd caused him.

"I'm already sure of my love for you, and I don't believe that saying. We haven't seen each other for three weeks. During that time, you've become even more distant."

He'd been the one who'd decided to stay away, but reminding him wouldn't help matters. "I'm sorry if I appear aloof. That isn't my intention. It has been a long and tiring day. The children were troubled to learn of my plans, and you are equally worried. My head aches, and there is nothing I can say that will make you or the children feel better about my plans."

"So there is no hope you'll change your mind?" When I shook my head, he jumped to his feet. "Then I suppose I should leave so you can take some headache powder and rest."

I didn't object to his departure. Truth be told, I was thankful he'd decided further argument wouldn't help his cause. When we approached the front door, I touched his sleeve. "Thank you for your kindness and understanding, Nathan."

His lips curved in a wry smile. "If you think I understand, you're clearly mistaken." He opened the door and glanced over his shoulder. "Should you have a change of heart, you know how to reach me."

I stood watching until he was out of sight and then closed the door on the life I'd known and loved for all of my twenty-two years.

CHAPTER 5

May 1881
Middle Amana, Iowa

My plan had been to glean further information about Amana during our train travels. Instead, I spent the hours caring for Mother. We'd been on the train only a short time when she became weak and needed to rest. Fortunately the doctor had given my father medication to use if she experienced difficulty during the journey. Although the medicine wouldn't do anything to cure her, at least it could relieve some of her discomfort and permit periods of fitful sleep. She ate only what I forced upon her, and when we finally arrived in the colonies, she appeared weak and pale.

Always a man who attended to details, my father had planned every aspect of our journey as carefully as any business transaction for his company. He had notified the elders of the date and time of our arrival in early May, and Brother Herman, one of the elders from Middle Amana, met our train. He was a kind man with sparkling blue eyes and a quick smile, and he welcomed us as though we were family. In some ways, I suppose he viewed us as such. Father had explained to me that everyone living in the colonies was considered equal—all brothers and sisters in Christ. And since I had no brothers or sisters, I found the idea appealing. Still, I wondered whether a village of strangers would ever become like true relatives to me.

My father had encouraged me to keep an open mind, and I agreed to do my best. With Mother ill, and I unsure of how I should behave in this new world, having brothers and sisters would be a good thing, even if I didn't know their names. But making the transition from English to German would take some doing. I hadn't understood my parents' determination to have me learn to read, write, and speak German when I was a child, but now I was pleased they'd insisted. While many of my friends elected to study French, I'd continued my German studies throughout my years in school, but I'd used it little since beginning my position at the orphanage. I would need my parents' help, for the dialect spoken here was different from the formal speech I'd learned in school. I leaned close and expressed my concern to Mother.

"In no time, you will have the language mastered." She spoke in German rather than English and I arched my brows. "Best to begin right now. We will speak no more English."

Brother Herman helped Father load our trunks into the wagon. "There is nothing more? You brought no furniture? I was told you were bringing your own furniture."

"The rest of our belongings will arrive on the train tomorrow."

"That is *gut*. Will be easier to adjust to your new house with some of your own belongings." He chuckled. "I did not mean the house is new—just that it is new to the three of you. You will share a house with the Hetrig family. Do you know them?"

My father hiked a shoulder. "I'm not sure. The name doesn't sound familiar, but we have been away a long time, Brother Herman."

"Share?" This was the first I'd heard of sharing a house with another family, but perhaps they would have a daughter close to my age one who could help me learn about the village and my new life in the colonies.

My father patted my hand. "Do not worry. It will be our own apartment—we will have separate rooms."

Before I had a chance to tell Father that the revelation had merely caught me by surprise, Brother Herman bobbed his head and smiled. "*Ja*, you will be on the first floor because it will be easier for you, Sister Almina." The elder glanced over his shoulder at my mother. "That's what we decided."

Some of the color had returned to Mother's cheeks, and she dipped her head in an approving nod. "I appreciate your thoughtfulness, Brother Herman." She continued to rally as we traveled from the train station toward our new house. She said it was due to the fresh air and the happiness of being home again. If that was true, perhaps she'd continue to feel even better once we settled into our new lives.

I stared in wonder as the horses clopped along the dirt road, pulling us into this unique new world—at least that's what it was to me. Rows of well-kept brick and frame homes lined the streets. The wooden sidewalks were flanked by thick unpainted board fences that produced a rare uniformity and style to the village. A variety of trees shaded the yards, and just like at home, flowers had begun to poke through the soft dirt that flanked the board walkways leading to each of the houses. Wide trellises were attached to the fronts and sides of the homes, and thick grapevines snaked their way through the wooden slats.

"You don't have enough land to plant your grapes?"

Brother Herman tipped his head back and laughed at my question. "*Ach!* I can see you know little about us. We have more than enough land for all of our crops—over twenty-six thousand acres are owned by our people. The grapevines on the houses are to help keep the houses cool during the summer and to provide extra grapes for jelly the sisters make each year. There is a large vineyard where we plant the grapes for making the wine." His broad smile revealed a row of even white teeth. "I am thinking you will help pick the grapes this year and sort the onions. Those are fun times, for sure. We are all joyful when it is time to harvest the grapes. The little ones sometimes end up with aching bellies because they eat more than they put in their baskets. And the sisters enjoy their time together sorting the onions."

While I'd never before helped with such tasks, I could imagine the laughter and visiting that the women and children must enjoy as they worked side by side in the fields. How my little students at the orphanage would relish such freedom. My heart squeezed at the thought. I could almost picture Matthew or towheaded Nettie plucking fruit from vines that had turned heavy with fruit. No doubt they would devour many of those grapes by the time they finished a day of picking.

I pulled my thoughts back to the present as the wagon rolled past several two-story brick homes, some larger than others, a number of thin-slatted frame homes that bore no sign of having ever been painted, and an occasional sandstone house. All appeared neat and tidy, but I'd seen few people outdoors. No women sweeping their porches or little children playing in the spring sunshine. None of the usual city sounds that had filled my ears each day back home.

I nudged my father. "Where are all the people who live in these houses?" The tranquility of the village surprised me. I'd expected to see women bustling in and out of shops, children tugging on their mother's skirts, and men rushing to and fro from one work site or meeting to another.

Brother Herman twisted on his perch. "They are at their work, just like in the place where you lived, ja?" He waved to a young woman carrying an infant, who gestured in return. "The women with babies are at home, but most of the sisters are busy preparing meals in the kitchen houses or working in the gardens. The men are in the barns and fields, caring for animals and tilling fields to plant crops, while others are at work in the woolen mill, lumber yard, or grist mill. All must work to provide for the needs of our people." He bobbed his head. "You will soon learn how everything is done."

"Do the people choose what work they will perform?"

My father's eyebrows scrunched low over his eyes, a sure sign he wanted me to cease questioning Brother Herman, but I couldn't seem to help myself. I wanted to know more about this new way of life.

When Brother Herman hesitated a moment, I wondered if, like my father, he thought I'd overstepped the proper limits of good manners. "The work is assigned by the elders in the villages, but we match the ability of the worker to the job. When the children are young, they go to school. In the morning they learn from books, and in the afternoon they begin to learn a trade. If they excel at working with animals, weaving baskets, making brooms, making clocks, or tailoring, then they continue with that work when they are older. You understand?"

"What if you don't like the work you're assigned? Are you given permission to do some other job?"

"Much would depend on where workers are needed, but we try to do our best to keep everyone content with their labor. For a man to find satisfaction in his labor is a gut thing."

I wanted to ask if I could visit the school and possibly assist the teacher, but I knew this wasn't the proper time. Even though women weren't permitted to teach, perhaps I'd be allowed to help in some way. It seemed a shame to let my education and experience go to waste. I hoped I'd have a chance to speak to one of the elders about my job assignment later in the day.

Brother Herman pushed his hat back from his forehead. "For you, we have considered your *Mutter*'s illness and know you will want to help with her care."

"Yes, that's very important to me." His remark caused me to wonder if caring for Mother would be my only work.

"Ja, is gut to care for one another, but you will also help one of the sisters with cleaning the quarters where the outside workers are housed. It is next to the woolen mill and not so far from where you and your parents will be living. Sister Margaret needs extra help, and the elders thought work close to home would be a gut choice for you."

I hoped Sister Margaret would also think me a good choice. I didn't have a lot of experience performing household duties, but I was pleased I wouldn't be far from home so I could frequently check on my mother. "I am pleased you were so thoughtful in your decision." I leaned a little closer. "Who are these outside workers you mentioned, Brother Herman?"

He slapped the leather reins, and the horses immediately picked up their pace. "Some are seasonal workers who come here to help harvest or plant. They stay only a short time and then move on. There are others who work in the woolen mill or at other more permanent jobs, and they stay with us longer. We have enough work to keep some busy throughout the year."

His explanation surprised me. For some reason I hadn't imagined anyone living in the villages unless he had joined the community. "And they all live in the building near the woolen mill?"

He shook his head. "Not all of the outsiders, but all the men who work in the woolen mill in Middle live there."

"With their families?"

He frowned. "*Nein.* They are all single men—no families. Would not be proper. You will see how it is. Sister Margaret will show you what is expected and answer your questions."

I leaned back and folded my hands in my lap. I wanted to ask more questions, but Brother Herman had sent me a clear message: Any further questions should be directed to Sister Margaret.

The horses immediately obeyed when Brother Herman pulled back on the reins. The wagon came to a halt in front of a large brick house, much like many of the others we'd passed along the way. Wooden flower boxes flanking the porch appeared to be filled with fresh dirt, and an occasional daffodil added a hint of color along the walkway. I was struck by the uniform neatness—so different from the city.

"Here we are. Your new home. I think you will find your space comfortable. Once your furniture arrives, it will be just like home."

Even though this house wasn't at all similar to our home in Kansas City, it was attractive, and the peaceful surroundings would provide a restful atmosphere for Mother. And Brother Herman was right: Once our furniture arrived and we'd arranged our belongings throughout the rooms, a sense of home would prevail.

Brother Herman waved us forward. "This way. Follow me."

After helping Mother from the wagon, my father supported her as she climbed the two steps into the small foyer of our new home. Two choices awaited us: Walk straight ahead and up the stairway or enter a door to the left of the front entrance. Brother Herman stood beside the closed door until all three of us squeezed inside.

With a bright smile, he pushed down on the heavy metal door latch. "Welcome to your new home."

I waited until Mother and Father entered before I stepped inside. I could feel Brother Herman's intense gaze upon me as I looked around the room. Except for a table and two chairs at the far end of the room and a multicolored woven rug that covered the majority of the pinewood floor, the room was bare. If the train didn't arrive tomorrow, we'd be living without a sofa or comfortable chairs, and I worried about Mother's comfort.

As if he'd read my thoughts, Father looked at me and then turned to Brother Herman. "We may need to stay at the hotel until tomorrow." He waved his hand toward the adjoining rooms. "We will need beds for tonight."

Brother Herman scratched his head. "You and Sister Almina can stay at my home. We have an extra bedroom, since our two sons have married." He glanced at me. "I will make arrangements for you to stay upstairs with the Hetrigs. They have a daughter, and you can share her room. I am sure Sister Hanna and Brother Werner will be happy to have you."

I swallowed hard. The thought of spending my first night with strangers in these new surroundings wasn't appealing. And wouldn't Mother and Father be more comfortable in a hotel? I waited, expecting to hear Father politely decline the invitation.

Instead, he nodded and smiled. "Thank you for your kind offer."

My mouth gaped wide enough to catch flies. *"Thank you for your kind offer?"* Was my father really accepting Brother Herman's proposed arrangement? Fixing my eyes on my mother, I cleared my throat and waited until she looked at me.

"I'm sure the Hetrigs would prefer to have me take a room at the hotel. They've never even met me." As a hint of fear took hold, I sent a pleading look in Mother's direction, hoping she would come to my aid.

"They're likely very kind, and it will give you an opportunity to become acquainted with their daughter. Perhaps you're close to the same age." She glanced at Brother Herman.

"Nein, but I'm sure young Madelyn will be pleased to welcome you. I think she is nine or ten years old. A sweet girl—you will like her." Brother Herman reached in his pocket and removed a pipe. "Your father said in one of his letters that you like young children, ja?"

"I do like children. I was a teacher in Kansas City, but—"

"Gut, then there is no problem. You and Madelyn will do fine together. There is no one at home right now, but I will take you to the *Küchehaas* and introduce you to Sister Hetrig. She works at the kitchen house where you will eat your meals. They are a gut family. Brother Werner is a supervisor at the grist mill, and their son, Brother Ritter, works at the woolen mill. Brother Ritter prefers to be addressed as Brother Ritt. You will like all of them." He gave a firm nod that signaled the end of the discussion.

Pleased or not, fearful or not, ill at ease or not, I would be spending the night in the home of strangers. Maybe Nathan had been correct. Maybe I should have remained in Kansas City. I pushed aside the notion. Wasn't I the one who constantly reminded the children at the orphanage to remain open to new experiences? Shouldn't I do the same? After all, nothing good would come from negative thoughts. No matter the circumstances, I wanted to be with my parents. I hoped our new neighbors would prove as likeable as Brother Herman promised.

"We will need to get you proper clothing. I will ask Sister Hanna if she will see to it."

After delivering my parents to his home and seeing to their comfort, Brother Herman gestured for me to follow him. "Come. I will take you to meet Sister Hanna and the other sisters who work in the Küchehaas."

After I bid my parents good-bye, Mother waved me forward as Brother Herman strode across the room.

He opened the door and waited for me to join him. "Your mother and father need to rest, but I am sure you want to see more of your new surroundings."

I did want to see more, and though I would have preferred to see it with my parents, I appreciated Brother Herman's kindness. For a moment, our departure reminded me of the day my parents had taken me to boarding school. When they'd departed to return home, I'd felt as though I'd been marooned on a desert island. Though it hadn't taken long for me to overcome the loneliness, I hadn't forgotten those feelings. As an inkling of those same feelings attempted to take root, I pushed them aside and forced myself to focus on Brother Herman.

"We will go this way. It is a little shorter." Taking long strides, Brother Herman escorted me away from his home. If he'd detected any reluctance, he didn't let on. Neither of us spoke until we neared a brick house that was larger than most of the others I'd seen. Brother Herman looked over his shoulder. "This is the Wieler *Küche*, where you will eat. We are going through the back door and into the kitchen, but when you come for dinner you will go to the front and enter through the women's door. I am thinking your parents have already explained that the men and women sit at separate tables to eat their meals, ja?"

When he arched his brows and waited for my response, I nodded. "Yes. But I don't know which door is for the women." There hadn't been much time to learn about the rules on our journey, but perhaps once our family was reunited, my mother would feel well enough to instruct me.

He smiled. "Just follow the other sisters, and you will be at the proper door." He tapped on the kitchen door, stepped inside, and gestured for me to step forward. "*Guten Tag*, Sister Bertha. This is Jancey Rhoder—the daughter of Jurgen and Almina Rhoder." Brother Herman tipped his head toward me. "Sister Bertha is the *Küchebaas*." He grinned at the wide-hipped woman. "She makes sure everyone gets plenty of gut food and that it is served on time."

"With the help of the other sisters. Without them, I could not manage." The gray-haired woman lifted an oversized metal spoon from a hook on the wall and lowered it into a kettle sitting atop the stove. She turned her gaze on me. "I remember your Mutter and *Vater*. Sister Mina was younger than I, but she could knit much better than girls twice her age." She continued to stir the contents of the pot. "Does she still knit?"

"Yes, when she's able. Her health hasn't been good for more than a year."

"Ja, I was sorry to hear." She looked at Brother Herman. "Sister Jancey will be working in the *Küche* with us?"

"Nein. I brought her to meet Sister Hanna. The Rhoders will be living in the rooms below the Hetrigs."

Sister Bertha stepped to a door that led from the large kitchen to the dining room. As she walked into the dining room, I peered around her and noticed long tables with benches arranged along both sides. A wide aisle separated the rows, likely the dividing line between the men and women. Sister Bertha stopped beside a woman with rosy cheeks. Soon, the two of them drew near, and Brother Herman stepped forward.

"Guten Tag, Sister Hanna. I would like you to meet Jancey Rhoder, the daughter of—"

Sister Hanna bobbed her head. "Ja, ja, I know who she is. Brother Ernst told my Werner the Rhoders would be moving in downstairs." She smiled at me. "Welcome."

"Thank you. I'm pleased to meet you, Sister Hanna."

Her lips curved in a broad smile that revealed a dimple in her left cheek. "*Danke*. And I am pleased to meet you, too."

Moving between us, Brother Herman pointed to the kitchen door. "We will talk on the porch so we do not interfere with the other sisters while they work."

Once outside, Brother Herman explained our circumstances to Sister Hanna. "Because their furniture has not yet arrived, Sister Jancey is without a place to sleep tonight. The simple solution is for her to spend the night with your family."

Sister Hanna appeared comfortable with the idea. "We will be happy to have you as our guest, but you might not get much sleep. Our Madelyn has always wanted a big sister instead of a big brother. She may keep you awake all night with her talking."

Before I could answer, Brother Herman shook his head. "Is not a problem. Sister Jancey has worked with children in Kansas City." He turned toward me. "Will be like Kansas City for you, ja?"

"A little." I smiled at Sister Hanna. "I'm sure I'll enjoy meeting Madelyn."

Sister Hanna gave a slight nod and winked. "And our son, Ritt, I think you will enjoy meeting him, too."

I wasn't sure what surprised me more—the comment or her knowing wink.

CHAPTER 6

To my utter amazement, Mother walked the short distance from Brother Herman's home to the Wieler Küche. Though she leaned heavily upon my father's arm, it had been months since she'd exhibited such strength. My heart soared as I caught sight of their arrival outside the kitchen house. Perhaps this move would prove to be the medicine that would cure her. If so, I would adapt to the necessary changes in my life. I would gladly give up the comfortable home in Kansas City and forgo a future of teaching at the orphanage. To see my mother restored to health would be worth any sacrifice.

"I can hardly believe my eyes," I said, hurrying to her side and taking her arm as they drew near. "I was going to bring supper to you at Brother Herman's house. Sister Hanna said it was customary to take meals to those who are ill, but I'm so happy to see you are able to walk this distance."

I shot a glance in my father's direction, surprised he'd permitted her to walk.

"Your mother insisted she was up to the walk, and I thought it would be good for her to try." He gestured to the group lining up at the other door. "I need to enter with the men, so you'll need to see to your mother."

A shade of rosy pink colored my mother's cheeks as she took hold of my arm. "It is good to be home again." She looked up at me. "Tell me what you've been doing since we parted."

While we waited to enter the kitchen, I told her about Sister Hanna and my arrangements for the night. "I haven't met the rest of the Hetrig family, but if they're as welcoming as Sister Hanna, I'll be fine."

"I'm sure they are a wonderful family, but I know this is a sacrifice for you, Jancey. If at any time you decide you want to leave the colonies, your father and I will understand." She squeezed my arm. "You'll tell us if you're unhappy, won't you?"

"Yes, Mother, but you should push aside your concerns. The only thing you need to do is continue to gain your strength." I leaned close to her ear. "And tell me what I'm supposed to do so I don't look like such an outsider."

"Just watch what I do and you'll be fine. And remember—no conversation during meals."

I was thankful for the reminder. Father had mentioned the "no conversation" rule to me on the train, but I'd already forgotten. There were lots of rules, he'd said, and I wondered how many of them I would break before I could commit them all to memory. Mother and I sat side by side on one of the long wooden benches, and though I expected the hard benches to cause her difficulty, she sat through the meal without exhibiting any problems. She ate far less than anyone else but appeared to enjoy the dumpling soup and parsleyed potatoes. When we stood for the after dinner prayer, Mother clutched my arm.

I dipped my head close to hers after the prayer. "Are you feeling weak?" I momentarily forgot and asked my question in English.

"Speak German," she said, patting my hand. "Just walk slowly and I will do fine."

When we arrived outside, Father was standing with Brother Herman, two other men, and a young girl. As we drew near, Brother Herman turned toward us. "Gut evening, Sisters. I want to introduce you to your new neighbors." He patted a tall, angular man on the shoulder. "This is Brother Werner Hetrig and his son, Brother Ritter Hetrig. And this is young Madelyn."

Brother Herman crooked his finger, and Madelyn stepped forward. *"Guten Abend."* The young girl's smile revealed a charming dimple in one cheek, just like her mother's. "Mutter says you will share my room tonight." Her blue eyes sparkled as she pranced from foot to foot.

I returned her smile. "I hope you won't mind having company in your room. I'll do my best not to snore."

Madelyn covered her mouth and giggled. "Girls don't snore, but my brother, Ritt, snores. Even with the doors closed, I can hear him all night long."

Her brother chuckled and raked a handful of dark blond hair from his forehead. I couldn't be certain, but I guessed Ritt to be near my age. Like his father, Ritt was tall and broad-shouldered with natural good looks. He possessed an easy smile, and his hazel eyes sparkled with laughter as he spoke to his sister. "Then maybe we should send you to bed an hour earlier, so you will go to sleep without my snoring to bother you, ja?"

"Nein!" She shook her head with such vigor, her cap slipped to one side of her head. "I like the sound of snoring."

There was an easy camaraderie among the members of the Hetrig family, especially between brother and sister. An undeniable longing settled deep inside as I watched the two of them. What joy I'd missed growing up without a sibling—someone with whom I could share my deep secrets, someone who would be my friend no matter what, someone who would protect me when needed. But my being an only child hadn't been my parents' choice.

After my birth, Mother hadn't been able to carry another child, a fact I regretted as much as my parents did. When I decided to become a teacher, Mother said it was my lack of siblings that had drawn me to the profession, and perhaps she'd been right. Though the children at the orphanage weren't like brothers and sisters to me, they filled a void. A slight ache squeezed my heart, and I wondered if they were missing me as much as I missed them.

"Did you hear me, Sister Jancey?" Madelyn tugged on my hand.

I shook my head. "I'm sorry. My thoughts were elsewhere." I leaned down to eye level with the girl. "You now have my full attention."

"I asked if you would like to go back to the house with us. We usually go home until time for prayer meeting."

Uncertain what I was supposed to do, I sent a questioning look in Brother Herman's direction. "Ja, that would be gut. You go with the Hetrigs. Madelyn will keep you entertained, for sure."

After placing a kiss on my mother's cheek and bidding my parents good-night, I joined the Hetrig family. Brother Werner gestured toward the kitchen house. "My wife will be home in a short time. First she must finish her work with the other women while they clean in the Küche." He raised his eyebrows. "You understand?"

With a slight nod, I stepped alongside Madelyn. "Yes, Sister Hanna described her work to me earlier."

"I would like to hear why you have joined us here in Middle Amana, Sister Jancey." Brother Werner glanced over his shoulder as he spoke. "I know your parents lived here long ago, but I am sure to come here caused you some worry, ja?"

"You're right. Coming here was a big decision for me, but I wanted to be with my parents. They are all the family I have. Brother Herman may have told you my mother's health is failing."

Brother Werner didn't indicate whether he'd been advised or not, but since I'd told Sister Hanna a bit about my past when we were together earlier, I thought it would be easiest to answer any questions from the rest of the family while she remained at work. It would save repeating the same things over and over.

"It is gut you want to be with your Mutter during her time of need, and we will do all we can to help you and your parents." He glanced at Ritt and then Madelyn. "Won't we?"

Both of them agreed. I didn't miss the sympathy in Ritt's eyes when he looked at me. "You should tell us whatever you need, and we will answer any questions you have. Do not be afraid to ask." His voice radiated a deep warmth and kindness that made me feel comfortable in his presence.

"Thank you, Ritt. I'm sure I'll have lots of questions until I learn how things are done and where everything is located."

He chuckled. "Will not take long to show you where things are. The village isn't so big, and you speak German, so anyone can help you if you get lost."

"Where did you live before you came here? Was it a big city?" Madelyn spread her arms wide.

"My parents and I had a home in Kansas City, Missouri. I consider it a big city, but it isn't as large as some of the cities on the East Coast. Still, it is much larger than Middle Amana."

Madelyn's eyes grew wide. "I would be afraid in such a big place."

Brother Werner turned toward me as we walked inside the house. "Did your father work in Kansas City, Sister Jancey?"

I nodded. "He owns Forsythe Construction Company, which is located in Kansas City, but sometimes his contracts would take him to nearby smaller communities. As soon as all of his current construction contracts are complete, the business will be sold."

Ritt opened the door to their parlor and waited while we entered. Once inside, we sat down, and Ritt leaned forward. "I am curious about one thing. If your *Vater* owned the business, why didn't he name it Rhoder Construction Company?"

I explained that my father and mother had come to own the business, as well as our house, because of the kindness of Mr. and Mrs. Forsythe. "They were like grandparents to me. Since they had no children, they treated our little family like their own. My father wouldn't have considered changing the name of the company when he took over. Besides, keeping the name helped remind him of all the good that happened to our family. We were very fortunate to have met Mr. and Mrs. Forsythe."

"Ja, is true, but I think Mr. Forsythe must have known your Vater and Mutter would carry on his business in an honorable way. He was a gut judge of character. I understand the business has done very well." Brother Werner removed a pipe from his pocket and filled it with tobacco.

"Yes, the business has prospered under my father's direction." The fact that Brother Werner knew about the success of Forsythe Construction surprised me, since he hadn't previously indicated he knew anything about our family or my father's business ventures. Perhaps Brother Herman had provided some details about our family.

Madelyn inched closer, and when I pointed to the empty space beside me on the sofa, she immediately filled the spot. "Did you work in a Küche like my Mutter?"

"No, I taught school at an orphanage a few miles from our home." I didn't know if my father had shared that bit of information, but I saw no reason to withhold the truth. Keeping my eyelids at half-mast, I ventured a glance at Brothers Werner and Ritt, curious how they might react to such news.

Madelyn gasped and clapped a hand to her lips, her eyes shining with disbelief. "You were a teacher?" Though her words had been muffled, I'd clearly understood her question.

"Yes, I had a wonderful group of boys and girls in my class, and I was sad to tell them good-bye." I inhaled a ragged breath, remembering each of the children's faces as clearly as if they were sitting in front of me right now.

Madelyn moved her hand from her lips. "What will you do? The sisters cannot teach in the Amana schools, only the brothers."

Her look of concern warmed my heart and I patted her hands. "I knew that before I came here, so you need not worry. Brother Herman has already told me that I will be caring for my mother and also helping to clean the quarters occupied by the outside workers near the woolen mill."

"You'll be helping Sister Margaret." Brother Werner took another draw on his pipe. "She's a nice young woman and a hard worker, but she is . . ." He hesitated for a moment, obviously looking for the proper word. "Clumsy. Ja, clumsy. She sometimes can make as much mess as she cleans. It will be gut for her to have help."

I snapped to attention at Brother Werner's remark. I doubted I could provide a cure for clumsiness, and any attempts to correct Sister Margaret could spell disaster. And I didn't think she'd like being corrected by an outsider.

During my first weeks at the orphanage, I'd learned that suggesting new ideas could lead to heartrending ostracism—something I wanted to avoid here. I would do my best to perform my job in a suitable and efficient manner, and I would do my best to help Sister Margaret, but unless requested, I wouldn't make suggestions. And I certainly wouldn't criticize her work habits.

"If you still want to teach, you could help me with my reading, couldn't she, Vater?" The color heightened in Madelyn's cheeks as she turned toward me. "I'm not gut at reading. Brother Wieler says I need more practice. He's our teacher. He is married to Sister Bertha at the Küche."

"If your mother and father agree, I would be pleased to help you with your reading, Madelyn, but I don't want to break any of the rules." I glanced at Brother Werner.

"Ach, would not be breaking rules to help her read. No different than to have her Mutter or me sit at her side and listen, but I can stop at the school and speak to Brother Wieler, so he will know you are helping Madelyn." He pushed up from his chair. "I need to go to my room for a few minutes. Please excuse me." He waved to the three of us. "You go on and visit with one another."

Ritt smiled at his sister. "The schoolwork is not so important, Madelyn. You worry too much about your reading and writing."

I stiffened at Ritt's comment. Did he truly believe education wasn't important? Or did he think it wasn't important because Madelyn was a girl? Either way, the thought annoyed me. A good education was the foundation of a productive future, for both men and women, and given his age and experience, Ritt should realize that. I folded my hands in my lap and tightened my lips into a strained smile. I didn't want to challenge Ritt in front of his sister, but if we were ever alone, I'd ask him to explain his remark. For now, I'd take another tack.

"If I remember correctly, Brother Herman said you work at the woolen mill, Brother Ritt." I turned slightly to my right and faced him.

"Ja. I have been there since I finished school. I hope one day that I will become a supervisor, but that will be a decision for the elders when a new supervisor is needed." He stared down at my folded hands before looking back into my eyes. "It is a gut feeling to help create our fine woolen products."

"Do you ever need to read or write orders or instructions to complete your work?"

"Ja, for sure. I have to write out the orders for supplies and check them when they arrive."

I arched my brows. "So you need to add and subtract, as well?"

"For sure. We don't want to have incorrect numbers in our inventory."

I could see he hadn't connected my questions to his earlier remark to Madelyn about her schooling. "I'm pleased to hear that you have put your schooling to good use at the woolen mill."

His smile wavered as he slowly grasped my meaning. "Ja, I use a little of my schooling to do my job, but is not the same for Madelyn. She won't be working in the woolen mill, and I don't want her to worry all the time about not being as smart as the others. Is not gut to compare yourself with others."

"You're right, it isn't."

Madelyn turned back and forth as she listened to our conversation. There was no doubt this little girl valued her brother's opinion, and I could see she wasn't certain what to believe at the moment. I'd likely overstepped my boundaries and needed to set the child at ease. I grasped Madelyn's small hand in my own.

"We are all different, Madelyn. Each of the children in my class learned at a different rate. Some were good at reading, so they learned quickly." Madelyn's smile drooped, and I squeezed her hand. "But those same students didn't learn their arithmetic as quickly as they learned their reading lessons. God has given all of us special gifts, but I encouraged my students to do as well as they could in all of their studies. And that's what I'm going to help you do—be an excellent student. We'll work well together, and you'll do fine. You just wait and see."

Shortly after Brother Werner rejoined us in the parlor, Sister Hanna returned home from the Küche, her cheeks rosy from the brisk walk in the coolness of the spring evening air.

Only moments after greeting his wife, Brother Werner gestured to Madelyn, Ritt, and me. "Come along. Is time for prayer service." I wasn't certain if Brother Herman or my parents expected me to attend prayer service with the Hetrig family, so I hesitated for a moment. The older man arched his brows. "Something is wrong?"

"My parents didn't say if I was supposed to attend any of the church services. I wasn't sure it would be proper."

Brother Werner waved a dismissive gesture. "Ach! You are

welcome to join us. Our prayer meetings are not long, but we attend every evening. Your parents told you this?"

I grabbed my shawl as we departed. "Yes. They said there would be meetings seven times a week and sometimes more during holidays."

"We have prayer service every evening. Is not like our Sunday meetings, but we gather in small groups to pray and read the Bible. And there is no reason why you should not be with us. Is always proper to meet with others for prayer and to worship our Lord, ja?"

I nodded my head. "I wanted to be certain I was doing the right thing, since I haven't yet learned all of your ways."

Madelyn skipped to my side and grasped my hand. "I'll help you learn. We can trade lessons, ja?"

I squeezed her hand. "That would be perfect, Madelyn. I can hardly wait to begin."

CHAPTER 7

I had expected to begin work the day after our arrival in Middle, but Mother's initial spurt of energy didn't last. Instead of starting my job, I remained at home to care for her. In some respects it worked to advantage for me. When Mother wanted to remain awake and visit, she told me about her early years in the colonies—how she'd worked in the large garden that supplied fresh vegetables to the Küche where she and her family ate their meals. At times she became surprisingly animated. When she talked about the delivery of bread and coffee cakes from the village bakery, she lifted her nose in the air and sniffed as if she could still smell the yeasty aromas. Though I wasn't excited to hear tales of butchering, my mouth watered when Mother spoke of the cured hams and the sausages, for I'd already tasted both during meals at the kitchen house.

She described how the women preserved and dried fruits and vegetables for the winter months. *"If you ask Sister Hanna, she can show you how things are stored in the cellar below the Küche and in the drying houses."*

Although not so different from the way things were done in the outside world, I couldn't imagine the enormity or the responsibility of preparing and storing enough food to feed so many people through the winter months.

All of it interested me, yet I wondered why Mother hadn't told me any of this years ago. Perhaps back then it hadn't seemed important. Now she likely hoped her remembrances would help me adjust and feel a sense of belonging. And they did help, but I believed both time and participation would teach me the most about this new way of life.

Worrying I might forget some of the Amana customs and regulations Mother spoke of, I began writing her recollections in my journal after she went to sleep. Whether good or bad, a memory, or a rule to live by, I wanted to retain her words.

Last evening I'd received notice that today I would commence my new job of cleaning the men's dormitory. So this morning I opened my journal, and to refresh my memory, I read aloud some of the rules Mother had mentioned during our visits: "Don't talk during meals; walk to and from church with the women; always enter the women's door; a single life serving God is preferable to marriage; a year of waiting is necessary after receiving the elders' permission to wed; a young man must be twenty-four years of age before marriage." My thoughts turned to Ritt and I stopped short. I barely knew him, so why had he come to mind rather than Nathan?

Across the hall, my mother stirred and I closed the book. I

wondered if the doctor had informed Brother Herman that my mother's health had shown some improvement over the past few days.

Since our arrival, time had passed quickly, and our small apartment now bore some semblance of our former home. The overstuffed sofa and three chairs, though somewhat less sturdy than those constructed in the colonies, looked quite nice in the parlor. I'd taken care to arrange small marble-topped tables near each of the chairs and topped them with vases and kerosene lamps. I'd become accustomed to the gaslights in our Kansas City home, but it hadn't taken long to adjust to the flicker of the kerosene lamps. If my parents experienced any difficulty readjusting to their earlier way of life, or if they missed any of the conveniences we'd once enjoyed, they gave no sign. In truth, they both appeared quite content.

For as long as I could remember, my father had read the daily newspaper each morning without fail. Now, instead, he read the Bible, and the only news from the outside world came by letter. Only one had come since our arrival, and it was from Father's lawyer. A brief note stating funds had been transferred from the sale of our house to the elders of Middle Amana, as previously instructed.

I had hoped to hear from some of my students by now, for I'd left a packet of addressed and stamped envelopes with Mr. Ludwig at the orphanage. Of course, I couldn't fault the children overmuch, for I'd written only one letter to them. If Miss Manchester was teaching all of the children, she wouldn't have time to help them pen letters. Still, I couldn't help worrying about Charlie and his arithmetic or about Bertie's progress in reading. And was Miss Manchester exercising patience with Henry? The boy needed a gentle hand. If he was pushed, he often stopped trying. Would Henry or any of the other children regress in my absence? My heart ached as I thought of each one.

During these past weeks I'd almost learned to schedule my life according to the bell that tolled throughout the village. The sound was a reminder of when and where I needed to be present throughout the day. Mother had said I would eventually enjoy the soulful clanging, and she'd been correct. It hadn't taken long to grow accustomed to the familiar sound.

I'd arisen and dressed early this morning, for I'd been awake most of the night. My shoes clacked on the wooden sidewalk as I accompanied Father to the Küche for breakfast. I doubted I'd be able to hold anything in my stomach. I hadn't been this nervous when I began my first day of work at the orphanage. I'd always been confident about my abilities, but this was different. I'd never before worked as a cleaning woman, and I worried I'd do something wrong. I cared little about myself, but I didn't want to cause my parents any embarrassment.

"So today you will begin your first day of work." My father walked alongside me. "I know this work doesn't put your education to good use, but you should remember that whatever we do, we are to do it heartily, as working for the Lord and not unto men—that's from Colossians." He smiled down at me as I hurried to match his stride. "I have no doubt you will do your very best. And you should know I am very proud of the way you have worked to adapt to this new way of life. I am sure it has not been easy."

I glanced down at the dark calico dress that had replaced the clothing I'd worn in Kansas City—colorful cashmere jersey suits, well-tailored skirts, lace-trimmed shirtwaists, as well as numerous day dresses and evening gowns. I offered a weak smile. "I am adjusting. I do miss teaching and the freedom of choosing my own schedule, but there is something to be said for this simple way of life."

He nodded. "And Nathan? Do you miss him, too?"

I hesitated, trying to decide exactly how I did feel about this separation. "I'd certainly enjoy the sight of a familiar face, but Nathan hasn't written, so he may have found someone else to occupy his free time." The thought that Nathan would so easily toss me aside bothered me a bit. I didn't know if it was pride or if I had cared for him more than I wanted to admit. Though he hadn't exhibited his best characteristics before I departed, Nathan could be fun and quite charming. During the early days of our courtship, he'd enjoyed attending parties and celebrations of every sort. It hadn't been until later that his raw ambition to become a successful businessman had outweighed his fun-loving side—the side I enjoyed and missed.

"And you? Have you taken up your pen to write him?"

I shook my head. "No. If I am to remain here, I thought it best to adjust to my new life rather than look back to what I've left behind."

"I see. But now you are not so sure?" He inhaled a deep breath. "You must remember that you are not bound to stay here, Jancey. It would be wise for you to make a decision before the sale of the business is completed. I could possibly make arrangements to set aside a portion of money for you if you want to leave. But if you wait . . ."

His voice trailed off and I nodded. "I know. If I wait, then I must find work to support myself or find a husband who is willing and able to do so." I reached for his hand. "I have no plans to leave, Father. Mother needs me, and I want to be with both of you." He didn't argue, but I saw the worry in his eyes. "And if Nathan writes, I promise I will respond, but please don't worry about me. In no time, you will discover I have completely adjusted to this new life."

I meant what I said. I was determined to do my best—for Mother's sake and for my own. I'd been heartened by her improved health and her ability to rally the day after our arrival. However, she'd taken a downward turn immediately thereafter. When she agreed that I should bring her morning meal back to the house, I knew her pain was greater than she'd told either Father or me. Though I hadn't mentioned it, I planned to seek Brother Herman's permission to extend my time at home unless she showed some improvement after eating her breakfast.

When we arrived at the kitchen, I walked to the rear of the building and signaled to Sister Bertha. "My mother is not well this morning, so I will need to take her breakfast to the house."

"Ja. Sister Hanna will see to it. This isn't her week to help clean in the Küche. She can take it to her as soon as she has eaten."

"No, I will take it." I tightened my lips.

Resting one hand on her ample hip, Sister Bertha shook her head. "Sister Hanna tells me this is to be your first day cleaning at the workers' quarters, so you must go to work. Sister Hanna is more than able to care for your Mutter now that she is not needed in the Küche all day." I wanted to remain in the kitchen and argue, but Sister Bertha waved her fork toward the dining hall. "You should go and sit down. The bell is ringing and I need to see to my work."

Clamping my lips together, I hurried into the dining hall and scanned the room for Brother Herman. My thoughts exploded like grease popping in a hot skillet. If Brother Herman should give me permission to remain at home, would Sister Bertha become angry? She'd made it plain that she'd send Sister Hanna to attend to Mother's needs. Yet when I'd first arrived, Brother Herman had been clear that I would be caring for Mother as part of my duties. Had I realized Sister Bertha might interfere, I would have spoken to Father on our way to breakfast. I sighed when I spotted Brother Herman sitting near the door. He would be out of the dining hall before I could gain his permission.

I took my place at one of the women's tables and was spreading jam on a thick slice of bread when Sister Hanna approached with a fresh bowl of fried potatoes. She leaned close to my ear. "Do not worry about your Mutter. I will give her gut care while you are at work."

Sister Bertha had wasted no time passing instructions to Sister Hanna. Perhaps she'd detected my unwilling spirit and worried I would attempt to defy her orders. "Danke," I whispered. There was nothing else left to do or say. Now that arrangements had been made for Mother's care, I wouldn't ask Brother Herman's permission. I didn't want Sister Hanna to think me ungrateful. Even worse, I didn't want her to think I believed her incapable of caring for my mother. For today, I would be compliant. But tonight, I would clarify my work instructions with Brother Herman. My mother's care was my greatest concern.

After the final prayer, I pushed up from the table and was surprised to see Sister Hanna hurry toward me carrying one of the pails used to deliver meals. My heart soared. Sister Bertha must have changed her mind and decided I should take the food to Mother, but when I reached for the handle, Sister Hanna turned so I could not reach it.

"I will carry the food to your Mutter, but I thought it would be gut if I first went with you to the working men's quarters. I will introduce you to Sister Margaret." Her lips curved in a bright smile that revealed her dimple. "It is not so far out of the way for me, and I thought it would make it easier for you if I went along on your first day."

My spirits plummeted when I realized I'd not be going home, but I thanked Sister Hanna for her kind offer. I had hoped to meet Sister Margaret before commencing my cleaning duties, but when Ritt told me she lived in another part of the village, ate her meals at a different Küche, and attended prayer services near her home, I realized there would be little chance to meet before I began working with her—and I'd been right. Our paths hadn't crossed. At least not to my knowledge.

"Sister Margaret is close to your own age and very nice, so I think you could become friends. Werner says she is prone to accidents, but I think she sometimes hurries to complete her work and her haste is the cause of the mishaps. She should be able to answer any questions you may have. If not, save them for me, and I will do my best to help however I can."

"I am thankful for your kindness, Sister Hanna." Even though I would have preferred to go back and tend to my mother, I knew Sister Hanna would see to her care as well as I could.

"Ja, and I am thankful for the time you take to work with my Madelyn. She is so happy to have you help her with her reading."

"I'm thankful for her help, as well. Your suggestion that she read from *Kinderstimme* has proved to be a great help to both of us. The book is teaching me the rules used to guide children in humility and simplicity." I didn't mention that I feared young Madelyn had memorized most of the rules and we should move on to something else. For now, we would use the book.

The wooden sidewalk ended and we walked down the dirt road until we neared the three-story brick mill. Sister Hanna pointed to a long frame building not far away. "This is where you will be working."

As we drew near the door, a loud crash sounded from inside the building. Sister Hanna hurried through the doorway, and I followed close on her heels. I nearly bumped into her when she stopped short.

"Watch out for the water! I spilled both buckets." A young woman wearing a dark plaid dress pointed to the floor. A brown smudge dirtied one of her cheeks, and strands of blond hair poked out from beneath her bonnet.

The room where Margaret had spilled the water was a large parlor or sitting room of sorts. At one end, there were two wooden tables with chairs around them, likely where the men played cards or wrote letters. Two overstuffed divans and another large chair had been arranged on the other side of the room. Small tables with kerosene lamps sat at either end of the massive divans. Though the room didn't reflect a great deal of warmth, it provided a place for the men to relax before going to bed, and with windows lining both sides of the room, it was brighter than the rooms where the children attended classes in the orphanage.

Sister Hanna smiled. "Well, you need only add some soap and you can begin to scrub the floors, Sister Margaret." She took a backward step as the water slowly spread toward her feet. She grasped my arm. "This is Sister Jancey, who has come to work with you. Brother Herman told you about her, ja?"

"Ja, he told me a long time ago. I almost forgot." She circled around the water. "If you come this way, your shoes will stay dry."

I bid Sister Hanna good-bye. "If Mother should need me, you'll send word, won't you?"

"She will be fine. Now let me get on my way so that your Mutter may enjoy her breakfast before it grows cold."

Sister Hanna was out the door before I realized she hadn't agreed to come and get me if Mother should take a turn for the worse. Though I longed to run after her and require she answer me, Sister Margaret had already thrust a scrub brush in my direction.

"It isn't the day I usually scrub the floors, but we have to clean up this water. Besides, if we do it now, we won't have to do it on Friday and maybe we can leave early." She dropped to her knees without regard for her skirt.

I remained a short distance from the pooling water. "Perhaps if we used a broom or mop to spread the water around a bit, it would be easier and not quite so messy."

"There's a broom in the corner of the other room you can use if you like. I'm already wet, so I'll just keep scrubbing." She sat back on her heels and signaled for me to wait. "I'll finish this mess I made with the water. No need for you to get wet, too. You can strip the sheets from the beds and put them in those baskets with the men's dirty clothes." She pointed to several large laundry baskets near the door leading outside. "You can use the fresh sheets stacked on that table in the corner to make the beds."

Carrying a large oval laundry basket in each hand, I strode into the adjoining room and placed one of the handmade baskets on either side of the room. They were sturdier than the ones we'd used at home, but like most things in the colonies, these baskets were woven by an Amana craftsman. They were created to withstand heavy use and endure the test of time.

As I stared at the rows of iron bedframes that lined each side of the room, I recalled the sleeping quarters at the orphanage.

The beds in this room were larger and of much better quality than those in the Charity Home, and I quickly observed the sheets and blankets weren't worn or frayed, either. In addition, bright sunlight shone through the windows above these beds and provided a sense of cheeriness—something the children would have enjoyed. Although the men might have little privacy in this dormitory, their lodging was finer than I'd expected, and much more pleasant than the stark and dreary accommodations provided for the orphan children.

Pulling the sheets from the beds and gathering them in my arms as I went, I made my way down the row of beds. After dumping the dirty linens in one of the sturdy baskets, I continued back up the row of beds on the opposite side of the room. Removing the sheets would take much less time than making each of the beds—especially for me, as I'd had little practice. However, it didn't appear the beds had been made with a great deal of care, and I doubted the men would expect perfection.

While I snapped a clean sheet in the air and watched it float onto the lumpy hog-hair mattress, I recalled the Bible verse my father had paraphrased earlier in the morning. I stared at the row of beds and wondered if there was any way I could heartily perform this work as an offering to the Lord.

Making the beds had taken longer than I'd expected, but I felt a certain sense of pride as I stood in the center of the room and stared at the perfectly aligned sheets and blankets. Using the corner of my apron, I wiped the perspiration from my forehead.

"They look gut. Better than when I make them, for sure. And you finished much faster, too. My Mutter says I'm slow as a snail, and my Vater says I try to move too fast. I guess they are both right, because when I scurry around I end up with a mess that slows me down." She glanced toward the other room. "I got the water cleaned up. As soon as it dries, we can dust in there."

It seemed Sister Margaret understood the cause of her mishaps, but she hadn't yet decided how to overcome the problem.

"Is there a schedule you use for cleaning, Sister Margaret?"

"Ja, except when I spill water or I drop a stack of folded sheets. Then my schedule is ruined." She giggled. "We are to scrub the floors and change the sheets once a week. Each day we sweep the floors, dust, straighten anything that is out of order, and put water in the pitchers. If I have time, I straighten the beds, since the men usually leave them unmade."

"Is that everything?" I inhaled a deep breath.

She shook her head. "Nein. And then there's washday. We launder the sheets and towels, and some of the men pay to have us wash their clothes." She pointed to the baskets where I'd placed the sheets. "All of those we will do tomorrow."

Laundry for all these men? What had I gotten myself into?

CHAPTER 8

Two weeks later, a letter from Nathan arrived. The envelope was balanced against one of the kerosene lamps in a conspicuous manner, likely the work of my mother, who had inquired about Nathan on several occasions. It seemed she and Father had teamed together to assure themselves I didn't regret my choice to join them. Neither seemed willing to accept my protestations that their decision hadn't interfered with plans to marry Nathan—or anyone else, for that matter.

I picked up the letter and tucked it into my pocket before peeking around the corner to see if Mother was awake. Since taking a downward turn, the doctor, Brother Rudolf Zedler, had called upon her each day. And though he couldn't do anything to cure her, he said we shouldn't be overly concerned. He believed she would soon feel somewhat better, though he'd advised we should expect these ailing bouts to become more frequent. Father didn't mention that we'd become quite accustomed to them back in Kansas City, but I could see the worry in his eyes. Like me, he hoped the doctors were wrong and we would see a recovery.

"I didn't know if I was dreaming or if I heard the door close." Mother forced a feeble smile. "Did you see the letter from Nathan? What does he have to say?"

I patted the pocket of my dress. "I haven't yet read it." Her eyes darted to my skirt. She wanted me to read the letter. Shoving my hand into the pocket, I removed the envelope and slid my finger beneath the seal. After quickly scanning the pages, I shrugged one shoulder. "He says that work is going fine and he has been very busy."

My mother frowned. "In two pages, that is all he said?"

"He also said that once they have finished all of their work, maybe he will come to Middle Amana for a visit. He asked if I am happy and said that he is still willing to offer marriage if I am so inclined."

Arching her brows, my mother stared at me. "And since this is not the life you ever intended for yourself, perhaps you shouldn't refuse his offer. I am feeling very selfish that you have given up everything to come here." She swiped at a tear that rolled down her cheek.

"Mother, please do not cry. Over and over, I have told you and Father that I have not agreed to marry Nathan. I don't know him well enough, and we have many differences, both in what we believe and what we desire for the future. I don't know how I can do anything more to assure you that I came here because I wanted to and I do not count it a sacrifice. If I decide that I can't be happy in the colonies, I will return to Kansas City. You have my word."

She inhaled a ragged breath and gave a slight nod. "Good. Then I will not mention this again." Her eyelids drooped. "Sister Hanna brought me my medicine a short time ago and my eyes are heavy."

I patted her hand. "You sleep. It is the best medicine."

Her soft snores reached my ears as I departed the room. I sat down in the parlor and reread Nathan's letter. He'd mentioned nothing of the children at the orphanage even though he'd promised to visit. Then again, that promise had been made before he truly believed I was going to leave. Pushing up from the sofa, I walked to my bedroom and sat down at the small desk we'd brought from Kansas City. Pulling a sheet of stationery from one of the drawers, I dipped my pen and began a letter to Nathan.

After thanking him for his letter and telling him of Mother's health and my work, I stared at the page, and then dipped my pen into the inkpot.

I don't know if you've stopped at the Charity Home since I've departed, but I'm eager for news of the children. If you have time, I'd be appreciative if you could stop and ask Mr. Ludwig if he would encourage them to write me. I provided him with stamped envelopes prior to our departure. I'd enjoy hearing from Miss Manchester, as well. I don't want to impose, but I would count it a great kindness if you could look in on the children and give me a short report.

As to your suggestion of a visit, please be aware that the colonies offer little in the way of entertainment. I recall how much you enjoyed attending parties and the theater when we first met. This is not a place where you will discover such leisure. Our lives are quite simple, and you will have to make do without many of the conveniences to which you are accustomed. Of course, the final decision is yours.

I looked at the closing at the end of Nathan's letter and shook my head. *Yours always, Nathan.* I tried to imagine him hunched over the piece of writing paper while deciding upon the final words to close his letter—much as I'd been doing for several minutes. I doubted Nathan would always be mine, so I needed to select something different. However, if I simply signed it *Sincerely* or *Your friend,* he would likely be hurt or take offense. Though I doubted we would have a future together, who could say for sure. Besides, I didn't relish the idea of hurting Nathan's feelings.

The sound of my father's footsteps jarred me to action. The bell would soon ring to announce we should depart for supper. I dipped my pen one last time and scribbled, *Always, Jancey.* Whether the simple word carried enough benevolence to please Nathan, I did not know. But under the circumstances, it was as much as I thought I should offer.

After the first few nights of Madelyn's lessons, Ritt had begun to appear. He'd sit quietly and listen while his sister read from *Kinderstimme.* After she completed her reading, I'd give Madelyn a list of spelling words to practice. Occasionally, he would offer to listen to her spell, but it didn't take long for me to discover that his spelling wasn't much better than Madelyn's. Unless he held the list of words, he didn't know whether she was right or wrong. Once I'd become aware of his inability to be of genuine assistance, I refrained from accepting any further offers from him.

I was glad my declinations hadn't stopped him from attending our sessions each evening, and I wondered if he was joining us in an attempt to advance his own education. The idea seemed silly, because I was certain he could read beyond the level of *Kinderstimme.* Yet why else would he continue to sit and listen while I instructed his sister? I didn't want to cause him embarrassment, but if he hoped to further his education, I wanted to help him.

I'd not forgotten his remarks that Madelyn need not worry about broadening her abilities, but I'd been thankful her mother and father hadn't agreed. Both of them had proved supportive of my efforts to help her. In fact, beginning next week two other children would join us for additional help. Sister Hanna had told the women in the Küche of Madelyn's progress, and two of the sisters asked if their children might be included. After inquiring of Brother Werner as well as Brother Herman and Brother Wieler and receiving no objection, it was agreed the two other children would meet with us three evenings a week after prayer service. I didn't know if the children would enjoy the extra lessons or for how long they might continue, but at least it would provide me with an opportunity to use my teaching skills, and for that I was grateful.

"So what words are on your spelling list this evening, Madelyn?" Ritter asked. "It appears Sister Jancey is busy correcting some of your lessons, so I will help you, if you'd like." He stretched forward to examine the list, but Madelyn snatched it away.

"I haven't studied them yet." After laying the paper atop the table, she stood. "I need a drink of water, but I'll be right back. Would you like a glass of water, Sister Jancey?"

I looked up and shook my head. "Danke, I am not thirsty." Once Madelyn stepped from the room, I turned toward Ritt. "I was wondering if you were joining us in the evenings because you are interested in some special lessons, Brother Ritt. Perhaps some advanced classes in mathematics or science?"

Confusion clouded his eyes. "Lessons? Nein, I have no interest in any more schooling. I was most pleased when those days of sitting in the classroom ended." He grinned and cocked his head to one side. "You really don't know why I sit here each evening, do you?"

I shook my head. "If it's not because you want to further your education, I have no idea."

He leaned forward and rested his arms across his knees. His hazel eyes flickered in the lamplight. "Because I enjoy being near you. You're different than other young women. I have a desire to know you better." He touched his palm to his chest. "I was hoping you would feel the same about me."

I had noticed Ritt's good looks and kind nature, but I'd observed nothing in his manner to denote he'd taken an interest in me. Then again, things were different between men and women in the colonies, so I hadn't expected to draw the attention of any man while living here. While many members eventually married, remaining single was considered preferable, because those who did not marry could devote more time to their spiritual lives without impediment.

His remark rendered me speechless and he chuckled. "I see I have surprised you. You did not know at all?"

"No, but I am flattered." Heat seared my cheeks. What a foolish reply. Now he would think I welcomed his attention. He was a nice man, but I wasn't certain how long I would be here. It would be wrong to encourage his attention. Then again, what if I decided to remain in Middle Amana?

"Maybe you would consider going with me to the river a week from Saturday for a picnic?" He waited a moment before hastening to add, "Not alone. There will be a group of people our age who are going to fish and enjoy the afternoon."

The idea appealed to me, not so much because of Ritt—though I wanted to know him better—but because it would give me an opportunity to become acquainted with some of the other young people in the village. Working with only Sister Margaret and caring for Mother hadn't provided much opportunity for me to interact with others.

"If my mother is feeling well enough for me to be away, I think I would like to go. Thank you for asking me."

"Go where?" Madelyn stood in the doorway. "Are you and Ritt going somewhere? I want to go, too."

Ritt frowned and touched his ear. "It is impolite to listen in on others."

"I wasn't. I finished my water and came back to study my spelling words. You're the one who shouldn't be in the parlor with us. You're not taking lessons. When Eveline and Anna and Bretta come for their lessons, you need to stay away. There won't be enough room for you. Besides, they'll be embarrassed to have you watching."

Ritt arched his brows. "And where do you think I should spend the evenings? Sitting in my bedroom?"

Madelyn didn't hesitate for a minute. "You can go downstairs with Mutter and Vater."

Since we'd begun her lessons, Sister Hanna and Brother Werner had been going downstairs to visit with my parents. Usually Sister Hanna took her stitching and sat in the bedroom visiting

Mother, while Brother Werner and my father visited in the parlor. I doubted Ritt would enjoy sitting with the two men, but Madelyn was right. The girls would take up most of the space, and his presence wouldn't be welcomed.

"It's true that the girls would likely feel uncomfortable with you present. The weather is warm. If you don't want to sit downstairs, maybe you could spend the evenings on the porch or in the yard." I was suddenly struck with a solution. "Better yet, you may have the parlor, and I'll take the girls outdoors for their lessons. Unless it's raining, of course." Now that they were halfway through June, the long, hot days of summer would become more oppressive. Even late into the evening, the upstairs rooms remained muggy and airless.

Ritt shook his head. "I would not expect you to go outside in the rain." He grinned at me and my heart did a strange flip that surprised me. "And the backyard is big enough that the girls should not mind if I sometimes come down and sit under one of the apple trees—in case I should need some fresh air."

Madelyn crossed her arms over her chest and pushed her lips into a pout. "You don't care about fresh air, Ritt. You just want to be near Jancey."

I snapped around and looked at Madelyn. Mischief danced in her bright blue eyes. She'd understood all along. It was only I who had been blind to his intentions. I cleared my throat. "This is Ritt's home, too, Madelyn. I am sure he will do his best to keep his distance when the other girls are here." I pinned him with an unwavering stare. "Won't you, Brother Ritt."

"Yes, Sister Jancey." His reply was in the same singsong voice used by children answering a schoolteacher, and I couldn't suppress a slight smile.

I pointed to the sheet of spelling words. "Now that we have that matter settled, you need to study your spelling words, Madelyn."

A light mist was falling as I hurried into the men's quarters after breakfast and greeted Margaret. Almost a week had passed, and Ritt and I were supposed to picnic near the river on Saturday. Ever since he'd extended the invitation, I'd been excited at the possibility of meeting some other people my own age. If the rain continued, I worried there would be no picnic.

Margaret stood in the sitting room, holding a broom in one hand. "You want to work in the parlor or the sleeping quarters? I already started in here."

We'd come to an agreement that we would switch back and forth with the cleaning duties, but whenever it was Margaret's day to change the sheets, she did her best to switch with me.

"It's your day to do the sleeping quarters, Margaret. You've changed the sheets only one time since I began working with you. Each time it's your turn, you find some reason to have me do it."

Truth be told, I didn't particularly mind changing the sheets, but it was the principle of the thing. If there was one thing I believed in, it was being fair. I'd consistently taught that to the children at the orphanage, and I tried always to be fair in my own dealings. Margaret had obviously come to believe I had no idea what she'd been doing—that thought annoyed me more than changing the dirty sheets.

Margaret thrust the broom toward me. "I didn't know you were keeping a log. There have been days when your mother was sick and I had to clean both the rooms."

My feelings of fairness subsided and shame washed over me.

She was right—there had been times when Margaret had been required to clean more than her share. "Never mind, Margaret. I'll take care of the beds." A clap of thunder sounded overhead and I glanced toward the ceiling. "I do hope this rain doesn't continue."

Margaret bobbed her head. "If it does, we'll have to dry the sheets inside tomorrow."

I stopped and stared at her. "You're right. I had forgotten about the wash."

"Then why were you worried about the rain?"

"I guess I was just hoping it won't rain Saturday—because of the picnic. Are you going?"

Margaret grasped the broom in both hands and swept across the wooden floor. "I might if the right man should ask me." She kept her eyes fixed on the dirt she'd swept into a small pile on the floor.

"Who's the right man? Do you have someone special?" My father had explained the rules regarding engagement and the year of separation. It was why he and my mother had left the colonies—they hadn't wanted to wait to marry. If Margaret had a special beau, I was sure they weren't yet engaged. Besides, she'd never before mentioned any interest in a man.

Her lips curved in a faint smile. "He works at the woolen mill. Now can you guess?"

I shook my head. How could she expect me to know?

"Brother Ritter, that's who."

I swallowed hard. "Brother Ritt is the man you want to ask you to the picnic?" My heard pounded and my palms turned damp.

"Ja. He is gut looking, don't you think? And very nice, too."

"He is," I croaked. "Has he invited you to attend other events with him?"

Her eyes clouded. "Nein, but I wave to him whenever I see him coming from the mill. Sometimes he waves in return. I am hoping he thinks I'm not too plain and will ask me." She shrugged. "If he does not, then I will stay home, which will please my Mutter. She wants me to help with the mending."

Swinging around, I waved toward the other room. "I'd better get busy and change the beds or we'll never get done on time." I hurried from the room before she could ask who had invited me to the picnic.

Yanking sheets as I proceeded down the first row of beds, I came to a dead stop when I reached the third bed from the end of the row. Still holding an armful of dirty sheets, I dropped to the side of the bed and stared at a tattered picture lying atop an old trunk stationed beside the bed. My fingers trembled as I picked up the blurred and faded photograph of a young girl. I rubbed my eyes and looked again. There was no mistake. The little girl with long blond braids was standing in front of the Kansas City Charity Home.

CHAPTER 9

I don't know how long I'd been sitting on the side of the bed staring at the unframed photograph. Had it been there all along and I hadn't noticed, or had a new worker arrived?

I startled when Margaret called to me. "You are not feeling gut, Jancey?"

With a quick turn, I waved her forward. "I am fine. It's this picture . . ."

Margaret approached and leaned over my shoulder. "Ja. What about it? A little girl standing in front of a building somewhere." She wrinkled her nose. "Not a very gut photograph, all fuzzy and discolored. I hope they didn't pay much money for it." She pointed across the room. "Some of the other men have better photographs than this one."

"Who sleeps in this bed?" I asked, patting the mattress. "Do you know?"

"Nein. I don't know the names of any of these men. I know only that the one who sleeps in that bed has the initials TK stitched in his clothes. We are not supposed to mingle with the outsiders. You know this, ja?"

I bobbed my head. Because I'd been the one who washed the sheets and towels while Margaret washed the men's clothing, I hadn't realized the men had markings in their clothes. Now that I knew, it made sense. I'd given no thought as to how the men identified their clothing once it had been washed and placed in stacks on the table in the sitting room.

"You are going to finish with the beds?"

Jumping to my feet, I laid the photograph back in place. "Yes, of course."

There was no need to confide in Margaret. My interest in the owner of the photograph hadn't piqued her curiosity in the least. She wanted only to see that the beds were stripped and remade, preferably without her help.

The rain continued to fall throughout the rest of the morning, and while thunder rumbled overhead, I tried to remember if I'd ever before seen anything lying on the trunk near the end of the row—or if I'd even noticed the trunk. I couldn't be certain. Surely that trunk had been there. How could I have missed it? While teaching at the orphanage, I'd been attentive to every aspect of the schoolroom, but my attention to detail had disappeared as I'd adapted to the cleaning routine here in the men's quarters. There had been no reason to be alert to my surroundings—or so I'd thought.

I waited until last to make the bed near the end of the row. After carefully tucking the sheets and placing a folded woolen blanket at the foot of the bed, I once again stared at the picture. Hoping to discover some detail that might reflect when the picture had been taken, I focused first upon the girl's appearance and then the building itself but found nothing.

The fact that I didn't recognize the girl didn't mean she wasn't still at the school, for she was older than the children in our section of the orphanage. And though I'd met many of the older children, I couldn't place this girl.

Perhaps she'd already come and gone by the time I began teaching, but the older children were seldom placed. Especially the girls. Some of the older boys would be adopted by families in the West with an eye toward help on their farms, but the girls were viewed as more of a liability than an asset by most. As potential families passed through the orphanage, I'd hear them comment that it didn't pay to take a girl. Their comments were always the same: *"As soon as you get a girl trained to be decent help, she runs off and gets married."*

"Didn't you hear the bell? Time to go or the noonday meal will be over before either of us puts our feet under a dining table." Margaret stood at the door with two umbrellas in her hand. "You can use this one. It's an extra that's kept here, so be sure you bring it back with you." She thrust a dusty umbrella in my direction. "I brought my own with me this morning. I hope that one doesn't leak. No telling the last time anyone used it."

With the rain descending in cascading sheets, I was thankful for any sort of protection. I peered out the window. Water stood in deep puddles and with no wooden walkway outside, our shoes would likely sink into mud up to our ankles.

I backed away from the window. "I don't think I'll go. I'm not particularly hungry. I can stay here and mop and finish dusting the furniture."

"What if Sister Hanna isn't able to take food to your Mutter? Did you think about that?"

With this downpour, Sister Hanna might expect me to offer. She would likely prefer to stay at the Küche. Before we hurried off in opposite directions, I gave her arm a slight squeeze. "Try to stay dry, and I'll do the same."

The corners of her lips tipped in a feeble smile as thunder clapped overhead. "Danke."

My shoes were soon wet and covered in mud. I had hoped there would be an opportunity to speak to Ritt and discover if he knew any of the outsiders who worked at the mill. But with the ongoing downpour, none of the men or women would remain outside to visit before the meal commenced.

Rather than take my seat at the table, I waited to catch sight of Sister Hanna. She smiled as she rounded the kitchen doorway and drew near. "If this rain keeps up, we will all need webbed feet to get around." Her gaze settled on my shoes. "Your shoes are soaked through. I have a pair of dry stockings in my mending bag you can borrow. Put them on when you get back to the men's quarters so you do not get sick."

"What about you? Are you going to remain at the Küche?"

Sister Hanna shook her head. "Nein. I will be going home until time to help with the evening meal. I will see to your Mutter's care." She motioned to the other room. "I have boots and an umbrella to protect me. Is gut we made lots of soup today. Even when it isn't cold outside, wet clothing causes chills." She motioned for me to follow her. "Come and get the stockings. Then I must ladle the soup. Brother Herman will soon begin the noonday prayer."

With the stockings tucked beside me, I finished the pea soup and then spooned a sizable helping of the radish salad and fried potatoes onto my plate. I helped myself to a small portion of pork loin and passed the platter to Sister Hulda. Hogs were raised in the colonies, so pork was frequent fare at our dining tables. And though I usually took a large portion, I wasn't particularly hungry today.

Without asking, Sister Hulda speared a large piece of pork and dropped it onto my plate. When I shook my head, she scowled and gestured that I should eat. Though I wanted to refuse, I refrained from doing so. To cause a scene wouldn't be wise. And though I wasn't hungry enough to eat such a large portion, waste was frowned upon. I would need to clean my plate. After so much food, I'd likely be longing for a nap by two o'clock.

During the meal, I let my gaze wander toward the outsiders who sat at a separate table on the men's side of the room. Though not all of them ate in our Küche, I looked at each one to see if I could detect a resemblance to the girl in the photograph. One young man was a possibility, but he had black hair and the girl's hair had appeared lighter. Even if he was an exact look-alike, what would I do?

I couldn't walk up to an outsider, tap him on the shoulder, and say, *Excuse me, but while making your bed I saw a picture of a girl in front of the Kansas City Charity Home and wondered who she might be.* Not cleaning my plate would pale in comparison to such forward behavior.

At the completion of the after-meal prayer, I departed with the pair of dry stockings tucked beneath my cape and the umbrella overhead. The winds had died down, and though it continued to rain, I didn't have to contend with the gusting sheets that had pelted me on my way to the Küche.

Margaret was waiting inside when I returned. "I am glad to see you remembered to bring the umbrella back with you."

I stared at her in wonderment. "It is still raining, Margaret. There is little chance I would forget the umbrella."

She giggled as she removed her shoes. "Ja, I suppose that is right. I am going to put my shoes by the stove. They are soaked. You should do the same." After dropping to one of the chairs, she untied her laces.

I removed both my shoes and then placed my wet stockings over one of the wooden chairs to dry. "Sister Hanna gave me a pair of dry stockings from her mending basket."

"Did you talk to Brother Ritt at the Küche?" Propping her elbow on the table, she rested her chin in the palm of her hand.

"No."

"I wish I lived in the same house with the Hetrigs. Maybe then Brother Ritt would notice me. I have tried my best to gain his attention, but with no success." As though struck by a bolt of lightning, Margaret jumped to her feet. "Maybe you could help, ja?"

My stomach lurched. I knew what she was going to ask, and I hoped to curtail any further talk of Ritt or his family. "I need to get busy in the other room. I haven't even begun to dust." I bolted toward the other room.

"Wait!" She grasped my arm. "I want to ask if you would speak to Ritt for me."

I sighed. There would be no escape. I looked into her expectant eyes and waited.

"Would you ask Brother Ritt if he has invited anyone to the picnic? To know would make it easier for me." She rubbed her fingers together in a nervous manner. "If he hasn't asked anyone, if you would mention my name, I would for sure be grateful to you."

What should I say? I didn't want to hurt her by saying he'd

invited me. Yet I couldn't lie to her. If I told her the truth, would it become impossible to work side by side in the future? I'd been looking forward to the picnic, but now I hoped the rain would continue and the outing would be canceled. That would solve this dilemma—at least for the time being.

"I can see my request has caused you discomfort." She bowed her head. "I should not have asked. To make such an inquiry of a man you barely know would be most embarrassing. Please forget that I asked you. If Brother Ritt desires my company, he knows where I live and work and he will ask me."

I inhaled a deep breath and forced a smile, thankful Margaret had withdrawn her request. Yet while I dusted the windowsills and iron bed frames, guilt washed over me. What if the rain stopped and the picnic went on as scheduled? What if Margaret decided to attend without an escort and I appeared at the picnic on Ritt's arm? How would she feel? I attempted to place myself in her position and knew I couldn't remain silent. To prolong the matter would only make it worse.

I tucked the dustrag into my apron pocket and returned to the other room. Margaret was stooped down in front of the stove, checking her shoes. She glanced over her shoulder as I approached. "Your shoes are dry so soon?" I asked.

"Nein, but I thought I would turn them around so the heat will reach the back as well as the front. Should I turn yours?"

I nodded and sat down on one of the chairs. "We need to talk, Margaret."

She arched her brows. "Ja? Something is wrong in the sleeping room?"

I shook my head. "Everything is fine in the other room, but I need to speak with you about Ritt."

She beamed with anticipation and dropped into the chair opposite me. "For sure, I would like that."

My palms turned moist and I wanted to run from the room, but I swallowed hard and forced myself to speak. "When you first mentioned Ritt and the picnic, I should have told you that he's already invited me." Her mouth dropped open and she leaned away from me, her eyes pooling with tears. I reached toward her and when she didn't withdraw, I grasped her hands and held them within my own. "I am truly sorry, Margaret. Please know I didn't intend to hurt you. If I had known you cared for Ritt before he asked me, I would never have accepted his invitation. I don't know what I can do to help ease your pain, but I didn't want his invitation to come between us."

A tear slipped down her cheek. She pulled one hand from my grasp and wiped the tear away. "I am grateful you told me. At least I don't have to keep hoping he's going to show up and ask me." Her lips curved in an awkward smile. "He has every right to ask the girl of his choice, and you have every right to accept. It's not as though he's ever asked to escort me anywhere." She inhaled a ragged breath. "I just kept hoping he might notice me."

My heart ached for her, and I longed to say something that might help. "If you like, I'd be most willing to withdraw my acceptance. With my mother ill, I'm sure Ritt would think nothing of it. That way, he might ask you."

"Nein." Margaret pulled away. "If you did that and he still didn't invite me, I would feel even worse. You should go to the picnic with Ritt and enjoy yourself. If Ritt is the man God intends for me, He will place me on Ritt's heart. If not, then I must accept that there is another plan for me."

I stared at Margaret, amazed by her discerning reply. Would I have been so insightful?

I remained at the men's quarters after Margaret departed. Following our talk, I'd moved at a slower pace than usual. And though I was the one who normally departed early, today it was Margaret.

Once I finished my work, I returned to the bed near the end of the row and stared at the photograph. The girl was a painful reminder of how much I missed the children at the orphanage. Even though I didn't know the girl, I longed to know who she was and her connection to the Charity Home and the unknown man who worked in the woolen mill.

No doubt Ritt would think me unwise to seek such information. I pondered whether I should ask him and finally came to a decision: I would write a note and leave it beneath the photograph. There was no need to involve Ritt.

After removing a sheet of stationery from a supply of paper and envelopes in the parlor, I sat down at the table and composed a brief note.

To the owner of the photograph that was placed on top of this note:

I am Jancey Rhoder, one of the colonists who helps clean the living quarters. I hope you will not think me meddlesome, but while dusting the top of your trunk, I could not help but notice the photograph. I was immediately drawn to the picture because I was a teacher at the Kansas City Charity Home before coming to Middle Amana. I do not recognize the girl in the picture, but I worked with the younger children, so there is a possibility I never met her. However, I am curious about who she is and if she still resides at the Charity Home.

You could write the information at the bottom of the page, but if you don't want to answer, I understand.

Sincerely,
Sister Jancey Rhoder

I folded the sheet of paper in half and tucked it beneath the photograph. I hoped the owner of the picture would be the one to find my note. Even more, I hoped he could read.

CHAPTER 10

The rain had ceased during the night, but the air remained heavy and oppressive. Brother Werner had declared the rain good for the wheat, corn, vegetable gardens, and vineyard. I was sure he was right, but I hoped my shoes would remain dry today. After drying them near the stove, they felt as though they had shrunk at least half a size. In spite of the rain and my pinching shoes, I was eager to reach the men's quarters, so as soon as Brother Herman uttered amen to the after-breakfast prayer, I rushed out the door.

Children scurried off toward the schoolhouse while a few adults remained outside the Küche talking before departing to their assigned daily work. I had gone only a short distance when Ritt shouted my name.

"Wait!" He jogged to my side. "What is your hurry? Has

something happened? You rushed away from the Küche so quickly I became worried."

"Nothing has happened. I am fine." Continuing at a quick pace, I strode onward.

He pinned me with a perplexed gaze. "But you didn't wait for me. Have I done something?"

I shook my head. Because the woolen mill and the outsiders' living quarters were situated in close proximity, I'd begun walking to work with Ritt. In my haste this morning, I'd forgotten that he would look for me. My mind whirled as I tried to think of a reasonable answer.

"I'm sorry. It is humid and once the sun comes out, it will be more difficult to breathe. I want to complete as much work as possible before it is unbearable inside." There was truth in my words, for in no time the men's quarters would turn hot and steamy.

"Ja, is the same in the mill. Maybe worse, I think." He kicked at a rock. "I'm looking forward to the picnic on Saturday. You are still going with me, ja?"

"Yes, of course." My heart warmed at the thought. Being around Ritt always seemed to lighten my spirits. Birds twittered overhead, and I leaned sideways as we passed beneath a hanging tree branch. "Do you know if any of the men have an interest in Sister Margaret? She is a nice young woman, and I think she would be pleased to have an escort for the picnic."

He hiked a shoulder. "No one has mentioned her to me, but that is not so odd. I think no one talks about who they ask because they fear the girl may say no." He tipped his head to one side. "It is embarrassing to be refused, and we do not like others to know."

"I understand, but should you discover one of the men is looking for someone to invite, you could mention her name. I don't think she would refuse."

Probably I shouldn't meddle in Margaret's life. She'd been plainspoken about putting God in charge of her future. But perhaps I could help God with this particular project. Maybe God wanted to use me to help Margaret find a man. At least that's what I told myself.

Ritt slowed his step as we approached the mill. "I will see what I can find out and maybe mention Margaret as a prospect. You are kind to befriend her. I have heard she isn't the best worker in the village—that sometimes she seems slow."

His comment annoyed me. In truth, Margaret was a hard worker. "I don't know why anyone would say Margaret isn't a good worker. She never leaves before her work is completed, and she does a good job, too." I shot a defiant look in his direction as we came to a halt in front of the mill. "And when you say she is slow, I'm sure you aren't referring to her intelligence, since she tells me she attended school through the eighth grade." I hesitated a moment. "Just like most others who live here, if I am remembering correctly."

For a moment, he appeared bewildered by my outburst. "Ja, but she had a little trouble with reading, I think."

I tilted my head and met his puzzled look. "But you're the one who told me that reading and writing weren't important."

He inhaled a deep breath. "Since seeing you work with Madelyn, I have changed my mind a little, but I still believe it is more important to be a skilled worker than to possess the ability to read with ease."

"Then you should not refer to Sister Margaret as slow, for she is as skilled at her work as anyone else in the village."

Ritt frowned and shook his head. "It isn't my wish to argue about Sister Margaret." He glanced toward the mill. "I must go to work. If an opportunity arises, I will mention her name to some of the brothers."

Shoulders squared, he turned and walked away as the work bell rang in the distance. What had come over me? I turned toward the outsiders' quarters and caught sight of Margaret entering the building. Instead of arriving at work before her, I had become embroiled in a silly spat with Ritt. What if she went into the sleeping quarters and discovered one of the men had left a note for me?

I raced toward the door. By the time I entered the building, I was gasping for air. I clutched a hand to my bodice, relieved to see Margaret in the sitting room cleaning ashes from the stove.

She glanced over her shoulder as my labored breathing continued. "You did not need to run, Jancey. This is not like working at the mill. There is no one to make sure you arrive on time."

"Maybe not, but we are still expected to be here when the bell rings."

She shrugged and returned to her work. "Ja, I suppose that is right, but so long as we finish before the men return for the evening, all is well."

I gathered my cleaning supplies and stepped into the other room with my gaze fastened upon the trunk where I'd left my note. After placing the supplies in one corner, I hurried down the aisle that separated the two rows of beds and stopped beside the trunk. My breath caught when I spotted a corner of the stationery peeking out from beneath the photograph. Either he hadn't discovered my note or he'd left an answer.

Leaning forward, I pushed aside the photograph and picked up the folded note.

"I'm going out to empty the bucket of ashes."

Startled by Margaret's announcement, I dropped the note and it fluttered to rest atop the rumpled sheets. My hands trembled as I wheeled around to answer, but she'd already departed through the open doorway. Relieved, I exhaled a slow breath and unfolded the note. Beneath my precise script, a short reply was printed in uneven bold letters: *Meet me at the pond after supper.*

There was no signature, not even initials. Just those seven brief words that were more a command than a request. A shiver raced down my arm, and I shoved the note into my pocket. For the remainder of the morning, I did my best to push thoughts of the girl in the photograph out of my mind. What difference did it make who she was? It wasn't as if I knew the girl.

At supper I scanned the table of outsiders hoping for some clue, but I saw nothing. When we prepared to depart after the evening meal, I remained unsure what I should do. A part of me still wanted to go, yet a modicum of fear mingled with the desire to unearth the mystery of the girl's identity. I continued to weigh the possibilities and said a silent prayer as I walked out of the Küche. Perhaps God would direct me.

"Sister Jancey, Sister Jancey, wait for me!" Madelyn skipped to my side and grasped my hand. "I know it's not our teaching night, but could you help me? I don't understand some of the schoolwork I need to have prepared for tomorrow." She pointed toward the Küche. "Mutter must help with the cleanup and won't be home until time for prayer meeting."

"I believe I've received my answer," I muttered.

Madelyn looked about. "Answer to what?"

"What I should be doing between now and time for prayer service." I squeezed her hand as we walked toward home.

When I arrived at work the following morning, another note awaited me. Once again, it had been placed beneath the photograph. At first I considered leaving it there untouched, but what if Margaret should read it and realize I'd been exchanging notes with an outsider? There was no doubt she'd feel compelled to report my behavior. I shoved the piece of paper into my pocket and set to work, unwilling to take a chance that Margaret might see it and question me.

When she went outside a short time later, I removed the paper from my pocket. The note bore the same uneven bold printing, but instead of a single sentence, he'd written a brief message. I quickly scanned the contents.

I'm sorry you didn't come to the pond yesterday. I've seen you cleaning at the quarters when I go to the Küche for morning break. I know who you are.

A knot formed in the pit of my stomach. He knew who I was, but I didn't know him. I wasn't certain if I should be frightened or if he was simply trying to form a bond with me.

I want to meet you. Please come to the pond after supper tonight. The girl in the photograph is my sister, and I need to get information about her. I hope you will help me.

Thomas Kingman

Learning the girl in the photograph was the man's sister and he wanted to secure information about her whereabouts convinced me. How could I refuse to help him?

After supper, I hurried from the Küche, determined to make my way to the pond before Madelyn or anyone else had an opportunity to stop me. I wasn't certain how I would answer if I should be questioned as to my whereabouts, but I knew I should have something in mind before I returned home. I hurried along a hidden path that Madelyn had shown me some weeks ago, a shortcut that she and her friends used when making their summertime treks to the pond. It would save time, and I wouldn't be easily observed.

The warm, humid air wrapped around me like a damp glove as I hurried along the trail. I stopped several times to gain my bearings. The rains had washed through, leaving portions of the trail rugged and undefined. The odor of musty leaves and damp earth filled my nostrils as I pushed aside tree branches and continued onward.

My spirits soared when I finally stepped out from a cluster of overgrown bushes and caught sight of the pond. I'd made it. I looked about, uncertain where Thomas would be, but I didn't have to wait long. He was standing near the water skipping rocks across the pond. He looked up and loped toward me with long, easy strides.

I narrowed my eyes to get a better look as he approached. He didn't appear familiar. He came to a halt a short distance in front of me and swiped a hank of tawny hair off his forehead. His eyes were as blue as a summer sky, and there was no denying he'd been blessed with rugged good looks. I guessed him to be at least three inches taller than my father. He cast a large shadow, and I felt quite small and somewhat frightened in his presence.

"Mr. Kingman?"

He chuckled and cocked a brow. "Were you expectin' to find anyone else out here?"

"No." My voice trembled.

I should have told him that someone would be joining me in a few minutes and we needed to make our discussion quick. Instead, I had just admitted I'd told no one, and I was now at his mercy. What if he decided to harm me? I should run. My brain told my feet to move, but nothing happened. I stood as still as a statue.

"You don't need to be afraid of me, Miss Jancey. I don't mean you no harm."

"That's good to hear, Mr. Kingman." I swallowed hard. "I need to get back home, so we need to hurry."

"Right." He nodded and stepped a little closer. "That picture you saw is my sister, Kathleen, when she was 'bout eight years old. She'd be 'bout fourteen now. Our parents died and I couldn't take care of her on my own so I took her to the Charity Home. I promised I'd come back and get her when I could."

His eyes radiated emotion, and I believed he was sincere in his promise to reunite with his sister. Though I wasn't always correct in my assessment of others, he appeared to be a young man who'd suffered a great deal of sorrow in his life.

He yanked a piece of tall grass from the ground and shoved it between his teeth. "Trouble is, when I finally got back there, she was gone. Nobody in that place would help me. Fact is, they wouldn't tell me much of nothing. Said it wasn't any of my business—that I had signed my name on the papers givin' up any rights when I left her there." He yanked the piece of grass from between his lips and tossed it to the ground. "That place needs to change its name 'cause they sure don't show much charity. Only thing I ever got was a door slammed in my face."

I wasn't certain anyone who worked at the home would have slammed a door in Mr. Kingman's face, but he'd made his point: He hadn't been well received. I'd worked at the orphanage long enough to know there were occasions when family members returned, but those events were rare. More often, the children never saw or heard from those who'd left them. I didn't pass judgment, for I knew the children were likely better fed and attended to at the Charity Home than with parents or siblings who were without means to care for them.

"I'm sorry for your difficulties, Mr. Kingman, but—"

"Call me Thomas. Ain't never been called Mr. Kingman, and it makes me feel downright uncomfortable." He gestured toward a stand of trees. "Why don't we go over there instead of standing out here in the open? You can sit on my jacket so your dress don't get stained."

"Thank you for your kind offer." I walked alongside him, but when we reached the trees, I remained standing. "I'll just lean against this tree. I'm not tired."

One side of his mouth curved in a perceptive grin. "Easier to run off if you stay on your feet—that the idea?"

I was surprised he'd so easily realized my motivation. I considered a denial, but he was shrewd. He'd see through any excuse I might offer. "Yes. No need to deny that I know I've placed myself in a bit of an unsafe situation, Mr. King—Thomas."

He chuckled. "It's more than a bit unsafe, but like I said afore, I don't mean you no harm." He dropped to the ground and looked up at me. "The only thing I want from you is some help findin' out where my sister might be. You think you can do that? Help me find Kathleen? She's a sweet girl, Miss Jancey, and I want her back with me. I'm able to take care of her now."

"I'm not sure what I can do. From what you've told me, she was gone from the home before I began teaching there. I do know one teacher who would have been there and might have known Kathleen. I could write and ask her if she can tell me any of the particulars concerning her whereabouts."

"I thank you, Miss Jancey. I'll be forever—"

I stretched out my arm to stave off his thanks. "I didn't say she'd be able to help or that she'd even be willing to answer my questions—only that I'd write a letter. You must remember that the records are not the best, and employees are not permitted to reveal information without permission from the director. However, she may have known Kathleen and possess some personal knowledge as to her whereabouts."

He nodded. "It ain't much, but it gives me a little hope. More than I had afore."

"You said you could support Kathleen if she came to live with you, Thomas, but you understand she can't come to Middle Amana, don't you? You'd have to give up your job at the woolen mill—unless you think she might be hired to help in the gardens or in one of the kitchens. Is that what you plan?"

"Naw." He stood and dug the toe of his boot in the dirt. "I have me enough money saved for us to begin over. No need for the folks at the orphanage to worry about jobs or money. If you find Kathleen for me, we'll be leaving and making us a new home elsewhere." He looked up with a quizzical look in his eyes. "How come you came here, Miss Jancey? Can't believe you'd rather live here instead of Kansas City."

I hadn't planned to reveal much about my past to Thomas, but it seemed rude to avoid his question. Especially after all he'd told me about himself. Without giving an extraordinary amount of detail, I explained my parents had previously lived in the colonies and, due to my mother's illness, had decided to return.

"I wanted to continue helping care for my mother. To have her so far away during her illness would have proved impossible for me."

"The minute I read your letter, I knew you had a good heart." He leaned one shoulder against the trunk of an elm tree. "Ain't nothin' more important than family. We gotta do everything in our power to take care of 'em. We got that in common, Miss Jancey."

The sun had begun to lower on the horizon. I'd been there longer than planned and needed to return before Mother began to worry. "I have to go, but I'll write the letter and post it tomorrow. I can't tell how long it will take to hear back, but I'll leave a message beneath the photograph if I hear anything."

"I thank you. And if there's anything I can ever do for you, just say the word."

I started off, but then returned. "There is something, Thomas. I need your word that you won't tell anyone else about this meeting with me. And if you should see me somewhere in the village, you shouldn't acknowledge you know me." I arched my brows. "Will you do that?"

He smiled and gave a nod. "Weren't no need to ask that, Miss Jancey. Ain't no one who could ever get so much as your name outta me. I know the rules about not mixing with outsiders—especially you womenfolk."

"Thank you, Thomas."

I hurried through the overgrown path, my heart pounding a ferocious beat. With any luck, I wouldn't be questioned about my whereabouts.

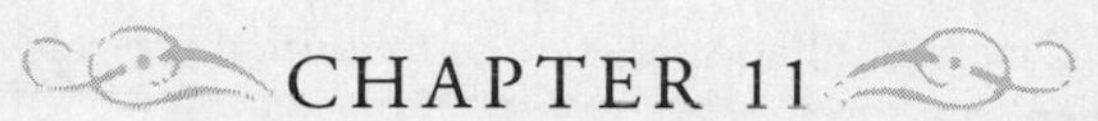

CHAPTER 11

Good fortune prevailed. When I arrived home from my meeting with Thomas, my mother greeted me in the parlor. I was pleased to see her up and about, for she'd been abed for the last few days. Her ever-changing health kept Brother Rudolf, as well as my father and me, on the alert, but I was most thankful whenever she had good days.

"I can see you went for a walk. Your cheeks are pink from the exercise." She cupped my chin in her hand. "I am pleased you are exploring on your own. It is good to learn your way around the village." She stepped toward one of the tables and picked up her Bible.

"You are going to prayer meeting?"

"Your father thinks it will tire me too much, but I have had few opportunities to attend prayer meetings, so I insisted. I will be fine. I'm going to read until time for us to leave." She sat down and opened her Bible. "Your father worries too much."

I didn't contradict her, but there was much for my father to worry about. In addition to her failing health, he was attempting to juggle a new life here while still tied to our former life in Kansas City. Unlike Mother, he'd been unable to walk away from the past. Our house had sold, but he remained the sole owner of Forsythe Construction. He wasn't present to oversee the projects, but he was still responsible for construction that must meet strict standards on a timely schedule. Not an easy task when he was present, but now that he was absent, his worries had increased tenfold. I wasn't certain his concern was well founded, for he'd left the business in capable hands, but I did understand the weight of responsibility that rested upon his shoulders. Here in Middle Amana, he'd been assigned to work with a crew constructing a new barn. Nothing that required much thought or effort after all the major projects he'd overseen in Kansas City.

"I'm going to my room and write a letter." I placed a kiss atop my mother's head.

"To Nathan?" She turned toward me.

A pang of guilt assailed me. Perhaps I should be writing to him rather than Lilly. "No. To Lilly Manchester at the orphanage. I want to inquire about one of the children." I rested my hand on her shoulder.

"You should write to Nathan. Your father had a letter from him yesterday. He asked if you hadn't been feeling well since he hadn't heard from you for a while."

I clenched my jaw, annoyed that Nathan would make such an inquiry of anyone other than me. I'd written him last, and if he wanted correspondence to continue, he should write to me rather than pass messages through letters to my father. "Father said nothing to me, but I'll write Nathan if I have enough time before we leave."

She reached up and squeezed my hand. "I don't think you'll decide to remain in the colonies, so if you care for him, you should be careful not to lose him, dear."

"If he is so easily dissuaded, then I doubt his love runs deep enough to survive a lifelong marriage. Don't you agree?"

I didn't wait for a reply. Right now, I didn't want to participate in a lengthy discussion about Nathan. Truth be told, my feelings for him remained jumbled—one moment I missed him and the next his behavior annoyed me. Trying to explain such mixed emotions to Mother would take far too long. Even if I tried, I doubted anything I said would make sense. Besides, I wanted to use this bit of time to pen a letter to Lilly Manchester and ask what she might know about Kathleen Kingman. I'd write to Nathan when I was less displeased with him.

Hearing the village bell ring a short time later, I set aside my pen and ink, folded the letter to Lilly, and slipped it into an envelope. I would mail it tomorrow. I hoped Lilly would be willing to check into the whereabouts of Kathleen. If she didn't know the girl, I had my doubts she'd make further inquiry, and I knew she wouldn't peek into the records on her own. Miss Manchester wasn't a rule breaker, and she certainly wouldn't risk losing her position at the orphanage after all these years. Unlike me, she had no other means of support and needed the income her work at the Charity Home provided.

I bowed my head and offered a prayer for God to intervene and help me discover Kathleen's whereabouts. "If it be your will," I added.

Before arriving at Middle Amana, most of my praying had been done in church, but I'd attempted to grow closer to God while living here. I'd been praying more often, but when answers didn't come quickly—and usually they didn't—I continued to seek my own solutions. In one of the prayer meetings last week, Brother William, one of the elders, said we needed to be patient and wait upon God, but some things needed immediate answers. I wasn't sure what I was supposed to do in such circumstances and I didn't ask. I might not like Brother William's answer. Though I admired the strong beliefs of the Inspirationists and prayed I would attain their ability to trust God in all things, I hadn't yet arrived at such a point. It seemed with each step forward, a backward step soon followed.

As I walked out of my room, I noted Father standing near the parlor door, obviously eager to depart for prayer meeting. "Your mother tells me you have been busy writing letters. Did you have time to finish them?"

"Only one. I'll write to Nathan when we return."

My father's inquiry surprised me, for he'd remained somewhat neutral about my relationship with Nathan. In my heart, I knew both of my parents desired my happiness, yet they both seemed certain that I would leave the colonies at some point in the future. Perhaps because that is what they'd chosen to do when they were my age and in love. But I wasn't in love with Nathan. I cared about him, but for those feelings to blossom into anything beyond caring, I would need to spend more time with him. Perhaps in time that missing spark would ignite. But given our separation, that was not going to happen—at least not anytime soon.

Along with the Hetrigs and a few other families, we attended prayer meeting at the home of Brother William. Small groups gathered for prayer at different places throughout the village, and generally the meeting lasted for less than half an hour. Following prayers, the presiding elder would make announcements regarding proper organization of work for the following day and communicate any other news the elders wanted passed on to the members.

Although this evening's meeting lasted only a short time, it had taken a toll on Mother. She'd attempted to do too much and would now pay the price.

"You see?" My father supported her arm. "I told you that you were pushing yourself too hard. You walked to the Küche, ate supper, and then walked home. The distance to Brother William's was even farther than the Küche, and you didn't have enough rest before attempting a second outing." He sighed and looked at me as we arrived home. "Help your mother prepare for bed. She needs to rest."

When Mother didn't argue, I knew she was every bit as weary as Father suspected, and I hoped this wouldn't cause the setback he predicted. I helped her out of her dark calico and into a nightgown before assisting her to bed.

After pouring a glass of water from the bedside pitcher, I stirred a packet of granules into the water and handed it to her. "Hold your nose and drink it down."

She smiled at the instruction, for it was the same one she'd always given to me as a child when I protested taking any medicine the doctor had ordered. She winked, clasped her nose between her thumb and forefinger, and downed the contents of the glass.

"There! Every bit gone in no time at all." She placed the glass atop the table and exhaled a long breath as she leaned back on her pillows and closed her eyes.

I pulled the sheet to her chin and kissed her forehead. "Rest well, Mother."

The quiet recitation of her nighttime prayers followed me to the parlor. As soon as I entered the room, my father removed his glasses and gestured for me to sit down. "I could see you were unhappy with me before we departed for prayer meeting. It was not my intention to pry, but there is something I must tell you." He patted his jacket pocket, his brow creased with concern. "I received a letter in today's mail." He cleared his throat. "From Mr. Millhuff, the man I appointed manager until the company is sold."

There wasn't any need for Father to expound upon Mr. Millhuff's position at Forsythe Construction. Nathan had spoken the man's name far too many times before we left Kansas City. In truth, Nathan had been overwrought when Father announced his decision. Even though Charles Millhuff possessed more experience and had been employed by my father for many years, Nathan had expected to receive the position of acting manager. Over and over, he'd privately expressed his unhappiness to me—until I'd suggested he take his complaint to my father. To my knowledge, he'd never taken my advice. I finally deduced Nathan had expected me to plead his case. I hadn't. And Father never changed his decision. Mr. Millhuff had been appointed to the position and entrusted with running the company.

"I inquired about your letters because I will be returning to Kansas City and can personally deliver them."

I gasped. "What? Returning to Kansas City?" I clutched my shaking hands together. "I don't understand."

Leaning forward, he patted my arm. "No need for you to be alarmed. I should have said I would be *traveling* to Kansas City. It's my hope that I won't be there for an extended period. A problem has come up, and both Mr. Millhuff and Mr. Hartzfeld believe my presence is needed to resolve the issue."

My thoughts swirled like flies on a hot summer afternoon. None of this made any sense. "What kind of problem, Father?" What could be so difficult that Mr. Millhuff or Mr. Hartzfeld couldn't handle it? "It must be serious if they need your assistance." I swallowed hard.

"I didn't mean to upset you." He scooted closer and pulled me into a comforting embrace. After releasing his hold, he glanced toward the bedroom. "I had hoped your mother's health would remain improved during my absence, but now I worry she may need to take to her bed again. I do wish she would have stayed home this evening."

I understood his concern for Mother, but I was anxious to hear what would cause him to leave my ailing mother and return to Kansas City. "I'll see to her care, Father, but please tell me what has happened."

"If you promise you won't reveal any of this to your mother. I've told her I need to return in order to sign some papers in regard to the business—which is true, but there's more, and I don't want her to worry."

"You have my word." If he didn't soon tell me, I thought I would burst from the anticipation.

"There's been a terrible accident at one of the work sites. There's an investigation in process, and the police want to talk to me." He rubbed his forehead. "I'm not certain what will happen, but I don't want your mother to be worried while I'm gone. Should it take longer than expected, I am depending upon you to calm her concerns."

"I'll do my best, Father, but what can I tell her? If she believes you're going to be gone only long enough to sign papers and you're gone for more than a day or two, she's bound to become fretful."

"Before I depart, I'll tell her there's a possibility I may be delayed if additional negotiations are needed before we sign the papers. Hopefully, that will allay her concerns." He exhaled a long sigh. "I dislike withholding this ugly mess from her, but I fear it could have a terrible effect upon her."

"What did Mr. Millhuff tell you about the accident? Was there a fire? Surely he gave you some details."

My father bowed his head. "Some sort of explosion occurred in one of the buildings the company was working on over on Sixth Street. None of our employees were present, but there were a number of people in the vicinity when it happened and some of them were injured. I'm not certain how serious the injuries were, but this gives rise to a multitude of problems."

My heart beat with such force, I clasped my palm to my chest. "This is terrible news. No wonder you don't want Mother to know. I won't speak a word of this. Did you talk to Brother Herman? He knows you'll be leaving?"

"Yes. As soon as I read the letter, I went to him. He spoke to the other elders in the village, and they are in agreement that I should leave tomorrow. The sooner I go, the sooner I can return."

Hoping to hide my fear, I swallowed a lump that had settled in my throat. "Why do the police want to talk to you? Since you weren't in Kansas City when the accident happened, what do they think you can add to their investigation?"

"I have no idea, my dear. There are a multitude of possibilities, but until I talk to them, I can't be sure."

I reached for his hand. "What kind of possibilities?" I couldn't begin to imagine even one.

"I'm sure they'll question me about my finances. Whenever something like this happens, there's suspicion someone will benefit financially. And who can say what will happen in regard to those who've been injured? Someone will need to take responsibility for medical expenses and the like." He ran his palm along his jaw. "There are a lot of loose ends that need to be tied together for certain."

"I'll be praying that it all goes well and you'll soon be back home."

"Thank you, Jancey. It does my heart good to know you'll be praying for me." He pushed up from the sofa. "I think I'll go to bed. Tomorrow will be a long day." He stopped outside the bedroom door. "If you have letters for me to deliver, be sure you leave them on the table beside the parlor door."

I settled at the small desk, dipped my pen into the thick, black ink, and began another letter to Nathan. My father would expect it—and so would Nathan.

We had finished breakfast and were on our way to work when I told Ritt my father would be leaving for Kansas City on the midmorning train. I merely stated his presence was required to complete some business matters.

Ritt's smile faded. "So this means you will not be going to the picnic with me tomorrow?"

"I don't think it would be wise. Mother wasn't well enough to come to the Küche this morning, and even if I see some improvement today, I wouldn't want to leave her alone for so long. Until she is doing better, I'll need to look in on her more often."

This wasn't anything new. Unless Sister Hanna went home

between meal preparations at the kitchen house, I often left work to go and check on my mother. When we had free time, Father was there to care for Mother, if needed. With him away, I had no other help upon which I could rely.

"I am disappointed."

"I am, too." I gave him a sideways glance. "If I'd known in advance that Father would be away, I wouldn't have accepted your invitation."

Stopping along the path, he reached for my hand. "Forgive me. I know you need to care for your Mutter. If my Mutter was ill and needed me, I would do the same."

As he squeezed my hand, a pleasant sensation raced through me. I could feel the heat radiating up my neck and across my cheeks. "Thank you for being so patient. I truly appreciate your kind manner."

He grinned. "And why would I be otherwise? You had no way of knowing this would happen."

He was right, but had I approached Nathan with news that I was going to cancel an outing, he would have pouted for days. I shouldn't compare the two men, but I found it increasingly difficult not to do so—and Nathan seemed to be coming up short most of the time.

Ritt came to a halt as we neared the mill. "If you should need me while your Father is gone, you can always come to the mill and leave word. There is usually someone near the entrance who would deliver your message."

"Thank you. I'll remember that." Though I remained disappointed I'd miss the picnic, Ritt's attitude had granted me a sense of relief.

Throughout the day, I made several trips home to check on

Mother because Sister Hanna was needed at the kitchen. Though Mother was sad about my father's departure, her condition remained stable.

As Margaret and I prepared to leave for the evening, she stopped me near the doorway. "I'm looking forward to seeing you at the picnic tomorrow. John Olson will be my escort." Her cheeks turned pink as she revealed the news to me.

"That's wonderful, Margaret. I'm so glad for you." I returned a smile. "Unfortunately, I won't be there." When I quickly explained my circumstances, she nodded her understanding. "I hope you have a pleasant time with John."

"I could ask my Mutter to come and sit with her if you'd like. I think she'd be willing."

A lump formed in my throat. "That is very generous, Margaret, and I do thank you for the offer, but I don't want to burden your mother. I'm accustomed to caring for her."

She bobbed her head. "Ja, I understand, but if you should change your mind, you can have Madelyn bring word to me."

I was certain I wouldn't change my mind, but my heart soared with the outpouring of compassion I'd received today. This was what my mother had missed and longed to experience once again—the generosity of spirit that bound this group together as brothers and sisters in Christ.

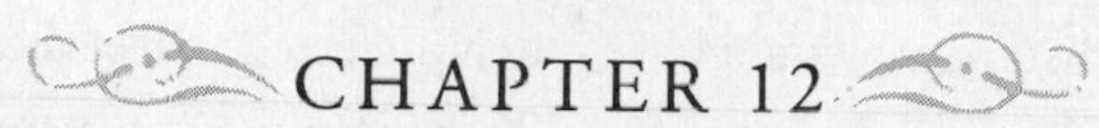

CHAPTER 12

The following morning, Ritt was sitting on the steps leading to his family's rooms upstairs when I arrived. He jumped to his feet. "I hope you don't mind, but I thought we could walk to the Küche together."

"It's a nice surprise to see you waiting for me." My heart fluttered when he reached forward and squeezed my hand.

He released his hold as we walked outside. "I wish I could hold your hand all the way to the Küche."

I chuckled. "I don't think that would be wise."

"For sure, there would be looks of disapproval if anyone saw us."

"I think there would be more than looks of disapproval. We would likely be required to explain our behavior to Brother Herman and the other elders." I shivered at the thought.

Using an exaggerated swoop of his arm, Ritt placed his palm

on his heart. "To hold your hand, I would be willing to take such a chance, but I don't want to get you into any trouble—especially since your Vater is gone and your Mutter is ill." He continued to press his palm to his chest. "You have my word that I will keep a proper distance."

Though I murmured my approval, I really didn't want him to keep his distance. I would have much preferred to feel the warmth and support of his callused hand holding my own. Instead, suitability prevailed and he stuffed his hands into his pockets while I clasped mine in front of my apron.

As we neared the Küche, Ritt gestured for me to slow my step. "I won't see you after we eat the morning meal since you must take breakfast to your Mutter, but I wanted to tell you that I will bring the noonday meal to you and your Mutter."

"You don't need to do that, Ritt. I know you want to go to the picnic with the others. I don't mind returning to the Küche for our meals."

His offer was kind, but after work ceased at noon, those who were going on the picnic would stop by the Küche to pick up their baskets of food before departing for the river. Taking time to bring food back to the house meant Ritt would miss joining the others until later in the afternoon.

"I have already told my Mutter that I will come by to fetch meals for you and your Mutter and carry them to the house, so you should not argue with me."

His lopsided grin warmed my heart. "I will do as you ask. I won't argue."

"Gut."

The final bell tolled as we parted, each of us running in opposite directions. I was the last to enter the women's door, but Ritt was faster than I—two of the older men followed behind him. Across the expanse that divided our tables, he smiled at me, and again my heart fluttered like the wings of a baby bird attempting to take flight.

As promised, Ritt appeared with two baskets shortly after noon. He handed the smaller one to me. "This is your Mutter's food. I have our food in this basket." He lifted the napkin that covered the contents of the smaller basket, and the inviting aroma of cotton soup, a mixture of chicken broth and eggs that had been slightly thickened with flour and butter, wafted toward me. "Sister Bertha sent the soup for your Mutter. She said it was left over from yesterday, but you should make sure she eats it, because soup is the best medicine." He tapped the handle of the other basket. "There is no soup in our basket."

"Our basket? I've already explained that I can't go to the picnic by the river with you."

Did he think that once Mother had finished her meal, I would leave for the remainder of the afternoon? I'd been clear with him. He'd said he understood and admired my willingness to put family first. Why would he believe I'd changed my mind and that sharing a picnic with him would lure me away?

"Nein. Not to the river. We will have our picnic in the backyard. While you help your Mutter with her lunch, I am going to spread a quilt on the grass. Then we can eat our picnic lunch and visit. My Mutter said it would be fine to use one of her old quilts, so you do not need to worry about that."

In my haste, I'd jumped to an incorrect assumption about Ritt's intent. Once again, his kind heart and gentle spirit surprised me.

I placed my hand on the large picnic basket. "I want you to take this and go to the river. Enjoy yourself and share your lunch with some of your friends." As the excitement in his eyes faded, I knew I'd wounded him. "I don't want you to miss having a wonderful afternoon because of me."

"Do you not understand that it won't be a wonderful afternoon unless I am with you? I don't care about standing at the water's edge and fishing or sharing my lunch with anyone except you." He tapped his index finger on the table. "You are here, so this is where I want to be." When I didn't immediately respond, he lifted his gaze and looked deep into my eyes. "Unless you do not want to be with me. If that is true, then I will leave."

"I do want to be with you, but—"

He touched his finger to my lips. "That is all I need to know. I will be waiting in the back of the house. You should take your time helping your Mutter." At the sound of a soft jangle, I glanced toward his hand. He'd reached into his pocket and removed a small metal bell. "Tell your Mutter to ring this if she needs you. With the window open, we will be sure to hear." He placed the bell in my hand and clasped his fingers around my hand with a gentle squeeze. "I don't want you to worry while you are outside."

His thoughtfulness touched my heart, and tears pricked my eyes. "Thank you, Ritt. It seems that is what I say most often to you, for you are constantly doing things for which I am grateful."

"It pleases me to help you." He gestured toward the other room. "Go take the food to your Mutter. I wouldn't want her to think I forgot to bring her meal." Holding the large basket in his hand, he turned and strode to the door.

I placed a wooden tray on the table, then poured the soup into a china bowl Sister Bertha had placed at the bottom of the basket. I arranged the silverware atop a neatly folded napkin beside the plate of boiled beef, peas, and creamed potatoes. After placing the small bell beside a cup of tea, I carried the tray into the bedroom.

Mother signaled for me to place the food on a small table that sat adjacent to a nearby chair. "I'd like to sit in the chair to eat. I feel strong enough."

She'd said the same thing yesterday, but she hadn't had the strength to make it out of bed. I didn't argue, for I'd learned such activity depleted energy—both Mother's and mine. Once she'd come to a sitting position with her legs dangling off the side of the bed, I slipped her feet into a pair of soft slippers.

Her color remained good, but I didn't want to take a chance. "Do you feel strong enough to walk to the chair?"

She nodded. I was surprised at the strength she exhibited as I helped her settle in the chair. Her gaze drifted over the tray while she arranged the cloth napkin on her lap. Using her thumb and forefinger, she lifted the small bell and gently moved it back and forth until the tiny clapper struck metal with a soft chime. She looked up at me and smiled. "Have we hired a maid?"

I chuckled and shook my head. "No. Ritt brought it when he delivered your lunch. He thought it would be helpful. If I'm not nearby, you can ring the bell to alert me. It will prove useful at night, too. While Father is away, you can summon me. I've been worried I wouldn't hear you call when I'm asleep."

"He's a thoughtful young man." She handed me the bell. "Why don't you put it on my bedside table? And do thank him when you see him this evening."

I positioned the bell on her table. "I'll tell him as soon as you've finished eating and have returned to bed."

"How so? I thought he was going to the river with the other young people."

"He was, but he decided to bring a picnic to the backyard. He asked me to join him so we could visit and enjoy the afternoon." A rush of heat ascended my neck and spread across my cheeks. "I told him he should go to the river, but he insisted."

She swallowed a spoonful of soup. "Do you like him?"

I turned and busied myself straightening the bedsheets. "Yes, of course. As you said, he's very thoughtful and kind."

"That's not what I meant, and you know it. I saw you blush when I asked about your feelings for him." She pointed her spoon toward the bed. "Sit down so I can see your face when we talk."

I sat down, folded my hands in my lap, and waited.

"While I eat my lunch, you can tell me about your feelings for this young man. Do be honest with me. You know I can always tell when you're avoiding the truth." She took a bite of the creamed potatoes. "Has this young man captured your interest?"

"Yes, he has. I like him very much. In many ways, he reminds me of Father. He has a kind and generous heart, and he isn't critical in the least. Not that he doesn't speak the truth, he does. But he is never harsh or insensitive." My mother continued to eat while I listed Ritt's attributes. "I don't mean to make him sound as though he has no faults—I'm sure he has as many as the next person, but he exhibits the virtues that are important to me."

My mother looked over the rim of her teacup. "Important in a friend or in a husband?"

"B-both. Wasn't Father your friend before you considered him a man you would want to marry?"

Placing the teacup on the matching saucer, she nodded. "Yes, but your father and I weren't living in two different worlds at the time. We had both grown up and lived our entire lives in the colonies."

"Ritt and I aren't living in two different worlds, either. We are both living in the colonies." There was little doubt what she was thinking, but I didn't want to hear words of discouragement.

"I don't want either of you to suffer the consequences of a broken heart." Her forehead creased with concern. "And what about Nathan? I thought the two of you might marry one day."

"I never . . ."

She waved me to silence. "He called on you at least one or two times a week until you told him you'd decided to come with us to Iowa. What else was I to think?"

"He was persistent. And he does have some good qualities. But Nathan changed. During the months before we departed, he was more interested in Father's business than in me. At least that's how I felt. I began to wonder if the business was more important to him than our relationship. Even though he'd been calling on me for some time, I began to doubt that I truly knew him. He's ambitious, and while that can be a good trait, it never appealed to me. Of course, I don't think I'll ever find a man more determined to marry me. Perhaps this time apart will help us discover whether we have any foundation for a life together."

"I suppose I took too much for granted." My mother frowned. "So now you believe Ritt may be a better match for you?"

"I'm not sure, but I find he has many more qualities that appeal to me."

"I won't tell you what you should do, Jancey. You're no longer a child, but remember that before you encourage Ritt, you should give serious thought to whether you could live in the colonies for the rest of your life. He is not a young man who would leave." She arched her brows. "You understand?"

"I do, Mother. It is not my intention to hurt him."

She extended her hand. "Help me back into bed, and then you should go downstairs before the ants have eaten your dinner."

Ritt sat with his back against the fat trunk of a large elm. His straw hat was pushed forward to block the sunlight from his eyes, and his left arm rested atop the picnic basket. He'd fallen asleep while waiting for me.

A branch cracked beneath my shoe when I approached, and he startled. His hat tumbled to the ground as he straightened his shoulders. I gestured toward the basket. "I'm pleased to see you were protecting our lunch from any stray animals."

"A man who falls asleep doesn't offer much protection, so I'm glad there were no attacks." He chuckled and placed a hand on his stomach. "I'm glad you're here. My stomach has been telling me it's past time to eat."

Hands on hips, I feigned indignation. "And how could you hear your stomach when you were asleep?"

We laughed together as I sat down beside him and lifted the napkin from atop the basket. Such a simple thing—enjoying a picnic in the backyard while birds twittered overhead. I couldn't recall an outing with Nathan when I'd experienced such anticipation and happiness. Though we'd attended the theater and dinner parties and taken walks in the park, none of those occasions had been joyful. Instead of pleasure, there seemed always to be a hint of reserve—on both of our parts. Would things be different if I allowed myself to relax in Nathan's company?

I tried to remember the last time Nathan and I had laughed aloud about something—anything. Yet I couldn't. Our times together had borne a sense of obligation rather than delight. Is that what I wanted for the remainder of my life? A man who derived more pleasure from his work than his family? On the other hand, I wasn't sure I wanted to wash dirty linens and scrub floors in the men's dormitory for the rest of my life, either.

And then there were the children.

I shook my head. Clearly I was getting ahead of myself.

Ritt leaned close and peeked into the basket. "Sister Bertha said she placed beef sandwiches, pickles, radish salad, cottage cheese, and stewed apples with raisins in each of the picnic baskets."

His breath tickled my neck and sent shivers racing down my spine. "Since you are so hungry, maybe you need a spoon instead of a fork to eat your salad and cottage cheese. It might let you eat faster." Turning toward him, I inhaled a slight gasp and quickly tilted my head away. Had I leaned forward by only a hairsbreadth, our lips would have met.

"I think I would like a fork for my right hand and a spoon for my left." He picked up the utensils, held one in each hand, and pretended to dig into the cottage cheese. "What do you think? This way is the very best, ja?" His eyes sparkled with mischief, and I joined his laughter.

"I think I should hurry and fill my plate before there is nothing left for me."

Ritt grinned as he placed one of the sandwiches on my plate. "I would never let you go without food. I would starve before I would let that happen."

He grasped my hand and looked into my eyes. Passion replaced the mischievous look from only moments ago. My mouth turned as dry as cotton batting, and I stared at him, unable to speak.

"I am sorry. I have upset you." He released my hand and looked away.

I reached forward and clutched his arm. "No! Nothing you've said or done has displeased me in the least." I touched my fingers to my neck. "My throat became dry and I couldn't speak."

"Then it is gut that I filled a jug with water." He filled a glass and handed it to me. "This should help."

I downed the water in giant gulps. "That helped. Thank you."

"Is your Vater in Kansas City to sign the papers to sell his company?" He scooped a mound of cottage cheese onto his plate. When I hesitated, he waved his hand in a dismissive gesture. "Is none of my business why he must go there."

I shook my head and pointed to my mouth as I swallowed a bite of the sandwich. "I don't object to answering your question." I hoped my smile would reassure him that he hadn't offended me. "In truth, I'm pleased to discuss what happened, as I'm very worried about what will occur while he's away." While we continued with our lunch, I explained what little I knew about the accident. "I don't know why the police want to speak with him."

"You are worried they think he was involved?"

I shrugged. "Yes. And I don't understand why they insisted upon his return when his lawyer is available to answer any questions. Mr. Hartzfeld—my father's lawyer—has already told the police that Father wasn't in Kansas City at the time of the explosion, so what could they want to ask him?" I sighed. "To make matters worse, we don't know how long he'll be gone. I worry my mother's health will spiral into a rapid decline if he doesn't return within four or five days."

"I am sorry this has happened, but maybe the police want to hear from your Vater's lips that he knows nothing. Then maybe they will let him return home. Ja?"

I wanted to believe that would happen, but I had my doubts. "We should talk about something more pleasant on such a pretty day."

"We could talk about Madelyn receiving some nice remarks on her school papers yesterday."

I perked to attention. "Did she? And she didn't even tell me!" I folded my arms across my chest. "You tell her that I expect a full report as soon as she returns from the river. I can't believe she didn't bring the papers to show me."

Ritt frowned. "I should not have said anything. If she comes downstairs with the papers, please act surprised."

"You have my word. Besides, whatever her teacher has written on the papers will be a surprise to me. You've told me only that she received a good report."

He stacked the dishes into the picnic basket. "She has gained more from your lessons than just gut remarks on her school papers."

"What do you mean? I've helped her with nothing else."

He pointed his index finger to the side of his head. "Is true you have helped her up here, but you have helped her here, too." Lowering his hand, he patted his palm against his chest. "She feels better about herself—not ashamed. Do you understand what I'm trying to say?"

I nodded. "Yes. I understand. Now that she is able to compete with the other children her own age, she feels more confident."

"So I think I must say I was wrong. For Madelyn it is very important that she be able to read and write."

I grinned at him. "Only Madelyn?"

"We will see. Maybe for everyone, but I should not rush too quickly in changing my mind. Then you would become too . . . what was that word you said?" He furrowed his brow. "Confident! That was it. Ja?"

I nodded. "Yes, that was it."

He leaned forward and wrapped his arms around his bent knees. "I would like to learn about your work at the orphanage. Tell me about the children and also your life in Kansas City." He grinned. "I want to know all about you."

His interest surprised but pleased me. Most men I'd been around were more interested in talking about themselves and their own accomplishments. As I spoke of the children, he asked questions and laughed when I related some of their antics. "They have been a very important part of my life."

"Ja, and that is gut. We all need to serve and use the talents God has given us."

A train whistled in the distance, and I turned toward the sound. "I hope my father returns very soon."

"We will pray for his safe return." He lifted the back of my hand to his lips and brushed a light kiss against my skin. His words comforted me, but my doubts remained.

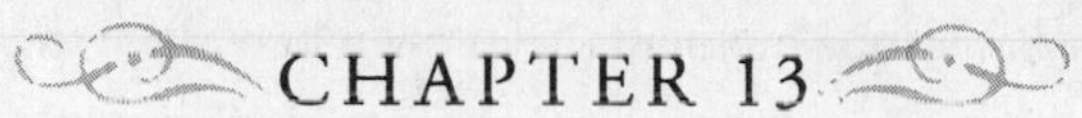

CHAPTER 13

Several days later, I stopped at the general store, where we received our mail. Though I didn't expect to hear from my father so soon, I'd promised Mother I would check to see if any mail had come for us. I, too, hoped there would be some word from him, but I was also eager for a response from Lilly Manchester. Father had promised he would deliver my letter to her as soon as he arrived in Kansas City. If he'd done as he'd said, and I was certain he had, she'd had sufficient time to write and post a letter.

Brother Traugott's bald head shone in the sunlight beaming through the front window of the store. I greeted him as I strode toward the counter, but my gaze was fastened upon the wall of boxes where the manager placed mail delivered to members of individual families. My heart picked up a beat when I spied an envelope in the box assigned to us.

"You are in need of some supplies, Sister Jancey?"

I shook my head. "I have come to pick up any mail for our family." My attention remained fixed on the cream-colored envelope resting in our mailbox.

"Ja, there is a letter for you." He removed it from the cubbyhole and looked at it for a moment. "Has been here since the day after your Vater departed, but you never came to pick it up."

My spirits plummeted. If the mail arrived the day after my father left for Kansas City, it wouldn't be from the two people I longed to hear from—Lilly Manchester or my father.

He tapped the envelope on top of the counter. "In the future, you should not wait so long before coming to get your mail. Could be something important. Who can say?"

"You're right. I've grown accustomed to my father picking it up. I'll stop by each day until he returns."

Brother Traugott turned the envelope facedown and pushed it across the counter. "Gut. We are praying for your Mutter's health and that your Vater will soon return to us."

"Danke." I picked up the letter and waited until I was out of sight to turn over the envelope. I stared at the return address. *Nathan.* I should have known. He'd likely written before he knew Father would be coming to Kansas City.

I shoved it into my pocket and strode toward home. I was deep in thought as I continued along the wooden walkway, and it wasn't until I neared home that I noticed Thomas waving to me. I glanced around, hoping no one would see him. Surely he realized he shouldn't act as though we were friends. I signaled for him to stop waving, and though he ceased his wild gestures, I wasn't sure if he thought that I'd waved in return or wanted him to put his hands in his pockets.

When he drew near, I muttered for him to meet me behind the house. He loped away and I exhaled a sigh of relief. Except for a woman and child I didn't know, the street remained empty. But who could say if anyone had been looking out a window when Thomas waved and approached. It would do no good to worry if we'd been seen, yet I couldn't understand why he'd been so careless.

I glanced around before walking to the side of the house and entering the backyard. Thomas was sitting beneath the same elm where I'd discovered Ritt sleeping on the day we'd picnicked together.

I gestured for him to get up. "Someone could see you. Move back to that stand of bushes."

He looked around and shrugged. "Who's gonna see me back here?"

"My mother, for one. Her bedroom window looks out at this tree." I pointed to the window. "Hurry and move."

Bowing his head to clear one of the low-hanging branches, he didn't stop until he was surrounded by brush and bushes. "Is this good enough?"

"Yes. Why did you approach me out in the open like that? You know I'm not supposed to have contact with you or any other outsiders."

"I've looked on my trunk every day, but there ain't been one word from you. Did you write a letter? Have you heard anything in return? I thought you said you'd let me know what was happenin'."

I didn't recall what I'd told him, but I'd never planned on giving him daily reports. "If I'd heard something, I would have left you a note. When I don't leave you a message, you can assume that I have nothing to report."

He scratched his head. "Well, did you write to that lady you told me about? That Miss Manchester?"

"Yes. And that's as much as I can tell you." I folded my arms across my chest. "She might not ever respond. And even if she does, there's no guarantee she'll be able to tell me anything about your sister's whereabouts. I believe I made that very clear." The bushes swayed and I glanced over my shoulder. "When we last met, you promised to keep your distance. You knew I feared being seen with you, but instead of showing concern for my welfare, you walk down the middle of the street waving at me." I rested my hands on my hips. "If you ever want to hear anything about your sister, you won't do that again."

"You got a mighty determined streak, Miss Jancey. I do like a woman who speaks her mind." He grinned, as though what he liked should make everything fine.

I narrowed my eyes and glowered at him. "And I like a person who keeps his word, Mr. Kingman. That means right now your name would not be included on the list of people that I like."

He shuffled his feet in the soft dirt. "I'm sorry for being careless. I didn't mean to cause no trouble, but I'm so eager to find Kathleen that I couldn't wait any longer. Please say you'll let me know if you hear something."

His plea bore a woeful ache that I couldn't deny. "If Miss Manchester sends word, I'll leave a message on your trunk. If I don't leave a note, it will mean I have not heard anything and you should not contact me. Are those instructions clear to you?"

"Yes, Miss Jancey, but I'd be mighty thankful if you'd consider writing to her again if you don't hear by the end of July." He reached into his pocket. "I got some money for stamps and paper that I brought for you."

I shook my head. "I don't want your money, Mr. Kingman. I'm sure you know we don't use money to make purchases here in the colonies."

"I forgot. Well, if you want, I could go buy a couple stamps at the general store. Old Mr. Traugott's willing to take money from outsiders. And I can buy some paper, too, if you like. You just say the word. I wouldn't mind one bit. It's the least I can do."

I wanted to agree that it was the least he could do, especially after his wild antics in the street a short time ago, but I didn't want to be further obligated. "No. I don't want any money or stamps or paper. If I haven't heard from Miss Manchester by the end of the month, I will pen another note to her, but that will be the last of it, Mr. Kingman. I do want to help you, if possible, but I think it's best if I set a limit on the amount of help I can offer."

"Thank you, Miss Jancey. I do appreciate what you're doin' for me, and I promise I won't bother you no more. Just leave me a note when you hear from that lady. And if you don't hear by the end of the month, I'm gonna trust you'll write her another letter without me asking you." He jammed his worn felt hat onto his head. "I guess that's everything."

"I believe so." When he started in the direction of the elm tree, I grasped his arm and nodded toward an isolated trail on the far side of the bushes. "Why don't you take the path over there. You can meet up with the main road before you get to your quarters. That way there's no chance you'll be seen leaving our backyard."

Using his hip and shoulder, he pushed his way through the tall bushes and disappeared. I rushed around the side of the house and, after entering the front door, stood in the foyer until I regained my composure. If I appeared distressed, Mother would likely assume there was some problem regarding my father.

"Is that you, Jancey?" My mother's voice drifted from the bedroom.

"Yes, I'll be right in, Mother."

After tucking a loose strand of hair into place, I entered her room. She was sitting in the chair near her bed. "Mother! I thought you promised you wouldn't get up unless I was here to help you."

"Sister Hanna came home for a short time. Before she went back to the Küche, she helped me into the chair. She was surprised you weren't here."

Hoping to ignore the comment regarding my whereabouts, I pulled Nathan's letter from my pocket. "I went to the general store to check on the mail. Nothing from Father, but I received a letter from Nathan."

"What does he have to say? Does he mention anything about your father?"

I shook my head. "Brother Traugott said it arrived the day after Father left for Kansas City."

Her smile faded. "It worries me that we've heard nothing."

"Father told you there was no reason for worry. He may be on his way home as we speak. Besides, worry will only rob you of your strength, and you've been getting stronger the past two days. Think how happy Father will be to see you feeling better when he returns."

I bowed my head and let a sigh escape my lips, thankful I'd

avoided further questions regarding why it had taken me so long to return home. "After I help you back to bed, I think I'll go to the parlor and read my letter."

"Maybe his letter will cause you to give more thought to a life with him." She lifted her brows and waited for my response.

Placing my arm beneath her shoulders, I smiled down at her, then helped her up and into bed. "I'm not sure one letter will do that, Mother."

"But you will tell me what he has to say?"

After arranging her pillows, I leaned down and kissed her cheek. "If there is anything of interest, I will be certain to tell you."

Holding the letter in my hand, I entered the parlor and sat down in a chair near the window. I stared at the envelope with no excitement or anticipation, another affirmation I'd been wise to leave Kansas City. I seldom thought of him anymore and didn't miss him. Rather than a delight, I found it a chore to correspond with him. This separation proved what I'd already suspected: Nathan and I were not well suited.

I slipped my finger under the seal and withdrew the letter.

My dear Jancey,

I expected to receive a response to my previous letter by now, and I write to tell you my disappointment runs deep. After receiving no letter from you, I have only to wonder if I have offended you in something I have written. If so, I ask that you tell me. I cannot right a wrong unless you tell me what I've done to upset you.

When you last wrote, you told me how busy you are, but it does not take long to pen a short note. My days are filled with work, as well, but because I care for you, I make time to write. I would never want to cause you to worry.

So far, his letter was nothing more than a reprimand. I sighed and continued reading. The next two paragraphs spoke of concerns about our future should the company be sold.

I am hopeful your father will reconsider and maintain ownership of the company. I am sure you miss the convenience of living in the city as well as your position teaching the children at the orphanage. I spoke with Mr. Ludwig, and he has not filled your position. He states he would be most pleased to have you return.

This separation has not been good for either of us, and I beg you to reconsider your decision and return to Kansas City. Please give my heartfelt plea your deep consideration.

Yours always,
Nathan

I turned over the page, certain there must be more. Nowhere in the letter had he asked about Mother's health. And though he'd spoken to Mr. Ludwig about my job, there was no other mention of the orphanage. In my last letter, I'd enclosed notes to the children. I could only guess that he'd given them to Mr. Ludwig rather than go to see any of my students.

My confusion deepened as I reflected upon the contents of his letter. He thought that he was doing everything in his power to force my return. Instead, he was pushing me further away.

During early July as the sun continued to bake the communal farmlands that surrounded the seven villages, my mother received a letter saying all had gone well and Father would return on the seventh of July. The letter contained no details about his meetings with the police or the investigation. Knowing Father, I wasn't surprised. He wasn't fond of writing long letters and preferred a personal conversation to correspondence.

Since receiving news of my father's impending return, Mother's health continued to improve. Over the past two days, she'd been able to sit in the parlor for several hours at a time before needing to rest.

"You're certain you want to remain in the parlor while I'm at the train station?" While I knew she wanted to surprise Father, I worried she'd overexert herself before he arrived.

"Absolutely." She pressed her hands down the folds of her skirt. "I don't know what I can say to assure you I will be fine."

"If the train should be late . . ."

She pointed to the side table. "I have the bell Ritt gave you. I'll ring it loud enough for someone to hear."

The windows were open, but there was no guarantee anyone would be passing by the house when she rang. I worried she might fall if she attempted to walk from the parlor to her bed without assistance. In some ways, I had worried less when she'd been confined to her bed.

"I'll leave the door to the hallway open. If the Hetrigs are at home, they will hear you ring." I glanced at the clock. "Madelyn should be home from school. I'll have her come down. She can practice her reading with you."

The children attended school six days a week, but unless Madelyn had gone to visit with a friend, she would be home by now.

She smiled and nodded. "I'd enjoy that very much. She's a sweet girl, and having her around reminds me of when you were a little girl."

I was thankful Mother agreed to the arrangement, and once Madelyn had come downstairs, I hurried toward the train station. I was early, but I wanted to be there to welcome Father when he stepped off the train.

I hadn't gone far when I saw Sister Margaret in the distance. I waved as she approached. Ever since she'd attended the picnic with John Olson, they'd been seeing each other with as much regularity as possible. "Off to meet John at the pond?"

She grinned and nodded. She'd told me the day before that he was going to meet her at the pond and they would try their luck fishing. "He says he thinks there won't be as many people at the pond as at the river and maybe we will catch more fish."

I chuckled. "I think he is trying to win your affections rather than catch a fish, Margaret."

"Ja, I hope that is true. You are going to meet your father?"

"I'm a little early, but I want to be there before the train arrives. I'm eager to welcome him home."

"And I should be going, or John will think I have forgotten him." Her eyes sparkled with excitement. "I will see you at work on Monday and tell you how many fish we caught."

Margaret hastened toward the pond while I continued at a steady pace. I wasn't long at the station before a whistle sounded in the distance and my excitement swelled. I longed to hear all that had happened in Kansas City, but having him return to us was what I desired the most.

Soon the train hissed and rumbled into the station. I hurried onto the platform and watched for the disembarking passengers. Two men, likely buyers who'd come to purchase items at the woolen mill, stepped down before I spotted my father.

Hiking my skirt, I raced down the platform, eager to greet him. I was only a few feet away when I stopped short and gasped.

My father turned and gestured over his shoulder. "Look who I brought with me."

My breath caught, and a dizzying sensation washed over me as Nathan stepped down from the train.

CHAPTER 14

In an effort to steady myself, I reached for my father's arm and leaned close to his side. "I do wish you would have written to tell me."

"There wasn't time." The brief response was all he could manage before Nathan was at my side.

"Jancey! It's so good to see you." His gaze traveled from my bonnet-covered head to the practical leather boots on my feet before he once again looked into my eyes. "You look . . . different."

"It's the plain clothing." I inhaled a ragged breath. "How long will you be visiting?" My voice cracked and I cleared my throat.

He shifted his leather bag to his other hand and pointed to the baggage cart across the platform. "This is more than a visit, but I'll explain later. I know your father is anxious to get home, aren't you, Mr. Rhoder?"

My father nodded, then turned to me. "Would you escort Nathan to the hotel so he can rent a room for tonight? Then the two of you can come to the house."

I wanted to go home with my father and learn what had happened in Kansas City. Although I knew I should be happy to see Nathan, his presence unnerved me, and until I could sort out my jumbled feelings, I didn't want to be alone with him. "Do you think it would be proper for me to go alone with him to the hotel, Father? If anyone sees me going into the hotel with an outsider, what will they think?"

"Outsider?" A frown thundered across Nathan's brow. "We're practically engaged to marry. How can you refer to me as an outsider?"

My father patted Nathan's shoulder. "Those who live or work here who are not members of the colonies are referred to as outsiders, Nathan. Jancey's comment was not intended as an insult."

Nathan's frown vanished. "I'm sorry. I don't know how things are done here. I shouldn't have been so quick to take offense."

My father nodded. "I understand. It will take some time to learn our ways."

My stomach tightened. Why would Nathan have any interest in learning about the colonies? Had he convinced my father he wanted to come here and become a member? I almost laughed aloud at the thought. Nathan had no interest in our communal ways. He wanted to own my father's company. So why was he here? And why was his presence creating such feelings of turmoil and confusion inside of me?

"Tell Brother Frederick at the hotel that Nathan is a family friend who traveled with me from Kansas City and needs to rent a room for the night. Then wait in the lobby while Nathan takes his belongings to his room. Afterward, the two of you will come to the house. It is all very simple." My father waited for my response.

I nodded my head. Escorting Nathan to the hotel might be easy, but having him here for a visit would likely prove complicated. The moment my father was out of earshot, I turned toward Nathan.

"The hotel is this way." I gestured to my left.

He didn't move. "We're walking?" He carried a large traveling case in each hand and an alligator club bag beneath his arm.

"It isn't far, but I can ask to have the cases delivered if you'd prefer." I pointed to the bag beneath his arm. "Would you like me to carry that one?"

"I can manage."

"Whatever you'd rather." I was willing to help, but I didn't argue. "We should cross to the other side of the street." I gestured to a building a short distance away. "The hotel is down there, near the curve in the road."

I hoped to gain some answers to the many questions that were popping around in my head like butter in a hot skillet. But I soon discovered the strain of carrying the baggage rendered Nathan unable to converse beyond a grunted yes or no. By the time we arrived at the hotel, Nathan's features had tightened into a grimace, and he dropped one of the cases near the front door.

I took the lead and entered the hotel. A bell over the front door jangled, and soon Brother Frederick appeared. Although my father hadn't anticipated I would experience any problems at the hotel, I wasn't as sure. I doubted Brother Frederick even knew me. As part of her assigned duties, his wife prepared meals for hotel guests, so Brother Frederick and his family ate at the hotel rather than a Küche. Their daughter, Bretta, was one of Madelyn's friends who came to the house for help with her reading, but I wasn't certain she'd told her parents about the lessons.

I stepped close to the desk and explained Nathan's presence and his need for a room. "You can help him?"

"Ja, that is why we are here—to rent rooms." He looked at Nathan. "Only one night, you want?" His English bore a heavy German accent, but all of the hotels were managed by colonists who could speak English.

"I might need more, but I'm not certain. Can I tell you later tonight?"

Brother Frederick nodded. "If it is better for you. The hotel is not full. One night or two—is up to you. There will be space."

While Nathan and Brother Frederick carried the bags upstairs, I sat in the lobby and waited. I hadn't been there long when Bretta appeared. Her eyes widened with surprise when she spotted me.

"Why are you in the hotel, Sister Jancey?"

"A family friend has arrived for a visit. He traveled from Kansas City with my father. I'm waiting while your father shows him his room. Then we'll go to my house so he can visit with my parents and me."

"That's very exciting. Does Madelyn know?"

I shook my head. "No. I didn't know he was arriving until I went to the train station to meet my father's train."

Her lips curved in a wide smile. "A surprise! I love surprises, don't you?"

"I'm probably not as fond of being surprised as you."

She plopped down in the chair beside me. "So we will not have any reading lessons this evening?"

"No, I won't be able to help you tonight." I'd completely forgotten. "Maybe you and the other children can help each other this evening." I grasped her hand. "Have you been improving in your classes?"

"Ja, I am doing better. My Vater says you have been a gut help for me, especially with the English. He says if I learn gut, then I can help *him*." She giggled.

"So your father knows you have been coming to Madelyn's house for lessons?"

A few strands of blond hair escaped and fluttered near her face as she bobbed her head. "Ja. Would be wrong if I didn't tell the truth."

"That's right. I'm very proud that you're doing better in school and that you always tell the truth."

At the sound of the men's voices, Bretta and I turned toward the stairs. "That is your friend?"

"Yes. His name is Nathan Woodward." I was certain Bretta would relay every detail to Madelyn. And though I didn't mind the girls discussing Nathan's arrival, I did worry what Ritt might think. I considered asking Madelyn to keep Nathan's arrival a secret but decided such a request wasn't a good idea.

Brother Frederick gestured to his daughter. "Bretta, you should be helping your Mutter with the dishes instead of sitting in the lobby visiting. Run along to the kitchen."

I was struck by a pang of envy as the carefree child jumped to her feet and skipped across the room without a worry. I pushed up from the chair and met Nathan at the front door. After thanking Brother Frederick, we departed and turned toward home.

I glanced in Nathan's direction. "You found the room to your liking?"

"It's adequate. Nothing like hotels in a large city, but it's very clean and will meet my needs for a night or two."

"And after a night or two, what are your plans? I must admit that I'm baffled by your unexpected appearance." Our shoes clattered on the wooden sidewalks. "Since you arrived with more baggage than you'd need for an overnight visit, you obviously have some sort of plan in mind."

When he reached for my hand and attempted to tuck it into the crook of his arm, I pulled away. Confusion shone in his eyes as he came to an abrupt halt in front of the general store. "You can't even hold on to my arm when we walk down the street?"

"No. I follow the same rules as everyone else, Nathan." I gestured for him to keep walking. "Please don't be offended. The fact that I won't hold your arm isn't an affront—it's simply the way of things here."

"I think it's foolish. What's wrong with being a gentleman?"

"Nothing, but it isn't permitted. We are not married."

"We could change that in a hurry, if you'd accept my proposal."

I had hoped we wouldn't get into a marriage discussion so soon, but I should have realized that was his plan. "So you've come here thinking we would get married and then return to Kansas City? Was that what you told Father?"

"I like that idea, but after receiving your letters, I knew you wouldn't agree to marry me right away. It's your letters that brought me here."

My mind whirled as I tried to think of what he might be referring to. I was certain I'd told him it would be best if he didn't visit—that he would find the colonies lacking in entertainment.

"Exactly what did I say that influenced your visit?"

He pointed to the smokestack that towered above the woolen mill in the distance. "You said they hired men to work in the woolen mill. I know you believed this separation would be a good test of some sort, but your letters revealed the opposite. Instead of writing that you miss me and long to return to Kansas City, your letters were filled with details of your daily life. When your father returned and I spoke to him, I knew this was the only choice I could make."

A wave of dread assailed me. I didn't want to believe my father had encouraged Nathan to come here. "Exactly what did you and Father talk about?"

"I told him I was concerned that our relationship might not survive this separation and you'd mentioned there was sometimes work available in the mill."

"Did you lead him to believe I'd suggested you seek one of those jobs?" I pressed down the anger rising in my chest.

"Not exactly, but I think he may have drawn that conclusion."

"And you didn't correct his assumption?"

He hiked his shoulder. "I didn't think it was necessary. After all, he knows that I care for you and am willing to do what's necessary to win your heart."

I stared at him. Was it my heart or my father's factory he wanted to win? I didn't want to misjudge his intentions, especially since he'd given up his position at the factory to come here, but I didn't think it mattered whether he lived in Iowa or Kansas City. I didn't believe he could win my heart—not unless I saw some dramatic changes in him. Being in his presence didn't spark any feelings of excitement or anticipation.

Not like Ritt.

I silently chastised myself. I shouldn't be thinking about Ritt—not now, not ever. At least not in any romantic way. Not until I was certain I'd remain in the colonies. A relationship with Ritt posed far greater obstacles than any I faced with Nathan. Or did it? My head ached as I attempted to sort out my thoughts and feelings.

"I've just told you I will do anything to win your affection, yet you have nothing to say?"

He appeared wounded and I wanted to cheer him, but I feared anything I said would only build false hope. Besides, he vowed he'd do anything to win my affection, but he hadn't remained in Kansas City as I'd requested. Would he return home if I asked him? A knot twisted and settled in my stomach.

"I believe a longer period of separation would have revealed whether we have any hope for a future together."

He shook his head. "I disagree. I want to spend time with you and prove my love for you. I asked your father if he would help me secure a job at the mill."

Confusion clouded my mind. If Nathan hoped to take over Forsythe Construction, it would have been more prudent for him to remain in Kansas City. Had I misjudged him? Was the business less important than I?

I was glad when we arrived home, where I might find some time alone to sift through my changing thoughts and emotions.

I gestured toward the house and forced a smile. "Here we are."

After we stepped inside the foyer, I led the way to our parlor. My mother and father were deep in conversation but ceased talking when we entered the room.

Mother smiled at Nathan. "It is good to see you, Nathan. I'm sorry we can't offer you a room with us, but I hope your room at the hotel pleased you."

"Of course, Mrs. Rhoder. The hotel room will be fine. It's good to see that you are feeling better." He waited until I sat down and then claimed a nearby chair.

"Jurgen tells me you hope to remain in the colonies and work at the mill. I had forgotten you worked at the Watkins Woolen Mill before Jurgen hired you at the construction company."

He leaned forward and nodded. "I hope my experience will be considered of value so that I can remain here."

My mother folded her hands and leaned back in her chair. "Before you accept a job, perhaps it would be wise if you became more familiar with our ways. After a day or two, I think you may decide to return to Kansas City." She reached for a glass of water and took a sip. "You will soon discover that life is very different here."

"Jancey has written me about the rules, but since I'm planning on staying only until I convince her to marry me, I'm not worried. I can tolerate most anything if I set my mind to it."

Since he'd followed me to Amana, I could only suppose he hadn't set his mind to accepting my absence.

My father chuckled. "You should listen to my wife. She is giving you wise advice. I have not yet spoken to the elders about a job. It would be wise at least to see where you will be sleeping and eating your meals before I ask about work for you. In Kansas City, you had comfortable rooms at the boardinghouse. In the men's quarters, you will find no privacy."

"At the Watkins Woolen Mill outside of Kansas City, I shared a third-floor bedroom with twenty-five men. I'm sure I'll be fine here." Before Nathan could finish his comment, my mother interrupted.

"And you must consider the food, too. There are no choices. You eat what is served or you do not eat. Concessions are made only for those who have problems with their health." She placed her water glass back on the table beside her. "I often heard you say you ate supper at a restaurant because you didn't like what was being served at the boardinghouse. Isn't that so?"

"That's true, but I'm willing to make a few sacrifices for the woman I care about."

I winced at his reply. If I didn't turn this conversation to another topic, Nathan would soon have us engaged and walking down the aisle. "I'm eager to hear about the investigation, Father. I hope you haven't already told Mother all the news."

"I've explained that there was an explosion, and I didn't want her to worry while I was gone." He patted my mother's hand. "I've told her enough to set her mind at ease. We knew you'd want to hear the details."

"All of it good, I hope."

"Yes. The investigation has been concluded. There were injuries, but the fault didn't lie with the men working for the construction company. Rather, it was caused by a company that had been hired to blast rock on the north side of the street. One of the men had placed a dynamite cartridge on a steam pipe to dry, and it caused the explosion. Most of the damage occurred at our construction site. The blasting company is responsible; we are not. Thankfully, there weren't other structures close by, or the disaster would have been much worse."

I still didn't understand why my father's presence had been required. "But why did they insist upon your return?"

"The blasting company was trying to shift blame on us and say we'd been using dynamite at our work site. The police wanted to question me about the kind of dynamite our company had used in the past. They believed it was important to ask me their questions in person." My father exhaled a sigh. "Although it was difficult being away, I'm glad I went. I feel more assured the matter has been put to rest. I also had an opportunity to speak to the prospective buyer of the company while I was there."

Nathan's jaw tightened. "I still think you need to wait until all of the current contracts have been completed before you make any definite agreement with him."

My father withdrew his pipe from his pocket. "The agreement isn't final, but I was concerned he might back out, what with the explosion and police investigation. There were any number of newspaper articles, and I worried he'd believe the publicity would damage the company's reputation."

"All is well that ends well." In spite of the heat, my mother pulled her shawl tight around her shoulders. "I am very happy you are home with us."

"You look tired, Mother. Shall I help you back to your room?"

"Nein." She reached for my father's hand. "Your father will help me. You and Nathan should visit until he must return to the hotel."

Nathan promised my mother he would come by to see her tomorrow if he hadn't already begun work at the mill. Obviously he'd taken none of her advice to heart.

Once the bedroom door closed, he turned to me. "I have a surprise for you. One that I think will make you very happy."

My breath caught in my throat. Even though I'd made it clear I didn't intend to accept a marriage proposal, I feared he was going to surprise me with a betrothal gift. An undeniable urge to flee the room overcame me as he reached into his pocket. I grasped the edge of the chair.

But instead of a ring or a gift, he extended a bulging envelope. "Letters from the children at the orphanage. I told them I was coming to see you and asked them to write you a note."

I stared in disbelief, then clutched the package to my chest.

How thoughtful of Nathan. Did he know I missed the children so much it hurt?

"Thank you." I gave him a heartfelt smile and he smiled in return.

Perhaps I had misjudged him after all.

CHAPTER 15

Until Nathan departed I maintained restraint, but the moment he was out the door, I hurried to my room and tore open the envelope. The children's notes fluttered atop my bed. Had my mother and father not been in the next room, I would have shouted for joy. Instead, I uttered a prayer and thanked God for this unexpected gift.

My fingers trembled as I opened the first letter, pleased to see it was from nine-year-old Caroline. She said she missed me, especially since the class no longer had story time, and she hoped I would soon return to teach at the orphanage. The notes from Matthew, Nettie, Charlie, and the other children were incredibly similar—so similar that I wondered if they'd been told what to write. I pictured Nathan standing in front of the class, holding a slate with a printed message for the children to copy. Was this merely a ploy to try to convince me I should return to Kansas City with him?

Shame pierced me, and I silently chastised myself for the ungrateful thought. I should give Nathan the benefit of the doubt. After all, how many different messages would the children write? They'd all be inclined to say they missed me and wanted me to return—I would have been hurt if they hadn't. But a part of me had hoped for more. A few personal sentences about themselves or a comment about Mr. Ludwig, even a remark about the weather would have pleased me. And though I'd have been delighted with more, I was thankful for what I'd received.

I thought there might be a letter from Lilly, as well, and was surprised she hadn't sent at least a note of some sort. Even if she didn't have any information about Thomas's sister, I found it odd that she'd not written at all. If I didn't hear soon, I'd write to her again. I liked the idea of playing a part in reuniting Thomas with his sister. During my three years at the orphanage, I'd seen how all the children longed for a family, which made Thomas's situation all the more poignant. He'd worked and saved, never forgetting Kathleen for all these years. Yes, the least I could do was write another letter.

The following morning, Nathan arrived at our parlor door before the bells rang to announce breakfast. My father invited him into the room and praised him for being so punctual. Although I would have preferred to have Nathan eat breakfast at the hotel, Father had suggested he join the outsiders at our Küche this morning.

Nathan traced his fingers through his still-damp brown hair. "You said I shouldn't be late. There are so many bells, who can sleep?"

My father chuckled. "If you stay, you'll become accustomed to them. There are bells to announce most everything. It helps keep us on schedule."

"I'm surprised there aren't bells to announce the bells," Nathan muttered. "Has no one heard of clocks and watches?"

"Of course." My father glanced at the grandfather clock sitting on the far side of the parlor. "But if we use the bells, we're all on the same time. A clock or timepiece can be off by several minutes. If that happened, we could have people straggling into the kitchen houses over a period of ten minutes, others would be late to work, and prayer meetings would be delayed. The bells prevent a multitude of problems."

Nathan nodded as he crossed the room and sat down. "I understand."

My father smiled at me and gestured toward the bedroom. "I'm going to see to your mother. I trust you will keep Nathan company until time for breakfast."

"Of course, Father." I sat down opposite Nathan and cleared my throat. "I read the notes from the children before going to sleep last night. I can't tell you how much I appreciate your thoughtfulness. Knowing they miss me touched my heart."

"Had I been thinking, I would have gone to the school a few days prior to my departure and asked Miss Manchester to have them write the notes. Unfortunately, by the time I conceived the plan, there wasn't much time and the children had to hurry." He smiled. "Some of them aren't very bright, are they?"

I stiffened at his question. "They're young, Nathan. You can't expect little children to dash off a note with the speed of an adult."

"No need to take offense. I was merely stating a fact." He leaned back in the chair. "Miss Manchester told me that the skills of the younger ones have declined since you left. Seems it's difficult for her to give them enough time since combining the classes and so forth. Both she and Mr. Ludwig are eager for your return."

I inhaled a deep breath and decided I wasn't going to let him bait me into a conversation about my return to Kansas City—especially not so early in the morning. "I was disappointed there wasn't a letter from Lilly."

Nathan's eyes opened wide, and he slapped his palm against his chest. "I forgot to give you the letter from Miss Manchester. She'd planned to post it the day I went to the school, but I told her I'd be happy to deliver it for her." He reached inside his jacket and withdrew the envelope. "And then I completely forgot."

My heart pounded in my chest. I didn't want Nathan to know about Thomas—especially if Nathan was going to live in the men's quarters. He wouldn't understand my desire to help an itinerant worker. My fingers trembled as I reached forward to accept the letter.

Deep creases lined his forehead. "Why does a letter from Miss Manchester create so much excitement that your fingers tremble?"

I willed my hand to stop shaking but met with little success. "I'm eager to hear what she has to say about the children, and I'm interested in her welfare, too. I consider Lilly a friend and we've had little communication since I left."

He arched his brows. "She said you'd written her not so long ago."

I swallowed the lump in my throat. "Yes, yes, I did. And I'm delighted she has answered." I patted the envelope, pleased to see it was sealed. "Did Lilly mention anything special about my letter to her?"

His lips curved in a catlike grin. "No. Is there something she should have told me?"

I shook my head. "Since she told you I had written, I was merely curious if she'd said anything else."

He cocked his head to the side. "Are you sure you aren't keeping secrets?"

"If I were, I couldn't tell you because then it would no longer be a secret, would it?" I worried whether my attempt to sound like a coy socialite would work, but I couldn't think of anything else that would stave off his questions.

His smile returned and he leaned forward. "Why don't you open her letter and see what she has to say?"

The bell tolled and I jumped to my feet. "There isn't time. That's the breakfast bell. We don't want to be late."

As my father returned to the parlor, I shoved the letter into my pocket.

"Your mother wanted to go with us to breakfast this morning, but I convinced her to wait one more day." He slapped Nathan on the shoulder. "Ready to eat?"

Ritt, Madelyn, and Brother Werner came downstairs as we stepped into the foyer. Ritt's focus remained on Nathan while my father made the introductions.

Brother Werner extended his hand to Nathan. "We are pleased to have you here. I hope you will find the colonies to your liking. For sure you will like the food that is served in our Küche."

My father translated Brother Werner's welcome into English as we departed the house. While we continued toward the kitchen house, he asked about Nathan's experience working at the mill outside of Kansas City. Nathan appeared pleased by Brother Werner's attention and didn't notice when Ritt dropped back to walk beside Madelyn and me.

"Bretta told us your friend had arrived. How long will he be here?" Ritt kept his voice low.

I shrugged. "I don't know. I didn't know he was coming until I saw him step off the train."

Ritt pressed his lips together in a thin line and stared straight ahead.

"You act like you don't believe me, but that's the truth. You can ask my father." In my desire to make him believe me, I'd spoken too loud.

My father glanced over his shoulder. "You and Nathan have much in common, Ritt. You are the same age and you both have experience working in woolen mills. I'm sure you will find much to talk about."

Ritt gave me a sideways glance. "Ja, I am sure we will, Brother Rhoder."

My father shepherded Nathan to the table where the workers ate their meals before returning to his own table. Throughout breakfast, I was careful to keep my eyes away from the workers' table. Although I worried Nathan might speak to Thomas and discover I knew him, I dared not turn in that direction. If Ritt looked my way, I didn't want him to think I was watching Nathan. He'd already drawn the wrong conclusion, and I didn't want to do anything to fuel that fire.

My father planned to speak with the elders after the morning meal and then take breakfast to my mother. Unless the elders immediately hired Nathan to work at the mill, which I doubted, he would remain with my father throughout the day.

Once we had recited the after-meal prayer and filed from the Küche, I strolled toward the path, hoping Ritt would catch up. I didn't have to wait long before he came alongside me. "Who is this Nathan Woodward? Is he the man you plan to marry?"

Coming to a halt, I perched my hands on my hips and pinned him with an angry stare. "I don't have plans to marry anyone, and you should quit acting like I had anything to do with his coming here. For your information, I wrote and told him he shouldn't come. Not that I expect you to believe me, since you're acting like a jealous schoolboy."

"You can try to act like there is nothing between the two of you, but I can see." He tapped his index finger alongside his eye. "He considers you more than a friend."

I sighed. There wasn't time to explain in detail, but I didn't know when we'd have another opportunity to be alone. "It's true that he has asked me to marry him, but I have refused. When I came here, I told him we needed to be away from each other and see if we truly cared for each other. He was unhappy with my decision, but I knew it was best. In my heart, I'd become more certain Nathan wasn't the man I should marry. I didn't write often enough to suit him, and my letters didn't say what he hoped to hear."

He frowned. "So he gave up his job and came here to work in the mill so he can convince you he is the man you should marry. Ja?"

"I think that's his intention." The bell clanged from the tower. "There's more to tell you, but I don't know when we'll be alone again. I need to know you believe me."

"I believe you." He smiled and tugged on my hand. "Come on or we'll be late to work."

Had Ritt accepted my explanation because he feared being late for work or because he'd truly believed me? The question nagged me as I raced into the men's quarters.

Sister Margaret turned and sighed as I clattered into the room. "If you did not visit so long after breakfast, you wouldn't have to run to work. You make yourself tired before you ever begin to scrub and clean."

"You're right." I waved and continued into the other room without stopping to visit.

Before anything else, I would read Lilly's letter. Then I would pen a quick note to Thomas. Even if Lilly's letter didn't contain any information about Kathleen Kingman, I didn't want Nathan to know I'd agreed to help Thomas. He would never approve and would likely tell my father. I sat down on the edge of the bed and massaged my forehead. So far I'd been successful in concealing my involvement with Thomas from Ritt. But now I had Nathan to worry about, as well. Unless Thomas could keep his lips sealed, having Nathan living here could prove to be my undoing.

Then again, if Lilly's letter contained Kathleen's address, Thomas would probably leave within a few days, and that would solve one problem. Bolstered with that hope, I sat on the edge of Thomas's bed and ran my finger beneath the sealed flap of the envelope. I scanned the letter, searching for any mention of Thomas or Kathleen.

Near the end there was a paragraph about Kathleen Kingman.

Kathleen's file reflects she was adopted by a family in Salina, Kansas, but the rules prohibit me from giving the name of her adoptive parents. There is a notation in the file that Thomas Kingman came here several years ago. He was told he need not worry about Kathleen's welfare as she'd been adopted by a family of substantial financial means.

He was also advised that we couldn't give him any further information.

If you wish, I could write to the family and ask if they are willing to release anything more to Thomas. If he is agreeable, you could forward me his address and I will send it to them. In the event they wish to contact Mr. Kingman, they could send their letter directly to him. You should caution him that the family may not answer my letter, but it's the most help I can offer. I'll await word from you as to whether he wishes to proceed.

I reread the paragraph. Thomas had told me basically the same thing: that his sister had been adopted, but they wouldn't give him any additional information.

Startled when Margaret's bucket clattered in the other room, I jumped to my feet. "I've tipped the bucket of water again," she called.

Shoving the letter into my pocket, I peeked around the corner. "Do you need help?" A pool of water was slowly spreading across the floor.

"Nein. It's my mess. I'll clean it. Once I finish, I'll take the linens out to the washhouse."

I didn't force the issue, for I'd become somewhat accustomed to such events. No matter how hard Margaret tried, she tipped over a bucket of water at least once every ten days. Besides, I hadn't yet stripped the beds. I yanked sheets from mattresses and muslin cases from pillows at breakneck speed, then tossed them toward the end of the room.

After gathering the dirty linens from the floor and shoving them into the wicker baskets, I gathered an armful of clean sheets and pillowcases. Margaret entered the room as I returned with the linens.

Her jaw went slack. "I cannot believe my eyes. You have not yet made the beds. Always you are done with your work before me. You are sick?"

My head ached, but I couldn't use that as an excuse. "I'm moving slow today. I have much on my mind."

She grinned. "Ja, I heard."

"H-heard what?" I dropped the armful of sheets onto a nearby bed.

"That you have a friend who has come all the way from Kansas City to visit. He came back with your Vater. Ja?"

I nodded, trying to digest the fact that she already knew about Nathan. Word had spread quickly. I wouldn't have been surprised about this if Margaret ate in our Küche, for she would have noticed Nathan walk into the kitchen house with my father. But she didn't. *Bretta.* She was friends with the family who lived in the same house as Margaret's family. Pleased to have news she could share, Bretta had likely told her young friend.

In truth, it didn't make much difference whether Bretta told her friend. If Nathan went to work in the mill, everyone would soon know of his connection to our family. The outsiders came here for the work, but Nathan was different. He'd come here because of my family, and mostly, because of me.

She tipped her head to the side and grinned. "John says Ritt will be jealous."

"You told John?" Margaret and John must be seeing each other more often than I realized.

"Ja, sure. He was interested in hearing about him. John thinks you'll return to Kansas City with your fellow."

"He's not my fellow, Margaret." I folded my arms across my waist. "You can tell John I'm not going anywhere."

Her smile faded. "No need to be cross with me. I told John you never mentioned having a suitor in Kansas City, but he says a man does not come all this way unless he is more than a friend."

I sighed. If Nathan remained in the colonies, I'd best get used to answering these questions. "He is a friend of the family and worked for my father. Before that, he worked in a woolen mill. He returned with my father to see if he could find work here."

Her eyebrows squished together. "So where was he working since you came here?"

"At my father's company." I snatched one of the sheets from the stack and pointed to the unmade beds. "I'll explain all of this later. We have work to finish."

She nodded but didn't move. "Ja, you are right. But I would rather hear your story."

I shooed her toward the door. "Later, Margaret. The laundry will still be wet come nightfall if you don't get started with the washing."

"Ja. And unless you start making those beds, the men will be sleeping on bare mattresses." She chuckled and strode toward the laundry baskets. "If you are done before I return, you will come and help me hang the sheets?"

While nodding my head, I snapped a sheet in the air and let it fall across the first mattress. I needed to write a note to Thomas, but this must come first.

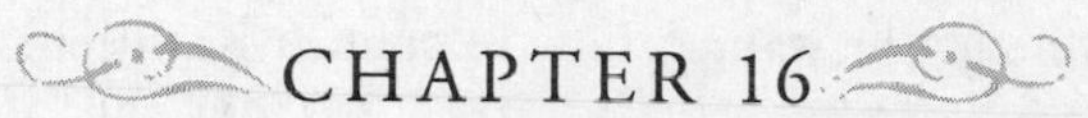

CHAPTER 16

Once I'd finished the beds, I sat down at the table in the men's parlor. If I didn't hurry, Margaret would come looking for me, and I didn't want her to catch me writing a letter—not when she'd specifically requested my help with the laundry. There wasn't time to contemplate exactly what I needed to say. I needed to be quick, to the point, and not forget anything I needed to tell Thomas. First and foremost, he had to keep any contact with Nathan to a minimum and never divulge the fact that I'd been helping him locate Kathleen.

I'd told Nathan that contact with outsiders was against the communal rules, and should he discover my dealings with Thomas, I was sure Nathan would point out the error of my ways. And who could say? With Nathan resolved that I should return to Kansas City, he might tell the elders, as well. I didn't want to take such a risk. Nathan had never exhibited a great deal of jealousy, but I didn't want to create any unnecessary problems. Not for Thomas and not for myself. He needed to understand the importance of avoiding Nathan.

Next, I informed Thomas what I'd heard from Lilly regarding his sister's whereabouts and then asked that he leave a note advising me whether he wanted Lilly to contact Kathleen's adoptive family. I dipped my pen in the ink and finished the letter with my final instructions.

You should leave your answer in the usual place. I cannot meet to discuss your decision. It is too risky.

I didn't sign my name. Thomas would know the correspondence was from me, and if any prying eyes should see the letter, I didn't want my name revealed. After folding the note, I carried it to the adjacent room and placed it beneath the picture on Thomas's trunk. I hadn't dusted or scrubbed the porch, but I could return to those tasks later in the morning.

I hurried outdoors, where the bright sunshine and warm breeze proved a pleasant change from the musty heat inside the living quarters. The gentle wind would dry the sheets in no time. Two large baskets of wet laundry rested on the grass beside Margaret. "It looks like I arrived just when you needed me."

Margaret rested her hands on her hips. "Ja, and I am sorry, but I will need you to hang these without my help. All of the work clothes still need to be washed. It will take me until the noonday meal before we can have those on the line." Using the corner of her apron, she wiped the perspiration from her forehead and turned back to the washhouse.

I usually enjoyed visiting with Margaret, but I was thankful we would be apart for the remainder of the morning. I was sure she would pepper me with more questions about Nathan and his sudden appearance. I didn't want to answer them—at least not yet. I still held out hope there wouldn't be a position at the mill and he would decide to return home.

I wondered what he would do if he was offered a job at one of the mills in Main Amana rather than in Middle. Main was the largest of the villages, with both a calico mill and a woolen mill, and there might be a greater need for an experienced worker in that village. If he worked in Main, we would have at least a degree of separation, and though he disagreed, I still believed that was what we needed.

Once the sheets were hung and blowing in the breeze, I returned inside. Despite the fact that I should have immediately finished my chores, I sat down at the table in the men's quarters and removed Lilly's letter from my pocket. I'd quickly perused the contents while seeking details for Thomas, but now I wanted to read the entire letter carefully.

After a brief paragraph saying she hoped her letter found me in good health, Lilly began detailing the problems she'd encountered since my departure.

I believe I am failing all of the children. Attempting to prepare and teach lessons for so many different levels is proving a monumental task. I fear the little ones will continue to fall behind if Mr. Ludwig does not hire someone soon. He says the directors of the orphanage cannot fund another position at this time.

I suggested that during the interim he teach the older

children and I would concentrate on your former students. I do wish you could have seen his face. You would have thought I'd suggested he jump from a bridge. He immediately informed me that he had been hired as director of the orphanage and that did not include teaching. I fear there is no solution to this problem. I don't wish to burden you with this dilemma, as I know family obligations must come first.

My heart ached, for it was clear she cared for the children more deeply than I'd thought. I truly admired the courage she'd exhibited, but I wasn't surprised by Mr. Ludwig's refusal to help. If the board of directors would occasionally visit the orphanage, they would see that beyond food and shelter, these children desperately needed an education if they were going to succeed.

I turned the page and laughed aloud as I read how Caroline, Charlie, and Matthew had convinced several other students to devote two weeks of their recess time to writing and practicing a play.

They did an excellent job, and I do wish I could make time to continue teaching them using stories, but it seems impossible.

I am certain you were surprised by Nathan's unannounced arrival. I was taken aback when he said he planned to remain in Iowa until he could convince you to return and marry him. Of course, I wished him well in the endeavor, as we all miss you and desire your return to us. The children were most excited to write notes that he would hand deliver to you. I do wish he would have come earlier so they would have had more time. I fear their handwriting is rather sloppy due to the time constraints. However, he willingly moved around the room and helped all of them.

I dropped the pages on the table. Just as I'd thought. The children had been instructed what to write. I didn't doubt they missed me, but I'm sure Matthew or Charlie would have written to tell me about their play if they'd had sufficient time. And little Bertie would have told me if she'd been having bad dreams. Why couldn't Nathan be honest with me?

Why aren't you honest with him? The convicting question twisted like a knife. I wanted to believe I'd been honest with Nathan, but perhaps I hadn't. Did I simply want to make sure he wasn't the man for me before I turned loose of him? Was I dangling hope in front of him like a carrot on a string as a means of protecting myself without considering his feelings? Nathan had some qualities I admired. Yet he could be abrasive and self-serving, as well. More importantly, he believed a reliance on God to be a weakness.

We'd argued over that particular issue on several occasions. I'd used my father as an example of a man who credited God for the success he'd achieved. Nathan had countered that the success of the company was due to Father's hard work, not to God. When Nathan asked if I credited God for my Mother's illness as well as my Father's success, I'd told him that I believed how we handled both the good and bad that entered our lives was a testimony to our faith. Handled properly, either could cause us to grow closer to the Lord.

He had dismissed my comment as mere foolishness, and we'd never again discussed God or faith. Had God directed Nathan to Middle Amana to strengthen his faith, or was this Nathan's final attempt to gain control of Forsythe Construction? Uncertain what to think, I folded Lilly's letter and slipped it into my pocket. Did God want me to help Nathan grow spiritually? At this juncture, I wasn't sure my own faith was strong enough to help Nathan—or anyone else for that matter.

Nathan was present at the noonday meal. Once again he sat with the outsiders, but there was no way to know if he'd been hired. There wouldn't be an opportunity to find out after we finished eating, as I'd promised to take the meal to my mother. By the time I picked up her food in the kitchen, the others would be headed back to their jobs.

When I entered the kitchen a short time later, Sister Hanna greeted me. "I have the basket waiting for you to pack." She gestured toward one of the worktables. "Your Mutter says I send too much food, but she needs to eat." Sister Hanna pinched the fabric along one side of her dress and tugged it away from her body. "Your Mutter's clothes are too big for her. You have noticed?"

"She has lost some weight, but now that she's feeling a little better, I'm hoping she will eat more." Twice I had offered to stitch tucks in Mother's dresses to provide a better fit, but she'd refused. She remained certain she would regain the weight by summer's end. I wasn't so sure, but I hadn't argued. I thought perhaps the medicine caused the upset stomach she so frequently experienced, but she needed the medication to help relieve her muscle aches and pains.

I carefully packed a generous serving of roast pork, creamed potatoes, and peas alongside the dumpling soup and a slice of thick dark bread slathered with butter.

"I wrapped a few prune cookies in a napkin and put them aside before we served dessert." She chuckled. "Otherwise, there would be none left. I think the men stuff extra cookies in their pockets before they go back to work." She handed me the cookie-filled linen napkin. "If she says she is too full for the cookies, you should tell her to save them until later in the day. Tell her Sister Hanna says the cookies will help to fatten her up."

"You're very kind. I'll be sure to tell her." I tucked a cotton towel around the edges of the basket, lifted it from the table, and headed toward home.

Laundry days were always the most tiresome, and if Mother was still feeling well, I'd return to help Margaret take down and fold the clothes. Except when a good shirt was needed for a special occasion, none of the current outsiders chose to have their clothes ironed. Margaret and I mended any holes, but ironing cost extra, and most of the workers didn't care to part with their money. At least not for pressed clothes. Instead, they gambled their extra money playing cards after supper. That's what Margaret had told me, and I had no reason to doubt her.

Holding the thick handles of the basket in one hand, I pushed down on the heavy metal latch and stepped into the parlor. "I'm home, Moth—" I startled and nearly dropped the basket. "Nathan! You frightened me. What are you doing here?"

He pushed up from the sofa. "I'm sorry. I didn't mean to scare you. Your father said I could wait here for you. I thought you'd be pleased to see me."

I forced a smile. "I'm not displeased, merely surprised. Does Mother know you're here?"

He nodded. "I knocked at the parlor door when I arrived, and she called to me to come in and wait until you arrived."

"I'll take Mother's meal to her, and then we can visit for a short time before I return to work." I motioned for him to sit down. "I shouldn't be too long."

Moving at a quick pace, I crossed the room and opened the bedroom door. My mother was propped against several pillows and waved me forward. When I didn't draw near enough to suit her, she crooked her finger. "Come closer." I placed the basket on the floor and sat down on the edge of her bed. "Why is Nathan here?" she asked.

I hiked a shoulder. "I'm uncertain. I'm going to talk to him once I set out your food. Father told him he could meet me here. Perhaps he didn't get the job and he's going to leave."

Grasping Mother around the waist, I gently helped her out of bed and into the chair.

"Is that what you're hoping?"

"I don't know, Mother." One by one, I removed the containers from the basket and placed them on the table.

She tipped her head and looked into my eyes. "You should be careful with the affections of others, Jancey. It would seem you have two men interested in a future with you. I'm sure you don't want to hurt either one of them. Am I right?"

"Yes, of course." I handed her a napkin and silverware, and then poured a glass of water from the pitcher beside her bed. "I know this sounds foolish, but when I'm with Ritt, I have this feeling deep inside that I can't explain—kind of like anticipation mixed with joy. He's kind and has a good heart. I feel as though I truly come alive when I'm around him, though he has never spoken of marriage."

My mother's lips curved in a slight smile. "I see. And when you're with Nathan?"

"I've never had such feelings with Nathan. He has some

qualitics that are admirable. He works hard and is interested in marriage and family—at least that's what he's told me from time to time. While Ritt is interested in what I think and what makes me happy, Nathan believes he can decide what will make me happy." I sighed as she took a sip of water. "What drew you to Father?"

"I respected your father, and we were unified in our beliefs." My mother returned the glass of water to the bedside table. "I suppose reasons people marry vary from person to person, but I believe that without those two ingredients, a marriage is doomed for unhappiness. Women thrive on affirmations of love, but men thrive on affirmations of respect. And how can you show respect if you have little or none?" She didn't wait for me to answer before she continued with another question. "Do you respect both of these young men?"

I contemplated her question. There wasn't any doubt I respected Ritt, but I couldn't say I completely respected Nathan. Perhaps because his primary interests seemed to center around work and purchasing my father's construction business rather than placing value on building our relationship.

My mother reached out and squeezed my hand. "Since you must give this some thought, I am sure you haven't developed a deep respect for at least one of these young men. Although I would love to see you marry before . . . in the near future, I believe it is important to take time and be certain you make the proper choice. You need to spend time in prayer as you attempt to make your decision, and I will do the same."

She inhaled a deep breath. "Now go and see what news Nathan has to tell you, and I will eat."

I dipped into the basket and placed the napkin-wrapped cookies on Mother's table. "Sister Hanna sent prune cookies for you and says you should eat all of them." I sucked in my cheeks. "She thinks you are too thin."

"I'll do my best." She gestured toward the doorway. "You go on. I'm fine."

I didn't know what news Nathan would have, but I did know Mother was right: I needed to pray about my future, and I needed to be certain I could always respect the man I married. As much as I wanted my mother alive to attend my wedding, I would do my best to wait upon God's direction.

I settled my attention on Nathan as I strode into the parlor. "How did your meeting go? Did you have a tour of the mill and meet with the supervisors?"

Nathan patted the empty space beside him on the sofa. "Sit here and I'll tell you everything."

Instead of doing his bidding, I sat down in the chair opposite him. "It is better if we don't sit close together."

A spark of anger flashed in his eyes. "There is no one here to see us. I think you are taking these rules too far."

I ignored his comment. I didn't want to argue. "What did you think of the mill?"

"It looks to be a good place to work. The ample windows provide a great deal of sunlight, and I was surprised to see vases filled with flowers on the windowsills." He chuckled. "They did add a nice touch to the rooms. The mill is larger than Watkins, but I don't think the men work at the same rapid pace as was expected at the Watkins Mill. That surprised me. And we didn't have midmorning and midafternoon work stoppages at Watkins to enjoy coffee and cake, either."

"What happened after you toured the mill this morning?"

He sighed. "I accepted a position."

"In Middle or Main Amana?"

"Why would I go to another village to work when I came here to be near you? That would make no sense, would it?"

I shrugged and gave him a faint smile. "I don't know, Nathan. Since you didn't discuss your intentions with me before arriving, how could I know what would make sense?"

"You say you don't know my intentions, but I've made them perfectly clear." He leaned forward and rested his arms across his legs. "You know I care for you, and if living here will prove that to you, I'm willing to do so."

He was right. We were going in circles and accomplishing little. "So you will be living in the men's quarters?"

He nodded. "One of the outsiders took me to see the quarters while we were on midmorning break. I thought I'd see you when we were there, but you were nowhere in sight." He leaned closer. "Where were you?"

His question sounded like an accusation. "I was hanging laundry near the washhouse located a short distance away."

He straightened and then leaned back. "It's hard to imagine you doing laundry. Is that really what you want to do with your life?"

"I don't know what I want for the rest of my life, but for now I'm content cleaning and doing laundry." I swallowed hard. "Have you met all of the other men who live in the quarters?"

"Since we're not allowed to talk during meals, I've met only a few of them. The ones who work in the mill."

My stomach lurched. He'd probably met and talked to Thomas. What if Thomas had already told him about his sister? Even worse, what if he'd told Nathan that I'd been helping him? "Which one of the men took you to see the dormitory?"

"Thomas Kingston or Kingman—something like that. Why do you ask?"

My heart pounded until I thought it would explode within my chest. "I didn't know how accepting the men were when someone new arrived."

"I didn't come here to make friends with the other workers, but he was nice enough. He said he planned to leave once he got some things straightened out in his life." Nathan chuckled. "I told him I planned to leave once I got a few things straightened out, too."

I wanted to ask what else he and Thomas had discussed, but the words stuck in my throat. Why had my simple life in Amana become so complicated?

CHAPTER 17

A short time later, Nathan departed for the hotel to gather his belongings and move them to the dormitory while I returned to work. Before going to the washhouse to help Margaret, I wanted to stop by the men's quarters. I wasn't certain of the time, but I'd remained at home far too long. I hastened my step. The stop wouldn't take much time, and I wanted to know if Thomas had retrieved my note.

Beads of perspiration dotted my forehead and upper lip by the time I arrived at the men's quarters. Taking long strides, I rushed through the sitting room and came to a halt beside Thomas's bed. There was no need to lift the picture of Kathleen. I could see my note was gone. I swiped the corner of my apron across my forehead and inhaled a deep breath. Thomas must have picked up the note when he'd shown Nathan through the quarters.

I didn't want to believe he'd mentioned the note or me to Nathan, but my timing could not have been worse. Everything had come together in the wrong place and at the wrong time. I tried to think what I would have done in Thomas's circumstance. I'd warned him not to mention our meetings to others, but would he think that included a new outsider—a man who had roots in Kansas City, knew me, and could possibly provide even more help locating his sister?

As I grasped the possibility, my knees grew weak and I dropped to the side of the bed. Thus far, Thomas hadn't proved to have a long memory when it came to the instructions I'd given him regarding the secretive nature of our dealings. I'd been strident with him the last time we'd talked, and I hoped he'd taken my warning to heart.

A horse whinnied and men's voices drifted through the open front door. I jumped to my feet as Nathan hollered his thanks for the ride. Without so much as a glance over my shoulder, I raced out the rear door and across the grassy expanse to the washhouse. I clasped a hand to my chest and panted for breath as I walked inside.

Margaret's mouth dropped open when she turned and looked at me. "Why you are running? Is not gut to run on a day that is so hot."

Still gasping for air, I leaned against the wooden doorjamb. "I'm late and I didn't want you to worry." The heat in the room was oppressive, but that hadn't stopped Margaret from lighting a fire in the stove. When I questioned her, she pointed to the tin coffeepot sitting atop the stove. "I like my coffee hot."

Though I couldn't imagine drinking hot coffee when the temperatures soared, I nodded. She clopped across the room, wearing the wooden shoes we donned to keep our leather shoes from getting wet when we laundered clothes. After changing her shoes, she pointed to the empty basket. "Already I hung out the work clothes, but together we will take down the sheets and fold them."

We each picked up a large woven basket and walked to the rope clotheslines that had been strung between cross-style posts. The wooden posts reminded me of the cross where Jesus had died for my sins, and in spite of the heat, I shivered. I couldn't imagine such a death—or such love. The enormity of His selfless act of dying to wash away my sins and provide a path to eternal life had become more evident to me since coming to Middle Amana. Throughout these past couple of months I'd begun to think of Jesus as a friend I could talk to—a personal intercessor who wanted to hear my problems and was never too busy for me. Perhaps it was the quietude and bucolic surroundings that drew me closer to Him. I couldn't be sure.

I was pleased by the modicum of inner peace I'd gained since my arrival, but feelings of guilt still plagued me. I should be completely honest with both Ritt and Nathan. I'd prayed for guidance and the ability to make a clear choice about my future, but I still hadn't received an answer. Why did it seem so easy for others to wait upon God, but not for me? Then again, maybe it wasn't easy; maybe they simply waited in silence.

Margaret nudged my arm. "You are going to help me or stand there and stare at the post?" She held one end of a dry sheet in her hand.

I stepped a short distance from her, removed the wooden clothespin, and walked toward her while holding my end of the sheet. We moved back and forth, quickly folding the sheets and pillowcases before placing them in our baskets.

"Your Mutter is not doing so well?"

"Nein, she is doing better. I think tomorrow she will be able to come with us to the kitchen house." As I unpinned another sheet, realization dawned on me. "I wasn't late because of Mutter. Nathan was waiting at the house when I got there, and he wanted to talk to me."

I hadn't wanted to discuss Nathan further with Margaret, but she deserved an honest explanation.

"If you tell me he is going back home, I know it will make Ritt very happy."

My heart skipped a beat. Exactly what had Ritt told John Olson? If I could keep Margaret focused upon Ritt, maybe she wouldn't ask so many questions about Nathan.

Instead of responding to her comment, I asked a question of my own. "Why do you think it would make Ritt happy? Has he been talking to John about me?"

She giggled. "Ja, but I am not supposed to know."

"What did he say, Margaret?"

She glanced over one shoulder and then the other. I smiled, uncertain why she thought anyone would be close enough to overhear. "He told John he likes you very much and hopes you will stay in the colonies. He thinks you have a gut heart."

"That's wonderful to know. I think he's very nice, as well." My cheeks warmed, and I dropped another sheet into the basket. "But please don't repeat to John what I've told you." I bent forward until we were eye to eye. "Promise?"

"Ja, I promise. But now you must tell me more about Nathan. If not for you, why else would he come here?"

There seemed no way to escape Margaret's questions. If I didn't answer today, I'd face the same inquiry tomorrow or the next day.

"It's true that he came here to try to persuade me to return, but I didn't ask him to come."

"So he is in love with you?"

"He says he wants to marry me, but I'm not convinced of his love."

Margaret's frown deepened. "This I do not understand. Why else would he want to marry you?"

I didn't want to tell her that my father's business likely interested Nathan as much, or possibly more, than I did. Margaret wasn't familiar with marriages that had been forged for power, money, or social status. After all, none of that mattered here, and I would never have enough time to explain the workings of the outside world to Margaret.

I tried to think of something that would help her understand. I touched my finger to the side of my head. "Up here, he thinks it would be good to marry me." I moved my finger to my heart. "In here, I am not sure he feels true love. When I came here, I told him it would be good for us to have time apart. He could discover if he really loved me, and I could do the same."

She bobbed her head. "Ja, like our year of separation when a couple becomes engaged." I agreed and hoped that would put her questions to rest, but when I reached for the basket, she grasped my arm. "What about your heart? Does it feel true love for him?"

I shook my head. "No. Not yet."

"That is gut for Ritt." When I lifted my hand in protest, she chuckled. "I will not tell him, but still it is gut."

I didn't have to wait long for a response from Thomas. The following morning, a note lay beneath the picture of Kathleen.

Once Margaret set to work, I picked up the letter, moved to the other side of the sleeping room where I was sure she wouldn't see me, unfolded the piece of paper, and skimmed the contents.

He asked that I contact Lilly and secure the name of the adoptive family and an address for Kathleen, if possible.

> *It would be easier if Kathleen could write to me instead of going through others. You can give them my address when you write. I hear you know Nathan, the new fellow who started work yesterday. Don't worry. I won't say nothing. As soon as you hear from the lady in Kansas City, leave me a note. TK*

In the future, both Thomas and I would need to be more careful with our notes. Granted, his note didn't contain my name, but if Nathan had picked it up, he would have known it was intended for me. After telling Nathan I was trying to live by the rules of the colonists, he'd have a lot of questions for me. Questions I wouldn't be able to answer to his satisfaction.

I tucked the letter into my pocket as Margaret rounded the corner.

She held a broom in one hand and a metal dustpan in the other. "I am doing my best to complete as much as I can today. You remember that you will be here by yourself on Monday. Ja?"

I stared at her, unable to immediately redirect my thoughts. "Myself?"

Her smile faded as she tapped the bristles of the straw broom on the wooden floorboards. "Ja, yourself. Unless it rains, onion harvest begins on Monday."

"Yes. Onion harvest. I'd forgotten."

Her frown deepened. "You would not forget if you were going

to be out in the hot sun on your hands and knees pulling the onions. Believe me, it makes for long, hard days."

I was surprised by her lack of eagerness. After hearing Madclyn's enthusiastic tales, I had volunteered to help with the onion harvest. But when the list of workers was announced, my name hadn't been chosen. Instead, I was assigned to take over extra duties at my regular job. Of course, not everybody helped with the onion harvest, but anyone who could be released from regular duty was assigned to the task. And for those like me, it meant extra work at our usual job.

"Madelyn tells me that onion harvest and grape picking are her favorite times of year. That's why I volunteered. I don't know why I wasn't chosen instead of you."

Margaret chortled. "Madelyn and the other children like onion harvest because they are released from school. For them it is more fun to pull onions in the hot sun than to sit in the schoolroom. When I was in school, I looked forward to time in the fields, too, but not anymore." She pointed to her knees. "Is hard on the knees and the hands, but the onion crop helps provide for all of us, so I should not complain."

One evening after I'd completed reading lessons with the girls, Ritt had explained that onions were grown in abundance in the villages. "We grow enough for ourselves," he'd told me, "but we also sell our Ebenezer onions and onion seeds to the outside world. Many seed companies want our seeds because the quality is very gut."

"And Sister Anna thinks her seeds are the very best," Madelyn had volunteered.

When I expressed my confusion, Madelyn told me that each garden boss, along with the other women assigned to work in the garden, planted and cared for beds of onion sets as well as the large plots that were planted to produce seeds. "When they weighed the seeds from Sister Anna's garden last year, she had almost four hundred pounds of seeds."

Ritt laughed when I gasped in surprise. "It's true. In Middle we sometimes harvest over two thousand pounds of onions," he'd said. I couldn't imagine such a mountain of onions.

Margaret handed me the dustpan. While I held the flat base against the floor, she swept a small mound of dirt into the metal container. "When it is time for the onion seed harvest in August, you should speak to Sister Anna. She might let you help. Is probably better you try the smaller harvest in the gardens before you try working out in the fields."

I stood and carried the dustpan outside and watched as the contents scattered in the wind. Margaret was right. Hadn't I always told the schoolchildren they couldn't read a book until they first learned the alphabet? If I was going to adjust to this new life, that's what I must do—take it step by step.

For the remainder of the day, Margaret accomplished as much as possible, and when we parted for the evening, I gave her a quick hug. On Sundays, she attended a meeting at a different meetinghouse than I did, so I likely wouldn't see her again until after onion harvest was completed. "Thank you for doing so much today. Your hard work will make it easier for me on Monday."

A rush of pink colored her cheeks and she brushed aside my words of praise. I'd learned Sister Margaret didn't easily accept compliments, but I wanted to show my appreciation. "I am glad I was assigned to work with you."

She bobbed her head and flashed a smile. "We have become gut friends, ja?"

"We have. You have taught me a great deal. I will be praying the sun will remain behind the clouds and a cool breeze blows across the fields next week."

Margaret squeezed my hand. "After the hot weather we have had this past week, I will gladly join you in that prayer, Sister Jancey. If you have any problems while I am gone, you should remember to go to the Küche. Sister Bertha will be able to help you."

After assuring her I'd be fine, we parted and I walked toward home. I hadn't gone far when I heard footfalls and glanced over my shoulder. I stopped when I saw Ritt racing toward me. The bells chimed in the distance as he came alongside me.

"I'm surprised to see you. Why are you off work early today?" I matched his stride as we headed toward home.

The hour wasn't early for most of us, but during the summer when large orders from the outside world arrived and needed to be filled before fall, all the mills remained open later. Recently many of the workers had been required to work until ten or eleven at night. The men claimed they didn't mind because they enjoyed the extra cash or store credits they received for their long hours at the mill. Ritt, however, hoped his longer hours and good workmanship would benefit him in another way. He wanted to become a supervisor in the weaving room.

"Because your friend said he was the best weaver at the mill where he worked, Brother William said I could go home, and he would see how well Nathan could weave on my machines. Is not right that I must give up my extra hours of work for that boastful man."

"Maybe you should speak with Brother William about your complaints. Or maybe speak to Brother William's supervisor regarding your concerns."

"Brother William is in charge of the woolen mill. His decisions are final." With the tip of his shoe, Ritt kicked a small rock down the wooden sidewalk. "For sure, I think your friend wants to become a lead weaver or supervisor. He wants the same job as I do."

There was a sting to his words, and I scowled. "You act as though this is my fault."

"He is your friend. If not for you, he would not be in the mill working at my looms."

"Brother William assigned Nathan to work at your machines, not me. He is an experienced and diligent worker, and I am sure Brother William wants to put Nathan's talents to good use."

"And you are very quick to praise and defend him." He pinned me with a cold stare. "I see how it is."

My heart froze as he turned and walked away. Had I just destroyed the possibility of finding true love?

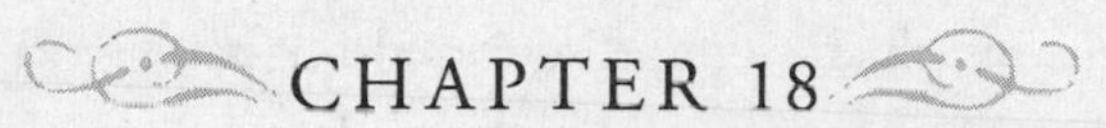

CHAPTER 18

On Sunday, Ritt remained detached. While he'd previously looked for opportunities to visit or walk beside me, since our talk on Saturday, he'd avoided me. Even though we attended different meetings on Sunday morning, he'd previously found opportunities to draw close and talk to me along the way, but not this morning. Inside the meetinghouse, I'd gone to sit on the women's side beside Madelyn. Like me, she attended *Kinder Versammlungen*, the meeting for those of us who hadn't attained full spiritual knowledge in the ways of the church.

The meetinghouse was a bit larger than other structures in the village, but unlike the large crosses and signage on churches in the outside world, the Amana meetinghouses remained plain and unassuming. There were no cushions to soften the pine pews, and the straight backs seemed angled forward rather than into a more comfortable back position. That, of course, was likely my imagination. But after sitting on the hard pews or kneeling on the pine floor, I'd decided nothing in the church had been created with comfort in mind. Hearts and minds were to be turned to God during worship, but my mind sometimes wandered to my discomfort rather than to God.

Madelyn reached over and squeezed my hand, and I smiled down at her. Moments later, we both stood to sing one of the songs in the *Psalter-Spiel*. I wasn't familiar with the tune, and without the benefit of an organ or piano to aid us, my voice faltered into an unharmonious warble. Madelyn clapped a hand over her mouth while I stifled a chuckle of my own. I didn't want to do anything that would cause either of us to be reprimanded for inappropriate behavior during worship.

After church, my thoughts immediately returned to Ritt and his unwillingness to let me further explain my comments. When he was nearby, he wouldn't look at me. I tried my best to find a moment when I could speak with him, but he made it impossible, and I finally gave up. While I understood his disappointment regarding his work at the mill, I could make no sense of his anger toward me.

My earlier response had not been meant as a defense of Nathan. Everything I'd said was true: Nathan did possess strong work skills and had proved himself to be an excellent craftsman. Had Nathan questioned me regarding Ritt, I would have said much the same about him, for I'd heard many of the brothers commend Ritt for his abilities.

Still, it seemed he wanted to blame me for decisions made by Brother William, and as Ritt's stubborn behavior continued, my anger mounted. Was he going to let his job at the mill come between us?

When Madelyn and I arrived home, she stopped in the foyer. "Do you want to come upstairs so you can check the lessons I completed?"

"Maybe later, Madelyn." If Ritt had returned from the meeting, I didn't want him to think I was chasing after him.

She grinned and bobbed her head. "Gut. That will give me time to finish learning my spelling words." She bounded up the stairs with enviable enthusiasm.

After the noonday meal, Nathan knocked on our door. Although his arrival was unexpected, I was pleased for the diversion. Rather than remain indoors and fret over Ritt's attitude, I agreed to accompany Nathan on a walk to the river. Besides, a stroll outdoors held much more appeal than forced small talk in the parlor.

However, I hadn't counted on the fact that other people would see me with Nathan. My stomach clenched when I caught sight of Margaret and John sitting together near the water's edge. While tugging on Nathan's arm, I nodded in the opposite direction. "Let's go down this way a little farther."

He shook his head. "This is the best place. I checked with several of the fellows, and they said there are flat rocks along here that provide a good place to sit near the water."

I knew he was right, for this was the area where I'd come with Ritt and Madelyn. "We don't have to be close to the water. I'd prefer a place where there was a bit more shade, wouldn't you?"

Nathan frowned and glanced about, but before he could answer, Margaret shouted my name. Jumping to her feet, she waved both arms high in the air. "Come down here and join us!"

Her invitation surprised me. Had she not noticed Nathan was at my side?

Nathan squinted and cupped his hand above his eyes. "Who is that calling to you?"

"Sister Margaret. She works with me cleaning the men's quarters. I've mentioned her to you."

"And that looks like John Olson from the woolen mill beside her. I've spoken to him a few times." He grasped my elbow. "Come on, let's go join them."

I wanted to run and go the other way, but refusing might give rise to questions about why I didn't want to socialize with Margaret. "Only for a short time and then let's look for some shade."

"I don't know why you're worried about the sun. You're wearing a huge bonnet and your arms are covered. I don't think even the brightest sun could penetrate your attire." His gaze traveled the length of my calico dress. "Don't you miss wearing fashionable clothing?"

"In truth, I don't miss fretting over which gown to wear or whether my hair has been coiffed in the proper style of the day. Of the things I have missed, fancy dresses would be near the bottom of my list."

He grinned as we drew near to Margaret and John. "Then I hope you'll tell me that I am at the top."

My shoulders tensed and I looked away. "That's impossible, Nathan. You're right here beside me. I no longer have a reason to miss you."

"Look at the fish John caught!" Margaret tugged on a line and lifted a flopping carp out of the water. "Isn't it grand?"

I was thankful Margaret interrupted before Nathan could rephrase his request. He would have been unhappy to hear that the schoolchildren were the ones I most longed to see.

"That's a wonderful catch." I bobbed my head with as much enthusiasm as I could muster and forced a cheery smile.

While John and Nathan exchanged greetings, Margaret tipped her head close to mine. "I thought you would be with Ritt, not with Nathan."

"Ritt is unhappy with me," I told her.

Nathan stepped to my side. "Are you going to introduce me to your friend, Jancey?"

I introduced Margaret and told him of her many kindnesses to me.

He nodded at her. "I'm pleased to meet you, Margaret."

"Welcome to our village. Have you decided that you like living in the colonies?"

"Living here is not what I would choose for myself, but I do like being near Jancey." He rested his hand on my sleeve. "And if it means I must live in the village to be close to her, then I am willing. Of course, it is my hope that she will return to Kansas City with me." He flashed a smile in my direction.

John's forehead pinched into a frown. "I thought you planned to stay in Middle, Sister Jancey."

"Look!" Margaret nudged John's arm. "A fish is nibbling on your bait. Don't let it get away." She leaned close and encouraged him as he landed the fish. "It is a gut one. Even bigger than the last."

While the two of them assessed their latest catch, I leaned toward Nathan. "They don't get to be alone very often. Maybe we should leave them to enjoy the afternoon by themselves."

We stood and Nathan gently squeezed my arm. "And I would like to enjoy some time alone with you, as well."

I immediately regretted my suggestion, but I feared a retraction would require an explanation, and I didn't have one at the ready. I gestured to Margaret. "I think we're going to walk a ways and sit in the shade."

"Please stay. The sisters who work in our Küche made extra cookies and sent some with me," she said, motioning to a small basket. "I am happy to share. There are too many for John and me, aren't there?" She arched her brows at John.

He nodded. "Ja, sit down. We have plenty. And I have a jug of water keeping cool down there in the river."

Without looking to Nathan for affirmation, I sat back down. "I suppose we could remain a while longer. I am getting a little thirsty, and that cool water sounds inviting."

Nathan dropped down beside me. "A cookie does sound good."

There was confusion in his voice, but I pretended not to notice and helped Margaret spread a small cloth. John propped his fishing pole between two rocks and came to sit near us.

He picked up a cookie and waved it in Nathan's direction. "So how did you like working the late hours with us last night? Is at least cooler in the evening. Ja?"

Nathan nodded. "I didn't mind, but I wouldn't want to work so many hours every day."

John took a bite of his cookie. "Ja, well you should be sure to tell Brother William you do not want the long hours. For sure it may change his opinion."

"Opinion about what?" Nathan helped himself to one of the date cookies.

John arched his brows high on his forehead. "About who receives promotions and is chosen to work extra hours. Is that not what we are talking about?"

"I don't mind the extra hours some of the time. Besides, Brother

William said the longer hours are necessary only when there are large orders for blankets and flannel. If it means a better job that pays more, then I wouldn't object." He shrugged as if such large orders would be of little consequence.

John frowned. "Our products are in high demand, and the long hours can go on for more than a short time. Each year we weave at least twenty thousand blankets and produce over half a million yards of flannel cloth. Our goods are highly prized."

"I'll do what I must, but who can say what the future holds for me." He glanced in my direction. "Or for Jancey."

"But if you do not know how long you will stay, it would be best if you didn't seek such a position, don't you think? A frequent change of supervisors is not so gut." John popped the rest of the cookie into his mouth.

Nathan shrugged. "If Brother William doesn't think it's a problem, why would I? The pay here is less than I made in the last woolen mill where I worked, so if I can be paid extra money as a supervisor, I wouldn't turn down the offer."

John hunched forward. "If you would receive such an offer, it would be gut to ask God's guidance so you have His direction in your life."

Shoulders taut and lips pressed into a tight seam, Nathan pushed to his feet and gestured for me to follow. There was little doubt he'd found John's suggestion offensive. Nathan wouldn't ask for God's guidance about a position at the mill—or anything else, for that matter.

The following morning, I walked to the men's quarters by myself. Nathan and the other outsiders usually departed earlier than the rest of us. I had hoped Ritt might seek me out after breakfast so that I could tell him about going to the river with Nathan and the visit with Margaret and John, but he left with two of the other men. I worried Ritt's anger would deepen once he heard Nathan's comments regarding work at the woolen mill. I had hoped there would be an opportunity to mend any possible wounds, but it seemed that would not happen this morning.

Today would be longer than most for me. There had been no rain, so Margaret would be in the fields pulling onions with many of the other women and children. The heat had subsided a little and I wanted to think my prayers had helped. Maybe God would help with Ritt and his stubborn attitude, as well. I glanced heavenward and uttered a short petition as I strode into the dormitory.

Without Margaret to talk to, my thoughts drifted like billowing clouds carried on the hot breeze. I thought about the children back in Kansas City and wondered what they were doing on this bright summer morning, I thought about Mother's health, I thought about making a permanent home in the colonies, but mostly I thought about Nathan and Ritt. When Nathan first arrived, it seemed Ritt viewed him as a competitor for my affection. Now, however, it appeared it wasn't me at all—it was competition for the position at the woolen mill. The idea gnawed at me as I picked up the broom and swept the wooden floor. Perhaps John Olson had misunderstood Ritt's comments about me, for since Nathan's arrival, it appeared Ritt's primary concern was a promotion at the mill and any thoughts of me had vanished from his mind.

The men's quarters always needed extra cleaning on Mondays, and today was no exception. On Sundays during the summer, the men sometimes went fishing or swimming in the river, but some of them remained behind to play cards, write letters, or read a magazine or book—and some remained behind and imbibed. From the appearance of the sleeping room, a few of them had gotten drunk last evening and then become sick during the night. The mess they'd made on the floor hadn't been properly cleaned, and the smell made me gag as I moved further into the room. I had hoped to wait until tomorrow to scrub the floors, but this wouldn't wait.

I worked my way down one side of the room, then stopped and went outside to the pump for fresh water. After placing the bucket of water on the floor, I arched backward and rubbed the center of my back. How it ached after moving only one row of beds.

Determined to complete the task before the noonday meal, I grasped the metal frame of Thomas's bed with both hands and yanked it toward the center of the room. The legs on the right side of the frame jostled, but one of the left legs wouldn't budge.

"What is wrong with this bed?" I muttered while tugging on the metal frame several more times. I released my hold on the bed and flexed my aching hands. Deep dents creased my palms. By tomorrow there'd likely be bruises. I dropped to the side of the bed, leaned forward, and rested my arms across my thighs. If anyone had told me a year ago that I would be scrubbing floors, washing dirty clothes for strangers, and moving beds, I would have laughed aloud.

After resting for several minutes, I pushed to my feet. "If I don't get busy, I'll be here when the men return from work." I glanced around the room. "Here I am talking to myself. If the workers pass by and hear me, they'll think I'm demented." I laughed aloud. If someone passed by, I wouldn't care what they thought; I'd beg for help.

Instead of another session pushing and pulling the bed, I

stepped around to the other end to get the trunk out of the way. Using the side of my leg, I gave the trunk a shove. Once I'd moved it a few feet, I leaned sideways and realized the problem. The leg of the bed was stuck on a piece of loose floorboard. Bending down, I locked my elbows, lifted the side of the bed frame, and gave the bed a hefty shove.

"Finally!" A whoosh of air escaped my lungs and my arms trembled from the exertion. I'd likely scratched a section of the floor, but I didn't care. I would worry about that later. Right now, I would take a moment to enjoy what I'd accomplished.

After pausing to take several breaths, I knelt beside the bed to examine the floor. If I'd ruined some of the boards, perhaps Nathan and Thomas could replace them. One look revealed some of the boards had recently been cut. It appeared as if someone had created a hiding space beneath the floorboards. Maybe Thomas had carved out the space to hide the notes I'd written to him.

I should have scrubbed the floor and moved the bed back into place, but my curiosity prevailed. I was determined to discover whether anything was hidden under the boards. Unfortunately, the loose piece of wood had dropped into place when I moved the bed, and now it fit snug against the other boards. Using the tips of my fingers, I attempted to lift one of the boards, but as I tried to force the board loose, a splinter lodged deep beneath one of my fingernails. If this continued, I'd end up with nothing but pricked fingers and bruised hands.

There had to be something I could use. I pushed to my feet and looked around the room. When I spied a pocketknife lying on the windowsill near Nathan's bed, my heart pounded so hard I thought it would leap into my throat. Grabbing the knife, I returned to my kneeling position near Thomas's bed and set to work. Using my thumbnail, I pulled out the short blade and pressed it into the crevice. Once the knife created enough leverage, the board began to lift and I reached for the rough edge, but the blade slipped and the board dropped back into place. I continued my efforts, but with each failed attempt, my frustration mounted.

I sat back on my heels and stared at the floor. One more try and then I had to get back to work. If I couldn't remove the boards today, I'd find a tool of some sort and try again tomorrow. After promising myself this would be my final attempt, I shoved the blade into place. This time I was careful to maintain the pressure of the knife against the board. As it inched up, I reached with my other hand and dug the tips of my fingers into the jagged edge and pulled. My stomach tightened into a knot as I lifted the second piece of wood and then the third.

Scooting forward, I peered into the dark hole below. I could barely see what looked like some sort of fabric. I reached out but then retracted my hand as I recalled the traps that Mr. Ludwig used to set to catch rats at the orphanage. What if there was some sort of trap down there? A rat trap could break fingers, and how would I ever explain such a thing? It would be impossible to deny that I'd been snooping where I didn't belong.

Even so, I'd come too far. I had to know. My hand trembled as I reached into the opening. Using the tips of my fingers, I tugged on a corner of the coarse cloth that lay wedged near the back of the space—likely fabric used to protect whatever had been hidden. My determination swelled, and I thrust both hands into the opening and grabbed hold. I wiggled and manipulated the fabric in all directions until it finally gave way. A yelp escaped my lips as I lifted a dirty canvas bag onto the floor beside me.

Eager to read the markings, I retrieved a handkerchief from

my pocket and swiped at the dirt. Though the letters were faded and difficult to read, I gasped and dropped the bag to the floor. Stamped across the canvas in faded black letters were the words *National Commerce Bank of Kansas City.*

My heart pounded an erratic beat.

I should put the bag back where I'd found it. I shouldn't look inside.

But I couldn't stop myself.

CHAPTER 19

The room swirled around me, and I collapsed against the side of the bed. I forced myself to breathe. Never in my life had I seen so much money. I didn't want to believe what lay before me, and I didn't know what to do next.

Inhaling a deep breath, I steadied myself. Thomas said he'd been saving his wages so he could provide a home for Kathleen. Could all of this belong to him? It appeared to be far too much money for one young man to accumulate. Maybe all of the men kept their savings in the bag together, but that made no sense. If they'd all placed their money in the bag, there would be no reason to hide it, for other than Sister Margaret and me, no one else ever came into the dormitory.

Maybe Thomas had come into a large sum of money before he came to Iowa. Or perhaps he'd worked someplace that paid exceedingly high wages, or maybe he'd been rewarded for some meritorious act. But with all this money, why hadn't he gone in search of his sister? Why had he come to the colonies instead? He could have hired a detective to help him find Kathleen. I'd heard my father speak of the Pinkerton Detective Agency, which would assist in locating missing persons.

Tracing my fingers over the imprinted letters, I attempted to think of some reasonable explanation for all this money, yet I could think of none. My father conducted the company's as well as his personal banking at the National Commerce Bank, and I'd seen him carry a similar, but much smaller, bag whenever he went to the bank. Yet that didn't explain why this large money-filled bag had been hidden beneath the floorboards of the men's dormitory in Middle Amana.

Maybe this money didn't belong to Thomas. The bag had been hidden under his bed and was from a Kansas City bank. And Thomas had lived in Kansas City, but that didn't mean it belonged to him. Someone else could have hidden it beneath his bed. While seeking a hiding place, maybe one of the other men discovered a loose board beneath Thomas's bed and then enlarged the space. Although unlikely, there was a remote possibility the money had been there for quite some time. Father always told me it wasn't wise to pass judgment without all of the facts.

As the noonday bell tolled in the distance, I jerked to attention. What if one of the men should return to the dormitory to pick up something on his way to the kitchen house? A shudder rocketed down the length of my body. I captured my lower lip between my teeth to stop the trembling. There wasn't time for fear. I needed to keep my wits about me.

In my haste, I dropped the bag and a quantity of bills and coins scattered across my lap and onto the floor in front of me. Among the bills, I noticed a ragged piece of folded newspaper and shoved it into my pocket. There wasn't time to look at it now, but I'd read it after lunch and return it to the hiding place later this afternoon. I thrust the bag back into the hole, pushed the floorboards in place, and heaved the bed into position. I exhaled a breath and clasped a hand to my chest.

If I ran, I might make it to the Küche before the second bell rang. There was no one in sight on the path, and I picked up my pace. It wouldn't do to enter the dining hall while Brother Herman was offering the mealtime prayer. Perspiration trickled down the sides of my face, and my hair felt damp beneath my bonnet. When the second bell tolled, I rounded the Küche and dropped into line beside one of the older sisters. I was still panting when she turned to look at me.

She gently patted my face with her palm. "Your cheeks are red as cherries. If you leave work when the first bell rings, you will not need to run."

"You're right, Sister. I'll try to remember."

She smiled and nodded as we began to move toward the door. My breath caught when I saw Nathan walking up the steps. He'd lived in Kansas City and he slept in the bed next to Thomas. Could Nathan somehow be the one who'd hidden the bag? But that idea made no sense. If Nathan had all that money, he would have offered to purchase my father's business. Wouldn't he?

My stomach churned like water being tossed about by a paddlewheel. I swallowed a bite of fried potatoes and instantly realized I'd made a mistake. If I ate anything more, I'd be sick for sure. My plate remained full when we stood for the after-dinner prayer.

Brother Herman had barely said amen when the old sister who'd admonished me for running now frowned and pointed to my plate.

"You could not eat because running upsets the stomach." She patted her hand against her midsection. "This afternoon you will be hungry." She forked the piece of ham from my plate and placed it between two thick slices of bread. "Wrap this in your napkin and take it with you."

I folded my napkin around the sandwich and thanked her before I departed. Several of the outsiders had gathered beneath a small grove of trees a short distance from the Küche. Both Nathan and Thomas were among the group, while Ritt stood a short distance away talking to several other men. Although I didn't expect Ritt or Thomas to acknowledge me, I wasn't so sure about Nathan. Whenever Ritt was around, Nathan tended to stay as close to me as a jealous child. I headed toward the shortcut hoping for a private moment to examine the paper I'd placed in my pocket.

When I neared the end of the path, I sat down on a nearby stump and withdrew the piece of newspaper from my pocket. I gasped at the caption above the article. *Two Bank Robbers Apprehended. Third Still on the Run.* The article stated that two men who robbed the National Commerce Bank of Kansas City had been incarcerated in the Kansas City jail and were currently awaiting trial. In the next paragraph, the article advised that a third man remained at large and was believed to be in possession of a portion of the stolen money. Near the end, the journalist wrote that he'd interrogated one of the criminals, Mr. Allen Dempsey, who'd declared the stolen funds had been equally divided among the three bank robbers before they'd split up and gone off in separate directions. The article went on to say that Mr. Dempsey had been unwilling to reveal the name and possible whereabouts of the third accomplice, but there was hope he might change his mind as the time for his trial drew near.

My heart thudded to a halt. Could Thomas somehow be involved in this robbery? If so, it made sense that he hadn't remained in Kansas to look for his sister. He'd want to hide out until he thought it would be safe to return. And what better place to hide than in the colonies? Who would think to look for him here?

I shook my head. I shouldn't jump to conclusions. Perhaps this was simply a clipping he saved because he had an interest in the case. I didn't even know how long ago this bank robbery had occurred. For all I knew, Thomas could have been a boy when it happened.

I turned over the piece of newspaper, but the only thing on the reverse side was an advertisement for St. Jacob's Oil, a potion that promised a cure for everything from rheumatism to frosty feet. I wished I had some of that concoction right now. Maybe a little St. Jacob's Oil would cure the disappointment I felt when I hadn't been able to find the date of the newspaper's publication anywhere on the clipping.

I tucked the paper into my pocket and tried to recall any talk of a bank robbery before we'd left Kansas City. Nothing came to mind, but I could have easily overlooked such an article. Father may have mentioned something, but if he had, I'd forgotten.

The bell rang and I sauntered toward the men's quarters while trying to remember if Thomas had told me when he'd first arrived in Middle Amana. I didn't want to falsely accuse him, but the possibility of Thomas Kingman being a bank robber kept filling my thoughts. A ripple of fear shot through me as I recalled meeting him alone in the woods. I closed my eyes and tried to picture him that day. He certainly hadn't acted like the sort who would rob a bank or do harm to anyone, but looks could be deceiving, couldn't they?

I entered the dormitory and glanced around. The realization that money that might have been stolen from a bank was hidden in this room caused my palms to turn damp. The few bites of fried potatoes rumbled in my stomach, and I thought I might be sick. I needed to make a decision. Earlier I had planned to return the newspaper article to the money bag, but now I wondered if that was a good idea. If I talked to the elders, it would be helpful to have the clipping in my possession to substantiate such an unbelievable story, and I doubted Thomas would remove the bag until he decided to leave the colonies. Besides, the idea of once again removing those floorboards made me as nervous as a cat stuck in a tree.

I patted my pocket and leaned back in the chair, but moments later startled to attention. I'd made my first decision without God's direction. Would I never learn to wait upon Him? I bowed and prayed for the Lord to direct me, determined I would remain silent about my discovery until I felt the Lord prompt me to do otherwise.

When the midafternoon bell rang, I was outside scrubbing the small porch and wooden sidewalk in front of the men's quarters. This wasn't one of my favorite chores, but today I didn't mind. There was little breeze, and being outside swishing water over the sidewalk was preferable to enduring the stifling heat inside the dormitory.

"Jancey!" I turned around to see Nathan marching toward me.

He pointed to the bucket of water. "How can you belittle

yourself like this? You shouldn't be scrubbing sidewalks. I can't believe you're willing to submit yourself to this way of life." He lifted his hand toward my face. "You're overheated and shouldn't be working in this hot sun."

I took a backward step before he could touch my face. "There are others watching, Nathan. You can't touch me in such a manner—not in public or private. I've told you over and over that it's not permitted."

His jaw tightened. "And I've told you that I don't like these rules. They're foolish. This is no way for people like us to live."

I arched my brows. "People like us? What kind of people are we, Nathan? Tell me how I am different from the women who live here. For that matter, how are you different from these men? We're all alike in God's eyes—created equally."

He thrust his chin forward. "You know what I'm saying, Jancey. We are different. You're playing word games with me. This is not the life you lived in Kansas City. You never scrubbed floors or washed sheets." In one swift motion, he reached forward and grabbed my wrist. "Look at your hands! They were once soft to the touch. Now they're rough and discolored, and your nails are chipped and dirty."

His harsh comments wounded me. "My hands have been in scrub water cleaning up after you and the other men who live here. This is the middle of the workday. Are your hands perfectly clean?"

My anger had risen and so had my voice. I hadn't intended to arouse attention and was surprised to see Ritt walking toward us at a brisk pace.

"Hallöchen!" Ritt waved in our direction as he drew near. He stopped beside Nathan, but his eyes were focused on me. "There is a problem?"

Nathan glowered at him. "Why do you think there's a problem? We were trying to have a conversation until you interrupted us."

"I am thinking there is a problem because I could hear angry voices when I started toward the path." Ritt's focus remained fixed on me. "You are all right?"

"Of course she's all right. You can see her, can't you?"

Ritt's shoulders stiffened. "I was asking Sister Jancey."

"I'm fine, but thank you for your concern." This was the first time Ritt had spoken to me since we'd argued about Nathan, and my chest warmed at the genuine worry that shone in his eyes. But while I was pleased Ritt no longer appeared to be ignoring me, having Nathan involved would likely make matters worse between the three of us.

"She doesn't need protection from me." Nathan clenched his hands and glared at Ritt.

"That is gut to know." Ritt nodded toward the path. "We are expected at the Küche for a snack. Unless you want to make Brother William unhappy, I think you should come with me. We are already late."

I nodded my agreement. "You should go, Nathan. You need to follow the rules if you are going to live here."

"Rules! That's all people think about around here." Using his shirt sleeve, Nathan wiped the perspiration from his forehead.

"If you are unhappy with the way we live, you are not required to remain in the colonies. No one is forced to live here." Ritt glanced at me. "Anyone who decides this life is not what they want is free to leave and make a new life elsewhere."

Nathan curled his lip. "Well, I can tell you this isn't the life I want for Jancey—or for myself, either."

Ritt hiked a shoulder. "For yourself you can speak, but not

for anyone else. Sister Jancey has the right to decide whether her future will be in the colonies or elsewhere." He stepped toward the path. "We must go to the Küche. If you and Sister Jancey want to talk, you should do it after working hours."

"Don't you see how foolish this is? Why should I need to talk to you tonight instead of right now?" Nathan stared at me.

"Because I have work that requires my attention." I leaned down to pick up the bucket, walked inside, and closed the door. I waited several minutes before I peeked out the window. When I was certain the two men had departed, I opened the door, thankful to once again gain a slight breeze.

Instead of setting to work, I dropped to one of the wooden chairs that surrounded the table where the men played cards and tried to steady my nerves. Discovery of the money bag had created a whirl of emotions, and the heated exchange between Nathan and Ritt further intensified my turmoil. This first day without Margaret wasn't yet over, and it had already proved more chaotic than I could have imagined.

I placed my folded arms atop the table and rested my head. Why hadn't I left those boards in place? If I hadn't been snooping where I didn't belong, I wouldn't be faced with this dilemma. Should I tell someone? Father? The elders? Ritt? Should I pretend none of it had ever happened? Should I attempt to discover more about Thomas on my own? After all, I couldn't be absolutely certain the money belonged to him, and I didn't want to bear false witness. The newspaper article was proof of a bank robbery and the fact that one of the robbers remained at large, but it wasn't proof that Thomas was that missing criminal. Everything pointed to him. But would a bank robber be the kind of man who wanted to locate his sister and build a new life? How

I longed to feel some nudging from the Lord—some indication of what I should do.

I needed to wait upon Him, for if I had prayed before I'd gone digging beneath the floorboards, I might not be in this situation. If I'd remember to wait before making decisions and then expecting God to get me out of trouble, I'd be much better off.

Some time ago, I'd spoken to Brother William about my occasional failures.

"None of us ever reach perfection, Sister Jancey," he'd said, *"but we must strive to remain in constant communion with God. That way, it becomes second nature to ask for His help when a problem comes our way."* His eyes had radiated kindness. *"It is pleasing to the Lord that you are trying to do your best and draw closer to Him. You will learn. I will be praying for you."*

I was certain Brother William had prayed for me every day since we'd had our talk, and though I sometimes remembered to first go to God with my problems, I still hadn't mastered the knack of remaining in constant communion with Him.

"You sick or sleeping?"

I jerked upright, my heart pounding faster than a woodpecker hammering on a tree. I hadn't heard footsteps. "Thomas! What are you doing here? Why aren't you at work?" I glanced at the clock. I must have fallen asleep.

His lips curved in a lopsided grin. "You don't need to worry. I won't tell anyone you were sleeping on the job." Using his thumb, he pointed over his shoulder. "I got off early, so you don't need to worry about none of the other fellows coming back just yet." He dropped to a chair on the other side of the table. "Brother William has that fellow of yours moving around the mill to learn all the positions. Looks like he's gonna make Nathan a supervisor.

Anyway, he's working in my area and I was in the way, so they said I could leave. Guess they thought you'd be done with your work over here."

Confusion blurred my mind. "I am. I mean, I shouldn't be in here with you. There's nothing that can't wait until tomorrow. I doubt the men will notice if there's a little dust on the window-sills." I jumped to my feet.

His gaze settled on my shaking hands. "There's no reason to be afraid of me, Miss Jancey. It's not like we don't know each other." He leaned across the table. "I been wondering if you got that other letter sent off to your friend at the orphanage."

My throat constricted as if a rope had been tightened around my neck. I croaked an affirmative response and massaged my neck.

Thomas pushed away from the table and pointed to the water pitcher. "Want some water? I'll be glad to get you a cup if you don't mind drinking after us men." He tipped his head to the side. "We don't worry 'bout unwashed cups."

I knew that much was true. The only time the cups were replaced was when Margaret or I carried the dirty ones to the Küche and returned with clean ones.

I swallowed and shook my head. "I'll be fine." I was pleasantly surprised when my voice sounded normal.

He settled back in the chair. "So how soon do you think you'll hear? I sure do wish I could find out something before much longer."

"I don't have any idea. Much will depend on the family with whom Kathleen is living, but as soon as I hear anything, I'll leave a note." I pushed away from the table. "I really should go home and check on my mother." I hesitated a moment. "When did you arrive in Middle Amana, Thomas?"

He scratched his head and looked toward the ceiling. "I don't rightly remember. Sometime this past winter."

I nodded. I'd felt a prompting to inquire, but I didn't know if it was my own curiosity or an urging from the Lord. I was uncertain how a person could know for sure, but I decided to continue with my questions.

"Had you ever worked here before? I've heard that some of the workers come and go, depending on the season."

He narrowed his eyes. "No. Why'd you ask?"

I fumbled with the corner of my apron. "Just curious. Back when we first met, you asked me about why I'd come here and I wondered the same about you. Seems there would have been better paying jobs in Kansas City."

"Seems you been thinkin' about me quite a bit, Miss Jancey. Not sure if I should be flattered or concerned." Using his right hand, he pushed his chair back until it balanced on the two back legs and looked straight into my eyes. "I was in and out of Kansas City, depending on work. Living here's as good a place as any."

"But it's a long way from Kansas City."

"No place is too far if there's train tracks, Miss Jancey." He pinned me with an unyielding stare and let the chair drop with a loud bang.

I jumped as though I'd been shot.

He'd made his point. Thomas Kingman had called a halt to my question-and-answer session.

CHAPTER 20

During prayer meeting that evening, I contemplated whether it had been the Lord nudging me to ask Thomas questions about his background or my own desire to discover the truth. I had a feeling it was the latter, but as we prepared to depart, I felt a distinct urge to confide in Ritt. I wasn't certain how the elders might react if I approached them with my findings—they might decide I wasn't the type of person they wanted living in the colonies. And I didn't want to tell my father. He had enough worries with Mother's ever-changing health; at least that's what I told myself.

In truth, I feared my father would step in and I'd never learn all of the circumstances surrounding Thomas or that hidden money—and I couldn't bear that thought. I didn't want to yield complete authority to anyone else, but I needed a confidant who could give me sound advice. Ritt seemed the perfect person. He'd been concerned about my welfare earlier in the day, so I hoped he now understood I wasn't to blame for Nathan's position at the mill.

I maintained hope that Thomas and Ritt had visited a bit during their work at the mill. At a minimum, Ritt should be able to tell me exactly when Thomas had arrived here. Then I could write to Lilly and ask if she'd stop at the bank to make an inquiry regarding the date of the robbery. Of course, there was a possibility Ritt would insist upon telling the elders. I contemplated that idea. Before I told him, I'd secure a promise that he wouldn't divulge anything I said. I wasn't certain what I'd do if he didn't agree.

First, of course, I would need to tell him about meeting with Thomas and writing the letters on his behalf. A part of me wanted to avoid that topic and tell him only that I'd discovered the money hidden beneath Thomas's bed. But Ritt was insightful. He'd ask how I knew where Thomas slept. It wasn't as if there were names on the beds in the dormitory. And, other than Nathan, I knew nothing about the workers who lived in the men's quarters. Ritt would think it odd that I'd know anything about Thomas. Yet the connection to Kansas City was an important part of why I suspected Thomas, so I needed to explain everything.

Thomas had already revealed Nathan would be working late this evening, so the timing would be perfect. As we walked home, Madelyn came alongside me and grasped my hand. "Are we going to read this evening?"

I smiled down at her and nodded. "And you should ask your brother if he would like to join us. He hasn't listened to you read for a while. I think he will be pleased with your progress."

Madelyn dropped my hand and skipped a few steps. "Can we sit outside under the tree? It will be cooler than sitting in the parlor."

The upper floor of the house was always warmer than our downstairs rooms, but when I'd suggested Madelyn come to our parlor for her summertime lessons, Sister Hanna objected. Though I attempted to assure her otherwise, she thought the activity would disturb my mother.

"I think that's an excellent idea." Plenty of daylight remained, and being outdoors would provide greater privacy when I spoke with Ritt about the money.

While Madelyn ran upstairs to fetch her books, I went into my bedroom and gathered a quilt for us to sit on. Mother hadn't been well enough to join us at prayer meeting, and I stepped inside her bedroom before departing. "How are you feeling?"

"As good as I can expect." She gestured toward the quilt. "You are going outdoors?"

"Yes. Madelyn asked if we could go outside for her lesson this evening. Is there anything you need before I go? Father should be down in a few minutes. He was talking with Brother Werner."

"No, you go on. Tell Madelyn she should come and read to me some evening. It will help me fall asleep."

"I think she would like that, but you should tell Sister Hanna. She thinks Madelyn's reading will disturb you."

Mother chuckled. "I'll speak to her. You go on now and enjoy yourself." She waved me off as she picked up her fork. I hoped she would eat well, even though I wouldn't be there to prod her along. These last few days, she'd been eating less and less, and I worried she wouldn't build her strength on so little nourishment.

Excitement bubbled deep within my chest when I caught sight of Ritt standing alongside Madelyn and two of the other children in the backyard. Hiking her dress a few inches, Madelyn bounded toward me and reached for the quilt I carried in my arms.

"I'll spread it out for us to sit on." She glanced over her shoulder. "Ritt said he wanted to hear me read."

I handed her the quilt. "I am pleased your brother wants to see how much you've progressed."

Madelyn spun around to face me. "I think he is more pleased to spend time with you." She ran toward her brother before I could correct her assumption.

My heart pounded an erratic beat as he waved to me. I hoped what Madelyn said was true. Had Ritt set aside the differences that had come between us? In my mind, there was no reason why Nathan or his job assignment at the mill should cause problems, but Ritt hadn't been so sure.

With the help of the other girls, Madelyn spread the quilt beneath a large elm tree and plopped down with her book. The group had formed a circle and only one opening remained. She patted the quilt as I approached. "You can sit between us."

I glanced at Ritt. "It might be better if you scooted over and sat between your brother and me. That way, we can both watch as you read and make certain you're not making any mistakes."

"This space is gut." Ritt tapped the same spot his sister had pointed to a moment earlier. "You are the teacher. I will close my eyes and listen."

I liked the idea of sitting next to him, so I didn't argue any further. If anyone saw us, we would both receive a reprimand, but I was willing to take the chance. A chance I'd been opposed to taking with Nathan. That truth settled in the back of my mind as I took my place in the circle. I had Madelyn read last so that Ritt wouldn't leave early. If listening while I worked with the other girls bothered him, he gave no indication. When Madelyn's turn arrived, he made a point to close his eyes and listen.

She made only one slight mistake while reading the lesson in English, and I praised her lavishly when she finished. "If you were in my class at the school in Kansas City, I would use my blue ink and draw a star beside your name. You did an excellent job with your lessons today."

Ritt smiled at his sister. "For sure, you have made great progress, Madelyn. Soon you will be able to read English better than I do."

I looked around the group. "All of you are wonderful students. You have worked hard to complete your reading and English lessons, but now it is time to work on your arithmetic." I motioned to a large basket I'd placed near the tree. "Would you bring that to me, Madelyn?"

Sister Bertha had given me permission to use a number of items from the kitchen house to help with our lesson. "Instead of repeating your addition and subtraction or going over your multiplication tables, I thought it might be more fun if we did something special."

Eveline stepped closer and peered into the basket. "We are going to cook?"

Madelyn giggled. "There is no stove. How could we cook? Why did you bring these things, Sister Jancey?"

I removed a loaf of bread that Sister Bertha had sliced for me, along with several large apples.

"We are going to have bread and apples?" Anna asked, her eyes radiating excitement.

"First we are going to see how many people we could serve from this loaf of bread. Each of you count and see how many sandwiches you could make from this loaf."

I watched as the girls carefully counted the slices. Anna's hand shot into the air and I nodded at her. "I could make ten if I didn't use the end pieces."

"I like the end pieces so I would make eleven. Besides, we shouldn't waste," Eveline said.

I chuckled. "Let's agree that we have eleven sandwiches, and we cut them in half. Then how many people will get a sandwich?"

Madelyn caught her lower lip between her teeth and frowned. Moments later, she raised her hand. "Twenty-two."

"Exactly right. That's very good. Now if we cut those eleven sandwiches into four pieces how many people could we serve at the noonday meal?"

Bretta shook her head. "That will not work, Miss Jancey."

I met the girl's intent gaze. "Why not?"

"Everyone would still be hungry, because they wouldn't get enough to eat."

Ritt burst into laughter. "She is right. What man would be happy with one-fourth of a sandwich?"

Hands perched on her hips, Madelyn turned toward her brother. "A starving man would not turn down one-fourth of a sandwich."

"Ja, you have an answer for everything, Madelyn." Ritt grinned at the girl and tousled her hair. "But this time, I will agree that you are right. A starving man would be happy for even a crust of bread."

After cutting the apples into slices, we continued to work on math skills. "I like subtraction the most," Anna said.

I chuckled and nodded. All of the girls wanted to practice subtraction when they realized they would be permitted to eat slices of apple or squares of bread. By the time they'd eaten the apples and some of the bread, I declared their skills improved and the lesson complete, but the girls decided they wanted to study spelling words.

"We're going to move over by the back steps, where the light is better." Madelyn picked up her books and gestured to the other girls.

I started to get up, but Madelyn shook her head. "You can stay here. If we have a question, we'll come and ask."

I agreed, certain the girls wanted a little time to share some secrets while they studied. Books in hand, they hurried away before I could change my mind.

"You are a gut teacher, Jancey," Ritt told me. "You are patient and kind, and that makes them want to please you. You have a special gift with children. I see how you help each one in a special way."

Ritt's words warmed my heart. "Each child has the ability to learn, and I try to remember that every child is unique. They learn in different ways. What works with one might not work with another. A good teacher keeps trying different keys until she finds the right one for each child." I turned my hand as if unlocking a door. "Once you find the right key, it opens a whole new world to them. You can see the excitement in their eyes, and when that happens, it thrills me."

Ritt pulled several blades of grass and twisted them between his fingers. "It is easy to hear excitement in your voice when you talk about teaching. I am sure you miss being at the school in Kansas City."

He held me with his gaze as the setting sun cast a gold glint in his hazel eyes. I swallowed hard and tried to look away, but I couldn't. A pleasant feeling tickled alive deep within my stomach, and I tried to concentrate on what Ritt had said.

"You're right. I do miss the children. Don't misunderstand. I very much enjoy being in the colonies, but teaching gives me a feeling of purpose. I have that same feeling when I'm teaching Madelyn and her friends."

He looked down at the blades of grass he held between his thumb and forefinger. When he didn't comment, I told him I'd received letters from some of the children at the orphanage. "I know it may sound silly, but reading their letters makes me feel closer to them."

"Nein. It is not silly. I can understand how it would help to ease the pain of leaving them. I am sure everyone at the orphanage misses you."

"There is a shortage of money, so they haven't hired anyone to replace me. Miss Manchester—she teaches the older students—wrote and said the younger children are falling behind." I sighed. "I do wish the board of directors would see how important it is to have a teacher for the younger children. You can't have so many children in one classroom and expect any of them to learn, but they say there isn't sufficient money."

Ritt frowned. "This I do not understand. They should have the funds you received when you worked there. Why could they not use that money to pay a new teacher?"

I shook my head. "I didn't receive any pay."

He tipped his head to the side. "I thought everyone who lived outside the colonies received pay for their work."

"I knew the orphanage had financial problems. My father suggested I work without pay since he could easily support our family. I considered my work an offering to the Lord—and the children."

"So at least one thing did not change for you when you moved to Middle Amana: You still receive no money for your work." He leaned back against the tree trunk and bent his knees until they almost touched his chest. "You have given up a great deal to be here among us. I saw the light in your eyes when you spoke of teaching at the orphanage, and I saw sadness replace that light when you told me the children are not learning so well now that you are gone."

"I won't deny that I miss teaching the children or that I am sad they no longer have the attention they need, but I am thankful for the opportunity to help Madelyn and some of the other Amana children during the evenings."

The glimmer I'd detected earlier in his eyes faded. "Ja, but it is not the same, is it?"

"Not exactly, but I want to be here. I couldn't bear to be away from my mother when she needs me. I made a choice to come here, Ritt, and I'm not sorry. Is that what you think? That I'm unhappy to be here?"

I needed to make him understand that I hadn't come here because I'd been forced to, or because I'd felt obligated. I wanted him to know that I came because I wanted to be here. I thought I'd made it clear before, but maybe when Nathan arrived, Ritt decided I hadn't been honest with him.

He tossed the pieces of grass aside and looked at me. "I want to tell you what is in my heart so there are no walls between us."

My heart skipped a beat and I bobbed my head, eager to hear him say he cared for me and was thankful I'd come here. "I would like that."

"I do not think it is a secret that I have come to care for you as more than a friend, but I have decided that I must put a guard on my heart."

My spirits soared but then plummeted so quickly that my stomach felt as though it had landed in my throat. "W-why?"

"I can see that you still have strong ties to your former life." When I opened my mouth to object, he placed a finger on my lips. "Let me finish and then you can speak. Ja?"

I didn't want to agree. I wanted to shout the objection that remained on my tongue, but I merely gave a slight nod.

"I cannot risk my heart when I am uncertain if you can ever be happy in Amana." He traced his finger along the stitches that formed a flower in the quilt. "And I could never ask you to give up teaching. If you remain here, you will never be able to go into a classroom and teach as you did in Kansas City. It is clear you are a gut teacher, and I believe you want to use the talents God has given you."

A sense of panic now assailed me. How would we ever know if we were meant for each other if he planned to distance himself from me? I needed to convince him he was wrong. "I may never be able to teach in a classroom again, but that doesn't mean I can't help some children in my spare time. I've been content since coming here, and I don't believe that will change."

Tenderness shone in his eyes as he looked at me. "I don't know if you can be completely honest with yourself right now. Your mother is ill and you want to be here to help care for her. But if the time arrives when you are no longer tied to the colonies by your mother's illness, you may want to return to the orphanage." He placed his hand over his heart. "Your heart may always be with those children. I can see how much you love them and what happiness they bring to you. Later, you may decide you cannot find that same happiness or contentment here. It is better if we remain only friends. To do otherwise could cause great pain for both of us."

I swallowed the lump in my throat. "I should go and check on the girls."

Pushing to my feet, I wondered how everything had gone so wrong so quickly. I had hoped Ritt wanted to mend any differences between us and move forward. I had hoped to explain that I never made a commitment to Nathan. And I had hoped to talk to him about Thomas and the hidden money. But none of those discussions would happen now.

The girls had finished their studies and were chattering about the onion harvest when I approached. "It's getting dark. I think it's time for you girls to walk home and for Madelyn and me to go inside."

The girls folded their papers, gathered their books, and scurried off with hasty good-byes. I turned and walked toward the front of the house while Madelyn chattered. I stopped short and glanced over my shoulder when Ritt called my name.

He was holding the folded quilt in his arms. "You forgot your quilt."

His hand brushed against mine when he passed me the quilt, and a shiver raced up my arm. How I longed to tell him he was wrong—that I could remain here if he would only declare his love for me and ask me to stay. But a look of determination shone in his eyes. I realized that nothing I said would change his mind—at least not tonight.

CHAPTER 21

Tears threatened as I bid Ritt and Madelyn a quick farewell. I turned and hurried inside, for I didn't want Madelyn to suspect anything was amiss. As I entered the front door, my father called to me from the bedroom. When I opened the door, he motioned toward my mother.

"Your mother has a terrible headache. She needs medicine from the apothecary. If you ring the bell near the front door, Brother Otto will come and help you. He knows what to mix for her. Brother Rudolf has given him the information."

I glanced out the window at the darkening sky. I didn't fear walking alone after dark, but it wasn't the custom for women to walk alone at night in the colonies.

"I would go, but your mother doesn't want me to leave her." He lowered his voice. "You'll be fine. If anyone asks why you're out, explain the situation and there will be no problem." His brow furrowed. "Is anything wrong?"

I forced a smile. "No. Why do you ask?"

He gave a slight shrug. "You appeared sad when you came to the door."

"Everything is fine. I'll be back as soon as I can." I turned and hurried away before he could quiz me further.

My shoes clattered on the wooden sidewalk, and my thoughts immediately returned to the recent conversation with Ritt. I didn't want to believe he was right, but maybe there was some truth to what he'd said. Maybe I wouldn't remain happy in the colonies. I knew Ritt hadn't wanted to speak of my mother's health, but what he was thinking had been obvious. Would I be willing to live here for the rest of my life? I'd thought I would, but now I wondered if he might be correct. Would I be content if I never was able to teach in a classroom again?

Unbidden tears streamed down my cheeks. I had hoped to gain Ritt's insight about Thomas and the money I'd discovered in the men's quarters. Instead, I'd lost hope of a future with him, and I had no one to guide me through this mess with Thomas. I became lost in my thoughts and yelped when a hand grasped my arm.

"It's me."

My heart beat an erratic rhythm as an arm circled my shoulder. I twisted around and looked up. "Nathan! Where did you come from?" Relief flooded over me, and instead of pulling away, I leaned against him. "I was so absorbed in my own thoughts I didn't hear you."

"I worked late tonight, and rather than going straight to the dormitory, I decided to take a walk and clear my head." He ran his fingers through his dark brown hair. "After listening to the noise of the machinery, I wanted to enjoy the quiet sounds of the night before I turned in. What about you? Why are you out here alone?"

Instead of his usual accusatory tone, his voice bore a hint of kindness and concern that both surprised and pleased me. Moonlight shimmered over us as he continued to walk alongside me with his arm around my shoulder. I explained Mother's need for medicine from the apothecary and her desire that Father remain with her. He reached around me with his free arm and wiped a stray tear from my cheek.

Gently squeezing my shoulder, he drew me to a halt and looked into my eyes.

"Are these tears because of your mother's illness?"

"Yes. She does well for a few days but then takes a downward turn. Each time that happens it takes longer for her to rebound. I'm worried that soon she won't be able to gather enough strength to . . ." I couldn't bear to say the words.

Nathan cupped my cheek and looked into my eyes. "I know this is very difficult for you, Jancey, and I haven't provided the love and support you need while going through all these changes. Since the other day, I've been doing a lot of thinking. I should be more thoughtful. I know you're very close to your mother. Sometimes that's hard for me to understand because I didn't share a close bond with my family. I suppose that's no excuse for my behavior, but—"

"But you want me to understand—and I do. However, you must give that same kind of understanding to me, Nathan."

He nodded. "I know. Even after I arrived here, I didn't give you the compassion you deserved. I was determined I could persuade you to return to Kansas City, so I didn't consider what you needed or wanted. I hope you'll give me another chance to prove my love."

I could scarcely believe my ears. This was a side of Nathan I had never experienced. Granted, he'd shown an occasional glimmer of kindness, but he'd never before requested forgiveness. I didn't know what had caused the transformation, but I wondered if God had been at work in Nathan's life. If so, it couldn't have happened at a more opportune time.

I wasn't certain I could trust this change, but he'd arrived when I'd most needed someone. With his ties to the outside, Nathan could be exactly who I needed to help me. He might even know of the bank robbery, especially since Forsythe Construction conducted all its banking at the National Commerce Bank. Perhaps he'd even talked to my father about the incident when it occurred. A sense of relief swept over me as I decided Nathan was the better choice to help me with this matter.

He was staring at me, waiting.

"I must agree that you've been less understanding than I would have expected."

His features tightened a degree. I hadn't said what he'd wanted to hear.

"However, I am pleased by this sudden change and hope it will prove permanent. I find you much more appealing when you're kind and thoughtful."

"I'm pleased to hear you find me appealing. Does that mean you've accepted my apology?"

He winked and brushed a loose strand of hair from my cheek. My pulse didn't quicken when Nathan touched my hand or squeezed my shoulder—not like it did when Ritt drew near. I tried to force thoughts of Ritt from my mind.

"I accept your apology, Nathan, and I do appreciate the things you've said." When a tear escaped and slipped down my cheek, he frowned.

"What is this? I thought you were pleased by the changes you'd seen in me. Is there more than the illness with your mother that's bothering you?" He lifted my chin. "You can tell me anything, Jancey. I want to help you however I can."

My emotions were a jumble. I wasn't sure I should confide in Nathan, but there truly was no other choice. "I have to tell you something important. Promise you won't become angry with me if I tell you."

"I don't know what could be so terrible that it would make you believe I'd become angry with you, but I promise."

We were only a short distance from the apothecary. "Let me get the headache powders for Mother first. I'll tell you on the way home." He started to follow me, but I held up my hand. "You should wait out here. It is better if Brother Otto doesn't see us together."

"You're right." He pointed to the side of the shop. "I'll stand over there, where I'll be out of sight."

I rang the bell outside the apothecary, encouraged by Nathan's unusually quick agreement. A few minutes passed before I heard footsteps and Brother Otto, who was also one of the elders, unlocked the door. He stood in the doorway and peered over his wire-rimmed glasses. "Your Mutter is in need of something, Sister Jancey?"

"She has a severe headache and my father sent me for headache powders. He said you know what the doctor prescribed for her."

He waved me inside. "Your poor Mutter is having a time with all this pain. Give me a few minutes and I will have it ready for you." He shuffled around the counter and withdrew several bottles from the shelf behind him. Using a mortar and pestle, he mashed up a concoction, poured the powder onto a piece of white paper, and secured the corners.

"Your Vater knows how much to give her." He handed me the packet before he pushed his glasses high on his nose. "I hope this will give her some relief."

After thanking Brother Otto, I placed the packet in my skirt pocket and departed. I knew Nathan was waiting for me, yet I startled when he stepped around the corner.

He glanced at my hand. "You got the medicine?"

"Yes." I patted my skirt. "It's in my pocket."

"All the time you've been inside, I've been trying to think what you are going to tell me. Please don't make me wait any longer."

I inhaled a deep breath and matched his gait. "This has to do with Thomas Kingman."

His eyebrows arched high on his forehead. "Thomas? The fellow who has the bunk next to mine in the dormitory?"

"Yes. I've been trying to help him find his sister, Kathleen."

Nathan stopped short. "How do you know his sister?"

I waved him forward. "We need to keep walking. Mother needs her medicine." He hurried and came alongside me. "I don't really know Kathleen, but she lived at the orphanage in Kansas City years ago." I explained how I'd seen the photograph on his trunk, and my subsequent meeting with Thomas.

Even with only the moonlight, I could see his features tighten into a frown. "You met Thomas alone out in the woods? How could you do something so foolish, Jancey? He's a complete stranger who could have done you great harm."

"I'll admit it wasn't wise, but when I saw that picture, I couldn't resist. I had to know who she was—and he has always been a perfect gentleman around me."

"Always? How many times have you met with him?"

"Only one time. After that, we exchanged notes." I hesitated.

"He did come into the dormitory one time while I was cleaning, and we talked for a few minutes, but I met him out in the woods only one time."

Nathan's frown softened. "I'm pleased you decided to write notes after your first meeting. That was wise."

My earlier tension took flight. His affirmation both surprised and encouraged me. Bolstered by his unruffled behavior, I went on and explained what I'd learned about Kathleen's whereabouts thus far. "Lilly is awaiting further word from the family that adopted Kathleen, and I've promised Thomas I'll pass along any message as soon as I hear."

Creases formed across his forehead and confusion shone in his eyes. "I don't understand why this has reduced you to tears. Do you think the girl has come to some harm?"

I shook my head. "No. That's only the beginning of what I have to tell you. Once you hear the rest, you'll understand why I'm in such a state."

He waved his hand in a circular motion. "You need not worry, Jancey. Whatever it is, we'll resolve it together."

Buoyed by his support, I detailed how the bed frame had been lodged on a loose floorboard and how my curiosity had taken hold when I examined the area beneath Thomas's bed. Nathan would likely believe me as curious as a hound dog sniffing a fresh scent—and he'd be right. If I'd practiced restraint, I wouldn't be in this dilemma. I recounted how I'd reached deep into the hole and tugged on the piece of canvas.

"Hurry—what did you find?" His voice quivered with excitement.

"A bag from the National Commerce Bank of Kansas City. And it was full of money."

He chuckled. "You're joking with me. Tell me what you really found."

I grasped his arm. "This isn't a joke, Nathan. If I hadn't seen that money with my own eyes, I don't suppose I'd believe it, either, but it's true." A sliver of moonlight shone on Nathan's face, and I could see the disbelief that flickered in his eyes. "And that's not all."

"You mean there's something else?" His voice cracked and he rubbed his fingers against his throat. "I'm not sure I can handle much more."

"Yes, there was a newspaper clipping about a bank robbery at the National Commerce Bank. I took it out of the bag and have it at home. I'll show it to you when we get back to the house."

"You removed the newspaper clipping, but you didn't remove any money, did you?"

"No, of course not. I'm not a thief, Nathan!"

"I know you're not a thief, but you did remove the clipping. I thought you might have removed a bill or coin to prove you actually discovered money." He massaged his forehead. "I do remember that a bank robbery occurred back in January—or was it December?" He shook his head as if to clear his thoughts. "I know it was cold when it happened, and I do recall your father mentioning it to me. He probably remembers when it occurred. He knows the bank officers, and I bet he recalls all of the details, too." He hesitated a moment. "Why didn't you speak to him about this?"

"Father has enough worries." I bowed my head. "Besides, I didn't want to tell him I'd been digging up floorboards and sticking my nose where it didn't belong."

I didn't add that I worried he would tell the elders and they might declare me unfit to remain in the colonies. If I admitted that possibility, Nathan might decide I should speak to one of the elders.

"Do you think you could mention the bank robbery to my father and find out exactly when it happened without creating suspicion? We're not even sure when it occurred, and I have no idea when Thomas first arrived in Iowa. I asked him when he came to Middle Amana, but he didn't give me a direct answer."

We stopped outside the front door. "First let me take a look at the news clipping. Maybe that will refresh my memory. Then we'll decide what to do."

I was pleased to see Father wasn't in the parlor. "You wait here while I take the medicine to my parents' room, and then I'll get the clipping from my room."

After a light tap I opened the bedroom door. My father had drawn the upholstered chair from the other side of the room to Mother's bedside. His chin rested against his chest, but when I tiptoed inside, he awakened.

"You got the medicine?"

I handed him the packet.

"Thank you." He poured a small amount of the medicine into a glass. "You are going to bed now?"

"Not right away. Nathan is in the parlor. He was taking a walk after work and saw me, so he escorted me home."

"He should not stay too long. He needs his rest and so do you. When the next bell tolls, he should go or he'll be late getting back."

"I'll be sure to tell him, Father."

As soon as I returned to the parlor, I glanced at the clock. There wasn't any time to waste. We only had fifteen minutes before the next bell. "I'll be only a minute. I need to get the clipping from my bedroom." Nathan nodded as I hurried across the carpeted floor.

Inside my bedroom, I picked up the Bible. My fingers trembled as I flipped through the pages where I'd hidden the clipping. When I didn't immediately find the piece of newspaper, my stomach knotted. Had Father used my Bible and discovered it? I sat on the edge of the bed and tried to calm myself as I continued my search. I silently chastised myself when I finally located it in the middle of Psalms, where it had stuck between the pages. I should have checked where I'd placed it before closing the Bible. Next time I'd be more careful.

I returned to the parlor and sat down beside Nathan. "Here it is." I extended the worn piece of news clipping.

"So they already captured two of the robbers." He scanned the remainder of the article. "Too bad there's no date on the article, but why else would Thomas have that money unless he was involved in the robbery?"

I shrugged. "He's very nice. He doesn't seem like the type of person who would rob a bank. He told me he'd been saving money so he could make a proper home for his sister. Maybe that money was what he's saved."

Nathan frowned. "I thought you said it was in a bank bag and there was a lot of it. I don't see how he could save a lot of money working in a mill. And why is he here? If he was living in Kansas City, why didn't he get a job at the Watkins Woolen Mill, where he would have made a higher wage?"

"I asked him the same thing. He said he'd been paying for food and lodging in Kansas City, so he wouldn't be making much more than if he worked here."

"Doesn't make sense for him to come all the way to Iowa. Train tickets cost money and his sister may be still living in Kansas City." Nathan shook his head. "I think he's hiding from the law, and this is the perfect place to remain concealed until he's certain it's safe to return. It's proved a stroke of good fortune for him that you happened to come here, found the picture of his sister, and agreed to help him. He's probably been quite pleased with all that's happened so far."

"You may be right, but I'm afraid he'll discover this news clipping is gone. He might become suspicious and take off. Then what?"

"If he leaves, it would solve the problem, but I don't think that's going to happen anytime soon. And he's not going to take a chance by digging around in that hiding spot—one of the other men might see him. Until he's ready to take off, I think he'll leave that bag right where it's at."

I twisted my hands together. "What if I hear from Lilly? Should I tell him?"

Nathan reached for my hand. "You're trembling. There's no need to be frightened. You rest easy and I'll take care of everything. On my day off, I'll rent a horse and ride over to Marengo and send a telegram to the newspaper office to find out the date of the robbery and see if there's any description of the third robber."

The bell tolled and Nathan pushed to his feet. "You don't know how much I hate all these rules. I can't even make a decision about what time I go to bed."

After acting and sounding like a new man only moments ago, I was alarmed to hear the animosity return to Nathan's voice. Had I made a mistake and told him too much? Maybe he hadn't changed after all.

CHAPTER 22

Since our conversation under the tree, Ritt had finally acquiesced enough to visit with me on a couple of occasions, but he'd been careful to direct the conversation toward neutral topics such as my mother's health, the weather, or work. He'd also refrained from attending any of the tutoring lessons with Madelyn and the other children or from meeting me on the path after meals. I missed spending time with him, but he was doing what he'd said—guarding himself against falling in love with me. However, when I looked into his eyes, I wasn't sure that I had protected my heart soon enough.

Last evening on the way to prayer meeting, he'd been particularly kind and I truly believed I'd received an answer to my prayer. I believed that God was urging me to tell Ritt about the money. However, I'd said only a few words when Madelyn skipped to my side, eager to tell me about a new math problem she'd conquered in school that day.

Later, I determined I must not have received urging from the Lord or Madelyn wouldn't have arrived to interrupt my conversation with Ritt. Perhaps I was supposed to keep the promise I'd made to Nathan. He'd said he would take care of everything, and I'd given my word that I wouldn't confide in anyone else. If I expected Nathan to keep his vow, then surely I was supposed to do the same. If trouble of some sort arose and Ritt was involved, he could be reprimanded by the elders, while Nathan wouldn't face such consequences. Nathan might be discharged from his job at the mill and told to leave the village, but those measures wouldn't affect his future in the outside world.

Although I didn't foresee any other explanation, I still held a modicum of hope that Thomas wasn't a bank robber. No matter what Nathan said, I simply could not envision Thomas committing such a crime. I'd offered any number of prayers that we'd discover the truth, but now I feared the truth would hurt not only Thomas, but his sister, Kathleen. What if her adoptive family granted permission for her to meet with Thomas and he was later arrested for bank robbery? The girl would be devastated. If I hadn't written that first note, I wouldn't have to worry. Twice now, I'd stuck my nose where it didn't belong, and twice it had delivered trouble to my doorstep.

Still deep in thought, I hurried inside the men's quarters and nearly collided with Sister Margaret. With the onion harvest complete, she'd returned to her regular work schedule at the dormitory, and I was glad once again to have her help. However, I hadn't readjusted to her constant presence. Since her return, she'd managed to startle me at least once each day.

After bidding me good morning, Margaret gestured toward the rear door. "I have to go out and heat the water. You remember we will do the wash today. Ja?"

I hadn't remembered, but I nodded. "You go ahead and I'll strip the beds and bring the basket of sheets when I finish."

When she reached the rear door, she picked up a basket filled with some of the men's dirty clothes. She wouldn't wash those until after she'd laundered the sheets, but her kind gesture would save me an extra trip to the washhouse later in the day. While the water heated for the wash, she'd prepare a pot of coffee that would be kept hot on the stove throughout the morning, and while I remarked that it was much too warm for coffee, Sister Margaret declared she hadn't yet seen a day when it was too hot for at least several cups of the strong brew.

Working quickly, I yanked the sheets from the beds, picked up any remaining clothes that had been left on the floor, and carried the baskets to the washhouse. Sounds of the clacking looms, the whirring spinning jacks, and the rumbling carding machine filled the morning air as I crossed the distance between the dormitory and the washhouse. I'd become accustomed to the muted sounds of the machinery, but I often wondered how the men inside the mill could tolerate the noise day after day.

I'd returned from my final trip to the washhouse and was cleaning in the sleeping room when the bell tolled to announce the midmorning break. After dusting the windowsills behind the beds, I turned and gasped when I caught sight of Thomas in the doorway. I didn't know how long he'd been standing there staring at me, but his eyes were as cold as ice. His lips were clamped in a tight line, and the moment I saw him, he spun on his heel and strode off.

My heart pounded in my chest and I tried to slow my breathing. Had Nathan been wrong? Had Thomas checked the money bag and discovered the newspaper clipping was missing? Was this his way of letting me know he'd caught me? My palms turned damp and I wiped them down the front of my apron. Any other time he'd caught me alone, he'd asked questions or at least spoken to me. But not today. Not any mention of Kathleen or any questions about a letter from Lilly—just a cold stare. I needed to remain calm, but how could I?

I wanted to talk to Nathan. Maybe he'd said something to Thomas. There wouldn't be time before the men returned from their break. Besides, I could hardly stand in the doorway and wave to Nathan. I could picture the workers' looks of astonishment if I should do such a thing. A nervous giggle escaped my lips.

"What is so funny?"

I jumped and pressed my palm against my chest. "Sister Margaret. You startled me again."

"You are the most easily alarmed person I have ever met. What is it that causes such uneasiness in you?"

"I-I don't know. I didn't hear you enter and you surprised me. There is no other explanation."

She tipped her head to the side and looked at me. "When I was a little girl, my Mutter told me such jumpiness was a sure sign I was hiding something." Her eyes gleamed in the bright sunlight that shone through the dormitory windows. "Are you hiding something?"

"No, of course not." I cleared my throat. "Is it time to hang the sheets?"

"Ja, the first ones are ready." Margaret grinned at me. "There was one other thing my Mutter used to say to me about jumpiness—do you want to know what it was?" I really didn't want to know, but she didn't wait for a reply. "Mutter said when I was quick to change the topic, I was for sure hiding something." She waved me forward and strode toward the rear door. "My Mutter is a very smart woman."

"I'm sure she is, but I'm not hiding anything. I only mentioned the laundry because . . ."

Before I could finish my sentence, Margaret had cleared the doorway and was out of earshot. She'd been quite observant, and I wondered if Thomas had been just as perceptive. Was she guessing or did she know what I'd discovered? No, that was impossible. Neither Thomas nor Nathan would have talked to Margaret, and she'd been busy with the onion harvest when I found the money. I was letting my imagination run away with me.

When the next load of wash was ready to hang, Sister Margaret returned and, from outside the door, hollered, "Don't jump, Sister Jancey, I'm coming inside!" I soon grew weary of her shouted announcements, but I could see she thought it great fun. I considered asking her to stop but decided I should let her enjoy herself—at least a little while longer.

We were in the midst of hanging another basket of clothes when the bell tolled, announcing it was time to depart for the noonday meal. "You go ahead. It takes longer for you to get to your Küche. I can finish hanging these shirts and still have time to get to the kitchen house in time."

"Are you sure? We can leave them until after lunch."

I leaned down and picked up one of the shirts and gave it a snap before pinning it to the line. "You go on. I'll make it with time to spare."

With a quick wave, Margaret turned and hurried off. I grabbed another shirt, snapped it in the air, removed a wooden clothespin from my pocket, and secured it on the line. Over the weeks, I'd developed a kind of rhythm and had grown to enjoy this particular task, probably because being outdoors reminded me of playing button, button, who's got the button or duck, duck, goose with the children at the orphanage.

I reached for the last shirt at the bottom of the basket, but a light tap on the shoulder caused me to startle. I jumped and my foot found a dip in the ground. My ankle twisted and I toppled to the ground, landing in a most unladylike position. I don't know if Thomas or I looked more horrified.

He stooped down in front of me, which only served to make matters worse. My skirt was bunched beneath me and hiked up as far as my knees. I'd never been so appalled in my life. Anger replaced my earlier worries, and I pointed a finger at his nose.

"Why do you insist on sneaking up on me? Now look what you've done." The joint throbbed inside my leather shoe. "I've injured my ankle because of you."

"It's not as though I pushed you down, so don't be saying it's because of me." He stretched out his hand and took hold of my shoe. "Here, let me take a look at it."

Before I could slap his hands away from my leg, a long shadow hovered over us. I looked up and gasped at the supervisor of the woolen mill. "Brother William!" Pain shot through my ankle as I pulled my foot free from Thomas's grasp.

"Sister Jancey." He gave a brief nod, then looked at Thomas. "You should go to the kitchen house, Thomas. We will talk later."

Thomas stood up. "But I want to—"

Brother William closed his eyes and pointed over his shoulder. "You will please do as I have asked or you may pack your belongings and leave. Which will it be?"

"I'm going to the kitchen house." Head bowed low, he strode toward the path without a backward glance.

Brother William kept his gaze turned from me. "You will please cover your legs, Sister Jancey."

I rolled on one hip, freed my skirt, and yanked it over my legs. My legs were covered by black cotton stockings, but my hiked-up skirt would have been considered improper even in the outside world.

The heat raced up my neck. "I am properly covered, Brother William."

Only then did he turn and look down at me. "Do you need assistance getting to your feet?"

Oh, how I wanted to say that I didn't need his help, but I knew I'd likely fall again if I tried to get up. "If you could bring me one of the wooden chairs from inside, I could use it to steady myself." I'd expected him to offer his arm instead, but he did exactly as I requested.

Moments later, Brother William returned and placed the chair beside me. "I will hold the back of the chair so that it does not topple over. Until you are sure the ankle is only sprained, you should keep weight off of it. Push up on your uninjured foot and sit on the chair." Once I made it onto the chair, Brother William gave a firm nod. "Take off your shoe in case the foot and ankle swell, and stay on the chair while I go to the kitchen house and get some ice. We will talk when I return."

I wanted to tell him I'd prefer to talk now and wait for the ice, but from the stern look in Brother William's eyes, I knew he would brook no argument. I leaned forward, removed my shoe, and propped my injured leg across my other knee. The ankle wasn't broken, of that I was certain. It had swollen a bit, but massaging seemed to help.

An eternity seemed to pass before Brother William returned. He carried a bucket containing small chunks of ice that had already begun to thaw in the rising summer heat.

"Sister Bertha was kind enough to give me ice from the cellar. You are fortunate this was one of her delivery days for the ice, or she would not have had this much to spare."

"I'll be sure to thank her." I offered a feeble smile, but his lips remained fixed in that same tight line I'd observed when he saw Thomas leaning over me.

He handed me a cotton towel. "Wrap some ice in the cloth and then hold it to your ankle." His eyes remained fixed on the bucket of ice. "Do you think you need Brother Rudolf?"

I shook my head. I didn't want to bother the doctor for a sprained ankle. "I'm sure it's only a sprain. By later this afternoon, it should be fine—especially since I have the ice." I smiled again, but he remained expressionless.

"Gut." He folded his arms across his chest and rested his back against a nearby tree. "Now you will tell me what was happening between you and Thomas Kingman. And be sure you are truthful, Sister Jancey, because I will compare your story to the one he tells me. I hope they are the same because I would not want you to add to your disobedience."

The ice had begun to melt and rivulets of cold water were dripping down my ankle—a near match for the icy fear that now gripped my heart. How I wished there was some way to know exactly what Thomas would tell Brother William, but I'd have to hope he'd do the same as I: tell the truth but keep the explanation to a minimum.

"It's all very simple, Brother William. I was hanging clothes and didn't hear Mr. Kingman approach. He startled me, and I think my ankle twisted when I turned around too quickly." I looked toward the clotheslines. "There may have been a slight dip in the grass that caused me to lose my balance and fall. I'm not certain. It happened so fast."

His arms remained folded across his chest. He nodded and tapped the fingers of his right hand against his left upper arm. "Go on. What happened next?"

I swallowed hard. "I, well, I fell down and Tho—Mr. Kingman, stooped down to see if I'd been injured. That's when you appeared."

"Ja, I see. So you will tell me please why Mr. Kingman was coming into the backyard to speak with you."

A hot breeze sailed around me, and I wondered if I might faint. No, I wouldn't faint. That would be too easy. Instead, I'd remain fully conscious and attempt to answer Brother William's questions in a suitable fashion—suitable enough that he would find me faultless. He arched his brows as if he'd tired of waiting for my response.

"I'm not positive why Mr. Kingman came to the backyard. He didn't have an opportunity to say anything before I fell down. As you know, I haven't spoken to him since then, so I think he could best answer that question."

"You should put fresh ice in the towel." He pointed to the bucket of melting ice and sighed. "I know it is difficult to learn our ways, Sister Jancey, but I am sure you have been told that meeting alone with any man, particularly an outsider, is not acceptable, ja?"

"Yes, Brother William, I have been told about that rule." After wringing out the towel, I retrieved several chunks of ice from the bucket and wrapped them in the cloth. "On a few occasions, the men return to pick up something they have forgotten or to inquire about their laundry and I must speak to them, but—"

He nodded. "Ja, and that is expected. You should not be rude to anyone and should always speak with kindness to those who are in our village, but you should not visit with the outsiders. They are lonely and could easily misinterpret your goodwill as an invitation to . . ." When he looked up, his cheeks had turned the shade of a ripe apple. "To become close friends, and that is not acceptable. Do you understand?"

My ankle throbbed and my head pounded as I nodded and mumbled my understanding.

He unfolded his arms and pushed away from the tree. "Sister Margaret should return soon. If you are unable to return to your work, you may go home and rest your ankle. I will leave that for you to decide." He stood a short distance from the chair and looked down at me. "Our life in the colonies is not for everyone, Sister Jancey."

His words stung. I thought I'd made great strides in applying the rules to my life, but it sounded as though Brother William did not agree. He was preparing to leave, but I couldn't let him go without asking the question that had been plaguing me ever since he'd seen me with Thomas.

"Do you plan to bring this before the other elders, or have I sufficiently answered your questions, Brother William?"

He looked down and the brim of his straw hat hid his eyes from my view. "I think it depends upon what Mr. Kingman tells me, Sister Jancey. If he has much the same story, then there is no need to speak to the elders." He raised his head and the stern look had returned to his eyes. "So long as you truly understand that you should refrain from being alone with the outsiders."

I wanted to mention Nathan and the fact that he was a family friend who visited our home from time to time, but I didn't think

Brother William would want to hear anything further from me at the moment—especially where it pertained to the outsiders.

"I will do my very best to follow all of the rules, Brother William, and thank you for bringing the ice to me."

"You are welcome. I will speak to Mr. Kingman, and if you are still at work this afternoon, I'll give you my final decision on this matter."

I mumbled my thanks. Now I was dependent upon what Thomas would tell Brother William. If he mentioned the letters I'd written for him and the notes we'd exchanged, Brother William would go to the elders before the sun had a chance to set in the western sky.

My hands shook as I wrung water from the dripping cloth. Surely Thomas would answer in a way that would avoid getting either of us in trouble. Still, I worried, for I didn't know if he'd discovered that the newspaper article was missing. What had he wanted?

CHAPTER 23

When Sister Margaret returned from lunch and found me sitting on a chair in the backyard, she immediately bombarded me with a litany of questions. I'd barely finished her inquisition when Brother William reappeared. Thankfully, he sent her back to the washhouse so he could speak to me in private.

His angular face didn't reveal what news he'd brought, but I continued to hold out hope that Thomas had been prudent with his answers. If not, he'd likely be headed out on the next train and I . . . well, I had no idea what might happen to me. That was the greatest fear of all. At the moment, the last thing my parents needed was another problem heaped upon them. Though I realized they would be supportive no matter the circumstances, I didn't want to be the cause of more distress in their lives.

"I took time to speak to Brother Rudolf before returning. He sent this roll of bandage and said you should wind it around your foot and up around your ankle to give support. If it doesn't feel better by tomorrow, you are to go to see him at his office."

I took the roll from Brother William and thanked him. If Brother Rudolf mentioned the sprained ankle to my mother when he called on her today, she would worry until I returned home.

"He won't say anything to my mother, will he? I wouldn't want her to worry."

Brother William ran his fingers along his jawline. "We did not discuss your Mutter, but since he is a physician, I am sure Brother Rudolf would not say anything that might cause her concern."

The look in his eyes indicated I should have known better than to ask such a foolish question. Our conversation wasn't off to a good beginning, so I could only hope it would soon improve. When Brother William didn't forge ahead and reveal the details of his conversation with Thomas, I decided to take matters into my own hands.

"I trust you've spoken to Mr. Kingman and he disclosed much the same thing as I told you earlier."

"Not quite."

I jerked my shoulders upright and leaned against the back of the chair with my spine as rigid as a broom handle. "What do you mean? In what way did our stories differ?"

Brother William once again assumed his position beneath the tree. "He said that you had been waving your arms, and he thought you were signaling to him." His eyebrows scrunched together and his forehead wrinkled into deep creases. "Did you wave to Mr. Kingman, Sister Jancey?"

I forced myself to remain calm, but anger boiled inside me like a kettle of bubbling water. "No, I did not. I don't know why he would say such a thing. I did shake out the shirts before I hung them on the line. Is that what he may have considered waving?"

Brother William hiked his shoulders in a dismissive shrug. "Perhaps, though he didn't mention the laundry—only that you waved your arms overhead and he thought you were in distress. He said he feared you had seen a snake or faced some other danger and needed help." He exhaled an exaggerated breath. "So this is not true?"

"I didn't signal him—at least not intentionally." My mind whirred like a child's spinning top. Thomas had protected himself with that story, but he hadn't done much to help me. "The only time I raised my arms was to hang the laundry."

"So you were in no danger?"

"Not until he frightened me and I fell and twisted my ankle. That's the only danger I encountered today."

"Well, I am thinking you will recover from your mishap, Sister Jancey." The hint of a smile played on the older man's lips. "I am pleased it was only a fall to the ground you suffered and not a fall from grace."

His final remark gave me hope. "So you will not report this to the elders?"

"I think not. I do not believe you were at fault in this matter. Also, I cannot say that I believe everything Mr. Kingman has told me. Whether he truly thought you signaled him or whether he hoped to befriend you remains a mystery to me. Unless I learn something to change my mind, I will not speak to the elders and Mr. Kingman will remain at his position in the mill." He stepped away from the tree. "I have warned him that he should not come around you, Sister Margaret, or any of the other sisters unless others are present. I explained this is for his protection as well as for the protection of the sisters. And now, I must return to work."

"If you have another moment, there was one other matter I wanted to mention to you, Brother William."

His shoulders slumped. "What is it, Sister Jancey?"

A persistent fly buzzed near his face until he swatted it away. For a moment, I wondered if he'd like to swat me away, as well.

"Earlier you mentioned I should not have contact with outsiders, so I wanted to remind you that Nathan Woodward is one of the outsiders working at the mill, and he is a friend of my family. He sometimes comes to our house to visit."

"Ja, your father has told me he is a family friend, and for him to visit with you is not against the rules. But you should avoid being alone with him when possible—the same as you would behave with any other man in the colonies. You should remember the rules of true godliness." He arched his brows. "You have learned them?"

"I haven't memorized them completely, Brother William."

"Ja, well, you should do so. Rule number three tells how we are to conduct ourselves with outsiders. You have read it?"

I nodded. "Yes, it says we should always conduct ourselves in such a manner so that outsiders have no reason to slander or shame the name of God."

"Ja, and what else?"

"That it is better to avoid the company of outsiders who might destroy our interest in the Lord."

"You see? You do know most of it." He patted his palm against his chest. "Now you must place it in your heart as well as your mind. Sometimes the head tells us one thing and the heart another. When both the heart and the mind are in agreement, it is a gut thing." He straightened his shoulders and prepared to depart.

"You should pray for God to direct your path, Sister Jancey. If you ask, He will show you in which world you belong, but you cannot have one foot in Amana and the other foot in the world."

I didn't tell him I'd been doing exactly what he'd suggested. Unfortunately, God's answers still didn't arrive with the speed I desired.

The ice and bandage had done their job, and by the time I'd finished my work for the day, I could walk with only a slight limp. I hadn't gone far when I heard the clatter of running footsteps and turned.

Brother William's recent warning rang in my ears as Nathan ran toward me. He was panting for breath when he reached my side. "Didn't you hear me call you?"

"No, but I've told you over and over that you shouldn't shout my name and come running after me like this. It isn't proper, and I don't want to get into any more trouble."

He tipped his head to the side. "More trouble? What'd you get in trouble for?" He grinned and tapped his finger on his chest. "I thought I was the only one who got in trouble around here."

I wanted to snatch back the words, but it was too late. "There was a misunderstanding while I was hanging clothes, but it's been resolved."

"What'd you do, hang the sheets the wrong way?" He chuckled. "I bet there's even a rule about how to hang the clothes, isn't there?"

I decided to give him only a meager answer and hope it would suffice. "Most women have a certain way they prefer to hang clothes."

"And I'm guessing Sister Margaret has been hanging clothes

for enough years that she can spot a crooked clothespin from a mile away."

I smiled and let him believe he was right, although I felt like a traitor for not defending Margaret. We'd gone only a short distance when he stopped and looked at my foot.

"Are you limping? What happened?"

His eyes shone with concern, and I didn't miss the alarm in his voice. He'd never shown much sympathy during my mother's illness, so I was taken aback that a slight limp would elicit such compassion. I never knew which Nathan would appear—the one who wanted to make me happy or the one who wanted to control me—the one who was considerate or the one who was insensitive. Since his arrival, he'd been as changeable as a chameleon, but I liked some of these recent changes and hoped they would continue.

"I twisted my ankle while I was hanging clothes. It's much better. By tomorrow, I'll be as good as new."

"Or it will be so swollen you won't be able to walk at all." He frowned. "I know you don't want to hear me say this again, Jancey, but this is no life for you. I want to give you the kind of life you deserve. A life where someone else takes care of household chores and you can do charity work at the orphanage or spend your afternoons enjoying tea with lady friends." He pointed to my sunbonnet. "Even wearing that hat doesn't completely protect you. Your complexion is already showing signs of too much sun. Can't you see this isn't where we belong?"

He'd been so kind and gentle, I didn't want to tell him there was no "we." Instead, I simply said he should feel no obligation to remain there. "I have prayed and asked the Lord to direct my future, and though I know what you want, I'm not sure where

He is leading me. I'm sorry, but I can't give you the answer you desire."

When he said he understood, I believed him—almost.

After going to bed, thoughts of Ritt, Nathan, and Thomas jumped around in my mind like a group of children playing hopscotch. All three of them had snatched a piece of my heart, but each in a different way.

Ritt's caring and kind heart, his truthful nature, and his dedication to the Lord made me want to consider a future in Amana. How could I find fault with a man who prayed for my mother and offered quiet strength to my life? Yet I'd been disappointed when he'd revealed his feelings for me but then pulled away. I admired the fact that he'd been forthright and told me he would not leave the colonies. And I knew he was right: If I remained here, it should be through God's leading, not due to the influence of others. In my heart, I had hoped he would woo me and tell me he couldn't bear to have me leave Amana, but he knew my commitment must first be to God. He was truly an upright man. A man who would make any woman a fine husband.

Rolling onto my side, I bunched the pillow beneath my head. I had to admit that Nathan had taken up a small corner of my heart, as well. Not because of his belief in God, for Nathan avowed he controlled his own path and didn't need religion or the church—unless it would provide him with the desired social contacts. His lack of faith plagued me, but I did admire his determination to be successful in spite of his early life. And though I'd observed occasional good changes in him over the past weeks, I'd also noticed they never lasted for long. I worried Nathan told me what he believed I wanted to hear rather than telling me what he truly believed. Without God, I wasn't sure Nathan could be the attentive, thoughtful, compassionate husband I desired.

And then there was Thomas. He wasn't a man who wanted to win my heart, but he'd stolen a small piece of it—not in any romantic way, but because of his desire to help his sister. Even though my association with Thomas had created all sorts of difficulties and recently raised some troubling questions, I still desired to help him if I could.

After a night of fitful dreams, I awoke with one thought in mind: I was going to return the newspaper clipping to its proper place. Perhaps Nathan would never ask to see it again, but if he did, I'd tell him the truth. Even though he'd told me to keep the clipping and leave everything to him, I no longer wanted the paper in my possession. I'd still depend upon him to investigate the bank robbery through his telegraph messages, but as soon as I found an opportunity, I was going to return the article to that bag hidden beneath the floorboards.

I had completed my breakfast when Sister Bertha signaled to me from the kitchen. As soon as we'd recited the after-meal prayer, I wove my way through the departing sisters. They were going one direction while I went the opposite, and for a few moments, I felt like a fish swimming upstream. "You wanted to see me, Sister Bertha?"

The plump woman swiped her hands on her apron and pointed to a basket. "I would like Sister Hanna to remain here so she can begin to make noodles for the noonday meal. You can take breakfast to your Mutter, ja?"

"Yes, of course." I grabbed the basket handles and departed out the kitchen door. I hoped Margaret wouldn't think that my ankle was posing problems and I'd been required to remain abed. She'd likely be worried when I didn't appear on time. Instead of turning toward home, I decided to stop at the dormitory and let her know before I headed for home.

I circled around the Küche and down the path toward the men's quarters. The other workers had departed before me, and the only sounds were birds twittering overhead. Soon the mill machinery would block out any birdsong, but for a few minutes more, I could enjoy the sweet music.

"*Psst.* Jancey! Over here."

I stopped in my tracks and looked toward the trees. "Nathan? Is that you?" A prick of irritation rose in my chest. Nathan had once again needlessly broken the rules. What if someone saw us?

He stepped from behind a tree. "Yes. I looked for you after breakfast, and when I didn't see you on the path, I was worried." He glanced down. "How is your leg? I thought it might be worse today."

"My ankle is fine. Surely you saw me in the Küche and could see I wasn't having any trouble. I'm not even limping."

He frowned. "You tell me you want a man who is caring, but you become angry when I am worried about you. After listening to you lately, I realize I wasn't a good suitor while we were in Kansas City, and I wanted to show you that I can be the kind of man you say you desire. I want to make you happy and provide you with the life you deserve. I've been doing everything possible to make that happen."

"Thank you, Nathan. I shouldn't have snapped at you, but both of us will be in trouble—particularly me—if we're seen alone out here. I need to stop by the dormitory before taking Mother her breakfast. I didn't want Margaret to worry when I was late." The warning bell rang in the distance. "If you don't hurry, you're going to be in trouble. Thank you for your concern, but please go on. I'll wait a minute or two before I continue down the path, just in case someone should be watching."

I could see that my words didn't completely appease him, but he departed. I waited by one of the tall pines for a couple minutes and then continued to the men's quarters. Margaret was standing in the doorway looking toward the path as I approached. I waved to her and picked up my pace.

"I'm sorry to be late." I lifted the basket a little higher. "I had to pick up breakfast for my mother. Sister Hanna needs to remain in the Küche this morning, so I'll need to go home for a short time. I didn't want you to worry about me."

Her lips curved in a generous smile. "I am glad you stopped by. Already I was worried your ankle was swollen and you would need to remain at home today." She glanced at my foot. "Is gut you are doing so well. Go on and take your Mutter's breakfast. I will be in the washhouse doing the ironing. It is cooler out there."

I wasn't sure it would be cool anywhere, especially with the fire already stoked to heat the irons, but Sister Margaret's news pleased me. If I hurried, I could deliver Mother's breakfast, return to the dormitory, and put the news clipping back in place, all before Margaret completed the ironing.

Thankful Mother hadn't needed me to remain at home with her, I walked to work as fast as my ankle would permit. Unfortunately, the quick pace wasn't wise. By the time I entered the dormitory, a dull ache had spread around my ankle and downward into the arch of my foot. I considered going directly to Thomas's bed but decided first to check on Margaret's progress. I didn't know how much ironing she had in her basket. If she hadn't much, she'd be almost finished, and I didn't want her walking in on me while I was in the midst of pulling up the floorboards.

I sat down only long enough to massage my ankle and then proceeded across the yard to the washhouse. I called out to Margaret as I approached and then stepped inside. "I wanted to let you know that I've returned. I'll go back and start cleaning." I looked in the basket that sat near the ironing board. "It looks like you still have quite a bit left before you finish."

"Ja, I will be here until time for the noonday meal—and maybe even after that. There is more ironing than usual this week." Removing a handkerchief from her pocket, she wiped away the perspiration that dotted her forehead.

A wave of guilt washed over me. "I can come out and relieve you in an hour or so if you'd like."

Sister Margaret chuckled and shook her head. "You remember the last time you tried your hand at ironing clothes? I had to dampen them down and start over."

"I won't learn unless I try."

She bobbed her head. "Is true, but you have other talents. Even with practice, I do not believe ironing is your gift, Sister Jancey."

I laughed and nodded. "You're probably right, but if you change your mind, I'd be willing to have you instruct me while I try again."

"Nein. We both have work to complete. There isn't time for lessons today." She turned back to the shirt and pressed the iron across the yoke.

Her return to work signaled our conversation had ended, so I strolled back to the men's quarters, relieved there would be sufficient time to return the clipping. Once inside the dormitory, I went directly to Thomas's bed, shoved it a short distance, and knelt down. I silently cheered when the floorboards lifted without much effort. "Probably because I loosened them so much the last time," I muttered.

I reached inside the hole, but my breath caught in my throat as I stretched my hand further inside and found nothing. No bag, no money—the space was completely empty. I captured my lower lip between my teeth, fear taking hold as I leaned forward to gain a better position. I spread my fingers, but felt nothing except an empty space.

I pushed back to my knees and stared into the dark, barren hole. Instead of returning the news clipping, I replaced the floorboards, shoved the bed to its former position, and dropped to the side of the bed. Panic gripped me and I glanced around the room, feeling like an animal in a trap.

Where was the money? Thomas must have decided to remove it after seeing the news clipping was missing. I stared at the trunk beside his bed and noticed a note beneath Kathleen's picture. My fingers trembled as I set aside the picture and unfolded the note.

"Where is it?"

I read the three words and gasped. Did he believe I'd taken his money?

CHAPTER 24

My mind was in a whirl. I didn't know what I should do. I'd prayed, but so far I still hadn't received an answer.

Telling Nathan wouldn't be wise. He'd instructed me to leave things to him, but I'd done the exact opposite. He was sure to be angry when he discovered I'd taken matters into my own hands. I could confide in Ritt if an opportunity presented itself, but I doubted that would happen. Besides, Brother William might see me and reprimand both of us, and I didn't want to cause problems for Ritt.

I needed to keep my wits about me and hope an answer would soon arrive. Above all else, I needed to avoid Thomas, even if it meant sticking close to Margaret's side until this matter was resolved. What if Thomas left work and came to the dormitory and confronted me? The mere thought created a shiver of fear that caused my entire body to tremble.

Instead of remaining inside any longer, I hurried out the back door to the washhouse. "How are you coming along on the ironing, Margaret?"

She looked at me as though I'd lost my buttons. "You were out here only a short time ago, and I told you I wouldn't be finished until noon. Nothing has happened to change that. You have finished your cleaning?"

"Not all of it, but I was thinking I'd really like to learn to iron. The cleaning can wait. I doubt the men will notice if I haven't dusted."

I wasn't sure she'd agree since she'd said ironing wasn't my gift, but I planned to stay until I convinced her I could learn.

Her lips drooped into an upside-down U. "I don't think it is wise. You've tried before and failed. Is easier if I finish the ironing and you clean."

"I don't think ironing is so much a gift as something that can be learned. Why don't you let me try one more time?"

She didn't appear pleased by my argument, but she acquiesced. "As soon as I finish this shirt, I will give you another lesson. You should sit there and watch. Maybe you will learn a few things before you actually begin."

I sat down and focused on each stroke of the iron. Perspiration soon trickled down the sides of my face, and I wondered how Margaret managed in this heat. She returned her iron to the stove and picked up the other one that had been heating. By the time she had finished pressing the shirt, my back was wet with perspiration and I wondered if I should have remained in the dormitory.

She gestured for me to stand. "Now, you can take a turn." She pointed to the basket. "Choose one of the shirts. One that is still damp." She'd sprinkled them earlier in the morning, and with the searing heat, I imagined they'd all be as dry as dirt, but I did as she said and dug deep into the basket until my fingers touched a slightly damp piece of clothing.

I pulled the shirt out of the basket and lifted it to the ironing board. I can't say that Sister Margaret was pleased with my finished product, but when I asked to try another, she didn't argue. Instead, she set up a second board and ironed my first attempt again. My second and third shirts weren't much better than the first, but I had improved enough that Sister Margaret had ceased starting over on the ones I had just pressed.

By the time the noonday bell rang, we'd finished the last of the shirts, and as we carried them back inside, Sister Margaret lauded my efforts. "I did not think ironing was your gift, but you have proved me wrong. Soon you will be ironing as gut as any Amana woman." She beamed at me. "Next week I will let you help me again so you can practice some more."

I hadn't planned to make ironing a part of my weekly routine, but I didn't offer any objection. If Margaret wanted my help in the future, it was the least I could do.

After Margaret left, I watched at a distance as the men departed the woolen mill. If I could walk close to Ritt or Nathan, Thomas wouldn't approach me. Moments later, I saw Thomas take to the path, and I stepped from the doorway. When I saw Ritt, I hurried to close the distance between us. Earlier I'd considered waiting until all of the men were out of sight, but then I worried Thomas might be waiting for me along the way. Better to avoid taking chances.

Ritt smiled as I approached. "You had a gut morning?"

"No, I mean yes. I mean, I suppose it was fine."

I longed to confide in him, but if I explained everything, we'd be late for lunch. Unless I had time to detail how I'd first seen Kathleen's picture and the meetings with Thomas, he'd never understand all that had occurred.

His smile faded and his eyebrows dipped low on his forehead. "You are worried about something. I can see it in your eyes."

I glanced around to see if Nathan or Thomas might be nearby. "No, there's nothing." I forced a smile. "I learned to iron this morning."

"Ach! So that's what's worrying you. Ironing shirts that meet Sister Margaret's high standards would make for a difficult morning, for sure." He grinned. "Brother John tells me that no one can iron a shirt as well as Sister Margaret."

"Brother John is right. She doesn't leave an unwanted wrinkle in anything that comes off her ironing board. I'll have to iron a lot more shirts before I can ever iron as well as she does."

We were nearing the doors to the Küche, and I broke off to go to the women's door, relieved that I'd been able to stave off any further questions about my uneasy behavior. I hadn't yet entered when Sister Hanna hurried down the steps and waved to me. I ran toward her, fear taking hold when I saw the dread in her eyes.

"Your Mutter is worse and you need to go back to the house. Your Vater is there, but he asked me to send you home."

My stomach tightened in a knot. "Has he called Brother Rudolf?"

"Ja, the doctor is there, but you should go."

As I ran for home, I didn't know if the drumming in my ears was caused by my hammering heart or my pounding shoes, but the sound made me run all the faster. I could barely breathe by the time I'd arrived home. Once inside, I leaned against the door and panted for air. I could hear muffled voices coming from the bedroom, and I strained forward. A part of me wanted to know what was being said, yet another part didn't want to hear, especially if it was bad news.

"Jancey? Is that you?" My father's voice drifted from the open door, and I inhaled a deep breath.

"Yes. Should I come into the bedroom?" If the doctor was in the midst of examining my mother, I didn't want to intrude.

My father appeared in the doorway and waved me forward. "Your mother will feel better if you are in the room with her." Instead of doing his bidding, I gestured for him to come into the parlor. He crossed the room in long strides. "What is it?"

"What has the doctor told you? How bad is she?"

"He says he can't be sure. Each time she has one of these episodes, she becomes more fragile. She is very weak right now."

"Does he think . . . ?" I let the question hang in the air. My father knew what I was asking without me saying the actual words.

Before he could look away, I saw tears begin to gather in his eyes. "He says he can't say for sure. If she makes it through the night, her chances will be greatly improved. He wants one of us to stay with her at all times. If you can stay here during the remainder of the afternoon, I'll take over after work."

"Yes, of course." I heard the doctor say something to my mother, and I glanced toward the bedroom. "Do you think Sister Hanna will send someone to tell Sister Margaret I won't be back to work this afternoon?"

"I'll stop to make sure she knows. Why don't you go in and speak to the doctor so he can give you instructions about the medicine." He hesitated. "I won't go back to work if you don't feel comfortable being here alone."

This wouldn't be the first time I'd been alone with Mother when she took a turn for the worse. That had been a benefit of teaching without pay: I'd never felt guilty when I needed to remain at home to nurse Mother. The village men were in the midst of raising a large new barn, and Father had been pleased when he'd been placed in charge of the project. I worried when I wasn't by Mother's side, but Father dealt with her illness more easily if he remained busy.

"You go on, Father. We'll be fine."

He pushed down on the heavy metal door latch and pulled open the door. "I'll leave early if work is progressing well." He turned and kissed my cheek before he departed.

When I entered the bedroom, the doctor looked up and greeted me. He touched my mother's hand. "Look who has arrived, Sister Almina. Jancey has come home to sit with you." He waved me toward the empty chair on the other side of the bed. The room was warm and smelled of medicine and illness. Beads of perspiration lined my mother's forehead, and I leaned over her to remove the quilt.

She touched my hand. "Don't take it; I'm cold." Her words trembled with frailness and I glanced at the doctor.

"She's having chills. I've given her medicine to help with the fever. Once her fever is reduced, the chills will cease."

My chest tightened as he told me how to mix the medicines and when each one should be given. With each downward turn of her health, the doctor added another medicine or ordered the prescriptions be given more frequently. I was thankful Brother Rudolf had written the instructions on a sheet of paper, for I doubted whether I could remember the exact time and amount for each one.

The doctor stood and patted my shoulder. "She's stronger than she appears."

His words gave me hope, and for that I was thankful.

I had drifted off while sitting in the chair and startled awake when the front door opened. Immediately, I looked at Mother and was pleased to see she had fallen into a restful sleep—likely the work of the laudanum I'd given her an hour ago. Her fever had broken and the chills had ceased by midafternoon, but the head and body aches had persisted, so I'd followed the doctor's instructions and given her the medicine.

I unfolded my legs from beneath me and stood. My legs and back throbbed and I stretched to release the soreness. I was massaging my lower back with my right palm when my father appeared in the doorway. I touched my index finger to my lips, and he retreated.

"I'm pleased to see she is resting." He kept his voice low. "The fever?"

"It broke midafternoon. I gave her some medicine, and she's been asleep for over an hour. I pray the doctor was right that when she wakes up, she will feel much better."

"That is my prayer, as well, but we must remember that your mother's health is in God's hands."

Although I'd wanted to hear my father say he was sure she'd be fine by this evening, I knew he was right. If my mother completely recovered from her illness, it wouldn't be due to doctors or medicine. Only God could restore her to full health.

At the first clang of the dinner bell, my stomach growled a loud protest. In the excitement of returning home to care for Mother, I had missed the noonday meal.

My father grinned at the rumbling noise. "You go to supper and ask Sister Bertha if you may bring supper home to me. If there is soup or broth, you should bring some. I hope your mother will be a little hungry when she awakens."

"I would be happy to wait while you go. . . ."

Father shook his head. "I think you need food more than I do. Besides, I want to stay here." He reached into his pocket and winked. "I stopped for the mail. There was a letter from Miss Manchester."

I perched on tiptoe and kissed his cheek. "Thank you." The letter from Lilly was the second good thing that had happened today. I considered putting it into my pocket and waiting to read the contents until I returned home, but curiosity got the best of me. I slid my finger beneath the seal and withdrew the letter as I walked to the Küche.

There were several pages, so I scanned the letter until I caught sight of Thomas's name on the last page.

Mr. and Mrs. Morgan, Kathleen's adoptive parents, are willing to have Thomas come for a visit with his sister. If Kathleen decides she wants to leave and make her home with Thomas, they will not stop her. They believe she is old enough to make the best decision as to where she will be most content.

The address of the farm outside of Salina was included, along with detailed directions. Below the address, Lilly had written another brief paragraph.

The Morgans will not tell Kathleen about any of this until they are certain Thomas is going to come to Kansas. They do not want Kathleen to be disappointed if he should change his mind. They ask that Thomas write or send a telegram detailing when they should expect him to arrive. Once they have received word from him, they will tell Kathleen her brother plans to visit.

After returning the folded letter to the envelope, I placed it inside my skirt pocket. I would read the rest later when I could savor the contents. While tucking it deep within, my fingers touched the note Thomas had recently left for me near his bedside. While I'd sat in the bedroom caring for my mother, all thoughts of the accusatory note had vanished from my mind, but now my earlier fears returned with a vengeance. Did Thomas truly believe I had taken that money? And if he did, how would I ever convince him otherwise? His curt note hadn't reflected the kind and gentle Thomas I'd first met near the pond. If he'd stolen the money, what prevented him from trying to use force to retrieve it? Then again, maybe he'd had only a minute to scribble the note before leaving for work, or maybe he'd been interrupted. Either of those reasons might have caused him to be abrupt. I hoped that might be the case, for I didn't want to believe Thomas was any less than the man I'd first met.

"Jancey!"

I shaded my eyes against the sun as Nathan came running toward me.

"How is your mother? Is she any worse?"

"She seemed a little better when I left the house. Her fever broke and that's a good sign."

Though I hoped it was my imagination, I thought he appeared disappointed by my answer. "Ritt asked some of the men at the woolen mill to pray for her. He said his mother told him your mother was very ill and the doctor was worried she might not make it through the night." He pushed his hat to the back of his head. "So you think she's going to recover?" Once again, I thought I detected regret in his voice.

"That is my hope. You sound unhappy to hear she is doing better."

He shook his head. "I don't want anything to happen to her, Jancey, but I do want you to be free to begin your own life with me in Kansas City. I don't mean to sound unsympathetic, but I know you won't leave until—"

My mind whirred. How could he be so callous? I held up my hand. "You shouldn't say anything more, Nathan. If you do, there is a strong possibility I may never want to see you again."

Jutting his chin, he met my gaze. "You're the one who says people should be honest. I'm trying to be truthful about how I feel. That's all." He thrust his hands into his pockets. "But I'll take your advice. I won't say another word."

As we drew near the Küche, Nathan offered a quick apology. I wanted to believe his words were heartfelt, but when he attempted to justify his earlier thoughtless comments, I had lingering doubts that he'd really transformed.

Nathan's own interests still remained at the forefront of his thoughts, and deep down I feared it would always be so.

CHAPTER 25

During the days following my mother's latest bout of illness, Ritt stopped by our apartment several times. He carried meals to us when Sister Hanna was busy at the Küche. He even stayed to pray with me and offer words of comfort. Throughout those days, he showered me with compassion and kindness that provided water for my thirsty soul. But now that Mother's health had improved and life had returned to a normal routine, he again withdrew.

Though I hoped he would continue to visit or would appear during Madelyn's lessons, he remained at a distance. There was no doubt he was a man of his word: He would be my friend, but nothing more. At least not until I made a decision about where I would spend my future. And though I couldn't fault him for remaining true to his word, I longed to have him spend more time with me.

If he'd give me an opportunity, I would tell him about my meeting with Thomas, the bank robbery, the money I'd found that had now disappeared, and the accusatory note that I'd received from Thomas. While Mother lay ill, I'd set aside thoughts of Thomas and the money, but now that the time had arrived when I must return to work, I needed advice from someone other than Nathan. Someone who understood how such a situation should be handled in the colonies.

A nervous giggle escaped my lips. How many times had wads of money been found under the floorboards of the men's dormitory? I doubted there was any precedent for such an incident. Yet in the past, other difficult problems must have arisen that required inventive solutions. Surely Ritt could draw upon those incidents to give me a general idea of how this might be resolved. But explaining my dilemma to him wasn't going to happen unless I could get him alone long enough to have a detailed conversation. And that didn't seem likely.

I hadn't been out of the house enough to worry over an answer to Thomas's note, and I wondered if he'd left any additional messages during my absence—ones that Margaret might have discovered while dusting. I could only hope that Thomas had heard my mother was ill and I was helping care for her.

"Sister Jancey! It is gut to see you. While you were gone, Ritt gave John and me daily reports on your Mutter's health. I am so happy our prayers have been answered and she is doing better."

I was taken aback when Margaret rushed forward and wrapped me in a warm embrace. Never before had she been so demonstrative.

"I know this has been a difficult time for you." After several pats on my shoulder, she released her hold and took a backward step. "You look tired. Did you sleep well last night?"

I hadn't slept well, mostly because I'd worried about seeing Thomas this morning, a fact I couldn't share with Margaret. "Not as well as usual, but I'll be fine. I'm glad to see you. Everything is going fine with John?"

Her lips curved in a shy smile. "Ja. He is going to ask permission for us to marry, but he will wait until the orders have slowed down at the mill. If he asks now, he's afraid the elders might decide to send me to another village, and he doesn't want me to be separated from my family. Once they catch up on work at the mill, they are more likely to send him to work at the woolen mill in Main."

"He's most considerate. I'm very happy for you, Margaret."

She bobbed her head. "Ja, I didn't think any man would ever take notice of me. For a long time, I prayed Ritt would one day look in my direction, but now I'm glad he didn't show any interest. John is the right man for me. We are gut together. You understand?"

"Yes. I've noticed how happy the two of you are when you're together." I gestured to the other room. "I should begin my work."

"Ach! I almost forgot. The day your mother took ill and you had to go home, that outsider . . . what is his name?" She stared heavenward and massaged the side of her head. "The one who has the bed next to Nathan." She strolled toward the sleeping room and stared at the row of beds.

"Thomas Kingman?" Though I wasn't supposed to be familiar with the outsiders, Margaret would likely assume Nathan had mentioned Thomas's name to me.

She bobbed her head. "Ja, Thomas Kingman, that is it."

"What about him?" I tried to hide my impatience, but Margaret's revelation worried me.

"He stopped by and I am sure he was looking for you."

I arched my brows and tried to appear surprised. "For me? Why? Did he ask for me by name?"

"Nein. He doesn't speak much German, so I didn't understand, but I think he wanted to know if you were coming back to clean the room."

I hiked my shoulders in an exaggerated shrug and forced a grin. "Maybe he was afraid he'd have to make his own bed if I didn't return."

"Ja, I have never seen that happen in this place." She motioned toward the rear door. "I will be in the washhouse if you need me."

While caring for Mother, I'd lost track of the days. It didn't seem possible washday had already arrived. It seemed like only yesterday that Sister Margaret was giving me ironing lessons. Now here I was all alone in the dormitory again, and today I couldn't hide in the washhouse. Tomorrow while she ironed, I might be able to join her again, but not now, not when I needed to be cleaning and stripping beds.

My gaze remained fixed on the trunk beside Thomas's bed as I strode to the far end of the room. Was he expecting a note from me when I returned? I stopped beside his bed. The picture of Kathleen was no longer lying atop his trunk. I stared at the shabby trunk and wondered what the missing picture meant. Was this another warning of sorts? Did he hope to unnerve me by removing the picture? If that had been his plan, it had worked.

Throughout the morning, I remained alert, turning to and fro at every strange noise. When the morning bell rang to signal morning coffee break for the men, I hastened to the far side of the washhouse, where I wouldn't be seen by Margaret—or any of the men who might expect someone to be near the clotheslines hanging laundry, particularly Thomas.

Once enough time had passed for the men to make their way to the Küche, I circled around the rear of the washhouse and returned to the men's quarters. I'd maintained a close watch on my return and nothing appeared amiss as I stepped across the threshold. I glanced about and exhaled a sigh of relief, thankful when I saw no one inside.

As I continued through the room, I glanced toward Thomas's bed and a fresh wave of fear grabbed hold of me. Kathleen's picture had reappeared and was lying atop his trunk. I clasped my hand across my lips to stifle the scream that threatened. He'd been in here while I was hiding at the washhouse. It was obvious he knew that I'd returned to work. And that picture was a clear indication he expected to hear from me.

What could I say? I don't know where the money is? He would never believe me, and such a remark might anger him further. I wanted to think he still might be the same friendly young man I'd grown to admire, but his last note had put me on edge. Why hadn't I figured out a plan during those days when I'd sat beside Mother's bed? Instead, I'd forced all thoughts of Thomas and the bank money out of my mind. I needed to speak to Nathan. Maybe he'd received a return telegram regarding the bank robbery and could tell me something that would help me decide what I should tell Thomas.

I waited near the door and watched for the men to return to the mill. If I remained in plain sight, Thomas couldn't approach me. I don't know why I hadn't thought of that earlier—maybe because I would appear as if I had nothing to do except stand and stare out the doorway.

As Thomas descended the path, he cast an angry look in my direction, but I averted my gaze and watched for Nathan. When he rounded the bend, I gestured. If he could avoid Brother William's watchful eye, I was certain he would come and speak to me. He glanced over his shoulder before he came running and ducked inside the doorway.

"Your mother is doing well, I hope." His lips curved in a half-hearted smile.

"Yes, much better, thank you." His comment didn't bear much enthusiasm, but right now I was more concerned about how I was going to respond to Thomas. "Have you received any word since you sent the telegram?"

"These things can take a little time, Jancey. I would have told you if I'd heard something." He shoved his hands into his pockets. "Is that all you wanted to ask me?"

"Yes. Can't you understand that I'm worried? What if he finds out that newspaper article is missing? He's going to think it was me. I'm the only one who has enough opportunity to go through things in here." Since I'd gone against Nathan's advice, I didn't dare tell him I'd attempted to return the clipping and discovered the money was missing.

"What about Margaret? She's in here by herself part of the time, too. It could even be one of the other men. There are times when everyone's gone on their day off. Even if he checks that bag, he's not going to know it's you. Besides, he probably won't even notice. Why would he give a second thought to an old piece of newspaper when he's got all that money?"

"Perhaps you could draw Thomas into conversation and he'd reveal something to you. Have you talked to him about his time in Kansas City?" I was grasping at straws, but I had believed Nathan was going to do something significant when he said he'd take care of the matter.

"He keeps to himself and isn't interested in talking to anyone. He doesn't even join in when the men play cards. I can't force him to talk to me."

His response surprised me. Nathan was one of the most persistent men I'd ever met, so it was difficult to believe he couldn't cajole Thomas into some sort of conversation. "You will let me know as soon as you hear something, won't you?"

"Of course." He patted my shoulder. "You worry too much." His patronizing tone matched the overconfident look in his eyes. He was treating me like a child. "I told you I'd handle this and I will. Just give me the necessary time."

There wasn't any use continuing this conversation. Nathan couldn't supply any information that would help me.

When the bell tolled for the noonday break, Margaret was still in the washhouse. After hanging the last sheet, I carried the empty basket and dropped it beside the wooden tubs. Margaret swiped her damp hands down the front of her apron. "I'm off to the Küche. I'll see you after lunch."

Standing in the doorway, I watched Margaret depart and wished I could join her. Instead, I'd eat lunch at Sister Bertha's Küche, where Thomas would be sitting with the rest of the outsiders. For sure, I'd be careful to avoid looking in his direction.

The parched grass crunched beneath my feet as I walked toward the dormitory on my way to the Küche. The lack of rain had taken a toll on the flowers and trees, but today the air had cooled a little. Though it wasn't yet August, I wanted to believe I could smell a promise of fall in the air.

The thought of a cooler season rejuvenated my spirits, and

I picked up my step. Deciding to remain outdoors and enjoy the fresh air, I circled around the end of the clotheslines rather than taking the shortcut through the men's quarters. I was midway between the washhouse and the dormitory, not far from the clotheslines, when the bushes rustled. Before I could take stock of what was happening, Thomas jumped forward, grabbed my wrist, and pulled me toward the brush, where we wouldn't be easily spotted.

Anger smoldered in his eyes. I tried to pull away, but he tightened his grip on my arm. I flinched and gritted my teeth. "Let go! You're hurting me." When he didn't release his hold, I narrowed my eyes. "I'm going to scream if you don't turn me loose. What will you tell Brother William when he comes running?"

"The men have already gone up the path. They won't hear you unless you scream very loud. If you do that, I'll have to cover your mouth, and I don't think you want me to do that, do you?"

My shoulders slumped and he loosened his hold a little, but not enough that I could break loose and run—not that I'd try. He'd be able to catch me before I made it out of the backyard.

"Just tell me what you did with my money and what you know about Kathleen, and we can part ways real quicklike."

"What money? I don't know what you're talking about." I swallowed hard in an attempt to keep my voice from trembling. "I saw that note you left last week, but I didn't know what it meant then, and I don't know what it means now. Why are you asking me about money?"

"How dumb do you think I am? You're in there every day snooping around while you're supposed to be cleaning the rooms. I've seen you over by my bed, and I know you found the money. Just give it back and tell me what you've found out about Kathleen."

I could barely believe this was the same man who had been so kind to me when we'd first met, but just like Nathan, Thomas had changed before my very eyes. "You need to think about your accusation, Thomas. If I knew you had money, why would I steal it? I have no need for money here in the colonies. Besides, my father owned a large construction company back in Kansas City. If I required any money, he could easily take care of such needs."

Although my father had divested himself of his wealth, if I truly were in need of financial aid, he'd contact people who would help me.

When Thomas still hadn't released his hold, I tried again. "I would never steal from you or anyone else. Since we met, I've done nothing but try to help you." I looked at his fingers still clenched around my wrist. "And this is how you repay me?"

He looked down at his hand. "It's the only way I can get you alone to speak to me. You didn't answer my note. What am I supposed to think?"

I gasped. "You knew I was at home caring for my mother. The men talked about her illness at work. You also stopped and asked Margaret about me while I was away."

"I think you could have found a way to leave me a message if you'd really wanted to—but you didn't."

"Because there was nothing I could tell you. If you had money somewhere inside the dormitory and it is gone, you need to ask someone else, because I don't have it."

He released his hold but remained poised to strike. "If you don't have anything to say about the money, what can you tell me about Kathleen?"

After the way he'd treated me, I now wondered if Thomas should be reunited with his sister. How would he act toward her if she did something that didn't please him? I could easily give him Kathleen's address right now, but I wanted time—time to decide whether Thomas would provide his sister with a happy home or if he'd wash his hands of her if she did something that didn't please him.

"There's nothing I can tell you yet."

"So you haven't heard nothin' from your friend in Kansas City? How long does it take for her to write a letter to those people and get word back to you? I just want my money and my sister's address. Once I got those two things, I'll leave here for good." He tipped his head to the side. "Things would be easier for you if I was gone, so maybe you should write another letter to that friend of yours." His jaw twitched. "And maybe you should do a little snooping and see if you can find out something about my money, too."

I ran toward the path, my heart pounding as loud as the strike of a blacksmith's anvil.

CHAPTER 26

Once I realized Thomas wasn't following me, I slowed my pace and continued walking toward the Küche. I'd been on the path only a short time when I heard branches crackling not far ahead. My breath caught. Was it wind in the trees or had Thomas circled around? I remained still as stone, inhaled a shallow breath, and listened intently for the sound of footsteps. Was he going to appear and level yet another threat? Prepared to run, I took a tentative step forward and gasped as a figure emerged.

"Ritt!" Fingers trembling, I covered my mouth. "You frightened me. I thought—" I stopped before I uttered Thomas's name.

Ritt's eyebrows pinched together. "You thought what?"

At the sight of him, the tightness between my shoulders eased, yet I floundered for an answer that would satisfy his curiosity. "I-I thought maybe an animal of some sort was going to attack me."

He tipped his head to the side. "Ja? Maybe a crazed squirrel was going to jump from a tree or an angry rabbit was waiting to jump out and nibble your shoes?" He wrinkled his nose and bared his front teeth.

His jovial reaction eased my fears, and I giggled at his rabbit imitation. "You can never be sure. There could be an angry bunny hiding back there in the brush." I absently massaged my wrist.

"If you see one, I think you could stomp your foot and it would run away." He grinned and took my hand. "I have missed you. I thought keeping my distance from you would build a wall around my heart, but it hasn't worked."

He dropped his gaze and his smile faded when he saw my wrist. Reaching forward, he cupped my hand in his palm. Gently, he rubbed the pad of his thumb across the red marks that surrounded my wrist. "What is this? What happened to you?" Concern shone in his eyes when he looked at me. When I hesitated, he stepped closer. "There is nothing to fear, Jancey. Please tell me what happened to you. I want to help."

I withdrew my hand and pulled the edge of my sleeve over my wrist. "It's nothing."

"Nein! I can see something has happened, and I want you to tell me." He shot me a pleading look. "You can trust me. Don't you know that by now?"

I forced a smile. "One of the men came into the dormitory before I left. Some of his belongings had been moved, and he thought I'd done it. I told him I hadn't, but he didn't believe me."

"So he grabbed you and caused that mark on your wrist?" Ritt scowled and shook his head. "Tell me his name. I am going to go and talk with him right now."

"No, Ritt. I don't want to cause him trouble. The outsiders

have very few possessions. Most of them don't know the Lord, so their possessions mean a great deal to them. To confront him won't reflect God's love."

"It is gut to show God's love, but love must be tempered with wisdom. Your compassionate heart is beautiful, but these men are wise to the ways of the world. If you are not cautious, they will take advantage of your caring ways." He pointed to my arm. "And this behavior is unacceptable. A man who does harm to a woman should not be working in the village. If you won't give me the worker's name, at least speak with Brother William."

The final bell tolled and I waved toward the path. "Run ahead of me so we don't appear at the same time. Or there will be talk."

He glanced at the path and then back at me, obviously wanting to remain until I agreed to speak with Brother William.

"Hurry!" I urged.

I sighed when he turned and ran. I wanted to be honest with Ritt, yet fear of his reaction caused me to vacillate. Would revealing the truth spell the end of our fragile relationship? Ritt wouldn't think me such a wonderful person once he knew I'd gone off to meet with Thomas and had unearthed hidden money in the dormitory—money that was now missing.

I was the last to enter the women's door of the Küche. Wooden benches scraped on the plank floor, and the shuffle of feet filled the room for a few minutes. The hushed voices silenced when Brother William bowed his head. Another shuffle of feet followed the prayer as we all sat down. Soon the clatter of forks and knives striking china plates played a harmony all their own, and I was surrounded by a symphony of pinging silverware. Throughout the meal, I refrained from looking toward the outsiders' table. I didn't want to chance locking gazes with Thomas.

As soon as we'd recited the after-meal prayer, Sister Hanna signaled to me. "I have a basket ready for your Mutter. I'm sorry, but I must stay and help with the canning."

The heat from the kitchen had colored her cheeks rosy. No doubt the kitchen would become even warmer by the time the sisters finished canning cherry juice this afternoon—one of the colony favorites, at least in Madelyn's opinion.

"I am always happy to take lunch to my mother. You should never apologize for being busy. Your work at the Küche must come first." I grasped the handles and picked up the basket, pleased I would be walking in a different direction than the men returning to the mill.

I did my best to remain focused upon how I should handle all of the problems that had taken root since the day I'd first picked up that picture of Kathleen. My thoughts leapfrogged from one incident to the next, yet I'd come to no resolution by the time I arrived home. I still didn't know if I should reveal the entire truth to Ritt, if I should wait on Nathan to do as he'd promised, or if I should give Thomas his sister's address in Salina. I had so many questions, but no answers.

My mother was sitting in the chair next to her bed when I arrived home. She'd arranged her hair in a tight bun at the nape of her neck, and a hint of pink colored her cheeks. She clapped her hands together. "How wonderful. I didn't expect to see you."

I smiled and leaned down to kiss her cheek. "I'm pleased to see you're feeling well enough to get up by yourself." After placing the basket on a nearby table, I lifted the jars of food from inside the napkin-lined container. "I hope you haven't tired yourself too much." I handed Mother a napkin and the silverware while I arranged the contents of the basket on a china plate.

She laid the napkin across her lap and placed the silverware on the small table beside her chair. "I feel quite good today. Do you have time to sit and visit for a short while before you go back to work?"

There would be more wash to hang, but it wouldn't be ready for at least another hour, and I'd completed most of the dormitory cleaning before lunch. "I can stay while you eat and I'll return the basket on my way back."

Mother picked up her fork. "You talk; I'll eat."

I fidgeted with the corner of my apron for several moments, then looked up and met my mother's gaze. "Have you ever been in a situation you didn't know how to resolve?"

My mother smiled. "I can think of several that have occurred throughout my life. Does this problem still revolve around Nathan and Ritt?"

"A little, but not entirely."

"Well, you've stirred my interest even more." She forked a bite of stewed chicken. "Exactly what is this problem you're trying to solve?"

I didn't plan to give my mother the particulars, but if I spoke in generalities, maybe she could lend some advice. "If you care for someone, do you think it's absolutely necessary to tell them everything that is going on in your life?"

My mother wiped her lips with the cloth napkin. "That's an evasive question. Would I be right if I guessed that you don't want to tell me the details?"

I grinned. "You'd be correct."

"You'll need to give me more than a snippet before I can provide any sort of helpful answer." She pointed her fork at the potato dumplings. "The dumplings are excellent." She leaned back in the chair. "How much does this secret you're keeping affect the person you care about? Is he—I assume you're speaking of a man?" I bobbed my head. "Is the secret something that involves him? You truly must tell me more before I can make any assessment, though I believe there are very few circumstances when secrets are a good thing."

I brightened at her last remark. "You believe there are some occasions when it wouldn't hurt?"

Her eyebrows pinched together. "I think you may be twisting my words to make you feel keeping a secret is acceptable, and that was not my intention."

"But you said there were a few circumstances—"

"A *very* few." Her frown deepened. "I need more specifics."

"This isn't something that affects the person directly, but he might be unhappy that I didn't confide in him and seek his advice."

"And why is that?" My mother arched her brows. "Because his advice wouldn't have been what you wanted to hear? Or because you had to make an immediate decision and there wasn't an opportunity to speak with him? Or perhaps because you don't completely trust him?"

"Oh no." I shook my head. "I trust him."

Mother tipped her head to the side and waited. "So?"

I sighed. "Mostly because I knew his advice wouldn't be what I wanted to hear."

"Ah, I see." She lifted the china cup to her lips and took a sip of the coffee. "In that case, I am sure the young man won't be particularly happy when he discovers your secret." After hesitating a moment, she looked deep into my eyes. "And he will find out, Jancey, either from you or from someone else. Maybe not right away, but eventually. If you have hopes of a future with this young man, you should remember that honesty and trust are the foundations of a good relationship."

Her voice bore a vaguely ominous tone that caused my stomach to lurch. She was right. How would Ritt feel when he learned the many secrets I'd been keeping from him? I tried to imagine how I might feel. I wanted to believe it wouldn't matter, that I would accept his apology and forgive him. But deep inside, I knew I would be hurt and angry. Even more, I'd wonder if I could ever trust him. I needed to prepare myself, for if I told him, he might well lose any trust he ever had in me.

My mother touched my hand. "Tell him, Jancey. Better that it comes from you than from someone else. Ask his forgiveness and promise you'll be forthright in the future."

"What if he doesn't accept my apology? What if I've destroyed any hope of a future with him?"

Giving my hand a gentle squeeze, she shook her head. "If you're meant to have a future with this young man, he'll forgive you. I'll be praying that you find the right words to help him understand why you didn't confide in him before now." She tapped the edge of the plate. "I can't eat any more. Tell Sister Bertha the food is very good, but my stomach doesn't hold much these days."

I repacked the basket, kissed Mother's cheek, and departed for the Küche, where I'd leave the basket before returning to work. "Thank you, Mother. I appreciate your insight."

"If I am any judge of character, I think Ritt will forgive you. Although he may be deeply hurt, I think he will choose forgiveness over anger. He is a fine young man with principles."

I stopped short. "How did you know I was talking about Ritt rather than Nathan or some other young man?"

My mother chuckled. "I am your mother. I've known for some

time now. I can see the love in your eyes and hear it in your voice when you speak of him."

I departed, still uncertain when or how I would tell Ritt. I knew Mother was correct: I needed to tell him—the sooner, the better. Perhaps there would be time after prayer service this evening.

All afternoon, I practiced what I would say to Ritt when I finally gained an opportunity to spend time alone with him. My plan to speak to him after prayer service didn't work as I'd hoped, for when we left the meetinghouse, Ritt and two of the other young men headed off in another direction. Unless he returned while I was giving Madelyn and her friends their lessons, there'd be no chance to talk this evening.

I wasn't completely attentive during the children's lessons. Each time I heard an unfamiliar noise or the sound of voices, I hoped Ritt would appear. Unfortunately, that didn't happen. I went to bed determined to find time to speak with him tomorrow—even if I had to slip him a note.

After tossing and turning, I finally drifted off to sleep. My dreams were fraught with visions of Thomas catching me in the woods and threatening me. While I tried to convince him I didn't have his money, it began to spill out of my apron pockets in endless streams, piling about my feet. His eyes flashed with anger as my apron turned into a large money bag stamped with the words *National Commerce Bank of Kansas City.* He bound me to a tree, yanked the apron from my waist, and stuffed the piles of money inside while I struggled to get free. A bell sounded and I screamed for someone to help me, but no one could hear because the bell continued to ring and ring and ring.

A door banged and loud voices called out. I pushed upright in bed. The bell was still ringing as I struggled to gain my bearings.

Outside the window, I heard people shouting. The mournful peals of the bell continued. I shoved my feet into the slippers beside my bed and opened the bedroom door in time to see my father bolt toward the parlor door.

Still shoving one arm into a shirt sleeve, he yanked open the door with his free hand and shouted.

"Fire!"

CHAPTER 27

My heart was gripped with terror. Shoving up on the wooden frame, I opened the parlor window. The acrid smell of smoke drifted on the nighttime breeze and carried into the room. Without thought, I shouted to a group of men running by the open window, "Where is the fire?"

A chorus of voices split the air. "The woolen mill! Fire at the woolen mill!" Shoes pounded on the wooden walkway, and the street filled with men running pell-mell toward the mill. I lowered the window back in place and hurried to close my parents' bedroom door. The smoke wouldn't be good for Mother.

Before I could close the door, my mother called to me. "I heard you shouting to someone. Did they say the fire is at the mill?"

I glanced over my shoulder, longing to don a dress and rush

after the crowd that would be gathering near the mill. "Yes, but I don't know any more than that."

"From the clanging of the bell, I knew the fire was here in Middle," Mother told me, "but if it's at the woolen mill, that could be very bad."

I hadn't learned there were different rings of the bell to denote fires in our village or other villages, but Mother appeared eager to explain. "Listen." She touched her fingers to her ear. "You hear how the bell rings with a constant beat? That means the fire is in our village. When the fire is in another village, the bell rings very fast, then slows up, and then rings fast again—it is called the *Sturm*."

Though I'd pushed the door closed behind me, I remained in place with my hand on the metal latch, poised to flee the moment my mother finished talking.

"When the bell is rung in the other villages, most of the men come to help, but watchmen must remain in each village to make certain there isn't a fire in their own village while the rest of the men are off fighting a fire somewhere else. I don't recall that two fires have ever happened at one time, but there is always that possibility. It is better to be watchful than to have a double tragedy."

My fingers itched to press the latch on the door handle and make my retreat. "It seems the elders have thought of everything." I rotated my shoulders, but my mother thwarted my departure with another comment.

"Not entirely. Your father and I are both strong believers in insurance. We always insured our home in Kansas City as well as the business, but here in the colonies, they believe that it is cheaper to rebuild than to pay for the insurance." She sighed. "I think that is true with the occasional small house fires that begin in a chimney, but with the woolen mill, it could prove devastating if the machinery is ruined." She pulled the quilt tighter around her, as if she thought the fabric cocoon would ward off further harm. "I do hope your father will take care. More than one man has been injured fighting fires."

Her declaration pummeled me like blows to the midsection. My eyes widened and I leaned against the cool wood door. What if my father or Ritt should be injured in the fire? I needed to go. "I'm going to the mill, Mother. I want to check on Father and the other men. There may be something I can do to help."

"I'm not sure that's wise, Jancey. You'll probably be in the way."

"Surely there will be some way I can help. If not, I'll come back home." There was a loud clunk as I pressed down on the metal latch. "I promise."

Before she could deter me any longer, I pulled open the door, crossed the parlor, and strode into my bedroom. Quickly donning a work dress and gathering a lightweight shawl, I hurried off. A twinge of guilt plagued me as I left Mother behind, but concern and curiosity propelled me down the street. Even at this distance, I could hear the shouts and cries of the men as they battled the blaze. The smoke turned thick as I drew closer to the mill, and my eyes began to water. While swiping the corner of my shawl across my eyes, I raced onward, spurred by the clamoring noise.

Controlled confusion appeared to reign at the scene of the fire. Horse-drawn pumpers were situated on two sides of the mill, with the water hoses unreeled from the hose carts and stretched to the mill race. The ladder wagon was positioned not far off, and I guessed the additional equipment had come from some of the other villages. Twelve to fifteen men lined each side of the pumper, their shoulders taut and muscles bulging beneath their shirts as they heaved the pumper bar up and down to gain enough power to draw water from the mill race and project it toward the blaze. In the radiating glow of the fire, the men's brows glistened with perspiration.

I glanced about, hoping to catch sight of Ritt and my father. After circling around the pump, I saw Ritt standing behind the men who were currently pumping. I gestured to him. He stepped toward me but maintained a watch of the men at the pumper.

Smoke billowed from the mill, but I couldn't determine how fierce the fire might be inside the building. "How bad is it?"

He shook his head. "Things are not going so gut, but we are doing our best. I need to stay close by so I can move up when it is my turn to take over and pump."

As Ritt spoke, his eyes remained trained on two of the men who were changing places at the pumper. If the exchange of positions wasn't accomplished with precision on the part of both men, torn fingers or broken arms could easily occur.

"Any idea how it started?" I held my breath as two more men swapped places at the pumper.

"No way to know just yet. There could have been hot ashes from a pipe or cigarette. The men know better, but sometimes they're careless in spite of the rules." He glanced toward the mill. "Or it could be spontaneous combustion. If nobody can find any other reason, that's what they usually list as the cause."

"How does that happen?"

After a pensive look toward the pumper, he turned back to me. "When the wool has been prepared with the necessary amount of oil for carding and heaped together in a way that won't permit the heat to escape, the temperature builds to a smolder. Eventually the wool becomes hot enough that there is a full-blown fire." He nodded toward the line. "I need to get back. You should keep your distance."

Several of the outsiders were lined up to man the pumper, but I didn't spot either Thomas or Nathan. Maybe neither of them had ever operated a pumper. And after watching the precision needed to change places, I doubted whether the experienced men wanted any novices unless absolutely necessary. With more and more men arriving from the other villages, it looked as though there were enough skilled men to help. And men were needed to help in duties beyond the pumper.

Ladders were hoisted but then withdrawn as the fire gained momentum. Wind and fire challenged the water spewing from the hoses as men covered with a shadow of soot hurried to and fro, fighting to control the blaze. Commands were shouted with the exacting authority of bugles directing men into battle.

I skirted the fringes, still seeking a glimpse of my father, but when I didn't see him, I ignored Ritt's warning and moved closer, hoping to find him among the crowd. I hadn't gone far when I spied Thomas. He was among a group manning a bucket brigade with leather buckets, though I doubted they were doing much good. Then again, I knew nothing of how to fight a fire. Perhaps their efforts were needed to keep the fire from spreading beyond the mill. One thing was certain: I didn't plan to do anything to draw Thomas's attention away from his duties. My father wasn't among the bucket brigade, nor did I see Nathan. Perhaps they'd been assigned duties on the other side of the mill. Maintaining a distance from the fire, I trudged to the far side and finally spotted my father with a group of men. As if drawn by a magnet, he looked up and came running toward me.

"What are you doing here, Jancey? You shouldn't be near this fire."

"There are other women out here. Surely you didn't expect me to remain at the house while the mill is burning. I couldn't sit at home while this fire is raging."

He frowned and shook his head. "There's nothing you can do. You can't man a pump, and there's a strong possibility you could be injured."

"I'm far enough from the fire that I'm not going to get hurt."

"Perhaps not, but you could get in the way of someone else and hinder his ability to perform his job."

I could see I wasn't convincing him, and if I didn't soon say something to change his mind, I'd have to return home whether I wanted to or not. "Have you seen Nathan? I've been looking for him, but he doesn't seem to be anywhere. I found you and Ritt, but there's no sign of Nathan."

"I didn't see Nathan when I first arrived, so I asked one of the men who lives in the dormitory. He said Nathan borrowed a horse from one of the outsiders and rode over to Marengo after supper, but he still hasn't returned." My father glanced into the distance as though he expected to see Nathan appear through the haze of smoke. "I'm worried he may have met up with some trouble, but there's no one able to go and check on him right now. Once the fire's under control, I'll talk to Brother William and see if I can borrow a horse and go look for him."

My mind whirred. Had he gone to Marengo to see if there'd been a telegram regarding the bank robbery? If so, would the telegraph office be open by the time he arrived? Though it made no sense, I hoped he'd return with news that would somehow eliminate Thomas as one of the men who'd held up the bank. At the thought of Thomas, I instinctively rubbed my wrist and recalled his menacing behavior. Even if Nathan had received word that Thomas wasn't involved, Thomas's changeable personality frightened me. Was he a man who could be trusted to treat his sister well, or would he become a brute whenever she did something that annoyed him?

My father's touch jarred any further thoughts of Thomas. "If you're going to stay here, move back with the other women and don't come close to the fire again. Otherwise, I'm going to order you back home."

I opened my mouth but caught myself before I said a word. I needed to follow my father's instruction—even if it didn't please me. I turned and strode toward a small hillock where some of the women had gathered. In truth, the spot offered a better view of the sad circumstances unfolding below. Each time the men made progress in one area, another fire seemed to flare and require their attention. They entered and then retreated when the flames or smoke overtook them.

With each attempted entry into the mill, worry overtook every woman in our group. The sounds of crashing timbers inside the mill caused us to gasp and cover our mouths.

"Ach! This is such a reminder of the fire in 1874." Sister Bertha wagged her head back and forth. "Such a tragedy."

"There was another fire? Here at the woolen mill?" I gasped at the revelation.

She heaved a sigh. "Ja, only seven years ago. For sure, that fire makes this one even more difficult to accept."

I stared toward the fire, unable to comprehend how much pain it must cause to see the woolen mill once again destroyed. "Did they ever determine what caused that fire?"

"I'm not sure. Probably the same as this one—something the men refer to as spontaneous combustion, but who can say? Maybe one of the men was smoking and tossed down a match."

"They are not allowed to smoke inside the mills anymore," one of the younger women put in.

"What they are allowed to do and what they actually do can be two different things. Ja?" Sister Bertha frowned at the woman, who quickly acquiesced, and soon our attention was drawn back to the fire.

We watched the men retreat from the building, and then I spotted a horse and rider approaching the mill. The pall of smoke hindered my view, and I moved a little farther down the hill.

Sister Bertha reached out and grasped my arm, stopping me. "You should stay here with us. If the men need food or coffee from the Küche, they will send someone to tell me."

I knew her grasp would tighten if I attempted to move, so instead I told her I was going to sit down. She nodded and released my arm as I lowered myself to the grass. Pleased that the smoke wasn't as dense from my new vantage point, I focused on the horse and rider. Either the horse was injured or it didn't want to get any closer to the fire—maybe both. The rider dismounted and began to run toward the mill. I narrowed my eyes. The man running toward the fire looked like . . . Yes, there was no doubt.

Nathan!

He'd returned and was safe. I continued to watch as he raced through the shroud of smoke. What was he doing? I jumped to my feet and moved several paces to the right, hoping to gain a better view.

Was he? Could he be? Oh, surely not! I couldn't believe my eyes.

Nathan was running headlong toward the burning mill!

Even from this distance, I knew I wasn't mistaken. Frantic shouts rang out, but Nathan didn't pay heed. I glanced over my shoulder. Sister Bertha and the other women were a short distance from me. Without further hesitation, I raced down the hillock, willing my feet to traverse the uneven ground through the moonlit semidarkness. What was Nathan doing? Why would he act in such a reckless manner? I needed to stop him!

My feet pounded the hard ground. With each step a heavy thud rang in my ears. Once I'd drawn closer, I inhaled a giant gulp of air and cupped my hands to my lips. "Nathan! Stop!"

He didn't turn. Instead he raced headlong into the burning mill. I continued running toward the fire. Suddenly strong arms encircled me, and I was pulled against a man's solid chest. "Jancey," Ritt barked, "what do you think you're doing? Even if you love Nathan, you can't chase him into a burning building."

I gasped for air. "I'm not in love with him, but I can't watch a friend burn." I struggled to free myself from his arms.

"Quit fighting. The men will get him out."

I watched as two men with handkerchiefs covering their mouths entered the mill through a door not yet in flames.

I sank against Ritt's chest. "Don't you know the only man I love is you?"

Ritt stroked my hair, then released me. "To hear this from your lips makes me very happy." He shook his head as another cloud of smoke billowed from the mill. "Even in these terrible circumstances, you have made me happy."

Ritt moved back to my side and I looked up at him. "What would make Nathan do such a thing?"

"I do not wish for anything bad to happen to Nathan, either. I do not consider him such a gut friend, but he is one of God's children, and I don't want to see harm come his way." He shook his head. "But why he would run into the mill is strange, for sure."

We watched and waited for what seemed a very long time,

though in truth it was far less. As three men emerged from the mill, I leaned forward and wiped my watering eyes. The men on either side of Nathan were dragging him from the building. His head hung low against his chest, and from my vantage point, it appeared he was either unconscious or . . . dead.

Several men gathered around Nathan, my father among them.

I tugged on Ritt's sleeve. "Should we go for the doctor?"

He gestured toward a running man. "There's Brother Rudolf." Ritt held me in place. "We should stay out of the way so the doctor can help him." I nodded, knowing he was right, but it didn't quench my desire to know what had happened. "I need to go back to the pumper, but you should stay at least this far away." He arched his brows. "Promise?"

"I promise." He started to walk away, but I grasped his hand. "We need to talk when this is over. I have much to tell you."

His lips lifted in a half smile. "That would be gut." He trotted away, back to the pump along the side of the mill.

Moments later my father stood and waved me forward. "Come here, Jancey! Hurry!"

Terror shot through me as I closed the distance between us. Had Nathan died? My father pulled me close. "He's going to live, but . . ."

I followed his gaze to the canvas bag that lay on the ground beside Nathan. My breath caught and I thought I might faint.

CHAPTER 28

My father tightened his hold around my waist. "The men had a terrible time trying to get him out of there. He kept shouting he had to get his money. I don't know how much is in that bag, but it looks to be bulging. I can't imagine how Nathan managed to save all that money."

My father's assumption didn't surprise me. Even though the money had been stuffed into a sack belonging to the National Commerce Bank of Kansas City, my father wouldn't imagine Nathan was a thief. He would believe Nathan had acquired the bag from the bank before leaving Kansas City. After all, Father had kept at least one or two of those money bags in his office for use when making large business deposits.

I swallowed hard and glanced around the group that had gathered close to Nathan's unconscious form. A chill raced down my spine when I looked up. Thomas stood directly across from me with rage flashing in his eyes. I squeezed closer to my father. Thomas looked at the money bag and then back at me. He likely believed Nathan and I had conspired to take his money. My father seemed to believe Nathan had saved the money. I, however, believed Thomas had stolen the money. Right now, only one thing was certain: That money didn't belong to anyone in the colonies.

The doctor looked about and asked for volunteers to carry Nathan to his office. My father stepped forward, and I was surprised when Ritt appeared and offered to help, as well. "I thought you needed to stay at the pumper."

"I just finished my turn." His breathing was labored, but I was thankful he'd agreed to help. I planned to walk alongside the men as they took Nathan to Rudolf Zedler's office. I didn't want to give Thomas any opportunity to be alone with me.

Thomas stepped close to Brother William, who had now left his firefighting position and come to check on Nathan. "I can take that bag and put it in Nathan's trunk, if you'd like, Brother William. He sleeps in the bed next to mine."

I sucked in a breath and waited for Brother William's response. If Thomas got his hands on the money, he'd be out of the colonies within minutes. Brother William leaned down and retrieved the bag. "Nein. I think it is better we put the money in a place of safekeeping for now." Brother William directed a pitying look at Nathan. "Sad that a man would risk his life for a bag of money."

"Ja, and jeopardize the lives of the men who tried to save him, as well," one of the other men said. "This is what the love of money can do to mankind."

A hum of accord filled the air, though I noticed Thomas didn't add his voice to the murmurs of agreement. Instead, his focus remained locked upon Brother William and the money bag. I wondered where Brother William would find a secure place within this village, but maybe he would take the money to one of the other villages for safekeeping. If so, I worried Thomas might follow him.

I needed to confide in someone before another disaster occurred. Yet, with the mill still burning and the doctor caring for Nathan, there was far too much commotion to speak with any of the elders right now. Worry and fear had become my constant companions, and I wanted to rid myself of both.

Once Nathan had been carried inside the doctor's office, Ritt and the men reappeared in the waiting area. Only my father remained with the doctor and Nathan. While the men scurried back to help at the mill, I grasped Ritt's arm. "Can you stay for a few minutes? I need to speak with you. It's very important."

He hesitated, his gaze following the departing men. "I should—"

"Please, it's urgent that you help me."

He stopped short. "Jancey, what's wrong? Let's sit down." We sat side by side in the waiting room of the doctor's office. I stammered, uncertain where or how to begin. "I have much to tell you, so please withhold your anger until I finish."

He arched his brows. "Anger? If you have something to say that will cause anger, maybe I don't want to hear. Ja?"

"No. You need to hear this." I inhaled a deep breath. "When I first began cleaning at the dormitory, I discovered the picture of a young girl."

Ritt listened intently while I recounted the entire story—how I'd noticed Kathleen's picture and met with Thomas. His eyes got wide when I explained I'd met Thomas in the woods, but he didn't interrupt. I told him that I'd written to Lilly Manchester in an attempt to locate Kathleen and I'd only recently received a definitive word back from her.

Ritt leaned forward and rested his arms across his thighs. "So Thomas is pleased that you have located his sister?"

"I haven't told him yet. That's the other part of my story."

He straightened and leaned back in the chair. "There is more?"

"Much more." I sighed.

Astonishment shone in his eyes when I revealed what I'd discovered beneath the loose floorboards under Thomas's bed. He inhaled a gulp of air. "And you gave that money to Nathan, and he hid it in the mill, and that's why he went in there! I cannot believe you would do such a thing, Jancey."

"No. That isn't what happened." I shook my head with so much fervor, I became dizzy. "Please. Let me finish." I grasped his arm, fearful he would take off before I could explain the truth. "This is the part I don't understand myself."

"Ach! It keeps getting worse." He drew in a deep breath, as if preparing himself.

I didn't want to leave out any of the details, but I feared Ritt might become impatient, so I did my best to quickly explain that I'd removed the newspaper clipping about the bank robbery, but I'd left the money where I'd found it.

"There was a bank robbery in Kansas City? And you think this is the money from that robbery?" His eyes were as wide as the china saucers in the kitchen house. "So Nathan robbed the bank?"

"No, not Nathan. I'm not sure, but I think Thomas helped rob the bank. I still have the newspaper clipping, but Nathan was supposed to wire Kansas City and get more information."

Ritt massaged his forehead. "And did he?"

I shrugged. "I don't know. He hadn't told me any news, but

I'm not sure why he was in Marengo tonight, either." I gulped a breath of air. "Are you angry with me?"

"How can I know if I should be angry?" He stared at me as though I'd lost my senses. "I don't know if I understand what has happened. You tell me all this so fast and expect me to understand, and then you ask if I am angry." His shoulders drooped. "First I should like to know why you told all of this to Nathan instead of talking to me." When I started to object, he held up his hand. "I know for sure you had to be the one to tell him about the money. He would never have found it on his own, because Thomas would not do something so foolish. So it had to be you. Ja?"

"Yes. I told Nathan, but that wasn't what I planned."

Ritt didn't appear convinced, so I mentioned the times I'd been prepared to talk with him, but on each occasion we'd been interrupted. "And then you decided to maintain a distance between us."

"Ja, because I didn't want either of us to be hurt when you left the colonies." He sighed. "So you talked to Nathan because of what I said, and for that, I am sorry. I wish you had told me instead of him, but that cannot be changed now." Placing his palms on his thighs, he pushed to his feet. "Thomas is going to want to get that money back. You told no one other than Nathan? Your Vater or Mutter maybe?"

I shook my head. "No. I was going to talk to my father or one of the elders, but Nathan said I shouldn't tell anyone—that he would take care of everything."

"Ja, well it looks like he was trying to take care of himself with that money. Instead, he may die."

I gasped. "Do you really think he's going to die? This is my fault."

Ritt dropped back into the chair beside me. "His greed is not your fault. Do you think if you had told me or your Vater, we would have acted in the same way as Nathan?"

"No, but—"

"Then there is no reason for you to take this blame on yourself. Nathan took money that did not belong to him. He hid it in the mill—at least that is what I am thinking he must have done. When he returned to Middle and saw the fire, he ran into the burning mill and put his life in danger, as well as that of the men who went in after him." Ritt tapped his index finger against the side of his head. "Not so smart."

"Do you think we should find Brother William and tell him?" I didn't relish the thought, but the elders needed to know.

The scent of smoke clung to Ritt's clothing and assailed me as he leaned close. "Ja, but only after the fire is out at the mill. Right now, there is enough to deal with."

"Ritt." I gripped his arm as he turned to go. "I meant what I said. I love you."

Despite his obvious exhaustion, he smiled. "I love you, too, Jancey, but I'd never force you to stay. If you cannot live with our teaching, I understand. Your happiness is more important to me."

"I've already chosen." I took hold of his hand. "Amana is my home now."

The fire was finally brought under control by seven o'clock in the morning. The haggard men went home to clean up before going to their respective kitchen houses for a late breakfast. As agreed, Ritt met me in the downstairs hallway outside our parlor door. He'd asked Brother William to meet with us before breakfast, so we headed to his house.

I hadn't slept and I doubted there had been even a few minutes for Ritt or Brother William to rest, either. Dark rings circled the elder's eyes when he answered the door to his parlor.

"Come in, children, come in." He directed us to the sofa, while he sat opposite us in a rocking chair. He looked me in the eye. "Brother Ritt says you can shed light on Nathan Woodward and how he came to possess all of that money he had hidden in the mill."

First I removed the newspaper article from my pocket and read it to him. Then I detailed everything, from the picture of Thomas's sister to how I found the newspaper article and the bag of money, and how I'd trusted Nathan. As I spoke, Brother William's expression changed from interested to concerned, to surprised, and then to horrified. When I finally finished my story, he rested his elbow on the arm of the rocking chair and cradled his forehead in his hand. I wasn't sure if he was praying or thinking—maybe he was doing both. Either way, I wasn't going to interrupt him. I'd said everything I could, and now he'd have to decide how to handle this whole mess.

Finally he looked up. "I spoke to Nathan a short time ago."

His remark surprised me. My father hadn't yet returned home, and I assumed Nathan remained unconscious. "So he is alive and well?"

"I wouldn't say he is well, but he is alive. His first questions were not about whether he would live or die, but about the money." The older man shook his head. "I asked him about it."

I nodded. "And what did he say?"

A sad smile tugged at the elder's lips. "He said it was his life savings, that he brought it with him when he came here and had hidden it in the mill to keep it safe from the outsiders in the dormitory."

I inhaled a sharp breath. "Was my father present when Nathan spoke to you?"

"Ja, he was there. Your Vater doubted he could have saved that much money, but Nathan insisted the money belonged to him."

"Did you or my father ask him why he went to Marengo?"

"Nein. He began coughing and Brother Rudolf said he should rest." Brother William waved his index finger back and forth. "And I do not argue with the doctor."

I glanced at Brother William. "I hope you secured the money in a safe place. I'm sure Thomas is eager to get the money back in his hands and flee."

"The money is safe for now. I will meet with the *Bruderrat* and see what they decide. I think they will want to talk to the marshal over in Marengo or Iowa City and maybe send a wire to the bank in Kansas City. I cannot say for certain what they will decide. One thing is sure. You should not say anything about this to Thomas. If he asks you any questions, you should tell him to speak to me. Even though it appears he was involved in the robbery, we have no proof."

Jancey frowned. "You have the money. Isn't that proof enough?"

Brother William shook his head. "Nein. Is true the money probably does not belong to him, but I cannot say for sure who robbed the bank or how Thomas obtained the money."

"Thomas has already threatened Sister Jancey and grabbed her wrist so tight it left red marks." Ritt leaned forward. "She should not be at work in the dormitory where he might find her alone and do more harm to her."

"I don't think I'm in danger now that he knows where the money is."

Brother William stroked his jaw. "No, Brother Ritt is correct.

You should stay with your Mutter until we have all the answers to solve this puzzle, Sister Jancey. If Sister Margaret cannot manage on her own at the men's quarters, I'll send another sister to help."

We walked to the parlor door, our footsteps muffled by the carpet. "One more thing, Sister. Someone will bring your meals to the house. I don't want you to walk anywhere by yourself."

"Is all this really necessary?"

"God would want us to make wise decisions regarding your care."

Ritt smiled and nodded. "Thank you, Brother William."

Despite my brave front, a wave of relief washed over me. Now that Brother William had confiscated the money, maybe Thomas would understand that I couldn't provide him with any information. Still, it didn't mean he wouldn't turn his anger upon me. If he was wise and wanted to avoid jail, he'd be on a train before day's end. I prayed he would be wise and leave the colonies.

That evening when my father returned home I greeted him at the door, eager for any news. He waved me toward the bedroom. "Let's sit in here. That way your mother will hear what I've learned." Once we were settled, he leaned back in his chair. "It's been decided that the fire was caused by spontaneous combustion."

"I'm glad it wasn't caused by carelessness. I can't imagine anyone living with such guilt."

My father agreed. "True, but the loss is great. The main building and most of the contents are a total loss, but we can be thankful there wasn't much wind and the surrounding outbuildings were saved."

"The mill will be rebuilt, won't it?" I thought of Ritt and his aspiration to become a supervisor. If the elders decided against rebuilding, he would be distraught.

Father folded his arms across his chest. "Yes. There was a meeting this afternoon. Sister Barbara Landmann came from Main Amana to attend."

My mother scooted up against her pillows, her eyes wide. "What happened?"

I hadn't met Sister Barbara, though I knew who she was, for my parents had previously spoken of her. They'd explained Sister Barbara had become the spiritual leader of the entire community after the death of Brother Christian Metz.

Father inhaled a sharp breath. "She said she'd had a word from the Lord. She presented a testimony at the meeting and told us that the community had fallen into spiritual decline, and there was a need for all to humble themselves in order to begin a spiritual revival. She added that more emphasis must be placed on spiritual growth rather than upon worldly success."

"But she agreed the mill should be restored?" I wanted additional affirmation. After hearing Sister Barbara's remarks, I wondered if the elders had ignored her testimony and decided to move forward without her agreement.

Father nodded. "Yes, but her words were taken to heart. I am sure there will be much said in this regard at future meetings." Reaching forward, my father placed his hand atop my mother's arm. "I have been asked to take charge of the rebuilding. The elders thought it would be a good use of my construction knowledge."

Mother tipped her head to one side, and I saw the hint of a question in her eyes. "That will be a project that could take quite a while."

"I estimate nine months to a year if all goes well."

"Then you plan to stay even after . . ." Her words hung between them like a sharp blade waiting to slice their lives apart.

"I haven't changed my mind. This is where I plan to live out the rest of my days."

A faint smile curved her lips. "And you will be happy?"

"I'll be as happy as I can without you at my side."

I felt like an intruder as I watched the exchange of both love and pain that passed between them.

As if he suddenly realized they weren't alone in the room, my father looked at me. "I asked to have Ritt work as my assistant on the construction project, and he has agreed."

My heart soared at the news. Ritt might not become a supervisor within the woolen mill in the near future, but this added responsibility could reveal he possessed the aptitude to be a good leader. I was already certain Ritt had the ability to be a good husband, but first I must wait to see if he believed I could remain content in the Amana Colonies—and if he would ask me to be his wife.

CHAPTER 29

The next morning, I learned that my prayer concerning Thomas hadn't been answered. According to Ritt, Thomas remained in the village. I guessed he still hoped to retrieve his money. Either he assumed I hadn't revealed my knowledge of the money, or he thought the elders would forgive him and overlook the possibility that he could be one of the bank robbers.

Brother William hadn't advised Ritt, me, or my father about what plans were being made, if any, in regard to Nathan, Thomas, or the money. Since I had to refrain from my regular work at the dormitory and had to eat my meals at home with Mother, my knowledge of happenings outside our front door remained negligible—other than what I could glean from Father or Ritt.

At noon, my father appeared with our meal. I was surprised to see him rather than Sister Hanna. "What brings you home,

Father? Are you not feeling well?" I jumped up from my chair and reached for the basket.

"I am fine, but I wanted to tell you that the doctor believes Nathan will reach a full recovery by tomorrow. He will keep him at his home for one more night to make certain his lungs are clear."

I lifted a corner of the napkin covering the containers of food inside the basket. "That is good." I was glad Nathan wasn't permanently injured, yet his betrayal had cut deep into my heart. "And now what happens to him?"

"I don't know, Jancey, but I'm sure the elders have set a plan in motion." He inhaled a ragged breath. "Nathan has asked to see you. The doctor gave his permission for you to visit him, but the choice is yours."

I shook my head. "I have nothing to say to him, Father. And nothing he tells me will restore my trust in him."

"Perhaps he wants to ask your forgiveness." My father's brows arched above his wire-rimmed glasses.

I was surprised by my father's response. "You think I should forgive him?"

"Forgive him, so you'll be able to trust again, Jancey. Don't let his actions take root and harden your heart. The only way to rid yourself of the pain he has caused you is to forgive. Then you can move forward. What do you think the Lord would have you do?"

"Forgive," I whispered. "But it is so hard, Father."

"I know, but holding on to the grievance hurts only you."

With Mother's latest downward turn, we couldn't leave her alone, so my father brushed a kiss on my cheek and bid me hurry to Brother Rudolf's office.

The breeze seemed to carry my prayers toward heaven, and I

found my spirit lifting despite what lay ahead. A rabbit hopped from a yard and crossed the walkway in front of me and I chuckled, remembering Ritt's teasing about a bunny nibbling my shoes.

At the thought of Ritt, I glanced toward the charred remains of the mill. The smoke still hung in the air and seemed to cling to everything. I turned back toward the road and gasped. "Thomas!"

"Where's the money?"

I glanced around. Surely he wouldn't do anything rash in broad daylight. "I have no idea. You know Brother William took the bag from Nathan the night of the fire."

He stepped closer, backing me against a post. "And my sister? Did you find out about those rich folks she's living with?"

My heart hammered an erratic beat. "Is that why you wanted to find her? Because you knew her family had money? Did you plan to rob them? Or maybe you were going to threaten to take Kathleen with you if her father wouldn't give you the money you demanded? Is that it? Did you care about her at all—or was it all about money?"

His features tightened and he inched closer. "She wouldn't have fit into my life, but I figured a time would come when that rich family would prove useful."

I shuddered at the impulsive decision I'd made to help Thomas. In my haste, I could have caused his sister and her family great harm.

"It is gut to show God's love," Ritt had said. *"But love must be tempered with wisdom."*

I looked into Thomas's eyes. A cold, calculating hardness now replaced the gentle man I'd first met, and Ritt's words haunted me. Anger burned in my chest. "I wouldn't tell you where Kathleen is with my dying breath. She's better off without you."

"Why you little—" He drew back his hand.

I shut my eyes, bracing myself for the strike. Instead, I heard a grunt. My eyes opened to see Ritt wrenching Thomas's hand behind his back.

"Ritt, where did you come from?"

"When your father didn't return to work, I feared your mother had taken another turn for the worse, and I came to check on you." Ritt eyed me critically. "Did he hurt you?"

"No." My voice caught.

"I'll take him to Brother William. The elders can decide what must be done, but Thomas has bothered you for the last time." Ritt held fast to Thomas's arm. "Were you on your way home?"

My lips trembled as the realization of what had happened began to take hold. "No, I was on my way to Brother Rudolf's office when Thomas stopped me."

"You are too troubled to go by yourself. Why don't you go home and see if your Vater will go with you?"

I shook my head and explained we couldn't leave Mother alone right now.

"My Mutter will be home from the Küche by now. She will come downstairs and sit with her." Ritt nodded toward the house. "Go on, now, and I'll talk to you later."

I hurried home and asked Sister Hanna to keep an eye on my mother. After hearing what had happened to me, my father wrapped me in an embrace. "I'll go with you. We can do this together."

A short time later the two of us walked to the doctor's office. Perspiration dotted my forehead, and my lunch tossed about like cream in a butter churn. A bell over the door jangled as we stepped into the waiting room.

"Ah, Brother Jurgen and Sister Jancey. I am guessing you are here to see Mr. Woodward." Brother Rudolf gestured for us to follow him into the back, where he took us into his parlor. "I'll have him join you in here. He is able to be up."

Moments later, Nathan stepped into the room. He extended his hand to my father and then sat down on the sofa beside me. "I didn't think you would come, but I'm glad that you did." There was a strange, raspy quality to his voice, likely caused by the smoke. Instead of looking directly into my eyes, he gave me a sideways glance.

"I asked you to come because I wanted to apologize for letting you down. I took advantage of your trust, and instead of doing what I promised, I took the money."

I inhaled a quick breath. "How could you, Nathan? I never would have believed you could do anything so awful. Was money so important that you would steal and then risk your life for it? What did you hope to gain?"

He covered his face with his hands. "I know it was wrong, but I wanted to have enough money to purchase your father's business. I thought that maybe then you would decide I was worthy of your love—that you'd return and marry me."

My father shook his head. "No. You will not cast this on Jancey's shoulders. She is not a young woman who bases her love on whether a man has enough money to shower her with a fancy home or gifts. Be honest with yourself and with Jancey." He inched forward on the chair and forced Nathan to look at him. "You stole because you wanted the power and prestige that you believe can be gained only through money, not because you thought it was a way to win Jancey's heart. Isn't that the truth?"

Tears streamed down Nathan's face. "Yes. I thought it would be easy, but now I've ruined all of my chances."

"I'm afraid that's true, Nathan. You made a bad decision that will change the entire course of your life."

Wiping his tears with his shirt sleeve, Nathan turned toward me. "Can you ever forgive me? I know there's nothing I can say that will make things right, but it would help to know you'll at least try to forgive me."

I met his faltering gaze. "I forgive you, Nathan." A swell of sorrow rose in my chest—sadness for the choices he'd made and the suffering he would endure because of them.

As we rose to leave, I stopped and turned to him. "Why were you in Marengo the night of the fire, Nathan? Had you gone to see if word had been received about the bank robbers?" I looked him in the eye. "And please tell me the truth."

He bowed his head. "No. I never sent any wires to the newspaper, or the bank, or to anyone else in Kansas City."

My throat caught. I'd suspected as much, but I hadn't been certain.

"I went to purchase two train tickets." His clasped hands rested on his legs.

"Train tickets?"

He nodded. "I was going to do my best to convince you to leave with me the following day. I bought the tickets in Marengo because I didn't want to take a chance buying the tickets or departing from one of the stations in the colonies. I figured someone would tell your father before we could get far enough away."

"And you thought I would do that? Leave with you and not tell my parents?"

"Not really, but I . . ." He hesitated. "I considered forcing you." When I gasped, he straightened his shoulders. "You said you wanted to hear the truth."

He was right—but I hadn't expected to hear that he would

have actually forced me to leave with him. Even when we lived in Kansas City, I was aware of Nathan's shortcomings, but in my wildest thoughts, I could never have imagined he would steal and consider making me go with him against my will. I placed my fingers against my mouth as a wave of nausea attacked. His revelation had physically sickened me, and I turned away.

My father stepped close and placed his arm around my shoulder. "I think we should go now."

"Do you know what will happen to me, Mr. Rhoder?" Nathan asked with a trembling voice.

My father squeezed my shoulder, and I stopped in the doorway. "The elders have not told me anything, Nathan. I am sure someone will come and advise you of what decisions have been made."

"If you could put in a good word for me, I'd sure appreciate it. I did a good job for you in Kansas City. You could tell them that—it might help."

My father looked over his shoulder. "I don't think anything I can say will help, but I will pray for you. It might be good if you did the same. You need to ask for God's forgiveness, Nathan. His forgiveness is far more important than ours—please remember that."

Though none of us had been informed beforehand, two of the elders had quietly departed for Iowa City, and this morning they had returned accompanied by a marshal and two deputies. Nathan, Thomas, the lawmen, and the money were all on the late afternoon train.

Father said they were taking Nathan and Thomas to Kansas City, where they would be tried for their crimes. With the lack of newspapers in Amana, I wondered if we would ever know the final outcome. Would Nathan write to me from jail? That thought gave me no pleasure. I sat down at the desk in our parlor and removed a sheet of writing paper. Lilly would wonder why there had been no word regarding Thomas and a possible visit to his sister. Once I completed Lilly's letter, I penned a letter to Kathleen's family in Salina, thankful they'd decided to wait until they heard from Thomas before speaking to the girl. The fact that Kathleen had been protected from further disappointment was the only good thing I could think of at the moment.

As I tucked each letter into an envelope, a knock sounded at the front door. I hurried to answer, worried the noise would disturb Mother. My stomach lurched when I opened the door. Both Brother William and Brother Otto stood in the hallway. I didn't know why they'd come, but I was sure it couldn't be about anything good. They'd probably come to speak with me about Nathan and Thomas. A lump the size of an orange lodged in my throat.

"Good afternoon," I croaked.

"You are ill, Sister Jancey?" Brother Otto backed away from the door.

I shook my head and touched my neck. "Something stuck in my throat." I swallowed hard and stepped to the side as I gestured for them to come inside. "My father is not here—only my mother and me." Thankfully, my voice had returned and sounded almost normal.

Brother Otto nodded. "Ja, but it is you we want to speak with." He and Brother William sat side by side on the sofa.

"Me?" The lump had returned and so had my croak.

The two men looked at each other, obviously uncertain about what ailed me. Once again Brother Otto took the lead. "There is an opening at the *Kinderschule* caring for the young children, and we were thinking you might enjoy this position more than cleaning in the dormitory."

Brother William nodded. "But if you prefer to remain at the dormitory working with Sister Margaret, you are not required to take the position at the Kinderschule. One of the sisters who worked there recently had another child, and she will not be returning for three years. With your experience teaching, we thought you might want to consider a change."

My excitement mounted at the prospect of caring for children. Granted, it wouldn't be the same as teaching in a school, but children were never too young to learn.

"I would be very much interested. How soon could I begin?" The lump in my throat had completely disappeared.

Brother William chuckled. "If you would like to begin tomorrow, that would be gut."

I hesitated. "Tomorrow is washday at the men's quarters. Sister Margaret might need my help."

"Nein. We will have one of the junior girls help her on washdays, but is kind of you to consider the workload of another sister." Brother Otto beamed at me. "I am pleased to see you are learning to embrace our way of life, Sister Jancey. I am sure it pleases your Mutter and Vater."

From his comment, I wondered if the elders had decided I would face fewer temptations working in the Kinderschule rather than the men's dormitory. Was that the reason for their offer? I pushed the thought aside, for it didn't matter what the reason. God had provided a place for me to work with children, and for that, I was most thankful.

The men stood and Brother William nodded toward the bedroom. "Your Mutter—how does she fare?"

"Today not so well, but we remain hopeful. Her health changes day by day. Brother Rudolf says it is to be expected."

"Tell her that our prayers are with her." Brother Otto led the way to the door. "Sister Belinda will guide you through your training at the Kinderschule."

I was so excited I wanted to kiss him on the cheek. Of course I would never have done such a thing, but I could barely contain my excitement. The minute the door closed, I tiptoed into my mother's room.

Though her eyes were closed, I whispered, "Are you awake?"

Her lips lifted in a meager smile. "I am now." Her eyes fluttered open. "You look very happy. What has happened?"

I told her of the visit from the two elders. "Isn't it exciting, Mother? I'll be able to teach again. I can hardly wait."

My mother reached for my hand. "You understand you will be caring for the little ones? Children who are three, four, and five—not the older children."

"I know it won't be the same as teaching in the orphanage, but working with younger children will be a new challenge for me. I'm excited to begin." I let the joy that bubbled within spread across my face. "And I'm pleased the elders considered me for the position."

Mother squeezed my hand. "I am pleased, too, my dear. And I'm certain by the time the little ones are old enough to enter the regular classroom, they will be well prepared."

I sat with Mother until she drifted off to sleep, my thoughts hopscotching over the many events that had taken place since we'd arrived in the colonies. Though there had been immeasurable changes in my life, I now understood the peace and sense of community that had beckoned my mother's return to this simple life.

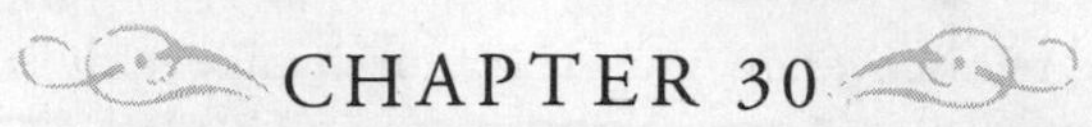

CHAPTER 30

April 1882

Although I sometimes thought it impossible to love Ritt any more deeply, my love for him continued to grow with each passing day. Through his kindness and gentle nature, I had learned the meaning of true love—the kind of love that existed between my mother and father. A love that flowed from the heart without the expectation of gaining anything in return.

The elders had agreed to our marriage, but because of my mother's health and Ritt's involvement in the construction of the new mill, we'd both been permitted to remain in Middle Amana during our year of waiting. If all went according to plan, we would marry in October.

Teaching the children at the Kinderschule had proved to be more fulfilling than I'd anticipated. Watching the little ones improve their vocabulary or learn to write a number gave me great pleasure. They exuded joy over something as simple as creating a small castle out of sand in the play yard or spotting a bird's nest in the orchard. Their eagerness to experience the world around them gave me more delight than I could have ever imagined.

Although I still missed the children at the orphanage, I'd been heartened to discover my prayers had been answered. Lilly wrote that the Charity Home had finally enlisted the help of a new volunteer teacher. The young woman had taught for several years at a girls' boarding school in Pennsylvania and recently offered her services to the orphanage. Lilly's letter bore nothing but praise for the new instructor, a fact that greatly pleased me. In closing, Lilly mentioned the children wanted me to know they liked their new teacher very much.

Over the past months, our ties to Kansas City had slowly dissolved. The sale of Father's business had been concluded, but Mr. Goodman, Father's business associate, kept us apprised about both Nathan and Thomas.

Upon his return to Kansas City, Thomas was identified, charged with bank robbery, and convicted at trial. Later, Nathan was convicted of larceny, and both men were sentenced to serve their time at the state prison in Lansing, Kansas. I couldn't imagine what life was like for Thomas or Nathan behind prison bars, but I continued to pray for them. I also gave thanks that Kathleen had been spared the pain of reconnecting with Thomas, for I was sure life with him would have proved a terrible disappointment.

This evening Ritt and Madelyn walked on either side of me as we returned home from prayer service, while my father, Brother Werner, and Sister Hanna followed behind. I had watched Ritt's excitement mount over the past weeks as the mill neared completion.

And finally, after an inspection a few days ago, the mill had been declared ready to begin production.

Ritt looked at me and grinned. "Tomorrow will be a special day, for sure."

Earlier in the month, an announcement was made that there would be a special ceremony at the opening of the new woolen mill. We would all gather for a prayer service to consecrate our lives and works to the furtherance of our work and beliefs.

I agreed, though I realized this unusual event would be more special to those who had lived here all of their lives. "Why do you think the elders decided to hold this prayer service?" I asked. "My mother said she had never before heard of such a thing in all her years living here."

We turned at the next corner, and Madelyn raced ahead of us. Ritt moved closer to my side. "My parents said the same thing. I think this is the first time. Vater believes the elders took to heart the words of Sister Barbara—we must not let material success become the goal of our villages." He inhaled a deep breath. "And maybe they feel a need to ask for God's blessing because this is the second fire at the woolen mill."

I nodded. "Sister Bertha told me about the other fire. I think the prayer service will be beneficial to everyone, especially to those who battled the fire and helped rebuild the mill in such a short time. I know how hard you worked."

"Ja, but your Vater was a great help with all his knowledge." Ritt tapped his finger against the side of his head. "I learned a lot from him. He has a gut way of leading men. He is a smart man."

We parted at the front door, and though I would have enjoyed spending more time visiting, Mother would need my help preparing for bed. We bid each other good-night, with a promise to meet and walk together to the prayer service at the mill tomorrow night.

"I'm home, Mother." I strode toward the bedroom door. Even in the dim light of the kerosene lamp, I could see a gray tinge to her complexion. "Mother!" I tamped down my rising panic and grasped her hand, but the clamminess of her skin escalated my fear. I leaned close and stroked her forehead. Her eyes fluttered open and she offered a weak smile. "I can see you're feeling much worse than when we departed for prayer meeting." She attempted to speak, but even that seemed too great an effort. I turned and poured a small amount of water into her glass. "Would you like a sip of water?"

She groaned, so I took that for a yes. Carefully, I slid my arm beneath her and lifted her shoulders as I held the glass to her lips with my other hand. When I heard the latch on the parlor door clank, I called to my father.

One look at my mother and he was by her side in four long strides. "What happened?"

I shook my head and looked at him. "I don't know. She took a turn for the worse while we were gone. Do you think she needs the doctor? I could ask Ritt to go for him."

My father glanced at the bedside table. "Did you give her medicine or just water?"

"Just water."

I silently scolded myself. My first thought should have been to relieve her pain, as the doctor had instructed us. I handed the small bottle of liquid to my father and waited while he helped Mother with the medicine. He handed me the bottle and I returned it to the table.

"Let's wait and see if this helps her. If not, we'll send for Brother

Rudolf. I don't know if there's anything else he can offer her other than what he's already provided."

I murmured my agreement, knowing he was right. Brother Rudolf had already explained that he couldn't do anything other than help relieve the pain through these final stages of her illness. Still, I always felt better having the doctor come whenever Mother took a downward turn. His reassuring manner and compassion appeared to give her a sense of comfort, and it did the same for me.

I nodded toward the door. "Why don't you go into the parlor and try to relax? I'll sit in here and finish some of my mending." From the stoop of his shoulders and weariness that shone in his eyes, I knew my father needed rest. If Mother had a bad night, he'd get little sleep.

"If you're sure." He remained near the bed, his gaze fixed on my mother.

"I'm sure. She's back asleep now. I'll keep a close watch. If there's any change for the worse, I'll call for you."

Mother's condition wasn't any worse by morning, but it hadn't improved enough that she could be alone. Father remained with her during the day while I taught at the Kinderschule, but I insisted he go to the special prayer service for the new mill in the evening. After playing an important role in the construction, his presence was more important than mine.

When he returned from the meeting, he came into the bedroom. "Did all go well?"

"Yes, but I'll let Ritt tell you about the prayer service. He asked if he could visit with you for a while. I thought the two of you might enjoy a little time together. He's waiting in the backyard."

My father settled in a chair beside Mother's bed and placed a worn Bible in his lap.

I leaned forward and kissed his cheek. "Thank you," I whispered.

The corners of his mouth curved in a slight smile. "He's a fine young man. I know he will make you a good husband. I hope you and Ritt will enjoy the same happiness your mother and I have shared all these years."

A hint of sadness framed his kind words, and I knew he must be thinking of the years ahead when Mother would be gone. Being without her would surely be hard for him, and I wondered if that was one reason he'd been willing to give up his life in Kansas City. In the colonies he could live a simple life surrounded by those who shared his faith. For Father and for me, I believed it would be easier here in Amana to adjust to the loss we would soon face than it would be anywhere else.

I glanced over my shoulder as I neared the bedroom door. The Bible lay open in my Father's lap, and he held Mother's hand while he read aloud from the Psalms.

Tears slipped down my cheeks as I hurried for the door. Outside, I inhaled a deep breath of the evening air and attempted to settle my mournful emotions. Moments later, I spotted Ritt standing beneath a large elm tree.

He strode toward me, his smile fading as he drew closer. When he arrived by my side, he touched his fingers to the dampness on my cheek. "What has caused you to cry? Your Mutter is no better?"

"No." I forced a smile. "In the past, she has surprised us and regained her strength. I am hopeful she'll do the same again. When the elders gave us permission to marry, she said she wanted to live long enough to see us wed. I have been praying that would happen, but with this last turn, I'm not certain." He grasped my hand, and together we walked to the elm tree. "Tell me about the prayer service."

His eyes brightened. "The factory workers, village elders, and many others attended. The gathering lasted for more than an hour." He grinned. "You probably already knew that since you were waiting on your father to return home."

I agreed, then urged him to continue.

"In their prayers, the elders emphasized the importance of the mill for both the spiritual and earthly survival of our people." He sighed. "It is a fine line that we must walk. It is important that our goods be of high quality so we can compete and sell to the outside world. The woolen and calico goods provide money to purchase what cannot be produced within the colonies, but we must always keep in mind that an accumulation of large sums of money is not our primary goal. I think the elders wanted to emphasize Sister Barbara's warnings that we must remain true to our beliefs."

We sat side by side on the quilt he'd spread beneath the tree, a reminder of the first time we'd sat there with Madelyn and her young friends. So much had happened since then.

Ritt squeezed my hand. "You're so quiet. What are you thinking?"

"About everything that has changed since my family arrived and about how much I have changed, as well."

"And you are sad because of all the changes? Are you missing the children at the orphanage and wishing to return?" He looked deep into my eyes. "Do you have regrets about choosing to remain here in the Amana Colonies? Please be honest with me, Jancey. I need to know."

A nesting bird warbled overhead as if calling to her mate.

"No. I am very happy with my decision to remain here, and I'm especially pleased that we'll soon be wed." I shifted on the quilt and faced him. "I will always miss the children at the orphanage, but I know they will be fine without me. They have a new teacher who will nurture and care for them, and I have the children at the Kinderschule. They fill my days with unspeakable pleasure. Except for Mother's health, I am happy and content."

Ritt cupped my cheek. "That is gut. Very gut." Leaning forward, he pressed his lips to mine, and my love for this man—this man who made me feel blessed and more cherished with every moment—deepened along with his kiss.

Ritt never told me if he had spoken to the elders, and I didn't ask, but two days later the elders spoke to my father and said that after conferring with Brother Rudolf, they all agreed that any additional waiting period should be waived, and Ritt and I could be married. My heart swelled with so much excitement I feared it might burst.

There hadn't been much time for preparation, but what I'd most wanted was going to happen: My mother would be present to see me marry Ritt. Because she remained bedfast, the elders agreed the ceremony could be conducted in our home.

God had answered my prayer. Though I'd been tempted to seek the elders' approval for an early wedding, I had resisted. A sense of contentment washed over me as I realized how much my faith had increased during these months in Middle Amana. I had finally learned the importance of relinquishing control and waiting upon God.

Sister Hanna came downstairs to help me prepare. She'd brought with her the dark shawl and black lace cap she'd worn for her own wedding and now offered them to me. Instead of the worry of buying an expensive wedding gown, brides in the colonies wore plain dark dresses and lace caps. Here, dark clothing was worn for marriage, while white was used to clothe the deceased. And though I didn't look like brides who married in the outside world, I felt as much joy as any woman could possibly experience on her wedding day.

"Let me adjust your shawl and then go show your Mutter." Sister Hanna shifted the fabric an inch or so before giving an approving nod. "You look lovely." She leaned forward and kissed my cheek. "I am pleased you will soon be Ritt's wife. I know you will continue to make him very happy."

"Thank you, Sister Hanna. It means a great deal to have your approval."

"You have more than my approval, Jancey. You have my love, as well." She squeezed my hand. "While you visit with your Mutter, I must go to the Küche and speak with Sister Bertha. With so little time to plan, she is worried there will not be enough food for the reception." Sister Hanna chuckled. "I told her the other Küchebaases would bring food, but she wants the best to come from our kitchen house."

Compared to the elaborate church weddings in the outside world, wedding ceremonies conducted in the colonies were small and simple, but a large reception was hosted afterward, with the kitchen houses providing refreshments for the afternoon of festivities.

I tiptoed to my mother's bedside and waited until she opened her eyes. A tiny smile lifted the corners of her lips as I performed a slow pirouette.

"You look like a beautiful Amana bride." She glanced at the clock. "Is it time for the wedding?"

"Not yet. I thought you might want your shawl and cap, so I came in to help you." The black cap and shawl cast a gray hue to her pale complexion, and I was once again thankful the elders had granted us permission to marry before a full year had passed.

Soon the members of Ritt's family, along with my father and Brother Otto, entered the room. Though it seemed odd to have the village pharmacist perform our wedding ceremony, the elders rotated their duties, so I was not surprised to have Brother Otto officiate.

Ritt and I locked eyes as he stepped to my side, and our gazes didn't waver throughout the brief exchange of vows. Even though the marriage hadn't taken place in the meetinghouse, we didn't kiss after the ceremony. It was not the custom here to kiss at a wedding.

As soon as the marriage service was completed, Ritt grasped my hand and whispered. "Come with me."

Holding tight to his hand, I followed him into the hallway and up the steps. "Why are we going upstairs?"

He glanced over his shoulder and winked at me. "I want a few minutes alone with you so that I can have a proper kiss before we go to the reception."

Once we stepped into the parlor, he tenderly gathered me in his arms. "You have made me the happiest man alive, Jancey. I hope you will always be content with me."

I placed my hand over his heart. "I can't imagine my life without you, Ritt."

He lowered his head and covered my lips with a lingering kiss that set my stomach whirling in a whole new way. His hands rested on my waist, and my heart fluttered as he looked deeply into my eyes and asked, "What are you thinking?"

I tipped my head and met his ardent gaze. "I am thinking that with you by my side, this change to a simple life will be filled with great joy." Placing my hands on his shoulders, I lifted on tiptoe and eagerly accepted another passionate kiss.

SPECIAL THANKS TO . . .

. . . My editor, Sharon Asmus, for her generous spirit, excellent eye for detail, and amazing ability to keep her eyes upon Jesus through all of life's adversities.

. . . My acquisitions editor, Charlene Patterson, for her enthusiastic encouragement to continue writing about the Amana Colonies.

. . . The entire staff of Bethany House Publishers, for their devotion to making each book they publish the best product possible. It is a privilege to work with all of you.

. . . Lanny Haldy and the staff of the Amana Heritage Society, for sharing history of the Amana Colonies.

. . . Peter Holhne, for answering my many questions about the Amana Colonies.

. . . Mary Greb-Hall for her ongoing encouragement, expertise, and sharp eye.

. . . Lori Seilstad, for her honest critiques.

. . . Mary Kay Woodford, my sister, my prayer warrior, my friend.

. . . Above all, thanks and praise to our Lord Jesus Christ for the opportunity to live my dream and share the wonder of His love through story.

Judith Miller is an award-winning author whose avid research and love for history are reflected in her bestselling novels. Judy makes her home in Topeka, Kansas.

If you enjoyed *A Simple Change*, you may also like...

To learn more about Judith and her books, visit judithmccoymiller.com.

In the quiet communities of the Amana Colonies, Karlina Richter and Dovie Cates are searching for answers. When they finally uncover the truth, can their hearts survive its discovery?

A Hidden Truth by Judith Miller
HOME TO AMANA

In the picturesque Amana Colonies, family secrets, hidden passions, and the bonds of friendship run deeper than outsiders know. As three young women come of age, must they choose between love and their beloved community?

DAUGHTERS OF AMANA by Judith Miller
Somewhere to Belong, More Than Words, A Bond Never Broken

Historical Fiction From Tracie Peterson and Judith Miller

To learn more about Tracie, Judith, and their books, visit traciepeterson.com and judithmccoymiller.com.

Romance and intrigue abound on beautiful Bridal Veil Island. Amidst times of change and disaster, three couples struggle to find hope. Will their love—and lives—survive the challenges they face?

BRIDAL VEIL ISLAND: *To Have and To Hold, To Love and Cherish, To Honor and Trust*

When three cousins are suddenly thrust into a world where money equals power, each is forced to decide what she's willing to sacrifice for wealth, family, and love.

THE BROADMOOR LEGACY: *A Daughter's Inheritance, An Unexpected Love, A Surrendered Heart*

BETHANYHOUSE

Stay up-to-date on your favorite books and authors with our *free* e-newsletters. Sign up today at bethanyhouse.com.

Find us on Facebook. facebook.com/bethanyhousepublishers

Free exclusive resources for your book group! bethanyhouse.com/anopenbook